DARKNESS

EVER

AFTER

TARA

MAJUTA

ALSO BY TARA MAJUTA

Riding With Darkness
Darkness In The Lion's Den

This one's for you, the reader!
Thank you for enjoying this series!

Now you know.
Nobody's ever loved anybody as much as I love you.
– Bella Swan, Breaking Dawn

CHAPTER ONE

Sunset

EVERYTHING HAD BEEN perfect. I had paid my debt, pennies at a time. I endured the year-long treachery of being a murderer. Kyle and I had healed. We were…thriving. Barely, at times, but we were. The nightmares had subsided enough to bring plenty of peaceful dreams. Settlement Island slipped from our minds and lips. The tenuous link our past held fell with each passing day. With it came a braver heart. A stronger spirit. Resilience. Hope.

This place was our safe haven. We loved it here. But we should have known. No matter how much we wanted a fresh start, that would never be possible for us.

My brows tightened against his smile.

Gavin Christopher Scott leaned back in his chair, folding his arms, as if I had inconvenienced him. His steel gray eyes waited for an answer to a question he hadn't asked yet. And I didn't budge. Not a gram of sympathy would be earned from me.

"Okay, honey, I made this one stronger than the last one because, well it's your birthday, and, oh my god!" Miguel nearly dropped the glass as he rounded the corner and became acquainted with my party crasher. "What are you doing here?"

Gavin's brows raised, "It's Catalina's birthday, my favorite day of the year."

"So, you drove all the way across country to see your *ex-girlfriend?*" Miguel moved his interrogation onto me. "You didn't tell me he was coming."

"I didn't know he was coming," I said. Gavin's head tilted at my words. The game was on.

"Ex-girlfriend?" Gavin said.

"Yes, ex-girlfriend," Miguel said. "Like as in, ya'll broke up last year after you got shot, she killed a guy, and—" The slip was met with a swift kick from me. He recovered after we both slyly glanced around the restaurant, ensuring no one had heard his damning outburst. To me, he said, "Noah's gonna be here any minute."

Intrigued, Gavin smirked, "Who's Noah?"

"Her new boyfriend."

"You have *another* boyfriend?" The hitch in Gavin's tone matched his wink. This was fun for him.

"Noah's actually a good guy." Miguel dropped my margarita down, spilling sweet liquor over the side, dragging salt onto the table. "Listen, you have no right, comin' into my family's restaurant, bringin' your shit from the past to sunny California."

"Miguel, I got this!" I said when he took a breath.

But Miguel didn't stop. He switched to Spanish, drawing the attention of his cousins who had migrated from the kitchen to see what had gotten him into such an uproar. In Spanish, I told him to calm down and motioned to the growing crowd of patrons who had abandoned their food for the show.

"Mijo, what's going on out here?" Great. Miguel's mother had joined the spectacle. She was not a patient woman; not when it came to disruptions in her business.

Aggressively, I yanked my phone out of the charger and threw everything into my purse. "So sorry." My apology unfazed her. In Spanish, she demanded to know who *Eyebrows* was. Miguel chuckled. "Just a friend." I put out my hand for Gavin, "Come with me." He hesitated. "Now!"

Eyeing Miguel then his mother, Gavin gave up his resistance and laced his fingers in mine. The softness of his skin threatened to bring up a memory. One from his birthday dinner last year. Us walking through the farmer's market, hand in hand, madly in love. For a beat, I wondered how he had spent his birthday this year.

Quickly, I drug him out the side door to the beach. The sun had clipped the ocean, drawing Gavin's eyes to the horizon. He'd never seen the magic of a California sunset before. The sand beneath his boots gave way, making him unsteady as I hunted for a spot where we could shout at each other in private. Alas, I found it next to an abandoned beach towel and two half-eaten tacos.

The punch landed hard against his shoulder, stealing his attention from the sea. "You need to leave."

Wincing, he chuckled, "I got shot there, remember?"

My fingers covered my lips on instinct. The blood was no longer taped to his skin. Aaron had dug into his flesh to release the metal, saving his life. I hadn't forgotten about his injury, I just wasn't thinking. "I'm sorry." He rolled his arm and relaxed, his hands diving into his pockets. I filled the silence between us with a question, "What are you doing here?"

"I'm here for your birthday."

"How did you get here?"

"Well, I got a map, and I got into my car…"

My eyes rolled, "How did you find me? Dad and Mother put a lot of money into making sure my whereabouts were kept secret." A bit of anger rose in my chest, "Did Cecilia tell you?"

His head shook, "No. I really thought I could get it out of her. Your entire family's pretty fuckin' loyal. So is Aaron."

"Aaron doesn't know where I am. Not completely." He knew I was in California. Beyond that, he wasn't privileged enough to know anymore. Especially since my last interaction with his brother left no room for loyalty or friendship between us. Ian Robert Porter was still coming for Kyle. And me. "It's kind of part of the deal."

"What deal?"

"Building a new life. I've spent this past year healing from everything that's happened to me since I met you."

He took the insult with a sigh. "How's that new life going? Meet any interesting people?"

"Like my boyfriend Noah?" I smirked, "Do you really want to know about my new relationship?"

Shifting his weight, he fought the sand until he became comfortable. "Speaking of relationships, Luke's pretty upset about you leaving Maine." Gavin stole a glance toward the ocean, "You should call him." I let my expression fall from annoyed to concerned, keeping up the appearance for Gavin. Luke had followed my instructions precisely.

When I first arrived in California, the guilt over leaving without saying goodbye to Luke taunted me. He deserved something, anything, that would explain everything I had done. So, I wrote him a letter, and then another, until I had a full bundle of notes sharing my regrets, prayers, fears, and uncertainty about the future. It was then that I mailed him my pleas for help wrapped in an apology package.

He called the night he received them, wrapping me in his love and friendship. I had saved his life and gotten him justice at a heartbreaking cost. Unlike Ian, Luke's debt to me didn't come with twisted, dark consequences. It was pure, full of love and light, and a bond that we tightened with every phone call and text message. He had become my sanctuary.

We found love over the line, born from companionship and forgiveness instead of lust and attraction. He forgave me for tugging on his emotions with every indecisive action I took. And I embraced him for who he was, not for the pieces I picked from him when I needed them. I was finally honest and truthful about everything. In the end, he guarded my secrets in exchange for a real chance at being friends.

Even then, after all the deception and frustration, he still wanted me in his life. So began our friendship affair.

Luke was the only person, other than my family, who knew what happened to me after I killed Blake and fled. Telling him seemed like a gamble. Today provided confirmation that he would never betray me. And Gavin was desperate enough to go to his former competition to find the girl who had left him to die on a hospital bed.

Back to Gavin. Flatly, I said, "It's hard keeping a low profile all the time. I can't burden Luke with any of this." Standing taller, I held onto my convictions, "Now, tell me how you found me, Gavin."

Gavin sized up my response. The ferocity behind my request would dissuade him from lying, I assumed. "Miguel, actually," he relented. "After months and months of looking for you online, James gave me the bright idea to search for your best friend whose family owns an award-winning Mexican restaurant in California." *Brilliant.* "Well, there are a lot of Miguels in California who have family members in the restaurant business. Eventually, I remembered his face from a photo in your room. From there, I was able to find the restaurant. Then, I got in the Nova and took a shot. I figured that you'd probably be with him on your birthday."

"It took you a whole year to find Miguel online?"

"Well, I spent some time surviving a gunshot wound, too." My insincerity needed to end. At my core, I was still levied with Gavin, gunshot wound or not. I was also compassionate, when I wanted to be. Waring with my feelings, I chose indifference.

"The Nova made it here?" I said.

Offended, he countered with a witty, "Why wouldn't it?"

"It's old."

"I take care of my cars, so that doesn't matter." His arms knotted across his chest, "You know, part of me thought this would go differently."

Our last conversation had obliterated any chance of this reunion being a happy one. Or a civil one. "We broke up. What did you expect?" I stepped closer, "We don't work. So, let's just move on."

He remained steadfast, "You know I shot Russ. Not even my closest friends know about that." Causally, he cased the beach, making sure we were alone, "I need you to tell me the full story."

"About what?"

"What you know about Russ's murder. Dixon showed you the file." His eyes darkened, mirroring the night that had crept up on us.

Gavin's big cross-country adventure wasn't about love. Selfishly, I thought he came here to make amends and fill in the holes he had dug in my heart. No, Gavin didn't love me anymore. The sternness in his eyes, the coldness in his touch, told me so.

Heartbreak didn't consume me. I had fallen out of love with him, too. So, my next words matched his mood. "What difference does it make? You killed Russ, and I killed his son because of you. That's the entire story."

From one killer to another, he should have known how secrecy worked. Yes, the story about what we had done wasn't complete. There was still confusion surrounding what happened with Russ and Hank, Gavin's father. Blake's obsession with ending the story was cut short by a bullet fired by me. Further proof that we, Gavin and me, didn't work. Also, it was my reason for keeping what I knew to myself. My parts of the story were not on display for him or for anyone. That's how survival works. At least that's how it works for me. His need to seek answers from me was misplaced. In its place should have been a hunger for redemption for the crimes he had committed. I wanted no part of that.

My pinky found Gavin's, grounding me as I said, "You don't have to worry. I'm not going to tell anyone about you and Russ. Can we just let go of the past?"

"Well, I never thought I'd see this sight ever again." My past liked to undermine my efforts to set proper boundaries. The man bounding through the sand was a constant reminder of this. Sunbathed and bone-tired from work, Kyle Workman joined us, taken aback by his long-lost best friend. "Brother." His arms wrapped around Gavin, not allowing him a chance to escape.

Gavin had been right; off drugs and with a thirst for life, Kyle was a gentle soul. Open and accepting of everyone. As Gavin closed the hug, Kyle held onto the relic from a time when he had put his shaky plans and revenge plots ahead of everyone he loved. Yet, each time, Gavin had forgiven him. Kyle's once enemy never tore him down for his transgressions. That was a nice sentiment; one I would never share with Gavin.

Gavin pulled away, fighting to find a smile to give his friend. "So, it's true? You two did run away together."

Kyle's arm draped across my shoulders, "She saved me." Kissing the top of my head, I leveled my face. He knew this look and what it meant. Gavin's brow raised as he tried to understand the closeness Kyle and I had. "With respect, Brother, we got a good thing goin' here," Kyle said with a roll of his shoulder. "If you're here to even some score, we're gonna need you to leave."

"I'm not here to fuck up anything."

"You being here puts Kyle and me at risk," I said. With a huff, I added, "I made my deal with Porter, and I brought him the men who destroyed his business. Your crew took them all out, so the debt's been paid. You, James, and everyone else are safe. As for me and Kyle," I paused to look at him. He nodded, "Porter wanted me to turn over Kyle, and I refused."

"That's where all your new-found courage is coming from," he snapped at me. "That's why you're here, Kyle?" There was the Gavin I knew. Moody and difficult.

Kyle glanced over at me then back at Gavin. "I gave Blake what he needed to infiltrate Porter's business. Then, we all know what happened next."

"That seems about right." Gavin's nod was pensive, "Now, you and I are forever even for all the shit you put me through."

Kyle accepted Gavin's statement with decorum. A step forward, "Thank you. I know I made things impossible for you; all the bodies, the broken promises, the shit that tore Settlement Island to shreds." His eyes glistened with tears, "I'm sorry about Logan. And for tryin' to kill James. I'm so sorry I put your life on the line to settle my debts." He let out a breath. "I'll never be able to repair that damage." Gavin put his hand on Kyle's shoulder. "You never turned on me.

Thick and thin, you were always my family. Even when I didn't deserve your protection, you saved me, anyway."

Gavin took Kyle into his arms. His tenderness almost made me jealous. "I don't hold grudges. You know that, Kyle." He squared up Kyle's shoulders, "Besides, you completely destroyed Porter and his business. Our crew is whole. Settlement Island is quiet." His embrace stiffened, "You did that."

I remained speechless. Gavin and Kyle had sorted out their issues before, but I never imagined they would actually make amends. But now I knew why they had.

Because of Kyle, Gavin had finally gotten what he wanted. Porter was out of business. No one was driven enough to withstand the violence and threats to replace him. Settlement Island had become a utopia, all because Kyle and I had left. A hurtful notion, but I couldn't deny it. Everyone was better off without us.

I invited myself into their conversation, "I'm happy you two are in love with each other again, but today is my birthday. And we have plans."

Kyle put his arm around me. "I'm sorry, Sweetheart." He handed me a small box, "Happy birthday." I opened it, revealing a gift card to my favorite bookstore. "Your TBR list is like ninety feet long, so I figured you could pick out a few books."

"That's so thoughtful," I pulled him into a hug. Before my eyes closed, I caught brown locks blowing in the wind behind his outline. I stepped back, focusing on the woman watching us.

"What is it?" Gavin said.

"Kyle, can you escort Miguel's new BFF into the restaurant?" I said. A frown collapsed his smile. Demi Woods would be his problem now. He nodded, giving Gavin another hug and inviting him to stay with us. Gavin politely declined.

"Then, I'll see you before you head back to Maine?" Kyle said.

Gavin shifted his weight, slightly, "Yeah, of course." Another hug, and Kyle advanced toward Demi, trapping her in a slew of compliments as he steered her into the restaurant. "Who's that?"

"Just some girl Miguel has a crush on," I hissed.

"And you don't like her?"

Not for the reasons he would think. Demi was a junior at UC Berkeley, majoring in Journalism. She had appeared in our lives around New Years, taking a special interest in me. She was getting into true crime, which was a threat against my entire existence.

Full of contentment, Gavin smirked again, "I never took you as the jealous type."

"I'm not." I brushed my curls with my fingers, preparing to see my new boyfriend. "Gavin, I need you to go."

"One full year without me isn't long enough?" My sigh lightened his mood. "I'm sorry for pouncing on you like this." My brows furrowed. "Okay, that was not the right thing to say."

My reflex was to smile, which he took as a reward. I dropped it, "I forgive you. But, seriously, you need to go."

"I'm not one to linger," he said, "but you can't get rid of me that easy. I need answers."

"Answers to what? And don't act like Kyle hasn't been feeding you information about me for the last year."

Gavin's hurt made my heart tense. "His loyalty to you is stronger than it is to me. For good reason." Shuffling his boots in the sand, he said, "You guys are happy here. Which is good."

His wavering infliction gave me an advantage. "You always said Kyle was a nice guy deep down. He's a good friend, too. I'm lucky to have him."

"He's protecting you?"

"I don't need protection here," my voice tightened.

"That's good." Gavin wasn't one to stall. So, why wasn't he leaving?

I addressed my curiosity with a question, "Why do you think I need protection?" He wasn't quick to shrug. Nor did he explain himself. "I'm tired of the games. Just answer my questions. With our history, we owe it to each other to be honest."

"That's a damn good point," he said. Still, he didn't budge.

"Just tell me."

"I'll tell you more when we can be alone. When can you make that happen?"

I hesitated. The wind had shifted, tangling my curls again, and blowing bits of Maine off his shirt. Scents of campfire and pines. I still missed that. "Before I agree to this, you have to promise me something."

"What do you want?"

I tucked my hair behind my ears, the last remnants of sunlight hitting my gold bracelets. "After we talk, you need to move on. No more me, no more drama, nothing. Just go find a happy life."

"I can't do that." The color slipped from his face, "Gary Porter was just paroled. He got out of prison yesterday, and I need your help."

A wave of nerves swelled over me. Gary had ties to Gavin's family. His father, Hank. Hank was the reason Russ had died. So, he was right; we did need to talk. "How did he get out?"

Agitation engulfed him, "It has to do with Russ and Blake."

My teeth clenched as I seethed. The emotions were stronger than I was.

"I know. But we can't ignore this. Gary getting out is going to create a bunch of problems for everyone, especially you and me."

"How so?"

"I thought you didn't want to talk about it right now."

He had caught me. My curiosity had derailed my plans for a quiet, meaningful birthday. One without him. I turned, pointing to a small café down the beach. "There. We can get breakfast tomorrow morning at eight."

"See you then."

I grabbed onto his arm, "I'm not agreeing to help you, yet."

"We'll see how you feel tomorrow." Gavin's eyes glanced down at my fingers. I relinquished him. His sleeve brushed my tender skin. "Happy birthday, Catalina." He whispered my name like a memory. Then he stepped through the sand and onto the boardwalk. I watched him disappear into the crowd.

It seemed so easy for him to just…leave. Like we were merely old acquaintances. My fists balled. I charged into the aimless families and beach goers, looking for him. But it was too late; he was gone.

CHAPTER TWO

Crusade

NOAH, MY NEW boyfriend, had to go back to work, so my birthday surprises would have to wait until tomorrow. After Gavin and I settled the score, that is. To prepare for our meeting, I would have to cut my birthday plans short.

Miguel knew the truth when I lied to his friends and family, excusing myself from my own party. I told them my boyfriend was MIA, and I wanted to catch up with my family before it got too late. I waited until everyone sang *Happy Birthday* before I dashed to the exit. Kyle caught me as I neared the door.

"She left already," Kyle said about Demi. "She stuck around for a bit, hoping you'd surface. You were out there for a while." He smiled at the bartender who offered him a shot. Declining drinks had been the norm for him. And me, too. We were setting out to have a sober night, much like most of our nights.

"Gavin wants my help with something."

Kyle put his back to the bar, making our conversation

private. "It's bad, isn't it?" I didn't give him a straight answer. "Catalina, I don't like this." His face came closer, "I trust Gavin, but whatever he's got goin' on can't be good for you."

"I'll handle it." He pressed his lips. "Seriously, I got this." Kyle's breaths grew tired. "I'm gonna head home. Can you cover for me?"

"Yeah, Sweetheart." Kyle conceded because it was my birthday.

Tomorrow, I'd have to listen to him divulge his concerns surrounding Gavin's visit and Gary's release from prison. Tonight was mine.

I got a pass from Miguel because his evening had taken a turn. He had to close for his cousin, so we'd have to postpone our plans for another day. There was so much I had to tell him, but I had the patience to wait. He had his suspicions after seeing Gavin, yet he kept his speculations to himself. For my sake. He wanted me to enjoy my birthday.

I kissed my best friend's cheek, and he held the door open. "Call me if you need me to kick his ass!" Miguel said. I waved his remark off, sauntering down the boardwalk to the seclusion of my home.

This beach house was my father's rental property, which he was gracious enough to let me live in. Kyle's construction job was miles away, so he would stay in a trailer on property for the next couple of days. A few months in, he made an arrangement with the owner to stay onsite and watch over the place at night in exchange for free lodging. A trained hunter, Kyle was more than qualified for the job.

Every couple of weeks, he'd stay in my guest room, so he could baptize himself in the ocean.

I slowed my pace. Vigilance became my priority. My safety net. I stilled my breaths when I stepped onto the porch. The inside was dark. Camera lights beamed down on me. Glass remained intact. I placed my key in the lock and turned it.

The beach house was undisturbed. Normally, I didn't stay out this late unless Kyle was with me. We had a system; he'd open the door and investigate the house before I came in. If I was alone, I would check every room of the tiny cottage several times before I locked up, set the alarm, and turned on every light.

This is how I slept.

I assumed no one would break into a well-lit house. Kyle agreed. And the gun sitting in my nightstand drawer was also something we agreed upon. It was on loan from Kyle. When he was here, he would reclaim it to protect us both. Exhausted, I pulled the drawer open, admired the humps of the gun sitting beneath a blanket of scarves, and closed it. Next, my bracelets came off. Then, I pulled Michelle's necklace from my jewelry box.

I had stopped wearing it some time ago. After leaving Gavin, it felt wrong to wear—

I jumped at my laptop chirping.

There were only a few people who had my new number. To hide my identity, my Aunt Eloise had added me to her phone plan. She had my number along with my immediate family. And they were all out of birthday wishes.

Cecilia was bombarded with inventory for her store, so

she sent a quick text and promises for a long chat tomorrow. Dad was on call, waiting for the hospital to give him details on his next surgery. His gift came this morning. The bouquet with long stemmed roses was too much. I knew it hadn't come from him, but rather Mother. She put me on video call while she visited Luke's mom for their local gossip exchange.

This is why he was calling.

"They're getting really bad," Luke said as he set his laptop down on his bed. He had gotten an apartment in Settlement Island proper this year, abandoning his condo in Anders. He wasn't too far from Cecilia, apparently. He settled onto the bed, his shirt barely hugging his chest, tearing against the muscles he had grown since his attack. Luke was strong, driven to take working out seriously after Blake's crew had beaten him almost to death. He wasn't going to allow that to ever happen again.

I adjusted my laptop, so he could see my face. "Our mothers constant gossiping helps us tremendously. We wouldn't know what we know without them." It was a painful truth; our mothers had given us a leg up in our investigation.

He wasn't convinced, "True, I guess. I just wish my mom wasn't so close with Adrienne's family. They went to brunch today, which is why your mom came over to talk shit."

"You went over to your parents' house? I thought you were going on a date."

He sat up, the shirt rolling down to his jeans, "My dad wanted my help with the boat. He's thinking about selling it." This was the same sailboat Luke had taken me on for my birthday two years ago. I hoped he hadn't remembered this detail. He continued, "I'm surprised you answered. I thought you'd be out with Noah."

Luke and I had agreed that we wouldn't have secrets anymore. It was the basis for our friendship. He knew about Noah, even though Noah didn't know about him. "He's working. Now, back to this whole date thing," I smirked.

"I didn't go because I just didn't want to get her hopes up. Cecilia met me for lunch instead." Luke had been out with this girl twice. She was smitten, and he was bored. I told him to give it another shot. Apparently, my advice was disregarded. "Melanie seemed to understand when we spoke over the phone."

"You broke up with her over the phone?"

"Your sister said it was better than ghosting her."

Things were worse than I had believed. Luke getting dating advice from my sister showed how desperate he was. "She has a point." I brushed back my curls, relieving my face. "How was lunch with Cecilia?" I teased.

"Good. She took me out to say thank you for helping her with inventory. We rearranged the entire store."

"She swindled you into working for free?"

"She paid me," he defended her. My shock made him chuckle. "Relax. It was just lunch."

"Beware," I warned. "Cecilia latches onto kindness. She'll use it against you," I said in a dramatic tone. Luke nodded haphazardly, ignoring my sage counsel. He grabbed his composition book and flipped through it. Now, we were onto Mrs. Dixon, Adrienne's mom. "Did your mom say anything about Officer Dixon?"

"Nothing that helps us. His mom hasn't seen him much because he's been working a lot. Some officers have quit, long hours, stuff like that." He looked up, "Any news on your end?"

"Gavin's here." Luke perked up as I said, "He said I should reach out to you since you're not doing too well." I leaned into the camera, "Thank you for keeping my secret."

"Of course." He tapped his notebook, "What did Gavin want?'

"Gary got out of jail."

Luke's attention sharpened, "I didn't hear about that." He snatched his phone off the bed, frantically shifting through screens.

This wasn't his fault. "Maybe the papers will have something about it tomorrow."

"Maybe," Luke said. "Gary getting out of jail would be big news for them. You know, because of his past."

"Do you think someone is covering it up?"

Luke didn't know. I stood and adjusted the laptop, so he could see *The Murder Wall*.

Miguel had named it my "Murder Wall" with glaring concern. Its purpose had been taken out of context. It wasn't a shrine to my life in Maine, as Miguel had assumed. This was my path to healing. Blake died, hurting for answers to close the case on his father's death. I knew who had killed Russ, but I didn't know why. How Hank, Russ, and Gary were connected.

This put me on a crusade to find out the truth for Blake. It was the least I could do.

So, The Murder Wall was born.

I had converted an entire wall in my bedroom into our living, breathing investigation board. We had pictures of Blake, Jude, Six, and everyone who had ever touched Gary, including Officer Jaime Dixon. Printouts of case files, news articles, and anything else that was related to Russ, Gary, and Ian. Thanks to Daniel's flash drive, we had more than enough clues to shift our investigation to Gary.

Gary getting out of jail was an impossibility. He had been convicted of murder. His sentence was life in prison, no parole in sight. So, how did he manage to overturn his conviction?

"Maybe you should have a conversation with Officer Dixon. See what he knows about Gary's release."

Luke rolled his shoulders, "I think he's onto us."

The disappointment hit us both hard. Officer Dixon came back to town a few months ago. He had been acquitted of any charges against him related to all the people he had killed for Blake. Witnesses had disappeared, alibis had been secured up, and all his fellow officers had given enough testimony to clear his name. And the officers who didn't support Dixon's return slowly quit or transferred to other departments, proving how powerful he truly was.

With my absence, Dixon had no reason to shy away from Luke's questions. Yet, getting Dixon's insight didn't come easy. Sure, Luke and Dixon had been civil since he broke Adrienne's heart. Her brother had seen through the lies and decided to side with him over her. But Luke's flimsy excuses for snooping around had caught up to us. Now, this alliance was in jeopardy, which was probably my fault.

"Well, let's not push him too far," I said.

"I think we're fine for now." His pen gestured to Gary's mugshot. "Jaime hates the Porters. If Gary's out of jail, I can use that to get the intel we need." He paused, "I can tell him that I'm worried for my family in the Club."

"That's good." Another thing came to mind, "Dixon hates Gavin, too." I walked over to the wall, pointing to Jaime's photo. "Although, before Gavin was shot, Jaime said something to me about Gavin's involvement in Russ's murder. It almost seemed like he was never convinced that Gavin was the killer."

"You think that's true?"

I shrugged. "Gavin killed Russ, I know that for sure. I think Dixon's using him to find the connection between Russ and Gary. Gary thought Russ was an informant to the police." I lit up, "Russ could have reached out to Dixon about Gary." I shifted through my notes, "Daniel told me that Russ had gone to the police after some of his property was stolen. He thought it was related to drugs. Then he was murdered. I think Gary covered for Gavin because Gavin had done him a favor. Russ talking to the police about Gary's business could create all sorts of problems. So, now we just have to figure out what Russ knew about Gary. Maybe Dixon found out something we don't know."

"How should I ask him? I mean, I don't mind asking him, if you really want me to. But I don't want him to shut down if he thinks something's up."

The stress on Luke's face didn't match his agreement

to approach Dixon again. "I'll ask Gavin tomorrow and see if I can find something that will help."

"You're going to see him?" This was more of an accusation than a question. He didn't have feelings for me anymore, but he still didn't approve of Gavin's intentions for my life. According to Luke, Gavin could live twenty lifetimes and never be good enough for me.

I felt the same way, "He wants to have breakfast and talk."

"About what?"

I tightened my words, "He needs my help. Gary getting out of jail affects me, I guess."

Luke's patience gave out. "Fuck Gavin." He barreled through my objections. "Don't defend him, Catalina." Luke's own objection stemmed from his support of my new, uncomplicated life, not the crush he had battled with. I had to remind myself of this sometimes.

"I haven't agreed to help Gavin, yet. He needs to help us, first. Then I'll decide." I looked up at the board. "I've heard so many things about Gary, but no one ever talks about the murder he committed." I pointed to the only information we had, "Richard Maverick Spencer. His street name was Maverick, apparently. I think he was a biker or something. He's not even a Settlement Island resident."

There wasn't much on the board about Maverick. Not for lack of trying, though. Most of the police files had been redacted. All we knew was his murder happened before Russ was killed. A few days before Russ's death. The killing could have happened closer to Russ's own demise; the coroner wasn't sure.

I plugged Daniel's flash drive into my computer. "Let's look in here and see if we missed something." Daniel's drive was stuffed with files, articles, videos, police reports, and ledgers. He must have spent hours on it. A testament to how much he loved me. "While I look into this, maybe you can find someone who knows something about Gary's arrest. That way you have something to talk to Dixon about." Someone came to mind, "Aaron might know something."

Luke halted the idea, "He's been spending a lot of time working. At least that's what he told Cecilia. She hasn't seen him in weeks."

I heard a key plunge into the front door lock. "See if you can find Aaron," I said once I found my breaths again, "And I'll let you know what happens with Gavin."

The door opened. Kyle announced his arrival. This helped ease my PTSD. After the break in, I always jumped when I heard someone at the door.

"Kyle's home?"

"How did you know?"

"You have that look of dread on your face." Luke understood that rush of fear when you weren't sure if the person coming through the door was a friend or a foe. "We're gonna get through this." He paused until I smiled at Kyle who had peered into my room. I motioned to the laptop. "Hi, Kyle."

Kyle advanced to the screen. "Hey, Luke. Ya'll workin' on case file stuff on Catalina's birthday?"

Luke let me answer. "We have a new development. I need to talk to you," I said to Kyle. Of course, he would know about Gary's murdering past. He had used Gary and Ian's enemies to give Blake an advantage in his war. Perhaps Maverick had a few surviving friends who Kyle had met from time to time.

"I'll get a shower, and then we can talk." He waved to Luke.

Once alone, Luke shuffled on the bed, getting ready for his goodbye. "Sorry for making this birthday about Gary."

It was better than spending it with my best friend's large and intrusive family. Hiding my past was exhausting. With Luke, I could be myself. "I'm good. Besides Miguel, you're my best friend. I like seeing you, even if it's over video chat to talk about the people who've been murdered."

To lighten the mood, he asked about my day. I gushed about my morning, only focusing on the good stuff. Painting, the ocean, a fulfilling therapy session.

Dr. Wong told me to stop overthinking about everything. To embrace my progress and look up instead of down. I was doing the hard work. I was crafting the life I wanted. And the proof was there. Up until I saw those blue-gray eyes, things had worked with me, not against me.

Gavin being here was not going to derail me.

I knew who I was, now. And I'd hold onto her at all costs.

Luke absorbed my enthusiasm. "I miss you."

"I miss you, too."

"Happy birthday, Catalina." Luke moved the screen closer. "I'll see you tomorrow."

"Likewise," I said. Luke hung up.

The timing was perfect. Kyle had emerged wearing

his signature sweatpants and a gray T-shirt. Tiredness laid in his eyes; he wouldn't last long. Quickly, I changed and prepared for bed. Kyle slept in the guest room when he stayed over, but tonight I asked him to sleep with me. "I thought you didn't want to have sex with me?"

I threw a pillow at him. "I have so much to tell you, and I'm pretty sure you're going to fall asleep while we're talking."

"You know me too well." He tucked the pillow behind his head. "Gavin's in town."

I climbed into the bed, leaning against the head board. "Gary got out of jail." His cool reaction gave him away. "Did you already know?"

"Mark told me. His mom called and let him know. She thought we should be warned."

"I thought we made a deal not to talk to anyone in Maine."

"You talk to Luke…"

"To get information to help us stay alive." I pointed to Gary's mugshot, "Is Gary coming for you? Gavin seems to think we need protection."

"Because of everything I did to Porter, I'm sure I'm somewhere on his list. First, he's gonna go after the people who put him in jail. Then, if no one kills him, he'll probably find his way to me."

"Who got him arrested?"

He measured his thoughts, "I have no idea." Kyle licked his chapped lips, "Is that what you're researching?" His yawn told me to hurry up.

"I just want to know what the tie is between Gary and Russ." Also, "Russ may have helped him get arrested."

"Gary's killed a lot of people who tried to jam him up. I don't think Russ, a square, would be able to catch him." He pulled out his phone and texted someone. "I asked Mark to see what he can find for you." Kyle's demeanor changed, almost to pity, "Here you are, on your twenty-third birthday, chasing down Gary. You should be doin' naughty things with your boyfriend." The teasing lasted a bit longer before he asked, "Do you want to talk about Gavin?"

Kyle had also earned my complete honesty. "I hate Gavin. And I don't want to see him." My nail stabbed my comforter, "I'm meeting him for breakfast tomorrow only because I need to know more about what's going on back home. You can come, if you want."

"I've got an early shift." Kyle pulled long hours, which paid well and left me alone a lot. His yawn told me sleep would take him soon. "What's Luke take on all this?"

"He's not happy about Gavin leaning on me for help. But he's gonna do what he can to support me, no matter what I decide to do." My fingers danced across his forehead, pulling his blond hairs back into place. "He's a good guy. Like you."

"You're too kind." Kyle tucked the blankets around his body. "Just be careful. I can't think of anyone out here who would want to hurt you." Another yawn, "But if you're looking into Gary, you might end up on Porter's radar."

"I'll keep that in mind."

This next yawn took him under. "I'm sorry, but I'm beat."

I kissed his forehead. "You go to sleep. I'm gonna stay up a little longer."

He snuggled into my blankets, as if he always belonged here with me, "Happy birthday, Sweetheart."

"Thanks," I murmured. The light flicked off, and I went to the living room.

The day was weighing heavy on me. My phone chimed with a notification. Noah had sent a few texts and a video. They were sweet, putting me at ease for a brief second. Yet, dread replaced it with no effort.

It was silly, but I thought about Aaron. He was the only person from my family who hadn't reached out to wish me a happy birthday. Last year, he had Cecilia send me a card. His signature looked rushed, but it was his. I had seen his writing so many times, I could mimic it in my sleep.

This year, there was nothing.

He had no reason to shut me out anymore. Sure, our relationship was a push and pull, mostly me pushing him away. Last year, I thought we had balanced out. He had been there with me when Blake took his last breath. We were trauma bonded, I thought. Still, he hadn't even tried to find me.

Was something wrong?

Gary got out of jail, and Aaron was suddenly unavailable? Knowing Aaron's relationship with Ian, this wasn't a coincidence. I reached out to my dad to see if Aaron was working tomorrow. If he was, I could get a hold of him at the clinic. Or Anders General. Dad shot back a quick reply, stating that Aaron was taking some time off. I asked when he would be back, and he told me we could discuss it tomorrow, when he wasn't on rounds.

Don't overthink it.

I'd worry about Aaron later. This sacred time was mine.

Before my birthday was over, there was one more thing I had to do.

I put my phone down and pulled out my notebook, brimming with letters to *him*. I had written him a letter every day since he died. Today's letter was an apology.

Daniel,

Today is my birthday. The second one I've had since Six killed you. Miguel had something big planned, which was more of a headache than I'm worth. I don't deserve to have a friend like him. Or his family. I ended up leaving early and chatting with Luke about Gary getting out of jail.

So many things are happening, and it's hard to keep up.

Gavin showed up, Gary got out of jail, and now I'm on high alert. Kyle doesn't think Gary's going to come after us, but Gavin doesn't seem to be so sure. I know you hate Kyle, but I'm happy he's here with me. He's helping me heal and come to terms with the past. With losing you.

He's not replacing you, though. No one could ever replace you. But maybe I should try harder to move on. Noah's great. You'd like him, I think. Or not, seeing that you were in love with me. You loved me. Do you still…

I'm sorry I never said it back. I'm sorry for everything, actually.

My only birthday wish is for you to be here, alive. I'd give anything to bring you back.

I love you, Daniel. And again, I'm so sorry.

Love always, Catalina

I closed the notebook. The loneliness of night always brought vivid memories of him. I'd lay down on the bed and see him lying next to me. Teasing me, of course. Reliving stories from my day, as if he had been there with me. And I'd feel full and rested, all at once.

Daniel was my soulmate. The disturbing peace that came with this thought always punched me hard.

My soulmate was gone. He had missed my birthday, and he would miss every birthday I would have. There was a silver lining, if you believe in those sorts of things. Without Daniel's gift, his ultimate sacrifice, I would have died that day in that barn. No bouquet of flowers or gift cards would ever match that.

It was unfair to compare them. Even worse, it was unfair for me to pressure Gavin to move on. I needed to move on, too. Hopefully, figuring out what was going on with Gary would help me do just that.

CHAPTER THREE

Blueberries

I THOUGHT BEING early would give me an advantage with Gavin. A chance to pick a table and get my bearings before I had to stare him in the face and tell him that Gary and Settlement Island were his problem, not mine.

After reading my letters to Daniel, I had made this decision just this morning. I laid on the couch, knees bent as I watched the ceiling. I had gotten enough sleep. The tiredness had faded some time ago. Emotions flooded my veins with shock, uncertainty, and then confidence.

Gavin needed my help, but I didn't owe him anything. In the end, he was the one who owed me. Settlement Island was a better place, thanks to my exodus. I had given up my family for him. I had taken away the reason for all his problems and provided Kyle with shelter. He was my burden now. So, what was left?

Gary Porter wasn't after Kyle or me. Not that we were aware of.

However, I could see how Gary was Gavin's problem.

I had gotten to know Porter's father with Daniel's help. On the flash drive was a short file on why Maverick's murder was his undoing. He couldn't escape the testimony of an unimpeachable witness. Someone he couldn't scare into covering up his tracks. Luke and I had speculated Russ may have been a witness, too, since Maverick and Russ were killed so close together. Kyle could deny this until his dying breath, but facts were facts. It was highly plausible Russ had set up Gary, and Gary took him out, just to ensure his freedom. A freedom that was still snatched from him justly.

There was a problem.

Maverick and Russ were killed by two different people. I had to remember that.

One killer was in the wind, while the other would sit across from me in a matter of minutes. This was the only motivation for me to attend this breakfast. After I learned what I needed to know from Gavin, we would be done.

I spied him sitting at a table, sipping coffee and reading a newspaper. Unassuming. Nerves wouldn't get the best of me. I pressed forward, bumping into two people, one of them a guy with long blond hair and biker leather. *Blood Diamond MC* was tattooed to his leather. The name felt familiar, but I had other things to consider.

We found ourselves chest to chest in the doorway. His eyes didn't leave mine as we shuffled past each other, the closeness inappropriate. He was examining me. I wanted to ask him why he was so interested in me, but he offered an, "Excuse me," before heading out into the sunlight.

He was alone. And so underdressed for the place we were, it was almost funny. He looked back at me. Normally,

I would duck and hide. This time, I knew he had seen something in me. It was my long curly hair with hints of honey against black. Or the bellowing blue sundress that showed him my full shapes. Perhaps it was my intimidating smile.

It was none of those things. His lips pressed into a line, eyes cut off by sun shades.

Gavin had abandoned his table, just in time to catch me when I slammed into him. "Someone has wandering eyes," he teased.

I straightened up, stammering for an explanation, then remembering he didn't deserve one. "You're already here."

"Got us a table," Gavin led the way and sat down. I joined without an invitation. He glanced up from the newspaper he had resumed reading as I waited for him in silence. I couldn't quite place the emotion on him. It was somewhere between contentment and curiosity.

"Good morning," he said as he folded the paper. "How was your birthday?"

"Long, but fun." He drew a sip from his cup, seeming interested. I said, "What did you do last night?"

"I tried pho for the first time." A teasing grin, "It wasn't what I expected."

"It's really good."

"Yeah, I know." Gavin put his cup down. "And I drove up to see The Observatory, but parking was a fuckin' joke, so I skipped that and went back to my Airbnb." He paused, "Then, I watched old movies until I fell asleep."

Old movies. That was our thing.

A twist of guilt arrested me. We used to have fun

together. Any other situation, and his first trip to the Golden State would have gone differently. *We* would have eaten pho together after I introduced him to one of my favorite eateries. *We* would have gone to The Observatory, and I would have found us parking. Afterwards, *we* would have gone back to our Airbnb. Then, *we* would have picked out a movie together. Or he would have let me watch *Casablanca* again and again.

The night would have been eclipsed by my full heart, falling asleep on his chest while he recited my favorite movie lines.

I had been so cruel, shoving him away from my party. That was a necessity. Now, we didn't have fun together. Gavin had ruined that for us.

Lost memories were not going to help me. I had to focus. "So, how long do we have?" I pulled out my notebook. "I've got a lot of stuff in here that could help us with the whole Gary thing, if you can fill in the gaps."

"We've got an hour. I'm driving to Stanford to meet with someone in Admissions this afternoon."

I pressed my hand over my lips, hiding my surprise. "Aaron said…"

"Yeah, I know. He told you about me getting into college and not going. Well, I have the money now, and I don't really want to stay in Maine, so I thought I'd see if they'd let me in."

"Stanford is far from here." This was a slip. I didn't want him to think I cared where he lived.

"I'm not here for you. We broke up, remember?" he said. I nodded forcefully. He leaned back, "I want my own life, and college seems like a great place to start." Gavin mistook my glare for anger. Instead, I was trying to imagine Gavin staying in California. Being so close. He turned his phone, showing me his calendar. "So you know I'm not lying."

"I didn't think you were." As he lowered his phone, I readied myself for my interrogation. "I guess we should talk about Gary?"

He pursed his lips for a beat, "Did you hear about his release from prison? Before I told you anything?"

"No," I admitted. "I keep up with what's going on in Settlement Island through Luke and Cecilia. Luke didn't know anything about it, either." Gavin clicked his tongue. I leaned in, "That's right, Luke lied to you. To protect me."

"I'm not mad," he said, even though he did a terrible job hiding his true feelings.

I ignored his anger and offered up a question, "Kyle said Mark's mom gave him a heads up?"

Gavin recovered, "Mark's mom is a lawyer. Gary's been trying to get parole for some time now. He had an army of lawyers who were looking for loopholes in his case. But no one ever thought he'd get out." I asked why he thought Gary didn't stand a chance in earning his freedom. "Catalina, love and loyalty won't save you from consequences. You fuck up enough people's lives, eventually, someone will turn on you."

I knew that very well. Love led to Daniel being murdered when he turned against Ian's wishes for my life. Loyalty had led to me fleeing Maine for California. When Gavin loved me, his loyalty was unthinkable. He got shot protecting me. All brave moves that had turned us into irreversibly broken people.

My heart shuttered, "Did you come here because of love and loyalty, too?"

"Are you asking if I'm still in love with you?" he said.

There was no point in hearing his answer. "I'm asking if you think you owe me something because of what I said about you ruining my life."

He shook his head, "No. Like I said yesterday, I need your help." Did help mean he thought I owed him? Gavin's attention turned to a waiter approaching our table. "What's good here?"

"Everything," the waiter said. I agreed. "What are you in the mood for?"

"Anything with blueberries."

Of course, the Maine boy wanted his blueberries. "Let's have two orders of blueberry ricotta pancakes and some orange juice," I said.

The waiter didn't ask Gavin for confirmation. He gathered up the menus and left us to our uncomfortable conversation.

"You're ordering for me," Gavin said as he poured more coffee into his cup, "I like it."

I crossed my ankles and pulled them close to my body, relaxing. "A lot of things have changed."

"New state. New boyfriend." His pause inferred he craved more information about Noah. When I divulged nothing, he continued. "Your brand-new life," his tone had dipped.

"How does Gary getting out of jail affect us?" I said without any hint of playfulness. "Am I in danger?"

Gavin cleared his throat, "Not yet. But you will be if we don't work together."

"What do we need to work on?" The sharpness in my words was unfair; I softened them, "I mean, I'm out of credit with Porter. Getting his people killed and running off with Kyle put me at the top of his list of enemies."

"Well," he sucked in a deep breath, "it's not Porter this time. I'm worried Gary might come for me."

"Aren't the Porters always trying to kill you?"

He rolled his neck, fighting the tension. "Gary suspected Russ was an informant to the police. I shot Russ, and Gary covered for me because of my dad. Hank was dealing for Gary at the time, and he thought Hank and I took Russ out to keep the cops out of his drug operation. Then, this other guy ends up dead, Gary's catching charges for that murder, and it seems like more than a coincidence."

My eyelashes fluttered several times. "You had nothing to do with Maverick Spencer's death, right?"

"No, but that's not the point." He sucked down another gulp of coffee and winced. "Russ and Blake were related. Blake tore apart Gary's business, trying to figure out how me and Gary were connected. Or that's what I've been told." I nodded, knowing the facts. "So, coincidences are starting to add up. I shot Russ, Gary goes to jail for another murder, and he swears Blake or Russ had set him up. Well, he did at first. Now, Gary believes someone else was behind the murder."

My shoulders shrugged. "So, what does that have to do with you and me?"

"Gary was able to get out of jail because he found evidence that linked Maverick's murder to Russ's. Apparently, you shooting Blake gave his lawyers a reason to reopen the case. The police were able to find the connection between Officer Jaime Dixon and Blake. Blake was Russ's son, so they believe Blake went after Gary to retaliate. Gary convinced some judge that he was set up by Officer Dixon who committed the other murder to frame him. That somehow, Russ was shot before Maverick was killed. And I shot Russ to help someone who wasn't Gary. Dixon was the responding officer the night I was arrested. Gary's lawyers twisted it, making it seem like Dixon and I were in it together. That I shot the wrong guy or something." I told him to hold on while I wrote everything down to make sense of it. He placed his hand on mine. "This is where you come in."

"But everyone knows Dixon was friends with Blake. You shooting Russ created a big riff between you and Blake," I said, my thoughts coming to life. "Dixon would have never agreed to silencing Russ, especially if he had dirt on Gary."

"That's true. The lawyers had to come up with another strategy. Instead, they claimed Dixon set up Gary for Maverick, and I shot Russ because Dixon told me to. He was playing both sides. Then, he turned on me, and he told Blake what I did. And I lied and said that Gary told me to shoot Russ, and that's why Blake came after me." A curse slipped from my lips. This was getting too complicated.

"They let him out based on these lies?" I said. Gavin

nodded. "Gavin, none of that makes sense. Dixon has chosen to side with Blake, and he stayed loyal. Even though he never tried to kill you, Dixon still held you accountable for what happened to Russ. He didn't have the full story. Neither did Blake. The secrecy surrounding his father's is what drove Blake to burn down Gary's business and confront you."

Hope gleaned on Gavin's face, "You know more of the true story than anyone. You were the last person to speak to Blake before he died. You know why Blake was after me. He had no idea why I killed Russ. He wasn't able to find a link between me and his father."

I took his hand from mine and wrote out a theory. That's when I knew. "You want me to prove Gary's lawyers wrong. I know Dixon didn't have anything to do with Maverick or Russ's murder. And I can corroborate your claims about Blake's involvement."

"The DA is working on filing new charges against Gary to put him back in jail. This time, they plan on using you to help them restore his original sentence."

"I don't know anything about Gary and Russ. Or who framed Gary for Maverick's death…if he was framed."

"Your police report states that Blake had come after Porter and his father's business. Gary's trying to show that Blake had reason to frame him. And Dixon somehow helped. He knows that you can fill in the gaps. With my testimony, he can plant seeds of doubt regarding Russ's innocence."

My head began to swirl.

"Together," Gavin continued, "if he has both of us,

he can keep me from talking about Russ and use you to discredit Dixon. Then, Blake takes the fall."

My pen tapped the notebook, "Our testimonies are enough?"

"Without us, the DA can still use the original signed witness statement from a man named Vincent Lloyd who saw Gary murder Maverick. So far, Gary's been looking for this person for years, and no one has been able to find him." Gavin tapped on his phone a few times, swiping through screens. "Here's his driver's license photo." The man was unremarkable. He would have been anyone. "Gary's lawyers think Dixon made the witness report to cover for himself."

"I've heard so many lies and rumors about Gary, and now I finally have the truth. Daniel made it seem like all this happened decades ago."

"Daniel Sullivan?"

I had given away a tell. But I didn't deny it. "Yeah, he was the one who helped me with my whole Blake investigation." I dropped the pen, tucking my nervous tics out of sight.

My reaction went unnoticed. "Gary went to jail shortly after I killed Russ. My dad left town, and Porter took over the business," Gavin said.

"What do you know about the man Gary murdered?"

"Not much. When they found his body, there wasn't much left. Apparently, animals had eaten parts of him." I had resumed writing until this moment. Gavin moved on, "They were able to find his identity because he was a felon. The police put up some flyers asking for leads. Then, they got a statement from Victor Lloyd."

I sat back. "Instead of finding Victor Lloyd, you'd rather have me get you out of testifying for Gary?"

"Something like that." Gavin's eyes softened, "You worked for Porter. Daniel took you deep into his drug operation."

"Not that deep."

"Well, deep enough where you can testify that Blake had nothing to do with that murder in the woods. And he was right when he targeted Porter's business. He was unhinged, desperate for answers about who killed his dad. And he wrongly assumed Gary was involved. But he never framed anyone. Because if he did, he would have never had Six shoot me. He would have never continued attacking Gary's business; not if he already got his revenge."

Telling the law what I knew was the only card I had to play. I also had the flash drive, crammed with files, ledgers, videos, and photos showing the operation. There was so much stuff, I hadn't been through it all. It was exactly what Gavin would need to make his case.

The only problem lied with my love and loyalties. Daniel had given me that flash drive as a good faith measure. It was meant to protect me, not pull me further into danger. If I used it, Gary would have a reason to kill me, just to keep me from using it against him. I'd be… erased.

Plus, there was something else Gavin didn't consider.

"My testimony could hurt you," I said. Gavin tilted his head, slightly deflated. "Gary and your dad were working together. Hank was there when you shot Russ; Gary could easily turn that evidence around and use it to prove that he covered for you and your dad. They could make it look like you committed the other murder and tried to pin it on Gary as revenge." I pulled out the last letter Hank had given him. "The scratched-out part says that your dad had gotten even with Gary. Do you know what that was about?"

Gavin held the letter to light. "No." He offered me the letter. "I don't want it."

I placed the paper back in my purse, "Why didn't the police just go to your dad for answers? I'm sure they saw a line between Hank and Gary."

"After Gary was locked up, my dad washed his hands of everything in Settlement Island."

"Don't you find that strange?"

Gavin shrugged, "Like always, my dad's being a deadbeat. I'd be surprised if he tried to help me." How tragic. His father should stand with him. Be on his side. "Since he's let me down, I was hoping you would get me through this," he said. Gavin's tension rose to the surface, "We need each other."

No, we didn't. "Gavin, we're not good together."

"I'm not talking about us dating."

"Neither am I." Bitterness rolled up my throat. "If I get involved, Porter will find me. And if I can't produce Kyle, he'd probably kill me." My hand flew up, silencing him. The next breath wasn't satisfying, "However, I'm torn. Blake only wanted to know the truth about what happened to his father. And we robbed him of that. Everything I've been looking into is for him."

"So, you're going to help a dead guy and not me?" he stressed. "What difference does it make? Blake is gone."

"But the mystery still remains." I had to know, "What happened between Russ and Hank? Why did Gary want Russ dead?" The rapid succession of my questions didn't end. "You killed a man, and you don't even know why. Doesn't that bother you? It bothers me every day. I have to find out," I said. "For me and Blake."

"So, you're going to be a fuckin' martyr again?" he hissed.

"I'm doing the right thing, for once." I closed my book and straightened my spine, "We have different goals. You want to defend yourself, and I want to get the full story for Blake. Then, I can move on, completely. With my life, my boyfriend, and whatever it is God has in store for me." That last part felt like a lie. Killing Blake meant God didn't want anything to do with me. But I could hope. "I can't help you." Gavin started an explanation, but I shut him down. "Good luck with Gary."

My choice to leave wasn't dramatic. Silently, I grabbed my purse and set it on my shoulder. He held my stare. This would be goodbye.

The café was crowded. I only made it a couple steps before his hand was on my arm. I flinched. "I'm sorry," he said in a breathy tone. "Really, I am." I fought the urge to look at him. "I wasn't gonna come here, but I ran out of options." Gavin took my hand, "Please, help me."

My intention was to tell him that he had an endless supply of options. When my eyes hit his, I couldn't bring the words to my lips. Gavin was broken. Scared. The same way he was when that bullet tore through his flesh, eating away at his life.

It was painful, but I didn't allow him to find any sympathy in me. "Gavin, no. I can't."

He leaned into my ear, "What are you afraid of?"

Fear and isolation were not the same thing. I had marooned myself here, so isolation could keep me safe. Yes, I had been on this crusade to find the truth for Blake, but that was on my own terms. No one would get hurt if I just played Nancy Drew with Luke from three-thousand miles away. Everything was within our control, just the way I liked it.

What Gavin was proposing wouldn't be on my terms. We'd have to find a way to work together, lean on each other for support. I wasn't ready for that.

I looked down at his hand, and he let go of me. "Just think about it tonight, and let me know tomorrow if your answer is still no. If it is, I will leave you alone. I promise."

I sighed, "Do you still have the same number?" He nodded. "I'll text you when I'm ready with my decision." My fate wasn't predetermined; I chose what happened to me. So, I would consider Gavin's offer after I had a chance to see if he still held any information that would help me.

Back to my murder wall. Given what Gavin had told me, I had renewed interest in Hank's role in Russ's death. Perhaps he knew something that would connect Gary to Russ and Maverick. I pulled out my phone to tell Luke of our new developments.

Noah had sent a text while I was with Gavin. He was on my doorstep, waiting for me. I had forgotten about his big plans for today. I bumped into someone while I replied to my boyfriend, forcing me to look forward.

I caught my blond-haired admirer meandering throughout the crowd on the boardwalk. His back turned to me, the name *Blood Diamond* etched into the leather.

Then, a memory and a fact stitched together.

Maverick Spencer, the guy Gary murdered, was also a *Blood Diamond*.

CHAPTER FOUR

Rose

"Yeah, he was a Blood Diamond," I told Luke as I walked slowly down the boardwalk. I had bought myself some time with Noah by telling him I was about fifteen minutes away. Now, I had nine, maybe ten minutes until he started wondering why I was taking so long.

Luke didn't care if Noah had to wait. He wanted to go through my event with the Blood Diamond again before he formed an opinion. Finally, he said, "Do you think he followed Gavin from Maine?"

"Not likely." I ran my hand through my hair, "Maverick didn't live in Settlement Island." The news article regarding Maverick's murder didn't yield much. And the police report referred to him as a non-resident only. "He could have been visiting someone up there. Another biker, maybe?" That had to be the link. "Are there any Blood Diamond biker gang members in Settlement Island? Or Anders?"

"I can look into it. But I've never heard of them."

"Okay, well, I'll see what Gavin knows." I put Luke on speaker while I surfed for Gavin's number. "The way he stared at me was so odd. It can't be a coincidence, right?"

"Calm down," Luke's request didn't match his tone. Our mysterious stranger's presence bothered him, too. "We're gonna figure this out."

Noah called, again. "Okay." Relief stretched across my body. Luke never let me down when it came to his promises. "I need to go. Noah's sitting on my porch, waiting for me."

"Make him wait." I scolded Luke for being rude. "Oh, Dixon said I can come by the station this evening while he's on duty. I'll ask him about the Blood Diamonds."

"You're the best." I could see Noah staring at his phone. "I'll look on the flash drive and see if I missed anything." My phone beeped again. "I'll call you later."

"Be careful."

"With Noah?" I laughed. "He's a good guy, remember?"

"As your friend," he preached, "I've met the guys you've been into, and I'm not impressed."

Neither was I, at times. "Noah's different. He's kind and sweet. And he's not from Maine."

"Ouch," Luke said. "That one hurt."

"You were born in Vermont?"

"Yeah, but Maine is my home," he said.

"Well, there you go." Luke had lightened my mood. But I did have to end our call. Noah couldn't know about my other best friend. The one who pursued the deadly things hiding in my past that I didn't want Noah to know about. "I'll call you when I have a chance."

"You better."

I put the phone away, so my boyfriend didn't know I was screening his calls. He caught me as the tension rolled off my shoulders. This would help me keep the attention off my growing concerns surrounding Settlement Island.

Noah was observant. If I was upset, or hiding something, he would uncover it. Such a great quality for a boyfriend. Today, I didn't want him to see a glimpse of worry on me. I brightened my smile. He met me on the boardwalk, his arm going over my shoulder. Noah kissed my cheek. "Happy birthday, my love," he said with little effort. Like loving me was so easy, despite my constant deflections.

"I missed you yesterday," I said while holding onto him. His skin always felt so good.

Sympathy crossed his lips. Missing time with me was like missing church. His parents had taught him to keep his commitments no matter what. He stuck to his values, which was impressive. His best qualities went on from there.

Noah was slightly older than me. Originally from Montana, he still had his cowboy roots. Blond hair, darker than Kyle's, eyes more brown than blue, he shouldn't have been my type. A working-class boy, he reminded me of Luke with his need to help others while having Dad's work ethic. But change was good, especially for me.

Today, Noah had left the cowboy hat at home, even though he needed a haircut. Ripped Levis tucked into worn boots, he rolled up his only button-down shirt and tossed my phone on the table next to the door after I let us in. It hit my mother's vase. The same vase that held my birthday flowers.

"I was using that."

"Your phone can wait." Noah laced my fingers into his and pulled me back into the living room. He appraised each item, "Is Kyle here?"

"He's at work. He'll probably stay on site for the next few days."

"Good. I brought this," Noah held up a bottle of wine and a cake.

When Kyle and I were together, which was often, I didn't drink, either. The sober solidarity was yet another thing that had created the bond between me and him. That and all the murdering and losses we had suffered in Settlement Island. Today, I would indulge in one glass only, to keep my senses sharp.

Noah squeezed my arm and gave me a hopeful smile. "I went by the restaurant on my way home, and Miguel said you had left already. I would have stopped by, but it seemed too late."

"Yeah, I came home and crashed. Had a long day." Now, I had to know, "How long did you stay at Miguel's?"

"Only ten minutes or so."

Good. Taking Noah out in public was a bit tricky. You see, Miguel and his family all knew me by a different name. They knew most of my past. So, I was always enduring various conversations with people who were eager to know why I had suddenly come back to California without an explanation, country boy in tow.

I dodged their questions, pivoting toward the high crime rates Settlement Island had succumbed to. "Yeah, but California is no different," they would say. Then came the long story about a friend or family member who had been carjacked at knife point. Or that one time someone got held up at a gas station. "Maine can't be that bad."

Every time, every challenge to my claims, was met with beaming confidence. "Yeah, I guess I missed home," I'd say. Pretty much everyone understood that.

Even when inquiries were dropped, the edge never left my shoulders. Each question or rebuttal came with increased risk. Noah would hear the wrong thing, and my plans would have to change. I had a go bag ready. Kyle did, too. Cash was tucked in an unused purse, along with passports, legal documents, everything we needed to disappear. Noah wasn't a threat, but he couldn't know anything. I had to be careful. One slip from an unknowing friend or family member could lead Ian to my door.

The gravity of this didn't seem to bother me during my debates with Gavin earlier. When I spelled out my crusade to absolve Blake from wrongful homicide. Emotions flew high, dulling my judgment. Again, I needed to be more careful.

Noah put the cake back in the box. "Let's eat this on the beach."

I gathered up a blanket, some glasses, and silverware. Noah opened the door, allowing me to exit first. He grabbed the wine and chased after me. Outside, we made a dash for the sand, the sun still high in the sky.

The beach was swollen with tourists. "Where did all those people come from?" I said as I dressed the shore with a little spot for us. I plopped down, pulling the sundress over my bent knees.

"Not sure." Noah gently positioned the box on the sand, opening it. Inside was a fondant cake with swirls and pretty decorations. He proceeded to light the candles. He sat behind me, pulling my body into his. The glow of flames would have been magical, if the sun hadn't drowned them out. "Happy birthday to you!" Noah sang with his country drawl.

After he completed his serenade, I blew out my candles. Noah surprised me with a kiss. A grateful kiss for having invited him into my life.

"If I was an insecure man, I'd be worried about you spending your birthday night with another man." Noah's smile was crooked.

"Kyle doesn't like me like that," I replied. Noah's head tilted. "We're just friends. He has a major crush on my sister."

He sighed, "All this time, I thought…in my defense, you just recently introduced me to him," he jabbed my side.

"It's only been three months. I don't even know if I like you yet."

Lips pressed to mine, he grinned. "Well, I like you, Rose. A lot."

Rose. My middle name. He didn't know me as Catalina. Only a few people here did. Each time that name rolled off Noah's tongue, I wanted to tell him the truth. Tell him to call me by my real name. Spend time with the real me.

Dr. Wong said Rose and Catalina were the same person. I didn't owe Noah anything until I was ready to tell him more. We were still getting to know each other. He had to earn my trust. This relationship should be…fun.

Noah and I were having fun. His sweetness saturated every action he took. He was a Christian, through and through. And a gentleman. Beyond kissing, he didn't try making a move for anything more. As he put it, "If we are meant to be, there's no reason to rush things." Although, it had been a year since the last time I had…

I pushed Gavin's bare chest and tight abs out of mind. "Wanna go back inside?"

"We just got here."

My fingers danced across his shirt, "I thought we could watch a movie or just hang out."

He gave me no pushback. Noah seized the cake as we made the very short commute down the boardwalk and onto the beach front properties, admiring the ocean.

As Noah opened the door to my beach house, he frowned again at Kyle's stuff sitting in my living room. My bedroom door was cracked, so I casually raced across to close it.

I hadn't covered up my murder wall since last night. A dire oversight. Normally, it hid beneath a beautiful drape I had found along Telegraph Avenue a few months ago. I loved it, but it was a pain in the ass to put up, so I didn't bother with it. Now, I regret my laziness. One peek inside and Noah would be on his way to tying the link between Catalina Rose Payton and Ian Robert Porter.

"Don't worry. I know I'm not allowed in your room," Noah said, stepping over Kyle's bag and sitting on the couch.

"It's a mess, that's all." Kyle's stuff went into the guest room. I sat down next to Noah. His eyes drifted back to the guest room. "He's just a friend."

"From Maine. Who moved out here with you?" Noah's tone was strained.

"I know what it looks like, but it's not that. We had a chance to hook up years ago," I said. This comment didn't soothe Noah's expression. "He was high, talking about how much he wanted to bang my sister, and he asked if I wanted him to be my first."

"That's inappropriate." Noah leaned back into the couch, "Did he have sex with your sister?"

"God, no! And I turned him down. He was just horny and coked out of his mind." I chuckled until my hand touched Noah's rigid body. My hand traveled to his knee, "Seriously, we haven't shared a soda or anything." *Except, I did let him sleep in my bed last night.* "His DNA has never been anywhere near my body."

"It's not that." He sat up, "It's not completely that. When can I meet your family?"

Why was he in such a rush? "It's only been like three months."

"I know," he said. "You've met my parents and my brothers and sister."

"That's because they came through town on their National Parks tour."

Noah licked his lips, "You've got your aunt who lives in Berkeley. Why can't I meet her?"

My stomach twisted. I wasn't ready for this discussion. Again, I really did like Noah. And I liked the way things were right now. I hoped a kiss, followed by another, would drop the subject. He held onto my head as I continued kissing him, tugging on his shirt. The spell was broken.

"Rose, what are you doing?"

"It's my birthday." A kiss. "Well, yesterday was." Another kiss, "I really like your outfit." Another kiss. "But you'd look better…"

He broke away and searched my eyes. "You're trying to distract me." *Damn you, Noah and your quick mind.* His fingers feathered my hair. "Why don't you want me to meet your family?"

I sat back, huffing a sigh. "It's complicated. We're complicated."

With reassurance, he said, "If they're anything like you, I'm sure I'll love them." He paused, cautious, "Is it because I'm white?"

I laughed, loudly. "My family is not racist. Not even close." I let the couch cushions swallow me, "My sister's boyfriend is white. Well, her soon-to-be ex-boyfriend, if he doesn't call her back. And so was my last boyfriend." I could see Noah quietly ponder what was wrong with him. "My last relationship left quite the impression on my family. Not a good one. I just don't want them to be concerned if they see me with someone new."

"They don't want you to move on?"

"I'm pretty sure they want me to move into a convent and become a nun."

"That bad?" I nodded. Noah cracked a smile, "It's a good thing you're not with him anymore."

Yes, it was. Noah's lips found mine. "I'm sorry I pressured you. Let's take it slow."

I kissed him again with more eagerness. "How slow?" He grinned and returned another kiss. We didn't hold back. A gentle hand placed me on my back. Noah's weight pressed me further into the cushions.

"Are you sure?" he said. I nodded.

A sea of kisses came over us. His shirt came off. He had a slender body, soft skin. I grinned, pulling him toward me. We had touched and kissed before, but this was different. The tenderness and impatient hunger between us was building fast. I tilted my head back as Noah kissed my neck, curls brushing out of the way. I was ready for this. Yearning for it. Even after seeing Gavin and his tight shirt pulling across…

And Noah was stopping. He sat up, finding his breaths, moving hair out of his face.

"Why did you stop?" I said.

His nervous chuckle dented the moment, "I think we should slow down." The mood died with his next words, "I just," he paused, "we should get to know each other more."

This wasn't about sleeping together. It had to do with my family. And Kyle. "You don't believe me about Kyle. Or my past." He didn't seem to have a pre-planned response. "It's because I won't open up to you, isn't it?"

Noah's hands rested in his lap as he scooted away a bit. "I feel like you're hiding something from me." I bowed my eyes. It was foolish to think he wouldn't see through them. I was a terrible liar, even now.

This was supposed to be fun. Dating shouldn't make you feel like you're losing an interrogation.

My phone buzzed, sparing him from more lies. "Sorry, I gotta get that."

"No, you don't."

The buzzing continued. "It might be one of those secrets I'm hiding."

And it was.

"Who is it?"

"My sister Cecilia." I only divulged her identity because I trusted her, not him. She was quick on her feet. Hearing Noah's voice would signal her to let me decide what he got to know about us. "Hey, I'm here with my boyfriend," I rushed out.

"Am I on speaker phone?" she said.

My brows scrunched together. Normally, she floated around her conversations with yards of playfulness. Something was wrong. Thankfully, Noah sensed it, too.

"Hey, Cecilia." He looked to me for encouragement. "It's nice to finally meet you. Rose has had nothing but good things to say about you."

"That's nice. Can you hand me back to my sister, please?" Noah complied.

"Hang on a second," I said to her and put the phone on mute. "I think something's wrong."

"Should I go?"

"No, I'll just be a minute."

He kissed my lips. "Take as long as you need."

I went into my bedroom and closed the door. Grabbing my earbuds, I took Cecilia off speaker while I fought the drape to cover the murder wall. When Kyle got back, I would have him put up a rod and some clips to make this process so much easier. "Hey, what's going on?" I said.

"Dad called me and asked if I knew where Aaron was."

I continued pushing the fabric and snapping it into the hooks nailed into the drywall, "Why is he asking you?"

"Apparently, he was supposed to be at work today. He didn't show up. He didn't go to Anders General, either. I'm driving over to his house right now while Luke watches the store." After everything that went down last year, my sister didn't like leaving the store unattended. Even with the expensive camera system in place.

"I talked to Dad yesterday. He said Aaron was taking some days off," I said. Thinking of it, my dad was supposed to call me with more details, and he didn't.

"Cat, this isn't like him. Yeah, he gets busy a lot, but he doesn't just stop talking to me. He definitely wouldn't ignore Dad and his patients."

She had a point. "You're going over there alone?"

"James, Mark and Oliver are with me."

Great. "Aaron doesn't like them."

"He has a newfound respect for them, you know, since they helped save Settlement Island and all. I would have brought Luke, but he's supposed to meet with Officer Dixon this evening. He offered to stay with the store instead, since it's really close to the police station."

My sister was craftier than I thought. "How long until you get there?"

"Five minutes."

"When you get inside, let's video chat. I want to see what you're seeing."

"I'll call you then."

Now, with my sister on her mission, I needed to get rid

of Noah. I stepped out of my room, allowing the worry to engulf my face. "What's wrong?"

"My sister's really upset about her boyfriend. He's ghosting her." I downplayed my concern enough to get him to worry but not want to stick around. "This might take a while."

Noah nodded. "Of course." He threw his shoes on and fixed his hair. "I'll give you your space."

"Thanks." I pressed a few meaningful kisses on his lips. "Tomorrow, can we spend the whole day together?"

"And will you tell me more about your family?"

"Yes."

Noah was a great kisser. I got lost in the sugary notion behind each stroke of his lips against mine. A few more kisses and Cecilia was buzzing on my phone. I turned Noah's attention to the door and opened it, regretting the fact that we couldn't take this further. He surprised me with another long kiss before I shut him out.

Then, I raced to my bedroom and tore the drape off the wall. "Cecilia?"

The first thing I saw was her bounding curls and perfect face. If she looked worried, it didn't show. Three figures moved in the background of the dark house. Like a true investigator, Cecilia combed Aaron's home thoroughly. All the curtains were drawn. No food in the fridge or scraps of food in the pantry. His bed was made. The place was immaculate, except for one thing.

"His suitcases are gone. So is his medical bag."

"He's running," I announced.

James took over the video, "What do you mean he's running?"

I unscrambled my thoughts. "I've been to Aaron's house before, and it was clean, but not that clean. It looks like he planned on leaving, not in a hurry. He had time. He must have known something was coming."

"Alright, Sherlock, do you think this has anything to do with Gary?"

James's question was a validate assumption, one I didn't quite have an answer for. "I don't know. If it does, he must've known Gary was getting out of jail." I pointed to the fridge and pantry. "When was the last time he stayed here?"

I saw Cecilia's face again, "He's been staying at the loft with me." James snarled. She shushed him. "He's disappeared from there, too. I thought maybe he came back home, but it looks like he didn't."

"Did he leave anything at your house? Like his suitcase and medical bag?"

"I'm not an idiot, Cat. That's the first thing I checked."

"Well?" I hissed.

"All his normal stuff is there. That's why I wasn't too worried until Dad called. I just thought he was working long hours and sleeping on the couch in his office." She looked back at his closet. "I bought him a set of really nice luggage for Valentine's Day, and it's missing. He didn't bring them over to my house, because he didn't need them." She turned the camera; Aaron's closet was empty.

James clicked his tongue, "He packed stuff from here, so you wouldn't notice he was gone." My heart sank.

Aaron really had vanished. "I'm telling you, Gary's the one behind this."

I shuddered, "Porter loves his brother; he wouldn't let anything happen to him."

"Well, you don't know him like I do."

Actually, I did. "Aaron's all that Porter's got. Besides, if he was gonna do something to his brother, he would have done a lot sooner."

"I wouldn't bet the farm on that," Oliver chimed in. "Fuckin' Gary's got a way with people. He can get them to do whatever he wants."

"Blind loyalty shit," Mark added.

Their concerns were strong, but Ian had his boundaries. "I don't know. I think…" I stopped. Ian had also vanished from Settlement Island since I saw him in the cemetery. Luke had confirmed this for me. "I think you're right." I gulped down a breath, "If Porter's missing, Aaron doesn't have any protection against Gary."

James took the phone. "We need to find Aaron before Gary kills him." Cecilia's face dropped. She was scared. "I'll let everyone know."

"If he ran to protect himself, he may be hard to find." I grabbed a notebook and a pen, starting my own investigation. "I'll call you the moment I know something." Cecilia sniffed, shielding her face from tears. "He's probably okay."

She nodded and said she loved me before hanging up.

First, I called Aaron. It went straight to voicemail. "Hey, sorry I haven't talked to you for a long, long time. My sister's freaking out, and I think you're on the run from

Gary." I sucked in my fears, "We just need to know that you're okay. So, give me a call or a text."

Then, I made the one call I didn't want to make. "Hey, Gavin." I didn't allow him a chance to say anything. "I need you to come over right away." There was a knock at the door. Painfully, I sighed and opened it. "How did you find me?"

Gavin smirked, "I followed you home." Of course, he did. "My meeting with my Stanford advisor was switched to a video call. I ended up sticking around after our breakfast, watching you and your new boy play on the beach."

"Gross," I retorted.

We stared at one another, "Are you gonna invite me in?" he said. I wasn't in a gaming mood. He picked up on it quickly. "Sorry for spying on you. I was curious about your little boyfriend. He's a lot skinnier than I imagined. Doesn't seem like your type." I grabbed Gavin's arm and thrusted him into my living room, locking the door. This time, my uneasiness brought his teasing to a close. "What's wrong?"

"Aaron's running from Gary."

CHAPTER FIVE

Russ

GAVIN'S BROWS GREW together. "Who told you Aaron's running from Gary?"

"Cecilia and James can't find him. It seems like he left around the same time Gary went free." Gavin's stance had tightened. Muscles ready for a fight. Wanting one. Last I knew, he and Aaron were still pretty distant, at best. So where was all this concern coming from? His extended silence killed me. "How are Aaron and Gary connected?"

"What makes you think I know anything about Gary and Aaron?" he said.

"A hunch?" My sarcasm deepened Gavin's bad mood. "They share a family member," I scoffed. "Gary owns the drug enterprise with Porter, which is something Aaron never approved of. I'm sure Gary and Aaron don't like each other. And you don't like them, so I figured you would have some clue about this." His confusion kept me going, "Your enemy of your enemy is your friend. If Aaron had something against Gary, he told you when you guys were cool?" The straws I was grasping for had faded.

Gavin tapped against his jeans. Maybe this was a nervous tic he had been hiding. "You said you were sharing details with Luke about what's going on in Settlement Island?" I nodded. "What have you figured out so far?" I took him into my bedroom and introduced him to the murder wall. "Holy shit, Catalina. This is…"

"…crazy? Over the top?"

His head shook, "Impressive." He admired the photos and the lines tying them to the other. Red string that made them one. "You're doing this because of Blake?" He turned to me. "To make amends for killing him?"

"It started with Blake." I stepped up, "He was investigating the relationship between Russ and Gary, right? Well, it goes far beyond that." I pointed to the printout about the murder Gary committed. "This murder is the focus of our problem with Gary now." Another look, "There is no tie between Gary and Aaron, except through Porter. So, why would Aaron run? Did he know about Maverick's case?"

Gavin backed away and took a seat on the bed. "My dad's up there." He paused. I assumed he was making sense of it all. "You spent a lot of time on this."

"When your life depends on it, you'll spend all the time it takes."

Inhaling a steady breath, he admired my work like art. Twisted art that had drawn him into this room. He pointed to Gary's photo, "Gary claims he was framed. Other people are starting to believe it, too."

Hesitation filled the room. "You believe him?"

"Why else would Aaron run?" Gavin kicked off his boots and pulled his knees up. His arms rested on his legs as he sighed. "Aaron never really talked about Gary. Not much, that is. He had his suspicions that maybe Gary and I would have it out since he pretty much killed my mom." I wanted to interject to get more details and clear things up, but he politely asked for my silence. "I was so young back then. A teenager. I didn't want to take on Gary myself. Besides, my dad was a part of his business. I figured if I got involved, it would make things worse."

"How could they get worse?"

"Hank was always trying to prove that he wasn't working with Gary. That he wasn't a drug dealer or the reason my mom was dead. He blamed everyone else, and they saw right through him. That night that Russ got killed, they were arguing. They were best friends, but I guess there are some lines that cannot be crossed."

"I'm sorry, but what do Hank and Gary have to do with Aaron?"

"Russ didn't like Gary. No one did. And we know Dixon was out to get him. I wouldn't be surprised if someone got the bright idea to plant some evidence for a dirty cop to find and put him away."

"You think Aaron was that person?"

The shrug he gave was sure enough to be convincing. "If Aaron helped whoever framed Gary, he would be at the top of his kill list."

"And your dad?"

"What about him?"

"What's your theory on your dad? Why did you bring

him up?" Gavin stroked his lower lip while he distracted himself with the wall. Family was a pain point, for good reason. Yet, *he* brought his father up, not me. I sat down next to him, my leg brushed against his jeans. "I've heard everybody's explanation about what happened that night with Russ. I read the report. But you never told me the whole story."

"I shot him," he chuckled darkly.

"I know," I turned, showing him that he was my only focus. "There has to be more. I just want to hear it from you." His silence was unnerving. "I shut you down the last time we talked about it. This time, I'm listening." Friendship wrapped around my voice. He could trust me. "What happened?"

Gavin started slowly, "It was my seventeenth birthday. Hank had been in and out of town, working as a trucker. I assume he did this because he was still running drugs from Gary. He never really confirms and denies when he was working for Gary, but I don't see how he could have made a respectable living with a high school diploma, about fifteen DUIs, and a glaring drug addiction."

"How could he get a job as a trucker with all these problems?"

"Gary needed people with no criminal record to transport his drugs out of state. My dad was sadly one of the cleanest dealers he had. Gary paid some lawyer to hide some of those DUIs and get him a not-guilty verdict for some of the other ones, just so he would be able to get his CDL. Then, it was only a matter of paying off cops and bribing people to get him the rest of the way."

"Is it really that simple?"

"James says it is. He was in and out of the drug world, going to jail, getting out, blah, blah, blah. He might tell you otherwise, but James going to jail was some of the best years of our lives. He made friends with everybody, including some of Gary's low-level dealers. They taught him all the tricks Gary used to get people out, so he used them to sweep his charges under the rug. As his best friend, he would tell me what was up. Help me keep tabs on Hank. And that's what led to what happened between me and Russ."

I reached over and grabbed my notebook. "Is it okay if I write this down?"

"Knock yourself out." Gavin walked over to the wall. He pointed to Russ. "Hank never really told me when he was in town. He would breeze in, start shit, and leave. James heard through the network that Hank was running some stuff up, and he'd be in town around my birthday. That night, Hank showed up. He called and said he wanted to see me for my birthday. He told me to meet him at the hotel he was staying at. On the way, I saw a fight. I recognized my dad."

"Did you see Russ?"

He nodded. "I didn't know it was Russ, though. I jumped out of the car and ran up to them. Russ was in way better shape than Hank, so he was winning. My dad started yelling at me to do something. He was afraid he was gonna die. I pulled out the gun, and I held it up. I was only going to scare him. But when he turned around, I saw the anger on him. He was coming toward me, and I pulled the trigger." Gavin licked his lips, "He fell." He sat down again.

I put my hand on his right hand, the one that had held that gun. Empathy for his gut-wrenching decision was a mirror we both held. I knew what this meant to him. To take a life. Kyle had made it look so easy. But I couldn't. It was beyond hard to live with yourself.

Gavin separated us, "Hank didn't hesitate. He jumped up and started yelling at me to get rid of the gun. If anyone asked, tell them he wasn't in town. And that I needed to destroy evidence. I hung around enough criminals to know what he was telling me to do. He wanted me to cover for him, even though I was the killer. So, I went to his truck and grabbed his notebook."

I went to my desk and pulled out Hank's journal. "This one?"

He nodded. "That's the one. He had it for years. I knew it had to be related to his drug dealing."

"Why did you think it was important?"

"If he tried to mislead the police about his involvement, I had proof. At the time, he went out his way to hide his drug dealing, but I caught on fast. My grandmother said he was driving for some company on the west coast delivering food to grocery stores. He would send her postcards with palm trees from places like Oregon, Seattle, San Diego, all coastal cities. Well, if he was working on the west coast, why is he keeping mileage and hotel records from here to Florida? Besides, James confirmed that all those locations were very close to where Gary and Porter had their operations."

"So, you put it together?"

"Yep." He sighed, "I grabbed the notebook. He had a duffle bag stuffed with money, so I grabbed a stack of hundreds. I told him it was my fee for saving his ass. Before I knew it, he was jumping in his truck and speeding away. The police got there because a witness saw Russ lying on the road. I couldn't get out of it. I hid the money and the notebook in a bush and picked it up after I got out on bail. I kept the gun on me because I thought it would help me in court."

"And you ended up getting off for self-defense?"

He shrugged, "I'm not sure how it happened, but Mark's mom was a bad ass." Shame was expected after he uttered his next words, "Word got to Gary about my situation. Not sure how he did it, but he used his friends on the force to help me stay out of jail. I was Hank's boy and all. Of course, Dixon wouldn't help him because of Blake."

Another mystery had to be solved, "His friend's dad was dead; there was no way he would let you get off. I still don't understand, though. Why…"

"…why would Gary help? Russ was popular. Eventually, the town would find out who murdered him. I was a drug dealer's son. Gary couldn't use any more bad press, so he made sure my record stayed sealed. Mark's mom worked with his lawyers to keep my identity a secret. That's where Officer Dixon comes in. He was there on the night of the murder. He asked me questions, but I didn't have any answers for him. Mark's mom wouldn't let me talk to anyone except the DA, who was friends with Gary. He ended up getting shot and killed shortly after my case was closed, so…"

"Is everybody's solution to a problem to kill someone?" I said. He shrugged, again. Moving on, "Dixon told me he didn't think you killed Russ. Was he trying to help you for some sick reason?"

"I killed Russ. It was self-defense. When Dixon arrived, I just threw a story at him. I said I saw Russ fighting with someone, and I shot the gun, trying to protect Russ, but I hit him by accident." Now, his toughness took a hit, "I was a mess. I threw up and started crying. I guess that was all the proof he needed. His demeanor changed once Gary started helping me. He knew things weren't right; the story I told him was probably a lie. He didn't confront me. No one goes against Gary."

The rest of the story I knew. "Russ had an issue with drug dealers because his house was robbed by some druggies. They were never caught, Blake never had the truth. He came after you and Porter because you two were involved in his father's death."

Then I killed him.

Thanks to Gavin's monologue, I didn't dwell for too long. Redemption for killing an unfortunate soul was the only thing I had sought for the last year. Now, I had found it.

I had satisfied my yearning for atonement for my sins and Gavin's lingering problem.

"Blake's vendetta wasn't wrong," I said. Gavin looked like I had just shot him all over again. "You and your dad are the reason Russ died. Blake felt justified in his attack against you and Porter, and Porter didn't even raise a finger against him."

"What's your point?" Gavin hissed.

"If he felt that way about you, we need to find a person who would have that level of hatred toward Gary." Yes, that was it. "This person is the one responsible for everything that has happened. If we find them and make them pay for the shit they pulled, we can feel better about what we did to Russ and Blake. We'll probably find the person who framed Gary along the way, if he was actually framed."

Gavin didn't quite know what to think. He searched for some words through pauses and stammering. "I don't know if it works that way." Quickly, he said, "You're falling for Gary's lie about being set up, too?"

It made the most sense. "Gary had a lot of enemies, I'm sure. Framing him for murder would be a great way to finally get back at him."

Gavin pondered my thoughts. "Catalina, this path is gonna be super traumatizing for us."

"We're already traumatized."

"This is gonna be different. Reliving it is going to be painful." Pessimism was the one trait he fell back on, "I didn't mean to kill Russ. I was protecting my dad. As shitty as he was, I still loved him back then. He was my only family." Deep reflection creased his forehead. "I regret Russ's murder every day because it wasn't worth it. Hank and I hate each other more than ever. It would have been better if I just let Russ take him out."

Sadly, Gavin meant every ungrateful statement he made on his father. Not selfishness but rather selflessness, and powerlessness, imprisoning him in the past.

When we were in love, Gavin was the most selfless

person I knew. That was before. I had no idea who he had become since then.

It didn't matter.

This story was an outcry for help. A twist to the originally proposed arrangement we were to make. Our alliance, if we formed one, would exonerate us both from the murders that still held us captive.

For me to do this, I thought beyond what I needed. I'd carry into this plan my crusade to get justice for Blake. Added into this mix was my duty to Aaron, wherever he had gone. I couldn't let him suffer for what we had done. "If Aaron is in danger because of me, I have to help him. He's been there for me, shielding me from his brother as much as he could." My voice hitched, "He tried to save Blake after I shot him. He held onto Blake's hand until he took his last breath."

Gavin looked at my wall again. An idea framed his brows. He walked up to examine the murder that Gary had been charged with. He tapped on the murdered biker. "This is where we start. We put Gary and this guy together. Then, we trace it back to Aaron."

My phone chimed with a video chat. Cecilia was trying to reach me. "Hey, did you find Aaron?"

She started to answer, but her head bobbed past me, "Gavin, is that you?" He winked at her. "That didn't take long."

"What didn't take long?"

"The two of you hooking up again."

"We're not hooking up," I said. She huffed. "Cecilia, what do you want? Did you find Aaron?"

Luke appeared in the video, too. "No, we haven't. We didn't have a chance to look for him." He murmured a curse, "I went to meet with Jaime Dixon at the station, and the police were all freaking out."

"Why?"

"Someone killed him."

Gavin and I bounced the news between us, unable to believe it. "Dixon's dead?" he said.

"Yeah. They found him in his patrol car. They think he was shot when he left to go on patrol. He was slumped over the driver's seat with a bunch of gunshot wounds."

"Sounds like Gary," Gavin added.

I held my answer, dreading the uproar it would create. Aaron was missing. Now, Dixon was found dead. This wasn't looking good. "Dixon was on the murder case involving Gary," I said to Gavin.

He nodded. "Luke, Catalina's gonna send you a phone number to an attorney. She's a friend of mine. She can get you access to the police reports."

But wait… "Why would Gary shoot Dixon if he had information on the murder that put him behind bars?" I said, "Wouldn't he want to torture him to get a name?"

"Maybe he didn't give it up," Gavin said. "Or, maybe he didn't want Dixon helping whoever it was that framed him in the first place."

Luke relented to the possibility. "If Dixon wouldn't give up the name, that could be enough to shoot him," he said.

Gavin agreed, "Either way, it seems like Dixon was more valuable to Gary as a dead man. Which means he probably got what he wanted and is now onto his next victim."

"Be careful," my sister said to me. "I don't like this."

"I'll be fine, Cecilia," I said. "Gary doesn't want me dead, I think." According to Gavin, we were safe for the time being. I chose to continue believing him. "Plus, I'm all the way over here."

She and Luke chatted about what they should do next. She leaned on him like a wife would her husband. Luke decided, "We're gonna see if the police know anything yet."

My concerns were short-lived. Luke was strong now. Determined and slightly jaded. He would be able to get the answers we sought without putting my sister in danger.

"I love you guys. Be safe," I said.

Cecilia blew a kiss and the screen went black.

I walked up to my murder wall. Painfully, I pulled a marker from my desk and wrote the word "Murdered" over Dixon's face, another life gunned down before his time.

Jamie Dixon wasn't that old. Not much older than Aaron. A young, good-looking man who would never start a family. Blake's friend. He would join him, wherever it was we went after we died.

I put the cap back on the marker, absorbing the news, and realizing another horrifying fact. "Gavin, if Luke and Cecilia talk to the wrong people, they might be mistaken for witnesses. There's nothing I can do if they get targeted while trying to get some information for me." I threw the pen down on my desk and dropped onto my bed. My head went into my hands. This was impossible. They were so far away, and I couldn't shelter them.

Gavin crouched down in front of me. He pulled my hands away, so I could see his face. He seemed so calm. How was that possible? I was on the verge of breaking down and never getting up again.

"I have a plan."

I rolled my eyes, "I think we need more than a plan now."

He smirked and pulled me up with him. We made yet another trip to the murder board. "Let's spread a rumor back in Settlement Island telling everyone that we're going to figure out who actually killed Maverick. We want to prove Gary is innocent." He wiped the making of a tear from my eyelash. "Then, if Gary finds out that Luke and Cecilia are helping us, he'll hold us accountable, not them. Plus, I think he'll be happy to know that we're on his side." He said sweetly, "He'd have no reason to hurt them."

Sure, that tied up the side of his plan that has come loose. The other issue was, "If we prove Gary's innocence, he's going to remain free. He'll be in charge of the drug operations, and we'll have two Porters to fight, not just one."

"Not necessarily." I wasn't following. "Whoever put Gary in jail can't have him roaming the streets looking for them. It's in their best interests to make sure he goes back as soon as possible."

"You're assuming this person isn't Dixon."

"If Dixon managed to frame him for murder, he would have planted enough evidence to take down the rest of his business in the process." He paused, "No, the person who framed Gary is an insider. An insider who benefitted from

Gary's business. A dealer or a supplier who would have lost big if it went down."

"Who could that be?"

"Gary's made a lot of people very rich over the years. He also cut a lot of people out of their territories. My guess is it was probably someone who planned on using this murder to get rid of Gary and sneak up the ranks. Then, with enough support, they'd strike when Porter was at his weakest, and take it for themselves."

A flaw knocked his speculations off course, "Blake already tried to do that. He failed."

Seriousness clouded Gavin's eyes, "True. However, Blake used forces outside the organization to strike. This person is smarter than that. More calculated. A threat that no one, not even Porter, can see." A nod to his own estimations cemented his dedication to this new theory, if that's what we were going to call it. Renewed hope looked good on Gavin, so I kept my challenges to myself. "Once the rumor gets out that we're looking into Gary's case, this person is gonna come looking for us." He laced his fingers in mine, "You in? If you are, I won't let anyone hurt you."

Gavin had hoped for a stronger reaction from me. Instead, I led with, "You're assuming Maverick's killer hasn't already gone underground. What if we can't find them?"

Gavin already had a conclusion in mind, "One way another, they're gonna come to the surface. According to James, Porter has posted high rewards for anyone who knows anything. The entire drug underworld is hunting this fucker down. Eventually, someone's gonna find him. Let's just hope it's us."

I had to give it to Gavin; his plan actually held water. "We follow the murders. We follow the trail that leads to Gary, Russ, and Maverick."

"Then, we'll find Maverick's killer, and we use them as leverage to get what we want from Gary."

But I didn't want anything from Gary. "I just want to save Aaron and get justice for Blake. I'm not interested in making deals with Gary for anything else."

"Fair enough."

I pointed to the obituary for the murder victim. "He was a known associate of the Blood Diamond motorcycle gang. If we can get the bikers on our side, they might tell us something nobody knows."

I remembered the man from breakfast. The one who shared a glance with me, as if he knew me. He was a Blood Diamond. He was the key. And I would find him.

CHAPTER SIX

Demi

EMPTY PIZZA BOXES littered the kitchen table. Instead of wine, sparkling water cans laid abandoned on the coffee table. Gavin and I had been at it for hours. We combed through what we knew about Gary and even got Cecilia on the phone again to double check our work. Luke chimed in on video chat for some of the conversation. By the time the sun was a distant memory, I still had no clue how Gary and the Blood Diamonds knew each other. Or how the man I had seen this morning played into anything.

Who was the man who was awkwardly holding the doorway hostage from me? The way he seemed confined by the mere sight of me spoke to my soul. Were we supposed to know each other already? Recognition, if I was lucky, was the only thing we had in common. I did spend a lot of time around these parts of the ocean. If I wasn't lucky—I couldn't afford to be unlucky.

In reference to the stranger, Gavin had a sharp remark,

"That fuckin' guy. He looked at you like you were some-thing to eat." I grimaced. "He was into you."

"Highly doubt it."

He eyed my sundress, "You need to give yourself more credit." My hand landed on my hip. "You're way more confident than you ever were when we dated. Night and day difference."

"It can't be that dramatic."

"Not dramatic," he said. "Just an improvement."

I snatched the control from him, "I always knew you wanted to change me."

He saw the defense, "That's not what I meant," he said, calming the mood as much as he could. "I always thought you were better than all the bullshit you were putting up with. Even before you came to Maine." I didn't cave. Blind words and compliments always came with red flags. Gavin was a testament to this. "You deserve to stand up for what you want."

"I do. No one runs my life but me."

He nodded, "It looks good on you."

"Well, therapy twice a week, some sunshine, and being sober has helped a lot. Being able to just be myself without having to hide and second guess my decisions, too." Yes, I was hiding my past and my first name from Noah, but I was still myself. I didn't hold back. I went after what I wanted. And Gavin found this person peculiar.

"Can I get to know you, too?"

"We don't work together," I asserted.

His chuckle was forced. "You've said that." The silence lasted too long. "We can't be friends?"

"Long-distance friends?"

"I'm moving here." Gavin's answer brought a frown to my face. "Don't be too happy."

"Stanford?"

"They're considering me for next fall. Gives me some time to get out of all this shit, pack up my house, and find a place to live here. Don't think I'm gonna do the dorms, because I'll be twenty-seven…" I stopped listening. Gavin wasn't supposed to lay roots in California. This was my world. My fresh start. I wasn't going to share it with him, even if he was hours away. "…we can maybe work out our problems." He hesitated on the next part, "I don't know if you'll ever love anyone again after me. I'd at least like a chance to make up for my role in your fucked-up love life."

That hole had been filled already. By Daniel. Those first months after he died were brutal. But now, my love for him was bearable. Dr. Wong had helped me understand that mourning was a part of life. I shouldn't run from it. For the first time in my life, I didn't. I embraced my feelings for Daniel. All of them. And they didn't kill me, not like how my love killed him. The guilt—

"Did you hear me?" Gavin ran his hand through his hair.

I blinked, "Sorry, what did you say?"

"Spacing out on me?" he said.

"Sorry, it happens. It's a trauma response. Disassociation."

"I have that, too." He leaned in, "Or so my therapist says."

Shocked, I said, "You go to therapy?"

He leveled with me. "I almost died and then my girl-friend left me. Kinda a lot happened." I grimaced. "Don't give me that look, I'm fine." He sighed, "My therapist says I have anger problems due to trauma? And abandonment?" I didn't say a word. "You can be honest with me. I was an asshole to you."

"Not when we were dating. Then, you were a dream come true." The compliments didn't last, "Before we started dating, you were the worst. And right when we broke up."

He slouched into the folds of the couch, "I don't remember much about that. I remember us talking about Russ and screaming at each other. Then, I woke up in the hospital. I asked where you were, and Aaron told me that you had left. With Kyle." A thousand-yard stare consumed him.

"Look, Gavin, I'm sorry that I didn't stick around."

His hand went to my forearm, "It's okay. We can talk about that another time." He considered the comment that launched this conversation. "So, how do we find your biker admirer?"

"He's not my secret admirer."

"Well, he's something." Gavin laid down on the couch. "He obviously knew who you were, at least."

I shrugged. "I've never seen him before." I didn't think I had. "If he was following me, how did he find me?"

"Same way I found you, probably." He gave a big yawn and closed his eyes.

"We should call it for the night." It was going on midnight. I wanted to get up early to see my boyfriend. I didn't like how things ended between us today. There was so much more we had to say.

Gavin sat up, "You're right." He looked around for his boots.

"How far is your Airbnb?" I said out of instinct. Kicking people out to brave the late-night streets of LA was not my style.

He thought for a minute. "Forty-five minutes from here."

I didn't want him to drive, not when he was this tired. That would be…irresponsible. "You can stay. I have a guest bedroom."

"Nah, I'm good. Besides, I don't have any of my stuff."

"Kyle has a closet full of clothes. And we have extra shower stuff." He shook his head. "Come on. It would make things easier if you just stayed."

"Do you think you'll need the protection?"

That wasn't a bad idea. "We can protect each other?" I offered with a smile.

Gavin smirked, "All I need is a toothbrush, some sweats, a pillow, and a blanket." I went to the closet and grabbed the items.

"You're gonna sleep on the couch?"

"If you want to be safe, I should be out here." His shirt came up, showing me his gun. The same one he always carried. He pointed to the sweats, "Those are clean, right?"

"Yes. My dad bought them when he came to visit last year. They have never been worn."

He took them and started unbuckling his pants. I

faced away, saying, "Seriously? We have a bathroom. Two, actually!"

"I'm too tired to walk." I could hear clothes being discarded on the floor. "Okay, you can turn around now."

When I did, I saw Gavin shirtless, his sweats hanging off his hips. The muscles were there, as they had been before. He hadn't lost them. I averted my eyes up, traveling to his face. On the way, I stopped at his shoulder.

"Does it hurt?" I said.

Gavin touched his wound. It was pink and red, angry like it should be. After all, it had almost claimed his life. "Sometimes. Mostly when I use my arm too much." I reached out to touch it, realizing that I had overstepped a boundary. My fingers recoiled. Gavin took my hand. "It's okay." My fingertips were placed on his flesh, feeling the imperfect dip in his smooth skin.

The cuts on my body from Ronda's blade were only faint now. Maybe Luke's dad could fix this for Gavin, too. However, I figured he wouldn't want to give up his scar. "Is it a reminder that you almost died?"

He nodded. "Something like that." He pushed my fingers around the outline of the scar. "It reminds me that I still have so much to live for."

Our eyes met. The deepest blue-gray. His breaths heightened. I pulled my fingers back. "I gotta get to bed."

Gavin dropped whatever emotion we were sharing and placed his gun on the coffee table. "I'll see you in the morning, then."

I stopped, "Hey, I'm sorry for being rude about the

whole Stanford thing. If it's really what you want, I hope you get in."

"Me, too." He laid out the pillow and blankets. Then, he looked at me, "I gotta go to sleep."

"Night." I headed toward my room. Turning, I had one more thing to say, "Thank you for your support with this." He gave me a salute and then climbed back onto the couch.

I closed my door and went to work. Starting with the Blood Diamonds was a good idea. To help with our research, I pulled Daniel's flash drive from its hiding place.

Before I began, I held it to my chest. "Please help me," I whispered. Before I jumped into the files, I opened my phone to see if Luke or my sister had texted over any new developments. My heart plummeted. I had several missed calls from my boyfriend. "Hey, did I wake you?"

Noah's voice was groggy. "Nah, I wasn't sleeping."

"Liar." I asked how his day was. Apparently, it was pretty full. He ended up going to Miguel's restaurant and hanging out with him for dinner.

"Demi was there." Noah then said he didn't know why I hated her so much. She seemed nice. Miguel adored her. In his eyes, that should have been enough. "She asked about you."

My tongue was quicker than my patience, "What did she want?"

"She said she saw you on the beach with Kyle and some guy?" Shit! "Who were you with?"

"That was a friend of Kyle's," I stammered. This wasn't a lie; there was no reason to feel any guilt. Not completely. "A friend from work. His name is Christopher."

"O-kay," he said. I wondered if he could feel Gavin in my house. "Miguel signed us up for brunch with him and Demi tomorrow morning at nine."

That didn't give me too much time to work with Gavin. Still, I couldn't lie to Noah, again. I had already lied about Gavin; it wasn't fair to keep making a habit of it. I owed it to my boyfriend to do the right thing.

"I'll see you then!" I mustered up enough energy to sound happy.

"I love you, Rose."

"I love you, too." The words felt foreign, but I meant them.

❧

When I woke up, Gavin was gone. He sent a text to explain his absence, even though I didn't ask for one. He had another video meeting with his Stanford advisor, and he wanted to look more presentable.

He always looked put together, no matter what time of day.

Don't overthink it.

A quiet house gave me the uninterrupted opportunity to get ready and prepare for my brunch with Miguel, Noah, and the girl I hated with all my heart.

"A double date?" I said to Miguel when I arrived at the same café where Gavin and I had abandoned our blueberry ricotta pancakes the day before. This time I wouldn't make the same mistake. Miguel was giddy. "Are you and Demi dating now?"

"Not yet. I think she's catching a case of feelings, too."

I scrunched my brows. "Give her a chance. She's really smart and really, really beautiful."

"Why are you downplaying the fact that I don't trust her?"

"Because not everything is about you." He scanned the room for her.

His excuse was appalling. "She has a habit of putting her nose where it doesn't belong."

"She's just curious, that's all."

"No, she's trying to figure out my real identity."

He put both of his hands on my shoulders. "You're over-reacting."

"And you're not reacting enough!"

He let go of my arms, "I can't believe you don't want me to be happy."

"I can't believe you would date someone who could potentially ruin my life."

"You already did that when you chose Gavin." I didn't need to scold him. "I'm sorry, that was mean." He kissed my forehead, "I really think you should give her a chance."

Miguel was high maintenance, which made dating really, really challenging. At first, I was hopeful that his new girl crush would be a great addition to our friend group. Then, I found out who she really was.

He came close to my face, blocking my view, "Just relax, *Rose*. Everything's gonna be okay." His smile landed behind me. My boyfriend had shown up right on time. He kissed my lips and asked about all the secrecy. Miguel didn't want to say anything in case he slipped and called me by my first name. "There she is," he said, nerves getting the best of him.

Noah leaned in, "He's blowing this out of proportion."

"That's who he is." If I didn't have my strong feelings against Demi, I could understand why he liked her.

Demi came toward us like magic coming to life right before my eyes. Her brown hair flowed with the wind, glistening even after she stepped out of the sunlight. Tight brown dress, sandals, and perfect makeup, I could see why she was a dream. Noah took a step back, having no idea what to say or do. I wasn't upset. She was a stunning girl, and she carried herself as such.

Miguel put his hand at the small of her back, "Rose, this is Demi. It's about time you guys actually met."

Familiarity sat between us. Even though I had dodged her, I still knew enough about her to go beyond the regular pleasantries. "Were you at my birthday party?"

Demi nodded, "Miguel invited me last minute. I hope that's okay."

I shrugged, "The more the merrier." I didn't mean to have a snap in my voice. But I had a feeling I was losing my best friend. "This is my boyfriend Noah."

The shake they shared was weak. I took it on account that he was trying to act uninterested. Every other guy in the joint noticed her. It was only natural for him to as well. I put some space between us, showing that I wasn't the jealous type. Yet, he still respected me by putting his back to her.

"Let's get a table," Miguel led the way for his date and me.

We shuffled past a few people, Demi being way too close for comfort. She smiled at a tall black man covered in muscles. "Okay, that was a little too much eye contact," she said, noticing her own misstep. Miguel was supposed to be her date.

However, I recognized the man as a famous model and YouTuber. He smiled at me, too, which was alluring. "You're not the only one," I teased back.

Noah shook his head, "I wouldn't even know how to compete with that."

California was full of gorgeous men and women. Way more attractive than me. Demi had nothing to worry about; every guy in the universe would always pick someone like her.

Noah leaned in, "I never thought of you as jealous." I patted his chest as we made our way to a beautiful beach side table.

Miguel sat next to his crush, and he winked at me. They looked darling together. Miguel was also stunning. He had done some modeling while we were in school. Guys and girls were always interested until they got to know him better. Then, the theatrics always pushed them to seek love elsewhere. Demi would be no different, if I didn't drive her away first.

After ordering breakfast, we started with some mimosas. Noah stayed true to our relationship and only had eyes for me, which felt alarming. It wasn't normal for a guy to only be into his girlfriend. He had to find Demi attractive. But instead, he focused on me.

"So, Rose, how long have you and Noah been dating?" Demi sipped her mimosa and patiently waited for my answer.

"Three months." I nestled into him, and he kissed my curls. "We met at the library." The story was fun and harmless to tell, "I was looking for a book, and apparently he wanted the same one, so we had a tiny fight." I laughed, "He ended up giving it to me."

"She's being modest. I saw her at the library, and I knew she went there almost every day. I wanted to know her. So, I set up that entire ruse, just so I could talk to her."

He was too darling. Demi squinted her eyes, "How cute." She turned to Miguel, "I absolutely love reading. Do you?"

No, Miguel didn't. He found it dull and uninspiring. As he fumbled through his response, I added, "I love reading, too. Who's your favorite author?"

This was a dare. I figured Demi would probably pick one of my favorite books, just to build some kind of rapport. Show me that we were very similar. In her nosy fantasy, I would be willing to share more about myself. I fought the urge to tighten my arms around my body. Instead, I relaxed, allowing myself to seem like I was truly curious about her answers, not for nefarious reasons.

"I have too many to count. I went through a classics phase, and a bunch of Jane Austen books a few summers ago. But I'd say I'm a sucker for anything that really moves me. I'm reading a Toni Morrison novel right now, and I can't put it down."

I nodded, "Which one?"

She thought for a long moment. This was not good. Anyone who was madly in love with a book would remember the title. Strike one, Demi.

"Don't mind Rose." My name felt jagged on Miguel's tongue. "She's a snob when it comes to books."

Demi accepted his explanation, "There's nothing wrong with that." She snapped her fingers, "I'm sorry, I'm reading *The Color Purple* by Alice Walker."

"I can see how you would get those two confused," I lied. Demi was hiding some type of truth in her words. She probably did like to read, but she was embarrassed to tell me what. "I haven't read that one in a long time." I smiled, "I'm really into romantasy right now." This was a half-truth. I had read a few books in the genre, but I didn't worship it. Not like Demi. Her eyes lit up, and I knew I had hit the spot.

"Have you read *A Court of Thorns and Roses*?" she said. I nodded. Demi squeaked, "Okay, so I am reading *The Color Purple*, but I'm also reading *ACOTAR*, and it's so good." Then came the long diatribe about other romantasy book series she was trying out and how she was hoping to find one to fall in love with. There was a long list of characters and crushes and predictions, and Miguel just nodded in bewilderment. He had picked the wrong girl, for sure.

"I'm reading *The Color Purple* for class, but it just breaks my heart too much. I needed something light to help me fall asleep, which is why I'm going through *ACOTAR*."

"Demi's studying journalism at UC Berkeley," Miguel swooned. I already knew this.

"That's awesome," Noah added.

"And you're reading *The Color Purple*?" I said.

"I'm taking a creative writing class just for fun. The instructor added it to the syllabus." She smiled, "Miguel says you took Creative Writing and English when you went there." Her lips pouted as she sipped her mimosa.

"I did. I read that book along with so many others. I have my full annotated copy at my aunt's house, if you ever want to borrow it."

"That's right. You lived with your aunt before you moved to Maine with your family?" I glared at Miguel. This is why I couldn't just *relax*. "Sorry, it's a journalist thing. I like to ask a ton of questions, so I can get to know people on a deeper level."

Miguel's chuckle didn't break the tension, "Before she agreed to go out on a date with me, she looked into my entire history to make sure I wasn't a killer."

My eyes narrowed at him. I was, indeed, a killer. And Miguel knew that. He winced at the off-color remark. Noah sat up straight, his body becoming rigid. Had he figured it out, too?

"Why did you come back to California if your whole family still lives in Maine?"

Noah turned to hear this answer. I couldn't stammer. I had to be strong with my execution of my thoughts or else I might give a damning detail away. "California is my home. I wanted to come back." I took Miguel's hand, "I missed my friends. I missed the ocean. And I missed the mild winters."

I couldn't tell if she was buying it. It didn't matter because our food had arrived. "Favorite author, go!" she said.

This was easy, "Grover Capshaw White."

Demi took a small bite of her fruit, "He's on the syllabus, too." She leaned in, "I bet you knew that."

Indeed, I did. "I've read all of Grover's work, both inside and outside of class." And because of Ian, I had a limited edition, annotated copy. The man was pure evil, but he had given me the most thoughtful gift I had ever received. "He writes soul-crushing poems."

"I'm sure you can relate. A lot of his poems take place in Settlement Island, Maine," she brought up, casually. My blood turned cold. "That's where you lived, right?"

Jackpot. Miguel choked on his mimosa. He clearly saw what I had been so afraid of. She had researched Maine and found Settlement Island. Soon, she would know my true identity.

I remained calm. Kyle told me that if someone figured out my identity to stay calm. The best way to lie would be to mix a lie with a truth. I couldn't deny that I had lived in Settlement Island, but I could downplay the whole murder angle. And sweet, beautiful Demi could not be smart enough to see the truth, right?

"Yeah."

"What did you hear about the murders?" she said.

Noah studied me. I shook my head, "Not much. My parents live in the country club, which is some miles from town. Me and my sister rented a loft off Maine Street, but we were pretty safe. And in our spare time, we went to this resort town called The Pines. Very nice. Great wine and food."

"If it was so great, why didn't you stay?"

Shit! I wasn't as smooth as I thought. "My sister's store

got broken into, and I was upstairs in the loft. It shook me to my core."

"Is she okay?" Noah said.

"Yeah, she's fine. My dad bought her some body-guards."

Demi pointed her fork at Noah, "I guess you'll have to be her bodyguard when she takes you over there."

He smirked, "If I ever get the chance to meet Rose's family."

Miguel and I shot each other a look. "I wish you were *this* interested in me," he teased Demi. "It's like you want to write an article on my very boring best friend."

She smiled, "I already grilled you about your life." She corrected herself, "Sorry for being upfront. I find people fascinating. When Miguel told me you went to the creative writing program, I had to learn everything I could about you. Plus, you're like a child genius, which I think is really cool." Her fork now landed on Noah, stabbing his skin, "Careful. Next time I see you, I might know your life history, too."

"I hope not."

Discomfort shadowed our table. This was all Demi's fault, and she didn't seem to know it.

"Well, let's move on from the interrogations and get hammered," Miguel put his hand up for the server.

"Can't. I gotta work this afternoon." Noah tilted his head in my direction. I winked at him, letting him know that I wanted us to make plans before he had to leave. Demi wouldn't be part of them. Not now, not ever.

"I gotta get back to school and work on my research,"

she said. Bluntness became her strong suit. "Rose, can I interview you?"

"About what?"

"Settlement Island is hitting national news, and my professor wants me to do a report on all the murders. Small town embroiled in bad drug crimes and murders is really good for publication." My rebuttal was steamrolled. "I know you weren't involved in all that stuff, but I figure you know something about that guy who got out of jail, and the cop that just ended up dead." She leaned in, "Coincidence? I think not."

She already knew about Gary? And Dixon? Gavin and I barely knew these things. Flushness rose to my cheeks. *Stay calm, Catalina.* "I don't really know much about that," I shrugged.

"Well, maybe you can point me to your friends or family, and I can interview them. You have friends over there still, right?" I didn't have to come up with an excuse. Demi paused me to check her phone. "Sorry, but I gotta go. I'm meeting with a source for my article."

"The one on Settlement Island?"

She nodded as she shuffled in her purse for her keys. "Yeah. I'm not sure how much help he's gonna be, but it's worth a shot."

"Really?" Miguel's expression wasn't apologetic. "You said you had the whole morning?"

"I'm really sorry, Miguel, but he just got back to me. He's willing to meet over to his side of town." She kissed Miguel's cheek. "I promise I'll make it up to you!"

Miguel was pissed for good reason. Demi had been

rude. I could handle that. But I couldn't handle the ending to our conversation. She knew all about Settlement Island and the murders. Plus, Gary and Dixon. Whoever this source was, I could use him, too.

Flash

"Demi seems...nice," Noah said softly as we walked to my house. Breakfast ended the moment Demi left to unravel the truth about Settlement Island. Miguel was on the phone with her, inviting himself to come along. At first, he was levied that she had just left him in favor of school. In a hushed conversation, I asked for him to stop her from ruining everything.

All of this was his fault. If he had taken my concerns seriously, we wouldn't have this problem. He thoughtfully asked what he could do to redeem himself. If stopping her wasn't an option, he would spy on her and feed me information. With these instructions, he stepped onto the boardwalk where he abandoned us.

Miguel was on Demi's heels. For Noah's sake, I released my control on the situation to be present with him. Yet, he was wiser than my ploy to get back to our plans for a fun, relaxing day. Demi had blown a hole in my cover, putting him on high alert. He was piecing things together, faster than I could bury them. Thankfully, he was called into work, giving me a chance to catch up to Miguel and Demi. "Do you think they'll last?" Noah said.

I shrugged, "I hope not. She seems self-centered."

"And very interested in you," he said. "I can see why you're a private person, especially when it comes to your family and your past."

Privacy was the foundation for my new life. It kept everything I had built intact. She wasn't allowed to break up that foundation.

"It's okay if you don't like her," he said.

"I don't like the way she treated Miguel. He deserves better." Noah seemed disappointed. "Seriously, that's it."

"You hated her before today." His sentence was not a question. A statement that connected into an ecosystem of lies that kept spreading.

I was tired of the constant deception. Not just with Noah, with everyone and everything. "I've always valued my privacy, even before I moved to Maine," I said. "I'm not hiding anything. I just want to focus on the future." My body nestled closer to his, "Preferably, a future with you."

This whole act between us felt slightly staged. Being with Noah had been easy until Gavin came back into my life. Now, I found myself hiding things, coming up with excuses, and back tracking a lot. And Noah was noticing. I knew that feeling that he didn't speak of. The one where you innocently want to grow closer to someone. In return, they repel you, "For your own safety," they say. Beneath all the hostility, you see mistrust. Selfishness. Distance that leads to hurt. For the one burdened with the secrets, they sat alone with emptiness and loneliness. Vulnerability that became a prison with no cellmates to share it with.

Sadly, Gavin's difficulties with intimacy were starting to make more and more sense to me. I could understand why he had kept so much of his life a secret. It was easier to just keep everything to yourself instead of trying to figure out if your words and actions were safe with the person who claimed to care about you. The relief of seeing them abandon you was satisfying until the prison built up around you.

He kissed me. "I want that, too." His embrace was warm and patient. "But I gotta go. See you tomorrow?"

I nodded, "Of course." The kiss I put on his lips was longer than his. "Have fun at work."

"I hope you find Demi." He left me at my doorstep, and I watched him walk away.

Time to act.

I thought about calling Gavin to come over, but I had an even better idea. I opened up the door and made sure Kyle was still working. I didn't want him to bother him with my worries until I had a plan for a way out. Also, if he knew what I had found, what Demi was searching for, he'd want to enact his solution right now, and we'd lose everything.

Kyle's solutions aligned with running away to Mexico. Or Canada. None of these were feasible. I loved California, and I wasn't ready to leave. Not without a fight.

Miguel shot back a text; he didn't know where she had gone. He was still looking for her, and he vowed to find her. Soon, for my sake. For him, I slowed his frantic apologies and pumped the breaks on his aggravations. He was off the hook until I could steer him in the right direction.

I had to think like Demi. *If I were researching Settlement Island, who in California would have information for me?*

I spent hours combing through the flash drive with no luck. Not one of Gary or Porter's allies or enemies came to or lived in California. The only one was Maverick, and he was dead, so…

I got on the phone with Luke. "Remember that girl I was telling you about?" He paused. "Luke, did you hear me?"

"Sorry, I'm with your sister."

"You've been spending a lot of time with her lately."

He told me to hang on. I heard the door close. "Okay, what were you saying about some girl?"

"That girl Demi. She's meeting with someone here about Gary and Dixon."

"Who?" I gave him an overview of my breakfast date. Luke backed up my concerns and saw Demi for the problem she was. "You need to be careful."

"There's no way she knows my part in all this," I said with shaky faith. "I mean, Settlement Island has been a blood bath lately. None of the newspapers or reports mention me."

He deflated my reasoning, "Seems like more than a coincidence."

I was starting to hate that word. I threw myself on my bed. "I'm screwed."

"Not yet. Have you tried being friendly with Demi? She might be more open to talking if you stop alienating her."

I shook my head. "Getting closer means she'll be able to write her report. If it gets published, it's all over."

Luke's sigh drew on for too long. "What if you gave it a try?"

"Why are you pushing this?" I said.

"Demi having some unknown source is good for you. It gives us a piece of evidence that we need. She's your best ally, Catalina."

I put Daniel's flash into my computer. "What if we already know who her source is? Then, she's not useful to us."

Luke was quiet for a moment. "*Then*, you answer the question of who from Maine traveled all the way to California to use her to get to you." He chuckled to something off screen.

"Luke, what is going on over there?" I hissed.

His attention came to my angry face. "Sorry, your sister's making us lunch."

"What?"

"Yeah. Spaghetti. She's getting it terribly wrong." I could hear Cecilia chuckling and shouting. He laughed back, "Anyways, we're gonna eat before we head back to Aaron's."

My shoulders slouched. Cecilia had to be going through a tough time, and I wasn't there for her. She had Luke. However, I wished she had me, too. "How's she doing?"

He neared the screen, "She's holding it together."

I imagined she would be spending more time with James, too. They were off from their romantic relationship, a small deterrent to his overall life plan. Their friendship was a weak catalyst to win her back. Aaron disappearing gave him another leg up, until her relationship with Luke became an obstacle. An unexpected obstacle that disturbed me. "Is James helping out a lot?"

"He's been in contact with your sister—" He was shut down, "Oh, I guess she wants to tell you herself."

"The thing with James is," she started, "Aaron and Porter are brothers. I don't think James really cares if we find him or not."

"Aaron might be an informant. That aids James in his crusade against…everyone."

"Well, that's only part of it." She pulled her long mane over one shoulder, "All in all, I think James will only help if Gary becomes a problem for him. Right now, Aaron isn't really his concern."

"Because James is in love with you?"

"I mean," she stammered, "he did build me a house."

"I find that pretty creepy. And desperate," Luke said.

"It's not desperate!" Cecilia put up her arm, so Luke couldn't join her on the screen. They bantered until I reminded them I had to get going soon. "Like Luke said, you should talk to Demi."

"Fine, I'll consider it."

My sister nodded her approval, "I'll let you know if we find anything new at Aaron's."

"Thanks."

She blew me a kiss. Then, they were gone.

Onto the flash drive. This time, I would carefully review every item within each folder. It took hours until I found a folder I hadn't seen before buried within two other folders. Unlike the others, this folder had four numbers: 0909. I opened it and only one file appeared.

File Name: For Catalina.

Within the archives was a familiar face. His grin was twisted, frozen in the video. Quickly, I pressed the screen.

"Catalina! I buried this video in here, just for you." He leaned into the camera, "So you could find me."

Daniel's voice soothed my aching heart. He was here, in the files, waiting. I paused the video.

The last time I heard his voice, *he told me he loved me.*

My fingers gently shut the laptop.

A moment felt like a lifetime.

Loving someone who was gone seemed easier as time went on. Their voice fades. Their smile and the little things that make them who they are disappears. You never expect to see them again, not in this life, anyway.

Daniel wasn't alive. I knew that.

I closed my eyes, calling upon several therapy sessions to get me through this. Dr. Wong had prepared me for the rush of emotions that would flood me if I came across a trigger.

Breathe deep.

Label the feeling.

Process it.

Don't overthink anything.

Release.

I did the exercise, not trusting it, nevertheless using it to uncover a fact I could lean on.

Daniel, my love, had been instrumental in getting me this far. His guidance was a necessity. I could get it, even if I got hurt in the process.

One more breath: No need to harbor any dread.

Another breath: The file was made out of love and protection. And I should be thankful for it, not avoid it.

Three breaths came in quick secession, and I opened the laptop and pressed play.

Daniel sat down on a desk in what looked like a warehouse. Maybe it was one of the warehouses Porter owned before Blake destroyed it. "Listen, I don't know if you'll see any of this, but based on what's happening with our little research project, I thought you might need it later."

He dropped his playful nature, just for a second. "This flash drive has the truth about Robert Porter and his business. He's been my friend for a very, very long time, but something has changed in him over the last year. Not to hurt your feelings, but I think that has to do with you."

He sighed, "You're a good person, Catalina. Despite all the odds, you manage to do the right thing." He dropped his head before picking it back up. "I want that for my life, too. I'm done with this. All of it. The dealing, the lying, the death. It's not worth it." Another pause. "Every night, I look up at the stars, and I think about what my life could have been like if I had never gone into this business. Would I have been a dreamer, like you? Or, would I have…" He gave me his sexy grin, "No, I don't wanna tell you. It's too personal."

"Daniel, for the love of God, just say it!" I said to the screen.

"Just know that whatever it was, it was gonna be good." I huffed a sigh. "Fine, I'll tell you." He leaned into the screen, "I thought about being a cop. One of those rugged, good-looking ones you see on the cover of those trashy romance novels I know you read." I rolled my eyes. "Seriously, I do wonder what my life would have been like if I had chosen a different path. Regardless, I'm going to do the right thing now."

He sat up again. "You deserve a beautiful life, Catalina. A happily ever after. And as long as you're working for Porter, you'll never have that. Take this flash drive and use it for some good. Take it to the Feds and show them everything that we did." He paused. "Now, I know what you're thinking. *Daniel, what about you?*" he said in his mocking voice. I could kill him all over again for making fun of me. "I have my own leverage. Gary has enemies everywhere, and they are willing to offer me a handsome reward if I share my files with them. Of course, that means I can't stay here." He moved closer to the camera, "I'm not going anywhere until I know you're safe. After you turn in the flash drive, go back to California and look for a biker gang called the Blood Diamonds. They can offer you protection in exchange for these files. Make a copy and use it to buy your freedom away from all this bullshit."

I ran around my room looking for a pen and paper to capture my new lead.

I looked up at Daniel. He was licking his lips from nerves. "I love you, Catalina. I don't know if I'll be able to tell you in person, but I need you to know that. Take this flash drive and go start the life you deserve."

The screen went black.

I sat down on the bed. All this time, the answer was

there. Gary did have a connection to the Blood Diamonds. Or a vendetta.

My intention was to get started on my investigation into the Blood Diamonds, but I sobered up. The therapy exercises slipped away. Daniel's haunting words replaced them. I replayed the video to savor his voice. To etch his face onto my heart. And it…crushed me.

I put down the computer before it fell out of my hands. The wave of pain, love, happiness, and fear knocked me to the ground. I let my body slide to the floor as I cried for the first time in a very, very long, overdue, time.

It was inevitable, really. I couldn't go on believing I had gotten over him. The letters to him were kind, masking the denial I would feel once I heard his voice saying that he loved me.

Daniel knew what was to come. He had made this flash drive shortly before his death. He made it because he knew he was going to die. Not the when and how, but knowing that his time was up.

I stayed on the floor for over an hour, leaning into the pain. Building the strength to keep going—the door opened. I sat up, hoping it was Kyle. If not, I didn't have it in me to fight an intruder.

The intruder stepped forward, the wood creaking under his boots. "Are you okay?" Gavin said.

I wiped my face, "Yeah. Just a rough day." I got up and closed my laptop, shielding Gavin from Daniel's face. "How did you get in here?"

"I know how to pick locks." Yeah, that was right. "Why are you crying?"

I swept makeup across my face, mixing it together. "It's just getting to me, that's all."

Gavin leaned against the doorway. "Wanna talk about it?"

I couldn't tell Gavin the truth, so I kept on with the questions. "What are you doing here?"

He sighed, "I called and texted you, and you didn't respond. So, I got worried."

"Sorry," I wiped my face for a final time. "I had brunch with my boyfriend, my best friend, and this girl he likes that I can't stand. Then, I came back here to do some work on Gary's thing, and I lost track of time."

"Ah, the boyfriend," he said with some attitude. "Why do you hate this girl?"

"It would take too long to explain." I got up and pointed to the bathroom. "I gotta wash my face." Gavin followed me and watched as I got ready for bed. When I finished, I felt refreshed and ready to talk. "I got a clue on our Blood Diamonds. Apparently, they had beef with Gary." I opened my computer and typed in the biker gang into the search bar. Several news articles appeared, along with a familiar face. "That's him! The guy from breakfast the other day!" His name was Charlie Gardner.

"He knows Gary?"

"I hope so. Maybe he'll be willing to meet me."

"I'm coming with you."

My head shook. "No, I want to do this one alone." My only in with Charlie would be to mention Daniel. And I couldn't do that with Gavin coming along.

He shifted his weight. "I think that's a terrible idea."

"I spent a lot of time with murderers and drug addicts last year. I should be fine."

"Help me out with this one." He tilted his head, "You want to meet with a motorcycle gang member about Gary because you managed to not get killed by some drug addicts? The only reason you're still alive is because the murderers murdered each other, Sweetheart."

Placating me wasn't going to reward him with an invitation. "I'll be fine." I walked back to my bedroom, and he followed. "I'll meet him in a public place, if that will make you feel better."

"I'd feel better if you would let me come with you."

"Not a chance." Realizing it was way past my bedtime, I walked out to the living room and to the door. "I'll let you know how it goes." He pursed his lips. "I promise."

"You know, you have a bad fuckin' habit of picking the wrong people to trust."

I couldn't tell him this was Daniel's idea. Daniel would never do anything to hurt me. "Gavin, please. I'm very tired, and you broke into my house to have this conversation. Can we talk about this after I meet with this guy?" He sighed and fought to find some words. "I'll be fine."

"Alright." He conceded. "I'll back off."

I gave him a smile. "I'll call you the moment I'm done with my meeting."

Disobedience roared inside Gavin. "You know what, no."

"No?"

He shook his head, "You're not going to do this without me."

"I'm sorry, but that's not up to you."

A massive wave of frustration left no room for compromise. "Last year, you threw yourself at Porter and his fucked-up deals to make things right, and I just let you do it." He didn't hesitate for a second, "I told you I would help you, so I'm going to do that."

"Gavin…"

"I failed you, Catalina. And if I want a shot at being friends, I need to support you and tell you when you're making bad fuckin' decisions." He blinked a few long times. "Let me make things right. At the very least, you deserve that."

"What I deserve is your trust." This was a lie, "Actually, I don't need your trust." I stepped up to him, "Gavin, I never asked you to come here. Not tonight, not ever."

"Except you asked me to stay the night last night, after you invited me over to work on Gary's thing." A contradiction he had figured out. "You wanted me here then. Now, you're pushing me away because of what? Your boyfriend?"

"Noah has nothing to do with this." My finger jammed into his chest, "This is about me following a lead without your attitude or your pity."

"You think I pity you?" He closed more distance between us, "I'm angry that you think you have to do all this alone. I want to help."

"Why? So you can have leverage over me? Is that how this works? You want me to make sure I'll save your ass from Gary?" Like always, Gavin wasn't willing to fight when it came to being honest with me. "I don't need to explain myself to you. Just let me do my thing." He put his hands up and walked over to the door. I grabbed his arm, "I mean it. Please don't get in my way." He smirked. My grip tightened, "What do you really want, Gavin? Because if you're just here to trick me into forgiving you, that's just cruel." His glare softened. "Say something, dammit!"

Gavin released my fingers from him, "I'm not playing games with you. I'm just not used to you being so fierce. Determined."

"Well, I had to toughen up last year. Working for Porter isn't for the faint of heart."

He didn't refute my words. "I should get going."

Flustered, I said, "Stop that."

"Stop what?"

"Whatever it is that you're doing."

He nodded and opened the door himself. Before he left, he turned. "I miss the days when you used to trust me." He pondered for a moment, "I wish I didn't fuck that up." Gavin stopped, but then he simply said, "Goodnight."

I closed him out and didn't linger. He wasn't worth it.

I wouldn't go to sleep while thinking about Gavin, so I turned to work. I typed Charlie's name into my search engine and his rap sheet came up. Along with his address and phone number. It was a gamble, meeting with him alone, but it was one I was willing to take.

Charlie, this is Catalina Payton. Daniel Sullivan told me to reach out to someone in the Blood Diamond club if I was ever in California. I got some dirt on Gary Porter, if you want it. Are you willing to meet?

The message was read. I saw him typing a response. Then, he stopped.

CHAPTER EIGHT

Noah

DODGING NOAH WAS becoming harder and harder. He wanted to meet this morning, but I had plans to stalk Charlie. My text to Charlie remained unanswered. So, I texted him again. And called. In my message, I explained my situation with Gary and the work I did for Ian. I was an asset to the bikers, and I had information for them. As an added measure, I told him to meet me at Miguel's restaurant at six. Then, I hung up.

Now, Noah was coming over. He didn't care what we did, as long as we saw each other. The stress in his voice put me on edge, marking the beginning of his suspicious behaviors. He came into the house, pausing in the doorway, like he didn't think he was invited in.

"What are you doing?" I said.

Then came the terrified wrinkles surrounding his eyes and forehead. A stance that made me feel unfortunate for even thinking a relationship with him was possible.

I hadn't been dumped before. The closest thing was

Gavin and I shouting at one another before we toppled to the ground. This felt like that, except Noah was the one falling, not to the ground, but out of love with me.

Noah took a deep breath and asked that we sit on the couch. I complied. Hands in mine, he said, "What am I doing wrong?" My brows crunched. "I feel like you're not into this anymore."

"Into our relationship?"

He nodded, "You seem distant." The weight of the situation pulled on him, "Miguel keeps avoiding me, too."

I could understand why Noah thought we were breaking up. Or that I didn't want him anymore. I had a lot going on, but I really liked him. His loyalty and light-heartedness lingered in my home for days after he left. He'd pray for me when things hit me hard. Abstinence was an unnecessarily great feature, though a slip and slide into bed occasionally would have been preferable.

Such a blessing of a man.

Uncomplicated.

Deserving of a woman who stroked his ego, letting him in.

"We're not avoiding you." *Pace yourself*, "There's just some stuff going on back home." His eyes told me that he wanted to know more. "A lot."

"Does this have to do with Demi and her research?" Fucking Demi, ruining everything.

His labored breathing broke me. He expected some type of honesty and truth. We couldn't go on like this. Not if we stood a chance of having a future.

Where to start? I thought about Daniel and how he

was so honest with me from the jump. He kept things from me for my safety, but he was always thinking about how things would affect me. If his choices would damage me. And that's why I loved him.

I could show Noah the same amount of respect, too.

Time to come clean. If I did, I could finally have a full relationship with him. "My name isn't Rose. Well, it is my middle name." Nice swallow breath, "My first name is Catalina."

He paused, allowing things to settle in. His eyes squinted. "Okay. Why did you lie?" He corrected himself, "I mean, I guess you didn't really lie. You didn't tell me the truth, either."

I skipped this step, trading wordy explanations about my name for momentum to finish what I had started. "I didn't leave Maine because I missed California." He stayed silent, patiently waiting for another turn to ask a question. I said, "I had to leave because of what happened last year." Understanding melted into fear on his brows. "I probably shouldn't tell you about it," I almost whispered.

"How bad is it?" he said. "Are you a criminal?"

"Kinda." His hand tore through his hair. I sped up the intrigue and got straight to the point. "A year ago, I killed someone in self-defense. He had taken me hostage because of a drug thing in Maine." He absorbed my confessions with little concern for the trauma that still lingered in my heart. "I kinda brought down his entire drug business. And they killed the man I love in the process."

Noah stood. "What do you mean it was self-defense?"

"I was working with someone to help stop the criminals

who had beat up my best friend Luke. Those same guys shot my ex-boyfriend." It sounded as bad as it seemed. Worse, even. "So, I left Maine to start over."

His fingers rubbed his forehead, massaging the tension. "Okay, I have a question for you. And don't lie, please." I nodded. "I was walking up to Miguel's on your birthday, and I saw you and Kyle talking to some guy on the beach. He was wearing boots and a jacket." His eyes narrowed, "Who was that?" The way he couldn't get past Gavin seemed suspicious. "The way he stared at you, I could tell you had history. You mentioned having an ex-boyfriend who was a big problem, so I figured that maybe it was him. Then you started acting all weird…"

I shut down his speculations, "That's my ex-boyfriend. He drove all the way here from Maine because he wants me to help with another problem that has come up since I left. I-I don't want to drag you into it." There was only one way to save Noah from this certain fate. "So, um, I guess this is goodbye." Before he could counter, I added, "You shouldn't be a part of this. I already lost two friends to this bullshit, and I can't put you in danger, too."

Molly wasn't really my friend, but I felt responsible for what happened to her. Daniel's death was squarely on me.

"That's why you didn't like Demi," Noah said. "She's a threat."

"If she hasn't figured it out yet, she will eventually know who I am and what I've done." Demi nailing my identity, and tying it to my past, made me a target for her source. The same source who had inside information about Settlement Island's murderous landscape. "I need to leave."

"What?"

"Like you said, Demi is looking into me. So, I need to get out of here before she guides someone to my location."

"Who?"

"Anyone who might want to hurt me or you." Or Kyle. I got out my phone and sent Kyle a text, letting him know that we had a situation. Then, I walked over to my room to grab my go bag.

"What are you doing?" Noah said as he followed me. "Where are you going?"

"I don't know." I went to the bathroom and started gathering things. When I returned, Noah had paused at the murder wall. He scrutinized it, like an art dealer trying to find the hidden meaning behind a piece of work. "What is this?"

"It's a project me and Luke are doing." I rushed through my room, gathering everything else that would be important to me. In my purse went Hank's notebook, Daniel's flash drive, my computer, and a stack of cash I had been hiding in my bathroom. The gun had gone missing. I sent another text to Kyle, asking him if he had our weapon. When I didn't hear back, I grabbed his go bag from the guest room. In my room, Noah sought a way to halt my efforts to get away.

"What kind of project is this? Is this why you have to leave?"

"It would take too long to explain."

"Try!" he yelled.

That's when I realized I was scaring him. "One of the bad guys from Maine got out of jail, and he's connected to an unsolved homicide that he says he didn't do. Luke and I don't know if he's lying or not."

I left Noah to his assumptions as I finished loading up two bags and my purse and put them in the living room. I needed to find my gun, but Noah had advanced to the living room with me.

"What's happening?"

"Like I said, I'm leaving." My final move was to unclip his apartment key from my keyring. I placed it into his palm. "Noah, listen to me carefully. There are going to be some really dangerous people after me. And they might come to see you, so I don't want you to panic. Just act normal and tell them everything that I told you. That I admitted to being a murderer, and I'm working on finding someone who killed some biker. You freaked out and dumped me, and I left." He tried to hush away my story, but I didn't have time. "I need to go."

Noah stood in between me and the door. Shock and denial gripped him. This wasn't the goodbye I wanted for us. He had been sweet to me. The best boyfriend I had ever had. This departure was insincere, I knew that. In the end, it was all I could give him.

I passed him, coming to a stop immediately. His hand, not quite firm on my arm, pulled me back in front of him. "Rose." He corrected himself, "Catalina. I, um…"

I shook my head, "It's okay."

He didn't relent. "Are you breaking up with me because you don't wanna be with me anymore? Or is it because you think I don't wanna be with you?"

Such a stupid question, "You heard me when I said I killed someone, right?"

"Yeah, I heard that part." He shifted his weight, still blocking my exit. Cautiously, he added, "Did you mean to kill him?"

"Yes," I whispered. "He left me no other choice. I had to defend myself."

Time was running out. My safety was on the line. Noah's eyebrows drew together. "What happened between you and the person you killed?"

I didn't have time to explain. Nor did I want to. "Let's just leave it at that." I tugged my arm away and pushed past him, seeing the door. Just within my grasp.

However, I didn't reach it.

Noah intercepted me again, putting his back against the wood. "Noah, this is serious. I need to get out of here."

"I've been dating you for over three months." His eyes fought what he was seeing, the evidence to get me to stay was not working. "I know it's not that long, but I care about you. You can't walk out on me like this."

Reality, much like emotions, is such a messy thing. It will always catch you off-guard, when you need it to stay hidden the most. "Noah, I'm probably being hunted. The last time someone I cared about tried to help me, he died. I don't want that to happen to you."

Noah read my fear. "I can't."

My head shook violently. "Yes, you can."

"We can go somewhere," he bargained. "I have like two-hundred vacation days saved up. And a very large savings account. We can disappear."

"This isn't about you saving me, Noah. I'm saving you!" I thought this would sober Noah up, but he remained steadfast against the door. "Please. I don't want to end up losing you, too."

His fingers went to my shoulders, releasing my bags from me. "That's a risk I'm willing to take." His head lowered toward mine, "I'm not gonna let you leave like this." He tilted my head upward. There was something like love in him. But it wasn't enough. I fought for the door handle. He didn't yield. "What are you going to do now? Are you going to find Charlie? Or are you going to try to find Demi?"

Charlie was a no-go. He still hadn't gotten back to me. Neither had Kyle. Demi was my next move, but I thought about Gavin. If I was going to run, it might be useful if he and I got Kyle and we all ran together. I'd hunt for them after I got Demi's source. I couldn't leave California without it.

"Um, Demi, of course." I texted Miguel and asked for her number. I mentioned that he couldn't block her until I had a conversation with her first. Back to Noah. "You don't want to be a part of this. Trust me. You'll regret it."

Noah fought for me instead of telling me that my decisions are shitty. "Catalina Rose, I love you. I care about you. This can't be the end of us. You need people. You need help. You need me."

This guy was stepping up. Gavin had taught me that guys were victims of weak characters. They ran at the first sign of trouble, especially if they were the root cause. Gavin ran. Kyle ran. Aaron ran. Every time, they fled, sacrificing the women to be the victors.

I shouldn't run alone. Noah would be a good addition to our team. There would be safety in numbers.

"Are you sure?" I said.

Noah nodded. "Yeah." He kissed me, "Now, let's do this."

I pulled him into a kiss, feeling complete. And protected. This is what relationships were about. Support and acceptance. Love and devotion. The kiss was warm, soft, and…

I had almost missed it.

Noah had given something away. Something he shouldn't know.

I broke the kiss and stared at him. He froze, "What is it?'

"I didn't tell you about Charlie."

His expression took on a mixture of different emotions. Then, he said, "Yeah, you did."

"No, I didn't. I didn't get his name until last night."

He chuckled, "It's on your murder wall."

"No, it's not. And I didn't call it my murder wall to you." He came to the realization and I pulled back. "Who are you working for?"

"Catalina Rose, I…"

"Who are you working for?" I shouted. Fueled by intimidation, I took on the menacing face I could find. No holding back, no hiding, he was going to give me what I wanted. "What is your real name?"

He put his hands in front of him. "My name is Noah."

"Who do you work for?"

Noah wasn't going to give up his employer. Not

without a fight. And since my life was on the line, I was ready to fight him to the death for the name on his lips. "Robert Porter."

Ian had found me.

I wouldn't slip into fear. "How did he find me?"

Noah pleaded again, "He doesn't want to hurt you. He just wants to know what you were up to."

He was after Kyle. "He can't have Kyle!"

Noah hushed me again, "He's not looking for Kyle. At least that's not my orders. I'm just supposed to watch you and see what you know."

"About what?" Noah fell silent. "Noah, for fuck sake! What does Porter want?"

"I don't know. He just wanted me to keep an eye on you and share whatever I learned."

A lie. Our entire relationship was a lie. And a damn good one. I hadn't seen it. Neither did Kyle. Ian was here, the entire time, hiding in plain sight, like he did before.

"How do you know about Charlie?"

Noah looked over to my TV stand. And then to my bedroom. "Cameras. Porter had me install them when you first invited me into your house. I've been watching you this whole time."

So, he knew about Gavin coming over. Everything me and Luke had talked about. Where we were on our investigation with Gary. I felt violated, especially given the moment Gavin and I had shared. Where he told me all his secrets that now Ian knew.

I wanted to kill Noah for what he had done, but I had even bigger issues. "Tell me again; what does Porter want?"

Noah didn't waiver. "He just wants to talk to you. That's all."

"And not Kyle?"

"I'm not here for Kyle. I just want you."

The way Noah had said these words calmly let me know that he was going to kill Kyle. "Noah, you have to let me go."

"Not until you talk to Porter. He's waiting nearby."

Panic jumped across my nerves. "He's here in California?" Noah nodded. "No."

Noah stepped up, this time not in the good way, "That's not an option." His fingers tightened around my arm again. I didn't know he was this strong. "Now, you can come with me willingly, or I can drag you out of here."

Winning against Noah's loyalty to Porter was impossible. He was stronger. Unflinching. Not the man I had been kissing and loving for the last several months. Whatever Ian wanted was more important than the relationship we claimed to have.

Time for a plan. A quick one. One I wouldn't lose.

I thought about my victory over Blake. The focus I had enveloped to make sure I didn't make any mistakes. Then, I flew into action.

I didn't hesitate as Noah held onto me. The crystal vase and flowers from Mother sat next to the door. An unassuming weapon. The force against Noah's face pushed him away from the door. The sun blinded me as I hit the front yard, jetting onto the boardwalk.

I ran, full speed, ducking between tourists and cyclists. The pounding of my bare feet against the tiny bits of sand didn't slow me. I had to make it to the restaurant. Miguel would be there with his large family, a few members who had spent some sentences in prison, not jail.

The crowd closed in around me. Strollers came to a halt. Up ahead, a street performer was to blame. Behind me, my pursuer was shortening the distance between us. I could only go left, into the sand, which was a horrible idea.

Sand gave Noah the advantage. And so did my indecision. My mind was frozen, contemplating both horrible choices before me. Either way, if I found myself within his arms again, I'd lay into him. There would be another death struggle, and I would tear him apart.

I glanced down the boardwalk, sealing my decision. He wasn't too far. I broke through a family in front of me, taking a few steps to create more room. One more look back, and he had found his own way through. I turned, charging on, craving just a little more space.

And in that space stood a smirking Gavin, waiting for me to cross over. The smirk became a distant memory. He opened his arms, catching me.

It only took one word for him to put it all together. "Run!"

CHAPTER NINE

Chateau

I CHANGED MY mind. Corrected my previous thoughts about weaknesses and loyalties when it came to the men in my life.

Gavin had *never* run from anything in his life. He would occasionally drop out of contact, moving pieces of the game here and there in the shadows to secure his own destiny. To his enemies, his absence was perceived as a weakness. As it was to me. An infuriating weakness. He had gone dark on me so many times for the sake of a higher sense of duty. Or to feign my safety.

But not today.

Gavin held onto me as he squared up with Noah who had come to an abrupt stop. Arm outstretched, his silver gun kicked off little sparks of light against the sunrays. The kind boy I had known a few minutes ago knew he had met his match. Without a word, Noah put his hands up, but Gavin didn't take the shot.

"If I drop this, will you tell us what we want to know?"

he said. Noah complied, nodding without hesitation. Gavin tucked his weapon in his back pocket. "Who are you?"

Noah dropped his hands. "This isn't between us, Scott. I just want Catalina Rose."

"You can't have her."

By this point, I didn't need Gavin anymore. I let go of him and stood by his side, ready to protect myself. "I already told you, Noah. I'm not meeting with Porter."

Gavin chuckled, "Really? You've been pretending to be her boyfriend, so Porter can get to her?" He shook his head, "That's lazy."

"Where is he?" I said. I knew Ian's face after he had floated in and out of my life, right under my eyes. He would be recognizable to me, if I had known to look for him here. Nonetheless, he had tucked himself inside the crowds, somewhere, probably watching. Out of sight, at the top of my mind.

The game of possession between Noah and Gavin had to come to an end once I brought up Porter. Noah's bond to his boss kept him silent. "Noah, whatever you think you're doing for Porter, it's not gonna end well for you."

He advanced, but Gavin was faster. He stepped up between us. "I'm not helping Porter. This is my retribution. I'm sure you can understand that." No, I couldn't. I didn't owe Ian anything. Not anymore.

Beyond Noah, a couple of uniformed police officers soared up the boardwalk on bikes. "We need to get out of here," I told Gavin. To Noah, I said, "Tell Porter I will never help him ever again." I grabbed Gavin's hand, "Let's go!" We backed up into the crowd, our eyes still on Noah who staggered forward slightly. With my departure came Noah's sullen fate.

He didn't have what Porter wanted. I knew first-hand how this would play out. If he didn't end up murdered before the end of day, he would have to work harder to save his own life. Even though I had been in his situation before, I had no sympathy for him. He had lied to me.

And now, my life is over.

I had to leave.

But Kyle wasn't with me.

I took off running to my house, Gavin fighting to keep up. On the way, I called Kyle and left him a jumble message to not trust Noah and that we needed to go. Porter was in town. And he might already know where he was.

Gavin finally caught up as I rounded some tourists, heading toward my house. "Why are you coming back here?"

"There's something I need to get," I said.

"Catalina, police officers are after us." I looked back, seeing the bike cops abandon Noah in search of our whereabouts. They could wait; I needed my survival kit.

Gavin didn't deter from his path to evade the officers. So, I found the perfect place for us to hide. I grabbed him, and we sat down in a photo booth. We only had a few seconds before we could change direction. Heightening the illusion, I pressed my lips to his, feeling the sweet saltiness of his skin.

He parted his lips, allowing me to deepen the kiss. With each touch came a crush of familiarity and building intensity. I lived for kissing this man before. Our bodies enveloping the other as we sensed what we wanted without a single word. It was electric and need…we needed this. And each other.

Gavin felt it, too. He placed his hand over my back, my chest braking against his leather jacket. Soon, he guided me with each kiss, forgetting that we didn't love each other anymore. That he had declared his intention, and I wasn't a part of any plans he was making. He didn't come here for me. He didn't want me.

He wouldn't be able to hide behind his lies anymore. I knew the truth; he still loved me.

The curtain moved behind my head. I stayed in the moment with Gavin, pretending all this was normal. We were just two people, tearing each other apart in a photo booth. The curtain hit my head again, and I heard a male voice say, "It's not them."

I released Gavin as he leaned in for more. Sadly, I pressed my finger to his lips. "We can go now." I opened the other side, pulling Gavin into a group of college kids. By the time the cops doubled back to the photo booth, we were sailing away into the crowd.

"Good move," Gavin said as he glanced behind himself, staying close to me. "The Nova is in the parking lot up there."

"I can't leave without my bag."

"Why are you so fuckin' obsessed with this damn bag?" he pleaded.

"I need my case files." He wasn't convinced. "I'll go without you." I didn't give him a choice. I left down the street, toward my house.

"Fine," he hissed as he trailed behind me.

We headed away from the boardwalk. The ramp leading to the beach was steep, but we kept up the pace, even though we were both getting tired. From here, it was just two blocks on the street to my dad's house. We arrived at the back side of the property, leaning over so we could catch our breath.

"We have to keep going," I said raggedly. Head up, I examined the bathroom window. It was locked.

Gavin recovered and placed a knife in the seam. Soon, the lock released, and the window slid open. I had an arm inside when Gavin grabbed my other arm and pulled me back. "Let me go first." Gun at the ready, he slid inside.

Noah didn't own a gun, I think. Yet, I couldn't be surprised if he did. My assumptions had been so off. The clues should have come together. The fact that he wouldn't let up when I tried to leave. I just thought he was a nice guy. On my side. Willing to go the distance to protect me.

I pushed that thought away and followed Gavin into the house. He made sure I stayed behind him while he investigated the place. The gun went to his waist, and he told me to gather my things. "It's nice," he said as he watched me rush about.

"What's nice?"

"Your house." He paused, "I thought you and Noah would have torn this place up."

"I hit him with a vase and ran." Barefoot, at that. "Besides, Mother would kill me if I ruined her beach house. She had some famous designer pick out all the furniture, even the stuff in my bedroom." I picked up a magazine from the coffee table and handed it to him, "Check out page seventeen."

This distraction gave me enough time to scour the living room for anything else I would need. Gavin chuckled, "She spent over $100,000 on furniture and paint?"

"That's my mother." I neared the end of my search, yielding nothing. "She had to approve everything I brought in here. Said it was her job to make sure I didn't create any imbalances in the energy of the rooms."

"What the fuck does that mean?"

"When she comes to visit, she wants to make sure everything *feels* a certain way." I paused, "They're probably going to have to sell this place now."

Gavin shook his head, "Nah. Once we get out of here, Porter won't touch it." I made a move for the front door where Noah had abandoned my bags. Gavin told me to stop. "There's broken glass everywhere. Put some shoes on, and I'll get your stuff."

I threw on my converse high-tops, and Gavin locked the front door. Soon, we were back out the window and I was texting Miguel, letting him know not to come to my house for any reason. And to stay away from Noah. And Demi.

I sighed, "Noah's gonna know I left. He installed cameras, so he and Porter can see everything I do in here."

Gavin said, "Then, at least they know you're not here." He didn't wait for me to process his words. He helped me hoist up through the window, landing on the asphalt and ready to go.

The bathroom window was shut. Gavin took his elbow and smashed it. "What are you doing?"

"Call 9-1-1."

"Why?"

He rolled his eyes, "Call them and report a break in at your house. They'll send the cops, and Porter can't come anywhere near your murder wall."

"But then they'll see it."

"Which is a good thing. The cops will see all the people you are investigating, and they'll have a motive for the break-in. Anyone on that wall, including Porter, could be behind your disappearance."

"Which would keep him away from me."

Ian was smart. The police looking for me would lead them to him, too. The price for being caught in California, by police who didn't know him, would be hard to pay. Gavin's plan was flawless.

He knew everything. I guess that's what happens when you're always on the wrong side of the law. I accepted his idea as a fuck-you to Noah, too. He wouldn't have access to my murder wall. Or the cameras. He wouldn't be able to figure out what I was doing next.

I got out my phone and called my dad. He was already one step ahead. He had called me several times after he saw all the commotion in the cameras *he* had installed. Dad, being the caring father that he was, had already made arrangements for me.

"I called your Aunt Eloise, and she said you could stay with her until we figure this out."

Aunt Eloise still lived in the same house I had stayed in when I went to UC Berkeley. It was far enough away, but close enough for us to get there in a few hours. It was a safe move. But I didn't want to bring her into my problems. Besides, I couldn't leave without Kyle. I sent him a text as my dad continued giving me a plan for what to do next. "I don't want to put her in danger."

"I know my sister. She's tough. Plus, Irving used to play professional football, remember?"

I rolled my eyes, "There's more to this than that. Besides, I'd rather not involve them right now." I quickened my pace after Gavin.

"Well, your other option is The Chateau."

"Really? Don't you think that's a little over the top?"

"It's covered with security. The manager is a personal friend of me and your mom's. He won't let anything happen to you."

"How long have you had this plan?"

"Since you told me you were going back to California. No matter what, I'll always take care of you."

I loved my dad. Having him prepare a place for me made my heart warm. "Thank you so much." Aaron came to mind, "Have you heard from Aaron?"

"No, I haven't. But don't worry about that right now. You get yourself to some place safe."

Between my aunt's house and a five-star hotel, I decided that the hotel was my best option. "I'm going to get a room for the night. Maybe two. Then, I'm going to head back to Maine."

"I'll set up the reservation, so it's not under your name. Give me twenty minutes, and I'll text you the details. Call me when you leave and when you arrive."

"I will. I love you, Dad."

"I love you, too. We're gonna get through this."

I hung up the phone. "My dad got me a room at the Chateau Marmont."

"A hotel? Is that the smartest thing for us?"

"Us?" I didn't mean to say it out loud, but it just came out.

"Yes, us. We need each other." This was his way of dragging me back into whatever it was we were doing over and over.

"Gavin, about that kiss." Yes, this was my fault. But I didn't want to lead him on. "It was just an act."

He nodded, "I know. You just broke up with your boyfriend, and Porter's after you. You were desperate."

"I wasn't desperate," I snapped. That's not how I wanted him to see me. "I just didn't want the police to catch us." He winked. "I mean it, Gavin. I don't want you to think I'm trying to use you or anything." I cringed. That's also not what I meant to say.

"How would you be using me?"

His question had merit. "The moment I had a problem, I went to you."

"Noah's a problem? Before you raved about how much of a good boyfriend he was," he teased.

"Well, he's out of my life now. You don't have to worry about him anymore."

"I just don't know what you see in him."

"I was just a job to him," I snapped.

Gavin chuckled, "Well, don't feel too bad. He probably thought you were really attractive," he added. He moved on, "The Chateau Marmont, huh? Maybe we should just check it out and then keep our options open."

"When you see it, you're not gonna want to leave."

"They have room service?"

"They have everything, including tons of security."

He nodded, "Okay, we stay there one night, then we go somewhere else. Now, call 9-1-1, so we can get out of here."

After my emergency call, Gavin suggested that we causally walk back to his car. Bike cops had swollen in size on the boardwalk. We needed to be as composed as possible, in case someone recognized the gun-wielding guy in the black jacket and boots hurrying to his black vintage car. Somehow, we had blended in with the surfers and their bikini-clad co-eds. I didn't want to take any more chances.

"Take off your jacket and boots."

"Why?"

I pointed to all the people walking around in bathing suits and shorts. "Because you stand out."

He groaned and peeled off his boots and socks. Next, he took off his jacket, his shirt tight against his skin. Then, the shirt came off. Teasing, he tossed it to me. "Hang onto that."

I shoved it into my purse. His jacket laid on top of my duffle bags which were carried by Gavin.

The Nova was closer than I thought. Out of habit, he opened his door for me and I climbed in. My stuff landed in the backseat. Gavin didn't bother to put his shirt back on. Or his boots.

Then, I broke down, not into tears, but into laughter.

"He was so nice. So sweet. I should have known." Gavin stared at me. "I'm talking about Noah."

"I figured." He turned the key and brought the engine to life. "That boy had Maine written all over him."

"What makes you think that?"

Gavin motioned to a few people around, "How many country boys have you met in California?"

I shrugged. "He said he was from Montana. I met his parents and his siblings."

"That's a pretty good cover story. He couldn't claim to be from California, because nothing about him says he's from California. Montana would be a better fit. As for the family, he probably went online and hired some actors."

"That's a little farfetched."

"Every time James has to go to court, he always hires a fake wife and kids to show the judge that he's a family man who has learned from his mistakes."

"And that works?"

"It did the first couple of times." Gavin winked, "Now, where are we headed?"

"Chateau Marmont. It's in West Hollywood, on Sunset."

"Like that's supposed to mean something to me."

"Don't worry, I know where it is." I put my seatbelt on, for good measure.

Gavin threw the Nova into drive, and we were off.

❧

"Your dad really doesn't know how much things cost, does he?" The room door closed behind him. I think he expected a palace of some kind. A rich man's lair. Instead, we were tucked into a little cottage right off the garden, adjacent to the pool.

"This bedroom is over $1000 a night."

"Oh, I know," Gavin peeked into the bathroom. "He could have rented a whole house for a week with that much money."

I absorbed the nostalgic vibes, "I always wanted to stay here."

My hint of sadness was rewarded. "After all this is over, I'll buy you a room here for the night."

"But you can rent an entire house for a week with that much money." I smirked. He nudged my shoulder playfully. "And you don't have to buy me a room here. I can cover it myself." If I wanted to quickly drain the small fortune I had amassed while working for my dad. Without his help, I would be completely out of money within three days.

"Sure, you can." Gavin went into the bathroom. The bathroom taps were turned on then off. I questioned him, but he ignored me.

Bored, I headed for the balcony as his arms went around my waist. Before I knew it, we had sailed through the air and onto the bed, ruining the crisp white linens. "Did you catch rabies or something?" He propped himself up on an elbow. "You've lost your mind."

Then came the kiss. A continuation from earlier.

Gavin's kiss held more ferocity. A sharp contrast to our play for the police. This time, he led us down a path to passion and sex. I broke away before we went too far. "Um, we can't do that," I said.

"It's just sex, Catalina." He searched my eyes. "I haven't been with anyone since you."

"Same."

His brows smirked, "Noah didn't…" I shook my head. "Oh, that's right. He was just pretending." The insincerity at my obvious embarrassment pulled him back. "I'm sorry he did that to you. But I'm glad he didn't lead you on too much."

That was a good thing. Something I was grateful for.

The hunger in Gavin's eyes remained. I had been mistaken before. He didn't love me; he just wanted my body. "You're leading me on right now."

"How so?" he said out of pure confusion.

"You fought me so hard when we talked about sex when we just started dating. Said you didn't want to take something from me in case you ended up being no good. Well, you're no good for me, Gavin."

A light licking of his lips, and he said roughly, "I've always wanted you, Catalina." His forehead went to mine. "And that kiss…" He measured his breaths, "If you tell me you don't want me, I'll stop."

He knew he was attractive. And fucking irresistible. I needed more than lust to get back into bed with him. The bar had been set by Daniel, and I wasn't lowering it anytime soon. "I don't want you." My voice was stern enough to seem believable.

But Gavin hesitated. Then, he traced my curls, brushing my mane from my face. A soft, sweet kiss touched my skin. "Okay." His head tilted toward my bags, "Which one of those are you willing to leave behind? In case we need to pack light."

"None of them." Everything I owned was a treasure.

With a "hmm," he was up, unzipping my luggage. I shot over, preventing him from looking inside. "Catalina…"

"This is private."

"You got some old love letters from the guy who was pretending to be your boyfriend?"

"No!" We wrestled, him getting the upper hand. The bag was tilted over, my things cascading onto the dresser. "Gavin, stop it!" He didn't let go. Not until my annotated copy of Grover Capshaw White's manuscript fell onto the floor.

Gavin released me and picked up the book. He fanned through it. "This is from him, isn't it? Porter?"

"Yeah. But I didn't know Groover was Porter's stepfather until I figured out who Porter really was." I said, "I can't believe it took me so long."

Gavin offered me the book, "I figured Aaron would have told you who his father was."

"No, he didn't." I sniffed, "It was perfect for Ian, though. His last name was Porter, but he led me to believe it was White." I turned to the dedication page. "Grover never dedicates his books to his family or friends. He always dedicates them to his readers." I cleared my throat and read, "*May your heart be broken by only the things that are worth it.*"

"You call him Ian?" My brow raised at his question. "Porter."

"That's his name. Ian Robert Porter." I rolled my head,

"I was such an idiot. He was right there the entire time, and I never knew. Then he came here, and I didn't even think that he would plant people in my life."

"Consider yourself lucky. You're still alive." Gavin fell back on the bed. "There aren't a ton of people who have met Porter face to face and lived to talk about it. And no one has ever gotten a gift from him."

"It was all part of the act." I tossed the book on top of my bag.

"Maybe, but he's also given you several second chances. And you know his real name. That's not an act."

I sat down next to him and crossed my legs. "He only did that because he thought I would lead him to Kyle." My breaths strained, "Kyle isn't answering any of my calls."

"Relax. I took care of it." He looked over at me. "He called me shortly after you tried him several times. He wanted to know what I wanted him to do."

"Why didn't he ask me? We're supposed to be really good friends."

"You are." He straightened up. "The conversation we had, he wouldn't be able to have it with you because of how much you guys love each other."

"What conversation was that?"

"Well, *Ian* is after Kyle. Noah said Porter only wants to talk to you, but Porter doesn't give up on his vendettas. Kyle's the reason why all this started, and he won't stop until he's dead." Gavin sighed, "Kyle's going to turn himself in."

"No!" I didn't go through all this heartbreak for nothing. "Kyle needs to give that up, right now!" Gavin tilted his head. "Porter doesn't want Kyle, he wants me. That's what Noah kept saying." My head shook, "Through Noah, Porter has known where Kyle is this entire time. If he wanted Kyle, he would have killed him by now."

Gavin saw my point. He knew that once Noah came into my life, Kyle would have died right away. As a result, I would have been kidnapped and brought to Ian without all these months of lying and hiding.

Something else had driven Ian to my door.

I went to my purse and flew through my notes on everything regarding Ian. To figure out what he wanted.

"I don't know if the answer you're looking for is in there."

"You don't know what I'm looking for."

"I know you better than you think." Gavin got to the point. "You want answers. To get those, we either need to find Porter or Noah."

He was right. "I need you to call Kyle." Gavin complied knowing Kyle would only take calls from him. After a few rings, it went to voicemail. "Hey, it's me, Catalina. Listen, don't go to Porter. He's interested in me, not you. He wants me." My words scrambled, "I don't know what for, but just don't turn yourself in. Or at least wait until I can dig deeper and find the source who gave us up. Please, give me some time, okay?" I sighed, "Just call me back, please!"

"That was very moving," Gavin said while he looked around the room.

"If he listens, he'll stay away from Ian until I can find…"
"Find what?"

A lead. I already had two: Charlie and Demi. Noah didn't have any answers, so I had to find another way. Evolve. My text to Charlie had sat on Read. I had only one other option: Demi.

Miguel offered her number up without any questions. He was done with her, and he didn't care if I ate her alive. I sent her a text, asking to meet up. We could talk about Settlement Island, and I could give her what she wanted. In return, she would give me the name of her source.

Demi wrote back. She was game for my offer. And her source had given her another lead.

CHAPTER TEN

Intimidation

I SHOT CHARLIE another text, letting him know I had changed my plans. Then, I finished my conversation with Demi. I proposed a late dinner, but she was busy. Not with Miguel, though. He had blocked her shortly after our brunch. We were both back to being single with no crushes on the horizon.

Miguel stepping out of the picture left me to get to know Demi on my own. I'd buy her breakfast as a friendly gesture. Then, the grilling would start.

For now, day turned to night.

My head was buried in my notebooks and my laptop. Gavin had propped himself up next to me, asking about my research. I went over everything I knew about Noah, looking for another connection between him and Ian. He had called over two dozen times, filling my voicemail with pleas to just give him a chance. I ignored them all, including the novel-length texts he had sent as well.

How could I have been so stupid to fall for him? Gavin

glossed over this fact and went straight to the problem at hand. We needed to stay focused on Gary. We were supposed to be finding Aaron. Ian being so close meant he could show up at any time. If he did, I should be ready with enough leverage to make him think twice about hurting me. The person who framed Gary or Aaron's whereabouts were my best bets.

After several hours of going back and forth with theories, we called Luke who was more upset with Noah using me than he was with Ian being in town. But he did offer some solid advice.

"If Noah is telling the truth, you can't brush this aside. You're going to have to find him and deal with Porter." He shrugged, "Maybe he's more useful than you think." Luke also told me to keep going with my investigation into Gary. Ian showing up to California around the same time his father was released from prison didn't add up. Perhaps it was Gary calling the shots, not Ian.

Gary was a good and likely candidate. The Blood Diamonds were at odds with him, according to the flash drive. He'd do anything to set that record straight, put them back in their place, if they were out of line.

We called it a night here. Luke had to get up early to meet Cecilia at the store. They had arranged a talk with Aaron's parents. She had called and texted Aaron a few more times, all going unread and unanswered. Tomorrow, she was going over to his parents' house to find out if they knew anything.

She was going to meet Grover Capshaw White.

I didn't have time to be jealous. This wasn't about

my infatuation with his writing. This was about his son. Besides, it was better that she went, not me. I would have been too distracted by sitting down with my idol to capture any good intel.

Tiredness was calling me to sleep.

Luring me to give up for the night and leave the rest until the morning.

Gavin still sat against the headboard, eyes closed, peaceful breathing.

I yanked my phone from the charger and grabbed a sweater. My feet padded out the door to the garden where I called Noah back.

"Rose!" he said after only one ring. "Oh, thank you for calling me back."

"My name is Catalina," I hissed, "and I only have a few questions for you."

"Okay," he said.

"Where is Porter?" Noah's silence was infuriating. "You came into my life after I had the worst year imaginable and lied to me. Pretended to be my boyfriend, someone who loved me." I waited, but he said nothing. "You have to tell me where Porter is."

"That's not how this works."

The flatness in his voice prompted me to say, "Then it was all fake? Everything we shared together meant nothing to you?"

"Catalina Rose, I don't know." He sighed, the phone shuffling, "Listen, I don't want to hurt you. And neither does he. All he wants to do is talk, I promise."

"You can't make promises for him, Noah." He needed

an education on Ian Robert Porter. "He never told you about what happened last year, did he?" I railroaded any attempt he made at answering, "Porter used me to find the man responsible for tearing down his business, piece by piece. His name was Blake. He was trying to understand why his father died." My fingers ran through my hair, relaxing the curls and moving them away from my face. "I stopped Blake, and in the process, Porter lost one of his best friends and allies. He blames me for his death. Said he would never forgive me." My voice cracked, "He's hunting me, Noah. You led him to my door."

"Catalina Rose, I don't know what to tell you." He seemed unaffected. "Whatever arrangement you have with him is between you two. My job is to bring you in, that's all."

There was an anchor tied between Ian and Noah. I could feel it weighing down his emotionless words. "What does he have on you? What do you owe him?"

"It doesn't matter," he said. "Listen, he's getting impatient. The sooner you meet with him, the sooner all this will be over."

"And if I don't comply?"

"You know what it's like when people don't give him what he wants."

The rattling of my bones fueled my anger. "He can't intimidate me. Tell him to man up and leave me alone!" I ended the call and walked back to my room, throwing the phone on the bed.

I expected Gavin to wake up and ask what was wrong.

He remained in his upright position, completely uncomfortable. I nudged him. "Gavin, you should lie down."

His eyes opened. His stare was long-winded. "Can you turn on the TV?"

"Yeah," I said slowly. I grabbed the remote, and he peeled off layers of clothing until only his boxer remained. I was too tired to protest him sleeping next to me with that much skin. "What do you want to watch?"

"Can you put on the channel with the old movies? It helps me sleep." He climbed back into the bed, pulling the comforter over him as his eyes collapsed shut again.

I found the channel. *The Bridge on the River Kwai* was playing. I listened to the rumbling of dialogue as I brushed my teeth and hair. An oversized T-shirt covered everything when I laid down next to Gavin. He was on his back, a hand on his chest, the comforter draped over his hips.

"Can you turn it up?" he muttered. "I like this part."

"Are you even sleeping?" I said.

His eyes opened, "Yeah."

I turned up the TV volume a few notches. "Better?"

"Yes."

I rolled over and faced him. "Do you have nightmares?"

He faced me, too. "Sometimes. Especially when I sleep in a new place."

"Why's that?"

Gavin blinked, lush lashes hiding his eyes before I saw them again, "I think it's because of the hospital." He moved the pillow. He chose to be closer to me in our enormous bed. "When I woke up, I didn't know what happened. I didn't know where I was. I was in a lot of pain, and it was dark, and I felt lonely." The next part took him a minute. "Like when my mom died."

My hand went to his. I was exhausted, on the verge of falling into sleep. But I'd stay awake to give him the friendship he sought from me. "What makes you think about your mom?"

"The paramedics rushed her to the hospital, trying to save her life. I remember peeking through the doors of the emergency room, waiting for her to wake up. Then she didn't." He didn't dwell, "The hospital was so cold. And dark because it was night. I waited for my dad to come, but he never did. Instead, my grandpa was the one who showed up. I guess I had fallen asleep, because when I opened my eyes, all I could see was the tiniest light coming from where they had taken her. The rest was darkness."

Gavin rolled his finger under his eyes, relieving the tears. I inched toward him. My arms inviting him in for a hug. He rested his head on me. Such a strong force of a man could be brought down by a memory of his mother. His one true love.

"We can leave the TV on forever, if that helps," I said.

His body rocked with a chuckle. His head came up to meet my eyes, "You're too sweet."

"I know."

I watched his chest rise and fall as he stared at me with hunger. In our past, this was the beginning of a long night of kissing and yearning for one another. I would relieve him of every article of clothing he had on, one by one, until the only thing I saw was skin. Tonight, I turned over and grabbed the remote, turning up the TV a little bit more.

His brows furrowed. "I like this part," I said.

He laughed, "I know you've never seen this movie before."

He was right. And the distraction took away the gnawing in my stomach. The heightening of my senses, compelling me to take this further. After all, like Gavin said, it was just sex. We could fill that void for one another. Just this once.

Gavin gave me a crooked smile, "You don't want me, remember?"

"I remember," I said, my fingers dancing up his chest. "And you don't want me."

"No, I fuckin' want you." He leaned in and kissed me. "I've always wanted you," another kiss. "I'll always want you."

We were engulfed in kisses. Gavin pulled himself on top of me, placing my hands above my head as kisses showered down my neck. A year had been too long. And having a nice boyfriend would never rival the bad one who knew the right way to feather his lips against your skin.

I took control of the kissing, my fingers lacing into his hair. My T-shirt was an obstacle. I pulled it over my head, Gavin tossing it to the edge of the bed. We drowned in more kisses, planting our lips all over each other's body.

Lust, hatred, passion, it all melted away. He stopped and looked me in the eyes, asking for permission. I nodded with a smile. He smiled back and kissed me, his body finding its place in mine. I gasped, feeling wanted and needed for the first time in a long time. The kisses came in a rush as Gavin gave into me, eager to please me in a way Noah couldn't.

This was more than sex.

It was more than having a little fun.

We both knew it.

It was threatening.

An undoing.

A mistake that could lead us back to falling in love again.

Silence became the norm for Gavin and me. We had woken up with enough time to avoid each other while we got ready to meet Demi. On the drive over to the café, Gavin had kept his eyes on the road. I spent my time trying Charlie again. Instead of texting him, I sent him my location for tracking. It was a terrible idea, but I figured he might be open to responding if he saw how much I wanted to talk with him.

Gavin opened the door to the café for me and grinned. "What's up?" I said.

"She has good taste." He leaned in, "I really like those blueberry ricotta pancakes." He pulled out his phone, his expression changing. "Kyle was moved by your message." He turned the phone.

Brother, tell Catalina that I'm not gonna see Porter. I'm on my way back up to Maine. James and the boys can use my help over there with Gary.

"What's going on with Gary now?" I said.

Gavin shrugged, "I'll look into it. It can't be too bad if James hasn't called me." A girl jetted by us, her breast nudging his sleeve. "Let's focus on Demi," he said, ignoring her.

I didn't see Miguel's two-faced crush anywhere. However, she'd be able to spot us with little effort.

Gavin drew the attention of almost every woman in the restaurant. The girls at the hostess stand undressed him with their snickers. I remembered this. How attractive he was. How the girls wanted to throw themselves at him. And my assumptions were now proven true. I always knew he would do well in California as a model or maybe even an actor.

These thirsty girls could dream all they want. When I closed my eyes, clips from last night played for me. His touches, feathery kisses, the relief after not being desired by my phony ex-boyfriend. The gap had been filled by the man standing next to me, while women wondered what a night with him would be like.

I already knew.

Gavin leaned into my curls, tickling my face with his words. "Is that Demi?"

He had indeed spotted her. Another revealing summer dress stretched over her curves, legs crossed at the knees, she sat at a booth, her hair tucked over one shoulder. She was writing in a journal.

"Yeah, that's her." I paused, "How did you know?"

"I saw her watching us on the beach when we were with Kyle." My glare left nothing to the imagination. He knew she was this entire time, and he didn't say anything?

"Why didn't you say something before?"

"It didn't seem relevant until now. I remembered now

because she seemed interested in me before, and I thought I was overreacting. It's called hypervigilance." And it was a trauma response. He was suffering more than he led on.

Gavin dropped the subject and sauntered to the table. His voice softened, "Sorry to interrupt."

Her eyes drifted up to his. A hint of attraction hit her. Gavin slid into the booth, leaving enough space for me and my purse, which sat between us. Before we jumped into our interrogation, I watched the two of them.

Gavin had bewitched Demi, for sure. She sat up, smiling as she said, "No interruption at all."

"Thank you for meeting with us," his tone was pretty flat with flirty notes. He wasn't good at this. Not like Daniel.

Daniel was also very attractive. And he liked people, making them like him immediately. The allure, the promise of friendship and importance were his hook. Gavin's was dark and moody. Mystery and distance. She seemed to eat it up.

Gavin stuck to his act. He didn't trust Demi, even though he didn't know her. She seemed to overlook this fact and did her best to win him over.

"I'm sure you're wondering who this is and why we're here," I said.

"By the way you two are sitting next to each other, I'd say you used to date." She paused, waiting for a response.

We couldn't be further apart without sitting at separate tables. Gavin put the focus back on him. "Do you know who I am?" he said.

"Not really." Demi said, "But my guess is you're from Maine."

My brows furrowed, "If you were to guess, who do you think this is?" She shrugged.

I may have overestimated Demi. All her posturing may have been just smoke and mirrors. She may not have learned as much about me as she claimed.

"I've done most of my research on you, Catalina. But I'm still piecing everything together."

Demi had played along with my game to keep my identity secret. Her loyalty was impressive, I guess. I was actually more offended that she never had the decency to tell me to my face. "When did you learn my identity?"

"A few months ago."

Gavin raised an eyebrow at her response. "So, you're a journalism student, right?" I said.

"Yes, I am."

"How's school going?" Gavin added.

"Good," Demi drew some of her coffee. "We're only a few weeks in, and I'm already feeling crushed by it."

I nodded, "I'm sure you'll find your footing."

"Yeah," she said. She got over Gavin's good looks and started her interrogation, "Hey, so um, I'm gonna be honest with you. Before Miguel introduced us, I was already onto what was going on in Maine. I came across articles and reports last semester about murders and a massive drug ring that led to several arrests. All the articles kept mentioning Anders and Settlement Island, Maine. So, I looked further and further into it."

"How did you look into it?" I said.

"I subscribed to the local newspapers. That gave me my first clue. Dr. Malcolm Payton is building a massive healthcare center in Settlement Island and Anders, and he is always in the news. I decided to look further into him and see if maybe he knew anything about the crime. Being the town doctor, he probably had some of these people in his morgue."

Gavin tried not to look enthralled. Before I could ask my next question, Demi continued.

"Dr. Payton wasn't available to take my calls, so they transferred me to Aaron White." She watched as my expression changed yet again. Demi was smart. Smarter than I had expected. "He didn't tell me much. Said it was all confidential information, and he had to go. So, I decided to dig further into Dr. Payton. A successful black doctor living in rural Maine didn't make sense."

"I thought the same thing," I said about my father. But betting against him was a terrible idea. He had turned a farfetched pipe dream into a multi-million-dollar health-care conglomerate. And he did it without killing anyone.

"Dr. Payton got his start in southern California. He is married to retired model Sally Ann Payton. His daughter, Cecilia, just opened a boutique which was hit by some home invaders. And one of those home invasion suspects was Blake Huntington."

I could have died right there. It only took a quick search, and through my father and then my sister, she found me. "You saw my name?"

She nodded, "I tried to find a picture of you, but I wasn't able to."

"I asked not to be photographed." For this very reason.

"Who told you she came back here?" Gavin said.

"No one." Demi took pride in her answer. "I called your sister's shop, and she blocked me. So, I tried different stores and restaurants in Settlement Island and Anders, hoping that maybe you worked there. After weeks of this, I called the clinic back to see if maybe your dad would at least let me know where you had moved to. That's when the receptionist told me that you had moved out of state. I figured you came back to California."

Gavin showed how impressed he was. "California's a big place."

"I'm a journalism student. Following my instincts, the answers were there. Your dad went to college here, you probably did, too. Your school of choice was Berkeley. By the way, you're still on Berkeley's website. You and Miguel published a short story together, so he was way my in. His family owns a successful restaurant, and he was featured on the school's website last year."

Gavin laughed, "See, all roads to you came from Miguel."

I killed him with my glare. "You befriended Miguel, meeting me eventually."

"The rest is history. When I saw you, Rose, I knew you were the right person. Your backstory was flimsy. You resemble your dad and Cecilia. The nail in the coffin was your past. No one would ever talk about it."

I leaned in, "Why didn't you confront me sooner?"

"I waited until my professor accepted my thesis topic. My thesis paper is on you and Settlement Island, and I'm at an impasse. My source has run out of details. He directed me to you."

This was the perfect set up for my next question: "Who is your source?"

"His name is Ben Ryan."

Sleazy, inappropriate Ben Ryan.

"Who put you in contact with Ben?" Gavin said.

I shook my head, "Is Ben here?" Demi didn't know which one of us to answer. My question took priority. "You said you had to meet with your source the other day. Was that Ben?"

She took in the gravity of my question. "Yeah, Ben's here." All composure went out the window. Ben being here meant he was a member in Ian's army. "Relax, Catalina. Ben seems like a nice guy."

"Ben seems like an asshole," Gavin said.

"Have you seen him in person?" I said.

"Not yet. We were supposed to meet that day, but he had to postpone to…" She opened her journal which was filled with articles and information on me. There was a name that she had circled on a page as well. Before she flipped away, I saw another name next to it. "…he had to meet with his boss. Since he doesn't live here, I thought it was strange."

"He was meeting with Porter," I told Gavin. The two names I saw in Demi's notebook were Robert Porter and Officer Jaime Dixon. "Demi, have you ever talked with Robert Porter?" She shook her head. "What about Officer Dixon?"

"He was the one who put me onto Ben."

"And how did you meet Dixon?"

"When I was calling around, of course. He wasn't

interested in talking to me at first, but then the flood gates came open when I told him about why I was looking into you. He set me up with Ben. Ben was able to answer some of my questions about the murder you were involved in. According to him, you killed Blake in cold blood and all that, but he never told me why exactly. That's when I looked into the drug business, and I found out about Robert Porter. I wanted to connect with him, but everyone I spoke with hung up when I mentioned his name."

Gavin studied her notebook, "Do you write everything in there?"

"All my conversations and interviews are here. All my research is on my computer in my dorm room." She seemed proud, not realizing that she was in grave danger.

I went from being a pain in the ass to a concerned friend. "Demi, listen to me. Stop looking into Porter and Blake. These people you are talking to are very, very bad people. They are dangerous."

"Give me your side of the story. My professor loves my thesis, but I can't publish it without your side." Before she could offend me any further, her approach softened, "You killed that guy, right? Well, no matter what Ben says, I believe you aren't a cold-hearted killer. I think you had to protect yourself. And he gave you no choice."

"It wasn't that simple," I said. "To you, this is just a grade in a class." I put my hand on my chest, "This is my life. And because of you, Ben and Porter know where I am!"

She put her hand on mine, "Then there's no harm in giving me your story." She motioned in my direction,

"You're scared of them. But if you stand up to them, and give me the scoop, you get your power back."

Gavin scoffed at this, "You can't be that selfish."

"There is no story, Demi." I had to calm down. "So, stop talking to Ben. And stay away from Noah." She seemed perplexed. "Did you know about Noah before? That he has been lying to me about who he is?"

She faltered, "Noah lied to you?" I nodded. "No, he never came up."

"What about me? I'm Gavin Scott."

Demi was crushed, "They shot you." She paused, "You killed Russ Huntington, right?"

Gavin shook his head, "Dixon tell you that?"

"Like I said, he was more than willing to help me."

"Now Dixon is dead. And Aaron White, who works with my dad, is missing." It was coming together for her, I hoped. "So just stop, okay?"

"I can't just stop. My entire thesis is based on this. If I stop now, I won't be able to finish my project." Her desperation was in the wrong place. She was worried about a class, and I was thinking about all the people she had just put in danger. Gavin reached across the table and took her journal. "What the hell?"

"If you want to help, this is how." He put the notebook in my purse.

"That's larceny! I can have you arrested."

"I don't fuckin' care." Gavin grabbed my hand and pulled me out of the booth. "Stop investigating us." I snatched my purse before we left the restaurant. Once outside, I stopped him.

"Do you really think that was the best way to handle that?"

"She wasn't going to give us much information. Her notebook is what we really need." Like always, he was right. "If she was looking into the murders and Blake, we can use this along with your journals to create our own leads."

"Brilliant. I owe you some blueberry ricotta pancakes." I opened my phone and there was a long string of texts from Demi, demanding that I give her notebook back. I texted back, telling her that Gavin was a jerk and I didn't condone thievery. Then, I made her a deal. Since she wasn't going to give up her project, I wanted to use it in my favor. She had done a great job learning about Ben and Porter. So, I wanted her to stay in contact with them. Feed me information. And in return, when all this was over, I would give her an exclusive interview.

She agreed, bitterly.

Now, I had to get in contact with Luke and tell him what happened. But he beat me to the punch. He had some news on Gary.

CHAPTER ELEVEN
Hollow

LUKE HAD STUMBLED upon something big. Huge. I texted him the entire ride back, Gavin seemingly unfazed by the distance between us. Demi had pegged us for a couple. Like we were just friendly exes who just so happened to meet for breakfast on a casual Thursday. That our past didn't define the uneasiness we now shared.

Did he regret it?

The sex, I mean.

His attention to the road, the way he made sure we didn't touch, was his tell. A note on how much distance had grown between us. Sadly, I had hoped that we could at least be friendly. If only for the time we would spend together. Once Gary was gone, we could go back to fading away from each other's lives.

We were back at The Chateau, sitting apart on the bed. Luke had set up a video chat, adjusting his screen. "Okay, here's what I got on Gary and Maverick." He pulled up an old article from over thirty years ago. "Gary Porter was charged with drug possession while living in Los Angeles, California. He was part of a drug ring that was tied to the Blood Diamond motorcycle gang. He was a drug dealer for them."

"I didn't know Gary lived in California," I said.

Gavin shrugged, "I don't see how you would."

Luke kept going, "He didn't stay in California for long. I found an article from two years later where he was arrested in Anders for DUI."

"Gary met Maverick through the bikers. He started dealing drugs and ended up in Maine?"

My friend had already solved this discrepancy, "Gary was born in Settlement Island." Luke shuffled through some screens. "His dad worked at the lumberyard, like many of the people here. He died in Anders at the age of ninety, so my guess is Gary moved there sometime after he came back from California."

"Porter was born in Anders, right?" I said.

Luke shrugged. "Gary was," Gavin added. "Porter was in Settlement Island, but he was never a Settler. Aaron's mom has relatives who built the town. They weren't big fans of Gary, so they ran him out of town when Porter was a young kid."

"Gary would have gotten his DUI around the time the Porters moved." Luke flipped through articles. "He got his first drug charge twenty-seven ago."

"Porter would have been around seven or eight then," Gavin said. "Luke, Gary's dad owned a small construction company before he died. After he kicked it, Gary started using it to deal drugs."

"You read my mind," Luke continued, "Gary probably got into the drug business in California where he got his first drug charge. He gets out of jail and moves back to Maine where he's quiet for a bit before setting up his new drug company." He took a break to bring up a news article. "His dad won a lawsuit against the lumberyard for an injury on the job. My guess is he left the money and the business to Gary, and he used it to expand his construction company while selling drugs."

"Then he flooded Anders with drugs." Gavin and Luke were silent. Gavin came to a conclusion, "What if Maverick was his supplier?"

That didn't seem plausible, "Carrying drugs from California to Maine would have been too risky," I said. "And Expensive."

"My dad's a trucker," Gavin said. "What if he was picking up drugs from Maverick for Gary?"

"That could put Maverick in Maine for Gary to kill," Luke said. "Could have been a drug deal gone wrong." Gavin nodded.

The lead was hot. Blinding hot, even. Still, they had missed the entire point of our investigation. "Gary didn't kill Maverick."

"I know that was our theory," Luke said, "but Maverick and Gary having a falling out over drugs makes sense. It would explain why Maverick came to Maine. Why would Gary be the only person with motive to kill him? I mean, why else would Maverick be here?"

"He did it," Gavin said. "Gary killed this guy."

"Not necessarily." They both groaned at my doubts.

"We have to look at this from other angles." Enlightened, I posed another theory, "Someone else could have known about Maverick and Gary's business deal because they were a part of it. A silent partner who leveraged Gary's deals with Maverick and the bikers to get him locked up," I said.

Gavin shook his head, "I doubt it. Porter and his dad have contingencies for shit like this. They have moles everywhere, reporting back to them. James's friends with some of the moles who got the hell out after Blake burned the place down."

He didn't mean to, but he had strengthened my case. "Blake knew about Porter's entire operation, thanks Kyle who was coked out of his mind and drunk all the time. He was a nobody who made friends with the right people who pointed him in the right direction. No mole caught him."

"With an organization that big, they can't keep track of what everyone is doing," Luke said. "So, Catalina, you're assuming someone threw Gary into jail, so they could profit off Maverick's murder?"

"Something like that. Either way, Gary going to jail benefits a lot of people, especially the drug dealers who didn't work for Gary." I opened my notebook, "When Gary went to jail, there was a three-year period where Gary's business took a hit. Dealers were going off on their own, setting up new territories."

"Yeah, Porter had to build up some new allies," Gavin confirmed. "James was one of them for a time. That's where the rumors surrounding James selling for Porter came from. He had his own drug ties, but he was still on good terms with Porter to feed me information and to keep himself out of the morgue. They had their scuffles here and there, but Porter knew that killing James would cause a riot."

James was always a volume of information. I turned in my notebook, "James told me that if someone were to go after Porter, it would have to be someone at the bottom, not the top. He was right about Blake. What if the responsible party planned the whole thing and recruited someone at the bottom to actually kill Maverick?"

Luke sided with me. "I think you're on the right track. I'll chase that lead here. Since you're in California, you can press on the Blood Diamonds."

"Your-inside-job lead plus my biker lead will prove Gary guilty or innocent." I smiled, "Good work, Luke," I beamed. Now, onto my news. I told him about Demi, and Noah, and Porter's demands to meet me.

Luke sighed, rubbing his chin. His eye should have been twitching, but he gave that up long ago. "Catalina, you should slow down your side of the investigation."

"Why?"

"Because Noah put cameras in your house to spy on you. And Demi is talking to Ben about you. Porter's gonna find you soon if you chase your Blood Diamond lead."

"But I'm at The Chateau," I reasoned. "No one knows where I am. Or what I'm doing."

"They will if you find the Blood Diamonds."

"Once I find Charlie, I'll see if our theory about Gary and Maverick are true. Then, I'll back off into the shadows and away from Porter's radar." I could hear Luke sigh as I wrote more notes. "It'll be fine."

Luke shook his head, "Don't do it." I argued with him for a moment before he said, "Come back to Maine, where you can put some distance between yourself and those assholes."

"Why would I do that? The bikers are here, not there."

"Because Porter would never expect you to go back to the place where you are not safe. But you'll have me, your sister, your parents. Not to mention the entire Settlement Island Police Department. They are levied with Gary because they think he killed Dixon. You'll have their protection." He became stern, "I love you, and I don't want to lose you to this."

Luke's words were tough. Gavin shifted his eyes between us. "I'll think about it," I said. Luke wanted more commitment. "I just don't want to run from my problems anymore." He had to see it my way, "Hiding isn't enough. It's not the ending I want in this story." I was possessed by a dark possibility. "Porter will continue to haunt me until I end this, Luke. Until I confront him, on my terms, rewriting this horrible story he's been writing for me. If I don't stop him, I'm gonna end up with darkness ever after." And that story was one Demi would happily write.

"Darkness ever after? I've never heard of that before," Luke said.

"It's her way of saying everything's gonna go to hell," Gavin scoffed.

Luke put his hand to the screen, "You're gonna get your happily ever after, my friend." He leaned in, "We just gotta be smart about it. Don't rush into things. Be patient. And don't try to do everything alone."

"I'm not alone. I have you." My smile brightened, "If investigating Charlie turns into a bad idea, I'll give it up."

Luke said, "I'm going to check in with you every single day until you get back to Maine." But I hadn't made that decision yet. "Please, just come home." He had to go. After we said goodbye, I moved on to Demi's notebook.

Her hand writing was so beautiful. And her notes were pristine. There were so many things I had missed. She had pages on Ben and Dixon. Her interviews with some of the people in town who hoped Gary would go back to jail and others who also thought he was framed. There police report numbers, phone numbers for witnesses, and dates forming a solid timeline.

I loved Demi. And I felt really good that between the two of us, we could make some progress on whether or not Gary was buying drugs from Maverick. I smiled as I curled my toes against the comforter, turning the pages to this awesome book.

Gavin sat down on the bed next to me. "Luke made some really good points." These were the first words he had said to me directly. Since we had spent the night together. He took the notebook from my clenching hands. "This is getting really dangerous."

"At least no one's shot at us," I told him. My joke was cruel, and I apologized over and over after I said it. Still, "We're both on the same page, right? We're not leaving here until I talk to Charlie. After that, we head home." I thought about it, "I guess this is my home."

"There are so many resources in Maine that will make all this guessing go by quicker."

I sighed, "I can't run just because things are getting tough." Gavin had to understand, "I'm not that same girl you were in love with last year. I stand up for what I want, and I don't back down. Not from anything or anyone."

Gavin nodded, "I like the girl you were last year. And whoever you are now. But having common sense and wanting to survive are not weaknesses." He put his hand on mine, "You are the strongest person I know, Catalina."

He was gaming me, and I told him, "I don't need compliments."

"It's not a compliment," he said. "It's a fact. You stand up for what you believe in, and that takes a lot of strength." The softness of his hand faded when I pulled it away. "About last night," he said.

"It was just sex," my words snapped. I reached for Demi's notebook. He tossed it to the other side of the bed.

"No, it wasn't." Gavin had a way of finding the emotions I didn't dare feel. "First of all, it was really, really good." He chuckled nervously, "Secondly, we never really broke up, Catalina. Not like normal people do."

"We're not normal people. We're both murderers. It would be silly for us to think we could ever have a real friendship or relationship." Telling him that we didn't work wouldn't cut it. I opted to reason with him on his level, "You always said that you didn't really date. You never had a girlfriend because of the life you lead. I get that now. Us dating was wishful thinking. Something we need to get past..."

His lips touched mine, gently. Full of tenderness. When he let go, I could see his heart. His soul. "I never stopped loving you." He gave me another kiss, this one just as lush as the first one. "Every time I look at you, I'm falling in love with you all over again." He gave me a final kiss. "Don't forget that," he whispered.

We were wrecked if I didn't say something. Anything. Luckily, Gavin moved on, "What's in Demi's notebook?"

Flustered, I swam through everything he had told me and found some semblance of focus, "I just opened it." I reached over and grabbed it.

Gavin patted the blankets next to him. I resumed my position, leaving a gap. He crossed his legs, one over the other. I turned to the first page, and we read what Demi had written. Then, we talked about it. This continued page after page. We were in unison, turning pages in tandem as we discussed the notes.

Demi was a gold mine.

Her conversations with Ben gave me insight into how Blake got a foothold in Porter's business. Gary had a ton of enemies who were itching for his territory and customers. There were some questions about loyalty, and Ben made it clear. In the end, no one was loyal to the Porter family business, except for the two men who held its namesake.

Officer Dixon told another story. He didn't mention the murders he committed for Blake. Instead, he zeroed in on Russ's murder. Things that didn't add up from that night. He made the assumption that Gary was involved because of Hank.

There in her notes, Dixon had admitted to seeing

Hank's truck driving away from the scene. He had run the tags and confirmed that Hank Scott, known associate to Gary Porter, was involved. Gary was arrested shortly after for Maverick's death, so that's where the lead ran cold. Gary behind bars was good enough for him. And Gavin was under Gary's protection, so he became Dixon's nemesis. And Blake's, too.

"Gary thought he was gonna get out of jail," I said. Gavin asked why.

"It says right here that Dixon traced your dad to Gary. So, Gary covered his tracks with Russ's murder for Hank, which means that he didn't want to catch a charge for Russ's murder. He had to assume his lawyers would pull through in his Maverick's case. Or else he would have set up a stronger alibi for that murder, too."

Gavin tapped his lip. "I don't know. That could make sense." He yawned.

"We'll pick this up tomorrow." I looked over at the clock. "What should we do next?" I said.

"What do you mean?"

"I can't go back to the beach house. We can't hide here forever. So, what do we do?" I thought Gavin would have a better idea for a plan. But he didn't seem to know any more than I did. Charlie was a bust. I could reach out to Noah to press him about Porter, but that seemed fruitless.

Luke didn't have any updates on Aaron's whereabouts. Porter was where he always was…in the wind. Gavin shook his head and placed Demi's notebook on the nightstand, "I'm going to sleep."

Unlike last night, Gavin didn't play around. He turned

on the TV to the movie channel and emptied his pockets. Boots off, he laid down on top of the comforter, still dressed, eyes shut. I went to the bathroom and prepped myself for another night together. When I came back, I figured he would be waiting for me. His heavy breathing against the sounds of a black and white flick told me otherwise.

I sat down and looked at my phone, waiting for someone to text me. When it went unanswered, I picked up the book Ian had given me. Grover's annotated copy with several notes and ideas. I turned to a poem that seemed to fit my situation perfectly.

Hollow Men

Some people say the Hollow Men have lost their passion. They wander the earth looking for vengeance that never seems to come. Bitter souls that lose their value over petty things you and I ignore. They start fights to feel something, anything other than the hollowness within their hearts. While you and I scoff at their indifference toward things that matter, they find solace in their darkened souls. Souls, souls, souls, they are consumed by them. And it's not until you examine further that you find the truth. They are hollow because there is nothing. They already consumed everything, locusts feeding until there is nothing left. Starvation sets in, and they move on, slipping into hollowness until they feast again. If you were hollow, you would do the same, too. Compelled by the vast loneliness of being empty, you would consume everything until it consumed you.

Clearly, it was a work in progress. Not as rich and luxurious as his other work. It still felt good to read something that matched what I was feeling. Blake and his friends were my hollow men. So was I.

I looked down at Gavin. Eyes closed, hair still perfect. Wonderfully jagged and beautiful. The sex had been great. It tapped into my hollowness, the canyon inside that had missed him.

I didn't feel bad about jumping into bed with Gavin right after I had smashed a vase against my boyfriend's head. What Noah and I had was built on sand and lies. There was no place to grieve or feel guilty about what led to Gavin and I drawing from each other.

Daniel was another story.

I got up and pulled out my letters to him.

Daniel,

I'm sorry I haven't written to you in a few days. Things have been pretty shitty lately. Gary's out of jail, Ian has found me, and my boyfriend ended up being a liar. I'm sure you would have figured it out if you were here. You would have exposed Noah for who he is; a deceiver. So, I ask, what should I do? Gavin and Luke want me to give up on this cause and save my own life. But I can't. I won't run. I won't just let Porter intimidate me for the rest of my life.

So, what should I do?

I wish you were here to help me. I know you would make it all right...

This felt unfair. To go to him after my lips had pressed against another man's.

I slept with Gavin. And I'm sorry.

I slammed the book shut. Gavin moved slightly on the bed, murmuring something. A new flick was announced on the screen. *Some Like It Hot.* I had seen this one, and I did enjoy it. Daniel's journal was hidden away in my duffle bag. I curled up under the blankets, watching Marilyn Monroe deliver her lines with confidence and poise.

I made it through the movie and soon forgot about everything except how much I really liked old movies. And pizza. And sometimes the boy sleeping next to me.

Gavin woke me up with some blueberry ricotta pancakes for breakfast. They were good. Of course, every item on the menu at The Chateau was always good. We took turns getting ready and shielding our eyes from the other. By the time we were done, the aching question still remained; where were we going next?

"Charlie still hasn't gotten back to me, so I don't know," I said.

Gavin tapped his finger to his lips, "There's a club of Blood Diamonds close to here. Maybe we can just drive over there and see if anyone will talk to us?"

Why didn't I think of that one before?

I agreed, and we went downstairs to check out and get the Nova. I looked up the address for the Blood Diamond headquarters, which was difficult. They weren't listed online, so I figured we could go to a bike shop and ask around. The address to *Dirty Bags Bike Shop* was in the GPS, and I went back to reading Demi's notebook.

We had stopped on an entry where she had a conversation with Officer Dixon a few days before he died. He asked about me. Wanted to know if she had any luck figuring out what I knew about Gary. Demi's notes were sharp. She had challenged him and asked for more information about Gary, which he had been tight-lipped about. She lived up to the term *The Press*, not letting go until he gave her what she wanted to know. She was relentless.

His final concession came as advice. He told her that she was looking in the wrong place. She needed to look into Gary and his relationship to the murder he was charged with. Dixon believed Gary was guilty, and Victor Lloyd was the key. Get Victor Lloyd and get the full story.

I chuckled, "Gavin, Demi was grilling Dixon about Gary. She was onto him, too." I read him the passage.

He nodded, "And she talked to before he died?" I confirmed, "So, when did she start talking to Dixon?" I flipped back to the beginning of the notebook.

"Here. It seems like Dixon was one of the first people she had contacted when she was looking into Blake and his murder." Gavin nodded. "What are you thinking?"

"I wonder what he told her. I mean, he told her about me. But as we can see, Dixon knew way more about what was happening with Blake. He took those secrets to the grave." He paused, "Think about it. Gary and Blake were enemies. Dixon was Blake's best friend. Wouldn't he want to put Gary behind bars for good? As a cop, he would have the means."

This was a good question. "But Gary still doesn't know who framed him. If Dixon did it, his death would have exonerated Gary." Gavin's shrug put my attention back on the pages. Once I learned more about Gary and Maverick, I would be able to see how Dixon fit. I looked at the map to see how far away we were from Dirt Bags. We had overshot the exit by several miles. The phone was telling Gavin to circle back, but he kept going forward. I looked at the road. We were on the PCH, heading north and out of Los Angeles.

"Where are you going?"

Gavin sighed, "Catalina, I know you want to keep chasing this lead, but we need to go home. Luke is right; we gotta go back to Maine."

He had betrayed me. I didn't have my car, and I was too far away from it. Without my own transportation, I'd remain his prisoner.

I had to think fast.

There was an exit for a rest area. I told Gavin to pull over, so I could call Luke. Reluctantly, he complied. Once we stopped, I got out, phone in hand.

Instead of calling Luke, I called Miguel. "Hey, I need you to come pick me up. I'm at the rest area over by…" I looked around, seeing Gavin's angry face.

"Get off the phone," he said. I shook my head. He lunged forward and grabbed me. I thrashed against him as he carried me back to the car. "Put me down, Gavin!" People slowed down enough to see what was going on. Yet, he didn't relent. I swatted his arms, "I mean it!" Strong, angry, and mission-oriented, he didn't budge. Desperate, I dug my nail into his bullet wound. That caused him to drop me, my back hitting the ground.

The pain tearing through him made me wince. It had been over a year. Why did the wound still hurt so bad? I didn't stick around to ask. I got to my feet and ran to the other side of the rest area. A few travelers had pulled off and stopped to offer their assistance. One was a blond fellow on a motorcycle, black leather strapped around his chest. He threw off his helmet and charged toward me.

"Do you need help?" Judging by the force in his voice, he would be a worthy match for Gavin. I didn't want to hurt him; I just wanted to get away.

"I need a ride, that's all."

The man looked over at Gavin, who was getting up. "Get on!"

I didn't hesitate. He got on and I climbed behind him, hugging his back. Soon, we were out of the rest area, heading south. I held onto his leather which read the words *Blood Diamond MC*. The hair, the face, the leather, they had been his signature in the few pages I had on him. This man was Charlie.

CHAPTER TWELVE
Bad Choices

STUPID, SELFISH BASTARD! My nostrils flared as I cursed Gavin's name and his intentions to derail my investigation. He may have been scared, but I wasn't. I clutched Charlie's back, having only ridden a motorcycle once. The Nova would be no match for the speed and agility of this bike. We whipped through cars, no regard for those sitting in the endless traffic.

I held on, feeling the sway of the bike moving back and forth. Without another thought, I placed my head on his back, breaking the wind from hitting my face like a knife. Charlie kept driving, no regard to me and my current position. This had been the worst idea I had. Especially when I realized I was missing my phone, all my money, and my purse. The same purse that contained Daniel's flash drive.

I cursed again. Charlie must have heard it. On the next exit, he pulled over to the side. I climbed off, my body shaking, me hating myself for being so stupid.

Charlie took his helmet off, "You're Catalina Payton?"

"Yeah. Please tell me you're Charlie Gardner."

"You kept calling me." He pulled out his phone, tilting it in my direction. "And you shared your location with me."

My stupid move had paid off. "Is that how you found me?"

He nodded, "Where's your phone?"

I motioned in the area of the long-gone rest stop, "I left all my stuff in his car. My phone must have fallen out during the struggle."

"So, you're stranded with no phone and no money?" He sounded like my dad.

I had put myself in the middle of a bad horror movie, "It looks like it."

"Okay, then." He leaned against the bike.

I seethed a sigh, "Charlie, I know this is going to sound strange, but you're not a murderer, right?" I didn't give him much time to answer, "I just learned that my boyfriend was not actually my boyfriend, but a mole for my enemy. And that enemy is in California. And my ex-boyfriend…" I hurried to the end of my story, "So, if you're gonna kill me, just get it over with." I sat down on the hard gravel and bottle shards. "You wouldn't be the first person to try."

His brows furrowed, "How many people have tried to kill you?"

"Three." I paused, "Well, I thought one of them was trying to kill me, but he was just going to use me as leverage against a drug lord." I frowned, "Same with one of the other guys." Then, I remembered Six. "Kyle and Noah weren't trying to kill me. But Six was, for sure. He pushed me off a waterfall. Then, Blake tried to shoot me…"

"I'm sorry," he said, "are you an actress in a movie?"

"No," I huffed, "but my life sure is seeming that way." I climbed up. "So, let's get this over with. Is it gonna be a gunshot, a stabbing, or just good old fashioned strangulation?"

He grinned as he said, "Neither?" He ran a hand through his long blond hair, fixing it back into place. "I've got six sisters and a single mother; I know how girls fight. I don't mess with women." He pulled out a pack of cigarettes and offered me one. When I declined, he lit it, and leaned against his bike. "That guy you were with; was he one of those people who was trying to kill you? Or not kill?"

"He's my ex-boyfriend. He drove across the country to find me." My tone was somber. "I know what you saw back there, but he wasn't trying to hurt me." I paused, "He was actually trying to keep me from finding you." *Bring it full circle, Catalina.* "You were looking for me?"

"I was tracking you from your cell phone. You said you wanted to talk about Gary Porter and Maverick."

I laughed, "What are the odds? I mean, I still can't believe you found me."

"It's not hard when you know where to look." Smoke escaped his lips, "What do you know about Gary?"

I wouldn't just give him my entire hand while I stood on the side of the road. There were still things I would need to get back to L.A. Charlie had become the unlucky carrier of this burden. Some vagueness was in order, just so I could lead him on, "Before we talk about Gary, I need to know what kind of person you are. Whether or not I can trust you. The people related to Gary and his son tend to be into dark shit."

He took a drag off his cigarette, "Like selling drugs?"

"And murdering people." Charlie looked me up and down, and I knew what he was thinking. "I don't do drugs."

"I can tell," he smirked. "I used to deal before I went to jail. Got out of it and got clean."

My skin tingled, "What did you go to jail for?"

"Drug dealing. Robbery. Battery on a LEO. Assault. Assault with a deadly weapon. That sort of thing. Did eight years only because I managed to get a plea deal. Without it, I would have done thirty-five years or more."

I looked at the leather on his back. *Blood Diamond MC.* "You're in a motorcycle gang, huh?" Another smirk and drag on his cigarette. I knew how to pick 'em. "Hmm."

"Scared?" he teased.

"After the last two years I've had, no. One of my best friends was a drug dealer I was trying to save. He ended up saving me." I didn't know what to do next. "Maverick and Gary. When can I meet your biker friends, so we can all talk?"

He dropped his cigarette butt and crushed it with his weathered boot. "Whenever you want. Based on the day you're having, maybe we should get to it now."

"What will it cost me? For your time and help?" Nothing in this life came free; especially not from a guy like this.

He approached, eyes square on mine. I wasn't afraid. At least I didn't want to be. "Whatever you think is fair." Then came the cursed wink that every bad boy gives the unsuspecting good girl who is totally over it. My negotiation skills were nominal at best. He leaned in, "Don't overthink it." He hopped on the bike, "You ready?"

"Yeah." I climbed behind him, clutching his middle.

"Before I bring the club in, I want to talk with you alone. Where can we go?"

"Do you like Mexican food?"

⚜

Charlie loved Mexican food. And margaritas. And coffee. The waitress asked what brew he wanted, and he said whatever they had laying around. I asked why he didn't ask for a fresh brew. He shook his head. Charlie didn't mind the taste of stale coffee. The bitterness made him sharp, he said.

The look on Miguel's face when I strolled in with my new biker friend was priceless. He thought he was never going to see me again. Here I was with another Gavin-like creature who seemed somehow worse. He pulled me aside, nails cutting my winded skin. "Where did you find him?"

"It's a really long story that I don't have time to tell." I peered over as one of his cousins seated Charlie in a booth. "Can he eat for free as payment for him bringing me back to town?"

"You don't have any money?"

"Gavin has my stuff."

Miguel's hand slammed into his thigh, "And where is Gavin?" he barked.

"I have no idea." I smiled, "But Gavin has my phone, so I can track him!" Charlie looked over at me, his head motioning for me to have a seat. Miguel glared. "Please, do this for me."

"Why?" Miguel shifted his weight, "You keep inviting

these horrible, horrible guys into your life. And I think you need an intervention."

"Miguel?"

"Noah fooled me, too. But Gavin and now this guy? And Kyle?" His brows narrowed, "You need to stop putting yourself in these people's shit."

"Look, I know I have worn you down in the blind faith department. But if you have faith in me, one more time, I'll make it worth your while." Miguel looked over at Charlie who was chatting with one of his cousins about the menu. "Please, just trust me."

"I don't need you to make anything worth my while." He danced from side to side, "This crusade has to stop. Make it worth your while to *not* do this anymore!" Convincing Miguel became impossible. My shoulders slouched. Miguel sighed, "Alright, fine." Before I left, he said, "Your limit is one margarita. And no steak."

"Thanks," I said softly and walked away to sit down across from Charlie. He crunched on a chip with a heavy amount of salsa. "My friend's mom almost got a Michelin star for that salsa."

"It's pretty good." He sat back. "I've heard of this place before."

"Yeah, it's a common haunt for people who want really good fish tacos." Miguel charged toward me, two margaritas in hand. He placed them down. "Thank you."

The biker pointed at Miguel, "Is this the friend?"

"Yeah, this is Miguel. Miguel, this is…" I had spent the past few hours with this man, and I didn't even know if he wanted me to give away his name.

He put out hand, "Charlie."

"He knows about Gary, Porter's dad," I chimed in.

Miguel shook Charlie's and glared at me. My poor life choices were now becoming his. "Relax, Miguel," Charlie said as he sipped his drink. In Spanish, he added, "I'm not going to hurt her." Language barrier or not, Miguel didn't hold back. In Spanish, he exclaimed about how I needed to stop picking up guys who clearly had Hepatitis C and go back to Boring Luke. Curious, Charlie said, "Who's Luke?"

"Just a friend," I brushed off.

"Is he one of those people who is trying to kill you?" Miguel's head whipped in my direction. Yes, I had told him about that, against my better judgement.

"No, um, just a good friend."

Charlie pointed toward me with a chip, "Not the drug dealer you're trying to save, right?"

"Oh My God, girl! Did you tell him your bra size, too?" Miguel snapped. I blushed.

Charlie popped the chip in his mouth. So casual, like we were just discussing if we should go see a movie later or not. "I live a really complicated life," I said.

He put his hands up, "I'd never judge you." Miguel's mother shouted for him to get back to work. Once he was gone, Charlie relaxed into the booth, one leg propped up against the wood. Yet, he was mindful of the upholstery. "Your friend seems pretty upset."

"I haven't made his life easy lately."

"What have you done?"

I didn't want to get into it. The sun was setting, and there were so many other things on my mind. Like where was I going to sleep tonight? If that was a possibility. "I need to find a place to sleep."

Charlie didn't hesitate, "You can crash at my place." That was out of the question. He could read the thought on my face. "I mean, you did share your location with me, hop on the back of my bike, tell me your life story, and then bring me to your best friend's restaurant. Sleeping at one of my houses isn't really that big of a deal."

"It is to me," I snapped. I was being rude, but I didn't mean to be. "I've been in this position before." Charlie tilted his head, "Last year, I was running around with this guy, sleeping in cars, in cabins, holding up in seaside resorts." I paused, "Showing him the stars," I whispered, remembering Daniel's glee when he learned the constellations. Sagittarius, his constellation. I'd never forget it.

"You loved this guy?" I snapped out of my daydream and started a rebuttal that never quite formed. "Well, I can't offer you a cabin or seaside resort, or car camping, but I do have an Airbnb in my backyard. It's all yours."

"You own an Airbnb?" I said with genuine surprise.

"Yeah, three of them. Nothing fancy like what you just described. There's a bed, half a closet, a shower, and a TV that's the size of a shoebox." I grinned. "Sounds good?"

I nodded. This was the best option I had, other than Miguel's. I wasn't going to put him in danger. Not with Ian stalking around. "If you give me your phone, I can send you some money."

He shrugged it off, "Don't worry about it." His eyes glanced toward the kitchen. "Do you think we can get some dinner?"

"Sure." I went to the kitchen, but Miguel wasn't in sight. I managed to order some of the house specials for us. When I returned, I thought Charlie would be gone. A figment of my imagination. Yet, he sat at the table, leg down now, texting someone.

I didn't ask who, but he offered up, "My sister. She's super pregnant, and the doctors are thinking of inducing her tomorrow."

I could tell he wanted to say more, but I barged past his sweet sentiment. "What do you know about Gary and Robert Porter?" He was taken aback by my abruptness. "Just tell me," I pleaded. "Because the sooner I can get information about Gary, the sooner I can get on with my life."

Charlie quickly figured out I was not kidding. Yet, he didn't relent, "We'll talk about Gary. Right now, I have some questions for you."

I sat up straight, "Fire away."

He made direct eye contact with me, "How long have you known me?"

This was a silly, irrelevant question. "A couple hours. What does it matter?"

Charlie's back settled into the booth. "You shared your location with me. And I offered you a place to stay, and you jumped on it, no questions asked."

"You think there's something wrong with me?"

"Not wrong with you," he said. "I'm curious to know why you were so quick to trust me when you don't know anything about me."

I perked up, "I know you are in a biker gang with Maverick. *Was. Were.*" I licked my chapped lips, "Maverick has ties to Gary Porter, the guy who is trying to ruin my life." And that's all I knew. Charlie's point soared toward me. I put my hands on my forehead and pushed my curls back. "You probably think I'm a crazy person, huh?"

"Not crazy. Lonely, maybe."

Such a short time together, and he thought I was lonely? "I'm desperate."

"How desperate?" he said.

I never liked where this question went. "I don't want you to get the wrong impression."

"I hardly know you; I haven't really formed an impression of you yet." He chopped another chip.

"But you said I was lonely?"

"I said you seem lonely. And a little too eager to jump into bed with a biker gang."

My eagerness was suspicious to him. So, I countered with a question, "You're all I have to work with." I sighed, "Seriously, I need your help. You're a really important member?"

"Sorta." He pulled his hair back, "I was vice president of the club until I went to jail. Youngest VP in history. Then, I got out of the gang."

"They gave you a choice?"

"Of course. Me getting locked up kept several other members on the streets."

"Sounds like you cared about them." I dunked a chip into the salsa, "Why did you get out of the club?"

Charlie stole a chip from the pile. "I had to, if I wanted parole and a different life. The club was my family for years. Before I got locked up, my mom and my sisters wouldn't talk to me because of the shit I was doing for them. I've never met my dad, but my mom said I was turning out to be just like him." He paused to look down. I knew that regret. It's the same one Kyle had given me in his cabin when he was telling me about all the people he had murdered. The regrets he would never outlive.

"They make you do stuff you didn't want to do?"

He shook his head. "No, I was happy to help out my club. A little too happy, I guess."

"Did they pressure you at all?"

Charlie's intrigue hardened, "What are your friends like?"

I was in a disagreement with all of them over one thing. Miguel and Luke wanted me to slow down on my war against Gary. Other than that, "Everything is fine."

"And the argument you just had with your friend over there? What was that about?"

"Why are you asking me all these questions?" I pressed.

"Why aren't you asking me more questions about myself?"

"You said you wanted to ask me questions first!" More chips entered his mouth as he fell into silence on me. "Everyone doesn't agree with what I'm doing at the moment, but that doesn't mean I can't think for myself," I finally said.

"I'm not everyone. I just think you should stop and wonder a little bit about…"

"…about what, huh?" My voice roared against his confidence. "I don't have time for this. I just need to know the connection between Gary and Maverick, that's all. Now, are you going to fuckin' help me or not?"

Charlie dropped his chip and folded his hands. His stare almost tore me down. No darkness crept into his eyes. No pity. Stubbornness was the likely culprit. I wouldn't know unless he told me, which he didn't do. Not right away.

I caught my breath, "That was a bit of an overreaction." My shoulders and back sank into the booth, "I don't know what's happening to me."

"What's going on?" he said. I buried my head into my hands. "I'm sure it's not that bad."

"You already know some of it." If I went into the details about killing Blake, my arrangements with Porter, Noah's lies…No, I was too tired to get into any of that. "I'm tired of my life, man."

"It sounds exhausting."

"It is," I chuckled.

"Take a break from it."

"There's a sense of urgency behind why I needed to meet with you."

"Gary's out of jail, and you're worried he's gonna come after you and your friends. Yeah, you made that clear in the three-thousand text messages you sent me." Annoyed, he continued, "Gary has a lot of enemies up and down each coast. Do you think you're the only one planning a move against him?" I hadn't thought about it. "Trust me, he's gonna get what's coming to him, one way or the other."

"You guys already have a plan?"

"Not yet. We're still figuring things out."

"I thought you were out of the club?"

"I'm an auxiliary member. In enough to help and out

enough to keep the Feds out of my hair." He ran a hand through this hair, bringing back some of the volume.

"Whatever you guys are doing, I'd like to be a part of it."

Charlie picked up a chip and pointed it to me, "We'll see." My brows didn't furrow for long. "I don't know you. And you don't know me. But I find it strange how willing you are to just throw yourself into danger with someone you just met. That's not a good sign."

"We already covered this…"

"What if I'm a serial killer? You said you already have three or four people trying to kill you. Don't you think it's a little reckless to put yourself in this situation with me? Besides, how do I know you're not working for Gary?"

Now, he sounded like Dr. Wong. She had been concerned about how careless I was with my life. But that was several months ago. I had outgrown that. "I'm deciding to trust you. Plus," I licked my salty lips, "you don't think I'm working for Gary or else this meeting would have gone differently. I imagine there would have been a lot of blood torture. Not chips and margs." He laughed. Seriously, though, "Are you a good person?" I said with concern.

"I'm a born-again Christian. I made a vow to God that if He showed me some mercy, I'd clean up my act. Instead of getting thirty plus years in prison, I got eight, and I got clean. I don't fuck around anymore, and I'm very cautious about who I work with."

"You think I'll be a bad influence or something?"

"Possibly." He leaned away from me.

I took the reins of the conversation, "How could I be a bad influence on you?"

"I'm an ex-addict. To track Gary, I gotta go back into the drug world cause that's where he thrives. The streets are his calling," he mocked. "Your gung-ho attitude is adorable, but you don't really know what it's like to be a criminal."

"I killed someone," I said with shame.

"Ever do any time?" I shook my head. "Then you don't know what it's like."

"If you're inferring that I didn't have to live with the consequences of my actions, you're wrong."

"That's not it." He set the chips aside, "We come from two different worlds. And I don't have space in my life to hang out with someone who is so careless with theirs."

Judging me was not the solution. An insult laid on my tongue. I hushed it. If I bothered winning his reconsideration, I'd have to…Tightness swelled in my chest. Defenses down, I saw it his way. The impression I had given him would have sent any smart person down this line of questioning. Addressed his statement with, "I'm not careless. I'm just motivated."

"You're motivated by greed," he said.

This guy was insufferable! A Know It All who would make me work for it. He had pegged a few of my least desirable traits. Greed did not hold a place amongst them. "Careless, I can live with that. I'm not greedy, though."

"Do you know the definition of greed?"

I didn't let this insult slide, "I am a child genius. I went to college when I was young, and I studied English and

Literature. Yes, I know what *greed* is," I said with utter confidence.

"Then what is it?"

This quiz was unnecessary. Again, we were wasting time. But I needed him.

"Greed means you want something. Usually it comes down to wanting money or power."

He accepted his answer and raised the stakes, "Greed is a selfish desire. When you want something so bad, you don't care about anyone else." Charlie pulled a fifty from his wallet, "I don't have room in my life for greedy people."

Charlie was leaving.

I couldn't lose him.

My hand trapped his on the table. "Please, don't go."

"Sorry, darling," his tone bordered casual and certainty. "I can't hang out with you." He pulled his hand back, "Good luck with your Gary thing."

Charlie had rescued me from the rest stop. Now, he was abandoning me? "You saved me!"

His boots hit the floor. He towered over me. "I wanted to know what you had to say. Now that I do, I've made my decision."

Scrambling, I filtered through everything I could offer this guy to get him to stay. My relationship with God was nominal, there was no way I'd be able to use that to gain some ground. I had money, lots of money, yet Charlie ended up paying a handsome sum for some chips and a saucer of salsa. My looks, my body, there had to be something that I could use to win him over.

Miguel had reemerged from the kitchen with our street

tacos spread. Disappointment sat on his brow as he saw me tugging on Charlie's arm to get him to stay. "Girl, if a man doesn't want you, you gotta let him go," he said. He stepped between us and placed the food down. Charlie became his focus, "You better eat this. If you don't, my mother will kill you."

The favor was obvious. We would be inconveniencing Miguel if he left. He was already upset with me for all the other hoops I had put him through. Not to mention the heart attack he had survived after meeting Charlie.

I chuckled, "I'm selfish," I announced. And I was a wreck.

Gary was driving me crazy. So was Ian. They were nowhere near me, but they somehow managed to propel me into this bottomless pit of problems and desperation. That was the loneliness Charlie had sensed on me. All my motivation, my purpose for breathing, was to hunt these two men and give them what I thought they deserved. The risk of losing everything was high, yet I had already reaping my rewards. In the process of my revenge, my selfishness had driven away all of my friends.

Miguel's mother shouted for him to get the next order ready. This left me and the biker alone.

"I don't know why I keep doing this," I whispered to myself. I clued Charlie in, "You're right. I'm greedy. Before you walk away, can I explain myself?"

"Yeah," he sat down. "Shot."

"I feel guilty about everything that's happened. A lot of it's my fault..."

Charlie hushed me, "What's in your heart?"

"Pain." My eyes glistened. Hiding my grief wasn't possible. "I've hurt a lot of people. Some of those people hurt me, too." This was a nod to Gavin, who was probably out of his mind worried about me. "It's like a vicious cycle of wrongs that lead to justice that lead to hurting people, and then it comes back around again, over and over." I wouldn't reveal my tears. Surprisingly, it was easier holding them in. "My life is not complicated, it's painful. I've been living with it so far." I could almost hear Daniel telling me to slow down. Feel it with my heart. "I can't go another day with this pain. I can't survive it anymore."

Charlie kept quiet. Silence built a space for me to rest until his throat bobbed. "What do you really want from me?"

Charlie was my connection to getting Gary back to jail. If I went down this path, I'd be selfish, like he had said. This was my truth. "I need your help with Gary."

"I don't know, Catalina. It still doesn't feel right."

His indecision was like a dagger in my chest. I wouldn't survive without his help. "Please. I'm begging you."

He was polite enough to wait until he gave me his verdict. "I don't like being used." I winced. Charlie got up for a final time. "I can't help you."

Nothing stopped him from leaving out the front door. My weak convictions were not enough to convince him. Except for maybe one. I got up from the booth and ran after him.

CHAPTER THIRTEEN

Savior

CHARLIE AND I had the same objective. His motives overlapped with mine. I didn't get the chance to tell him this. He straddled his bike, blocked by someone I wish I didn't know. Noah advanced toward me, grabbing my arm. "If you scream, you'll regret it."

Even if I did scream, Charlie wouldn't care. He wasn't going to help me. I was too selfish. Plus, my life was my own problem, not his. Motives overlapping, same objective, it didn't matter. However, he did seem to bend his view as our eyes caught. Noah walked me away from Miguel's, my feet slipping against the sand.

No time to freak out.

I couldn't be a victim.

I had to get some answers from my ex-boyfriend.

"How did you find me?"

"You're way more predictable than you think." The tension in his words tented my shoulders.

"If you do anything to Miguel," I said.

"You'll kill me, like Blake?"

Venom erupted from within. "How did you know Blake?"

Noah's lips stayed in a thin line. His fingers gripped harder. We were heading to a parking lot on the other side of the restaurant. My gaze went to a white Porsche SUV. Noah couldn't afford a car like this. I knew someone else who could, though.

Seeing him for the first time in a year felt like lightning striking me. Pain jolting through my bones, tissues, and muscles, sent down by the stark look in his glare. Noah had finally been a faithful servant. Ian had forgiven him because now he had made due with his promise.

Ian wore his black suit, no need to deviate from his everyday attire. His hair reminded me of Aaron's. Eyes black, opaque, hiding his God-less soul.

"Ms. Catalina Rose Payton," he said, voice twisting as he spelled out my name. "It's been too long."

Noah was like a statue as he held me in place. No running. No dream of hiding. I would face Ian with no plan or support within my grasp.

"Ian," I said. Now, he was arm's length from me. "You look well."

"I haven't been to California in years," he scrutinized the beach. "Nice place."

"Noah says you want to talk to me?" I said.

Ian motioned for Noah to open the door to the back-seat. "Let's go for a ride."

"I'd rather not," I replied.

"I wasn't asking," he hissed. Patience was not Ian's

strong suit. Gavin had been fooled; he thought Ian favored me for some reason. No, there was no way. The challenge in his stance, his towering demeanor, kept no love for me.

Noah plunged me into the backseat, slamming the door within seconds. Ian joined me on the other side. I found my bearings, sitting up straight, so I could breathe. Ian stared forward as he said, "Take us to the airport."

The airport? "Where are we going?"

"I need to know a few things, Catalina," Ian said. "Where is Gavin?"

Feigning ignorance would actually benefit me since it was the truth. "I don't know. I left him at a rest stop on the highway."

Ian nodded slightly. "Kyle?" A lie would buy Kyle some time, if Noah didn't know the truth. "Don't play games with me."

This was a test. "Kyle went to Maine, I think." His curiosity was not satisfied. "Your father getting out didn't sit well with him."

Ian pressed his fingers to his lips. He reminded Noah that he should start driving. Noah complied without hesitation. Emotions flat, concentration on the road, he ignored us. Or pretended to.

"Who was that man you were talking to?" Ian said as he turned to view my face.

Miguel or Charlie? Which one would I offer up? I would never betray Miguel. Nothing would force me to give any information about him. Charlie had refused to help me. He was on his own.

"He was a biker who gave me a ride after I left Gavin."

"You and Mr. Scott have parted ways indefinitely?"

"We stopped seeing each other last year," I said, glossing over the finality of our relationship. "Right before he got shot last year."

Ian surprised me with a question, "Because of Daniel?" My silence was my tribute to keep our relationship, our love, safe. "He put all this in motion." My brows knitted together. "That's why you came here, right? To follow the lead he had left for you?"

"I'm not sure I know what you are talking about?"

"Daniel was growing tired of the drug game. He would never betray me; not without the right leverage."

That leverage had to be me. "I never helped him betray you, if that's what you're saying."

"I'm not." He smoothed his suit, "You didn't know all the things that happened between Daniel and me."

Six didn't kill Daniel for Ian…it wasn't possible. "You had Six kill Daniel?"

The hurt lasted for a beat before he explained, "I would never hurt Daniel. His loyalty was paramount. It was his focus I worried about. You were a distraction, like you are with most of the people I put in your path." He blinked, "I was there when Daniel told you he loved you. The loyalty he had to you was unprecedented, rivaling his devotion to me."

"Jealous?" I snapped.

Ian chuckled, "Amused is a better word." His finger caressed his lip, "I don't understand why so many people are willing to die for you."

"As my father would say, 'my yoke is easy, and my

burden is light.' They don't have to give up anything for me."

"You think quoting a Bible verse to me explains your friendships?" He turned, catching my line of sight. "What about all those people who died because of you? People you tricked into helping you."

"You have killed more people than I have. And if I hurt anyone it was because you put me up to it." The narrowing of his eyes brought my tone down.

"Careful," he warned. "Don't forget who you are talking to."

"I know who you are," I said. "You're the man who ran the biggest drug operation in Maine. The amount of money you have made is…"

"…Flattery will not help you, Catalina," he said. "If you have a point, please get on with it."

"I'm not trying to flatter you, Ian." The chase was over. This could be a blessing, if I allowed it to be. "Why did you give me a copy of your stepfather's book?"

"He's your favorite author."

"Why would you care?"

Ian seemed trapped, "I was only trying to win your trust." Lint was picked off his pants. "You fonded over me like a silly school girl chasing an inappropriate attraction to her teacher."

"I didn't…" his brows tightened, silencing the lie. "Yes, I did have a crush on you when we first met. You shouldn't be surprised," I said.

"Is that so?"

"You wanted me to like you, so you became likeable."

A flicker of embarrassment hit him. "The book was a great move. Without it, I probably would have written you off."

"Why's that?"

"You're too old for me." I dared him to object. When he didn't, I said, "Does Grover know about your business?"

"He prefers to stay out of it. So, does my mother. My mother despises it, while Grover keeps his distance because we are rather different. He's a dreamer, much like my brother."

"Speaking of your brother, where is he?"

"I do not know. I was hoping you had a lead on him." He adjusted in his seat, "I saw your wall. Very impressive."

"I've been told," I said.

"By Gavin." Ian's lip flared, "I knew he would come for you, fucking up my plans in the process."

"What are your plans, exactly?" I sat up, turning to confront him. "I'm not going to give you Kyle. Never."

"As frustrating as that is, I'm not after Kyle at the moment."

Bargaining with the devil was always a bad idea. Seeing him face to face, I had to try. "Please, don't hurt him."

"He destroyed my entire business after fucking me over several times."

"I know," I said while shaking my head. Kyle wasn't making this easy. "He got what he deserved. He gave up his family, his friends, and he left."

"It's not enough. I've made too many exceptions lately, and I will have to set all this straight." Ian ignored me while he sent a text message.

Idle threats and promises of harm, that is what Ian was

good for. For two years, I cowered behind secrecy to protect myself and those that I loved. Now, the record would be set straight. "Why did you tell me your first name? Why did you give me so many exceptions?"

"I told you my first name as a test. To see if you would keep my identity hidden. Also, I wanted to know how far you would go to vindicate Robert Porter's business. You never told anyone about Ian, nor did you tell Ian about Robert. You stayed the course and didn't deviate from the objective except when you went to see Kyle." His next words stunned me, "I know everything that happens to the people who work for me. And you worked for me, whether you feel like you did or not."

"Working for you was never the problem." He mistook my statement as compassion. "I was willing to live with my fate for all the trouble I caused you. But I never had any loyalty to you."

"I know that," he said. His knee hit mine. We were getting closer, "I'd be a fool if I thought you did anything you did to help me. You know where your lines are, and I always respected that."

"No, you didn't. Because if you did, I wouldn't be here in this car with you, against my will."

"Really?" he said with amusement. "I only cross lines that don't exist. For you, your lines are probably written in sand. Most of them, that is." Ian's head tilted, "You are stronger now. More defiant."

"Defiance is a great survival tool." I straightened my shoulders, "I don't need defiance with you, I don't work for you anymore. And you are clearly not useful to me because you don't know what is going on with your brother and why he is missing. He's the only reason I'm still here." I added, "You already knew that because you've been spying on me."

"It was a necessary evil, I'm afraid." He tucked his jacket around him, "I never looked at any inappropriate images of you."

"You have cameras in my house without my permission. Everything about that was inappropriate."

"Well, I had to make sure you were safe."

"Safe? Why do you care about my safety?"

"I have my reasons."

"Nah, you don't get to do that." I stepped up, "You know all my secrets now. Tell me yours."

"That's not how I operate."

I got closer to him, and he didn't flinch, "I've done so many things for you, and I never asked for anything in return."

"You kept Kyle from me."

"Because you were going to kill him!" Noah jostled in his seat. "Look, these games have got to stop. Why do you want me so bad?"

"Make no mistake, I don't want anything sexual from you."

Joking only enraged me more. "If you're not going to tell me…"

He grabbed onto my arms, the strength undeniable. "Do not test me, Ms. Payton. I have been brutally patient with you because you are more valuable to me alive at the moment. But I will not hesitate to put you six feet under, when the time is right."

Heartless, soulless man. "I always thought you were going to kill me."

"You are leaving me no choice." His arms pushed me back away from him. "Continue challenging me and disobeying me, and you will see how far I'm willing to go when people disrespect me."

Useful. Valuable. These characteristics he had given me were only on loan until my certain death. "How am I valuable to you?"

"I do not have to answer your questions." His eyes slanted my way, "But you will answer my questions, if you want to keep everyone you love alive."

Ian had never made any claims of violence against my friends and family before. A shift had taken place. Stalling, I attempted to smooth things over, for the sake of those loved ones he planned to annihilate.

Hatred aside, I appealed to whatever it was he found interesting in me. "This is really hard to understand." My hand wiped across my face, "You had cameras in my house; you know everything I know. How can I still be valuable to you?"

"I know you have been tracking the movements of Officer Dixon, my brother, and a few other people in Settlement Island. I have a few guesses about what you're working on, but I don't know for sure."

I motioned to the driver's seat, "Noah knows everything. I told him the truth right before I smashed a vase against his head."

Ian found Noah's misfortune funny. "The glass shards did send a message, I'm sure. But in the end, he wasn't able to fill in many blanks for me."

"If I fill in these blanks, you're gonna kill me?"

"No, Catalina. Only if you keep challenging me."

"I challenge you because you keep threatening me and my family. And Kyle."

The slap took my breath away. Right above my left eye, it stung and pulsed uncontrollably. He allotted me a second, two even, to compose myself.

As I nursed my face, he fixed his suit once more, "I never enjoyed hitting women. I avoid it at all costs. But you have really worn down my patience." His throat cleared, "Now, where were we?" He paused to appreciate my throbbing face. His finger drew a line across the print he had left. "If you cooperate, the punishments will stop." My glare was taken as a sign of compliance. "Now, what do you know about my father?"

I let go of my face. Defiance wasn't the answer. Setting up Gary was. "He claims that he didn't kill that biker Maverick."

"And Gavin wants you to side with my father in order to keep him on my father's good side?"

"Gavin said that Gary helped him out when he was being charged with Russ's murder. He thinks Gary's gonna use that to hurt him."

Ian nodded, stroking his face, mocking me. "How can you help Gavin with this?"

I shrugged, "He said I knew the truth about Blake. Gary thought that my last conversation with Blake could pin him as a conspirator in Maverick's murder. Hopefully, if Gary didn't commit this murder, the real killer will find another way to put Gary back in jail."

My vagueness wasn't enough. "Has Gavin been in contact with my father?"

"I don't think so."

He pulled one leg over the other, "Your sister went to see my mother and stepfather looking for my brother. What did they tell her?"

"I haven't had a chance to talk to her."

"Because you went on the run from me." The smug arrogance of knowing how powerful he was brought my fists to a ball. "Where is Gavin?"

"I left him at a rest stop on the highway."

Ian peered out his window, "Then, you caught a ride with the Blood Diamond?"

The coincidence was uncanny. Motorcycles revved by us. My attention stayed on Ian. "He saw that I was in trouble, so he stopped to help."

"What are the odds? You were investigating the Blood Diamonds in connection with my father, and then one showed up to save you?" Leaning forward, he said, "Who led you to him?"

I was out of answers. Ian couldn't know about the flash drive that Daniel had given me. My pulse raced. *He did know about the flash drive.* Because of the cameras in my house. That is what he was here for. Luke and I had discussed it so many times. Now, he wanted to see it for himself.

"Luke, my best friend. He found the connection on

the internet from an article related to your father's time in California," I said, dodging any lead to the flash drive.

My explanation was plausible. Luke and I had talked about everything I found, including this link between Gary and the Blood Diamonds. Guilt crept over me for my disloyalty to my friend. The one who had done whatever he could to keep me safe.

Adding to the distraction, I touched my face again, feeling a welt. Ian appraised it without concern. He looked over at Noah who pretended not to eavesdrop. "Does this seem right to you, Noah? Is she telling the truth?"

"I believe so, sir," he said without a beat.

I let my hand fall from my face. Noah had been the biggest betrayer. And disappointment. He had lied and led me on in an unforgivable way. I hated him with all of my heart. Not just for his betrayal, but for not intervening when Ian hit me. And—

The vehicle jolted forward.

"What's happening?" Ian said.

"We just got hit, sir." Noah started by pulling the car to the side.

"We don't have time for this." Ian told Noah to keep driving. But he was being boxed in. The vehicle was being steered off the road and onto an off ramp. "What are you doing?"

"They're surrounding us," Noah's voice sharpened with panic.

The vehicle rolled to a stop. Ian said, "Who's surrounding us?"

Noah had his hands up as he looked out the window.

Ian pulled a gun from the console that separated us. My door flew open, a gun directed past me.

"Make your move," the intruder said.

Ian placed the gun down, but his hands didn't go up. The intruder latched onto my wrist, yanking me from the car, and positioning me behind him. The familiar embroidery on his back brought a smile to my lips. He nodded to the others who took a shot at each tire, disabling the vehicle.

Charlie peered his head in, gun still ready, "If you follow us, we'll kill you."

We swung wide, making a break for his bike. A warm glow filtered into my cold, shocked body. "You came back for me."

He motioned for me to get on the bike. "There's someone who wants to meet you."

CHAPTER FOURTEEN

Stripped

I WOULDN'T CRUMBLE into a mess. Not with so much more to do. Charlie had saved me from Ian and his unsavory plan. My head turned, shielding my face from the wind searing into my body. The sun was setting behind us as we took another freeway, our destination still ahead, I presumed.

The freeways soon faded into a business district. Drug addicts lined the streets, taking up residence on the sidewalks, their tents a reminder of the income gap between myself and them. If they knew how much money my family had, I'd be a target. One man leaned over and threw up on the crosswalk. Okay, maybe they wouldn't even notice me long enough to ask any damning questions.

Seven other bikers rode alongside us, encasing me in a layer of protection. I shouldn't have felt this way, but a growing sense of safety had enveloped me. They were an army, much like the Secret Service for the President. I wasn't that important. I mean, I couldn't be, right? Still, when we stopped at a traffic light, they cocooned me in a blanket of tough leather and no nonsense.

"We're almost there," Charlie shouted back.

Wherever *there* was, I had to prepare for it. Black ripped jeans, a white tank and red flannel shirt, I might be able to fit in. The Converse shoes strapped to my feet made me look like a kid, but I didn't feign against them. Downplaying my age could work with me, if these people had deadly ideas. Or it could lead to me being trafficked.

Charlie swooped into the parking lot of a building with neon lights and the silhouette of a dancing woman. The was, indeed, a strip club.

"I sure do know how to pick them," I said as I adjusted my clothes and stretched.

"It's not as bad as you think," Charlie helped me off the bike. He took one look at my shiner and growled.

"It's not as bad as you think," I said while smoothing over the conversation.

"Six sisters, remember?" I did. He tucked his anger back in. "Next time I see that son-of-a-bitch, I'll give him the slap of a lifetime."

The sentiment was darling, yet Charlie wasn't off the hook. "Why did you come back for me?" I said.

He leaned against his bike, arms crossing over his leathered chest, "When I saw that guy push you into the car, I knew you were in trouble. I was wrong. You're afraid, not selfish." I wouldn't call what he said an apology, but I took it the same. "That guy you were with; what is his name?"

"That's my ex-boyfriend Noah."

"The older one?"

"No, that's Robert Porter."

"Gary Porter's son?"

My nod brought a frown to his face. "Everything I told you at the restaurant was true. And now you know it," I said.

"I'm sorry, Catalina." Charlie's sullen eyes spoke of compassion and sympathy. "What you were proposing to me scared me to my core." He pulled out a cigarette.

"I was only asking for help," I said.

"I know you were." The cigarette dangled from his lips, "You've never been addicted to anything?"

Embarrassed, I denied my addiction at first. But Charlie didn't seem like the type to judge. At least not judge too much. "I used to drink a lot of wine...all the time." Didn't seem the same. "What was your drug of choice?"

"Alcoholic, too. I dabbled in drugs, but I never went full junkie. Jim Beam was my guy." I never called myself an alcoholic. Wine enthusiast, for sure. What twenty-something didn't enjoy a drink? Or Two? Or three? In quick succession. Charlie smirked at my contemplation. "Don't like being called an alcoholic?"

"Not sure if I am one."

"Regardless," another drag on his smoke, "it feels good to be out of it, huh?"

"True," I glanced over at the door. "What are we doing here?"

"Prez wants to speak with you," he enjoyed another puff and crushed the butt. "He's got questions about Gary."

If I didn't have the right answers, this would end badly. "I was hoping you had answers. Not the other way around."

"We'll take whatever you got." Charlie put out his hand. A notion for me to trust him.

I wanted answers more than I trusted Charlie. After all, he did claim he wouldn't help me not one hour ago. Yet, the flip-flopping with his commitments wasn't a huge issue. Whatever it took to get what I came here for was all I cared about.

Charlie's fingers felt like Brillo pads against my dainty fingers. An unlikely couple, no doubt. Me, this young black nerd with messy curly hair and a shiner, dressed like the Brawny man. Him, clad in leather and wind, he had too much edge for me. The bouncer didn't care.

He waved us in, the room dimmer than I imagined. Cecilia had worked at a strip club as a waitress shortly before we moved to Maine. The money was great, and the guys adored her, but she wanted more. A husband's worth more.

This place seemed sleazy, at first. Girls dropped their bodies to the ground, moving in rhythm with the music. Men bit their lips, daring to touch but not taking it too far. A bouncer stood at the base of the stage, hoping he would get the chance to throw any of them back into their seats. Only money could touch these women's skin. Anything more would have to be a secret arrangement out back or in an untold location.

Charlie had my hand, so he could navigate me through the men and showgirls who became annoyed by my presence. I wasn't competition, but somehow, the men were tempted to see what I was hiding under my flannel.

We went around the stage, through the chairs, and into the back of the club. Next, we entered a backstage area. Bare breasts and tight, bright fabric prompted me to shield my eyes. Charlie chuckled as he fired up a conversation with one of the girls. Lacy, I think. They seemed to be friendly.

"Relax, honey," she said, pulling my hand down. "We're got the same parts," she laughed. Luckily, she was clothed, slightly. "You know a girl named Cecilia?"

"Yes," I said. "How do you know her?" Regret filled my stomach, "She wasn't a stripper, was she?"

Lacy was adamant, "No! She said no guy could buy her like that. She did have the best coke, though." My sister was a drug dealer? Lacy denied this claim, too. "She had a hook up, and she would share it with us. You know, as a little pick me up."

Charlie amused himself with my anger. "How do you know I'm related to Cecilia?" I said.

"She had photos of you up in her locker."

"Here?"

Lacy slouched a bit, "Nah, it was at *The Velvet Club*. Really classy place."

"And my sister's a classy gal." I turned to Charlie's ear, "Please, get me out of here."

"Sweetheart, we gotta get to a meeting," his sweetly saturated words appeased her. They shared a kiss.

On the move again, I asked, "She your girlfriend?"

"Nope," Charlie said. Back to business. We stopped

outside a black door, music pulsing behind us. "When we get in here, let me do the talking." I pumped my curls. "You're still super cute," Charlie said as he thrusted a small bag into my busy hands.

"What is this?"

"You said you were broke. This is a finder's fee. If your information is good, you can keep it."

I threw the bag over one shoulder, steadying my breaths. This was it. Charlie walked with confidence, completely secure.

He opened the door, leaning against it, waiting. To his surprise, I walked right into the room, which had a lounge area, windows, and several tables. It seemed more like a living room than the backroom of a shady strip joint. On the walls were photos of bikers, different insignias for the Blood Diamonds, and various car parts. An odd selection for décor. Mother would have loved to remodel it. And they would have relished in watching her do it.

Then, I realized I didn't know who *they* were. We were alone in the room.

I put the bag down on the counter, "Where are the others? The guys who rode with us here?"

Charlie nodded toward the stage area. "They're not privy to this conversation."

Engines revved in the back-parking lot. Charlie opened the back door. I followed, curious to see who I would be reckoning with.

The road was littered with bikers riding in formation, all turning to enter the small lot. Girls, tougher than I could ever dream to be, straddled angry men, all who possessed the right to be feared. I leaned closer to Charlie, forgetting that he is one of them.

The bikers kept rumbling in until the lot was full. They stood outside, joking around in their matching leather, like they hadn't seen one another in years. Slowly, they filtered into the room, coming home to do business.

Charlie made the rounds, hugging his brothers with jolly affection, leaving me to cling to the wall. I was an outsider amongst a band of outsiders. These people were from the far edges of society, having found one another over the years. They were a family, and I was jealous.

The bikers settled into booths and tables, their women helping a few waitresses collect drink orders from the bar that was just outside a different set of doors. Snake Eyes, the bartender, stayed occupied by various members who came up to catch up. I heard snippets of conversations around how old kids were, who was still in prison, and how much different riding gear cost.

All the while, I watched Charlie navigate his way through the crowd, making sure he had at least one conversation with everyone. Then, after drinks were delivered, and Charlie was out of folks to chat with, he returned to my side.

"Everyone!" his voice boomed, reaching beyond his normal calm cadence. Attentions turned to him. "This is Catalina. She's the reason why I brought you all together." He turned to me, waiting for my response. "Feel free to ask her whatever questions you have about Gary Porter." This was beyond my comfort zone. My nails latched onto Charlie before he could leave me alone with these wolves.

"If you walk away from me, you're a dead man."

The next breath I took wasn't satisfying, even with his support. Neither was the one after that. Charlie nudged me. "Hey, everyone!" I gave a nervous chuckle, hoping it would help. I was met with dead eyes. "So, I'm not sure what Charlie told you…"

"Louder!" shouted one of the women.

I thought Charlie would take over or give me some words of encouragement. The stillness of the room reminded me that they were waiting. I cleared my throat. "I'm not sure what Charlie told you," I boomed. "My investigating…I'm investigating Gary Porter." Several people shifted in their seats. "I lived in Settlement Island for almost a year, and I met his son, Robert, who you might know as Porter. I worked with him last year, helping him uncover a threat to his business."

"You killed a guy?" shouted someone else.

They knew more about me than I thought. "Yes. I killed Blake, who was trying to bring down Porter's business." I shook off the images of that night, "Anyways, Gary's out of jail for the murder that he committed against one of your members, and I'm trying to get to the bottom of that."

Silence returned. Either no one knew anything, or they didn't care to share it with me. Charlie stepped up, probably because he felt bad. "She believes Gary didn't kill Maverick." The crowd rumbled. Why didn't I think to tell them that?

"Gary Porter's one sick son of a bitch," said a man. He stood, towering over the others. I didn't quite understand how large he was until he approached me.

His patch said President. He was in charge. Charlie conceded the floor to his president. The man addressed me, "He killed Maverick."

Disagreeing with someone like this was not a good move. But I had to know how he could be so confident. "Gary's sole goal has been to clear his name for this crime. He hasn't tried to cover his tracks with all the other things he's done; so why this one?"

"I'm not a cop, and I don't care." The room captured a light hiss of laughter.

"Don't you want to know who the real killer is?"

"No, because we know it was Gary. He's had a grudge against us for years, way before Maverick got killed. And it cost us business." President leaned against the counter, facing me. "Gary started his drug dealing here. He'd go down to Mexico and bring back all sorts of stuff, mostly cocaine. This punk kid, barely twenty-one, started selling around town, stepping on the feet of some of our dealers. When we went to shake him down, he stood up to us. Made us a business offer."

It seemed that business had always been in the Porter genes. "Gary was moving back to Maine, where he was from, and he wanted to set up shop there. He had this idea about bringing in drugs from out-of-state and selling them in this place called Anders. They had some low-level dealers, but what he wanted to build was gonna blow our fuckin' socks off."

That sounded like Gary. "He used the family construction company to launder drugs and money, right?" I said.

President nodded. "It was his dad's. Gary had come

out to California to get a business degree. His dad said he could come back and run everything. So, he went back home, started working for his dad, and moved drugs for us. He got married, had a kid, and then his dad died. After that, Gary started bringing on new dealers, building a bigger operation. Then, he got divorced, and took things to new heights."

"He moved on to setting up businesses in other states, all up and down the east coast," I added. Daniel had told me this. I refocused, "His son, Robert, took over the operation when Gary went to jail."

"By the time Gary JR had gotten involved, we were on the outs. Gary was no longer supplying us with business opportunities. Instead, he was hiking up profits for himself and cutting us out of deals with our connects. When we went to settle things with our distributors, he jammed us up. Got the cops involved and some of our guys ended up doing serious time. He did this to hurt our business, knock out the competition."

I shook my head, "It seems like everyone is trying to kill each other and steal their territory. Drug dealers don't get along, do they?"

President chuckled, "There are no rules in our line of work."

"Apparently not." I wanted to move this conversation along, "So, that's why Maverick came to Settlement Island? To confront Gary?"

"Gary didn't want us anywhere near his current operation, so he set up the meeting somewhere between Anders and Settlement Island. We were down on numbers because of the drug bust, so only three of our members could make the drive. Maverick was president, so he went. The other two members were long-standing Diamonds, great with a gun. Last time I spoke with Maverick on the phone, he said they were getting close to town. Gary was gonna be there in an hour. Then, all three of them went missing."

My heart had been shot. There were three murders, not one like the reports had said. "Who were the other victims?"

"Joker and Sting Ray."

Adorable names. "Do you know what happened to them?"

"We weren't too concerned, at first. They were from a chapter in Seattle, and we thought they had just gone back up that way once they were all done with Gary. But when Maverick didn't get back in touch, no one heard from Joker and Sting Ray, either. That's when we knew something was up."

I grabbed a pen and a napkin from the counter. "What are their real names?"

"You a cop or something?"

Did I look like a cop? No, I didn't think so. "I'm just trying to see if I heard anything about them." My disbelief was spilling all over him. "From what I've found out, the police only charged Gary with Richard's...Maverick's murder. The other two victims weren't even listed on the report."

"Sounds like there was a police cover up," someone shouted.

There was only one officer who I knew was capable of covering up a murder. "Officer Dixon."

"Who's that?" President said.

"He was an officer with the Settlement Island Police Department," I said. "Gary killed him, I think. Well, someone killed him."

President squinted at me. He had figured it out, too. "You think Gary killed this officer because he planted evidence to put Maverick's murder on him?"

"Not only that, there was a witness." The name escaped me. "Some guy who said he saw Gary kill Maverick."

"Have you met this guy?"

"No one has. I think Dixon made him up."

President looked to his fellow members for a verdict on my fate with the club. To decide if they accepted my need for help. I was no competition for President or all the other people in this room. If I hadn't carried my weight…I didn't want to think about what they would do to me.

Charlie put his hand on his friend's shoulder, "What do you think, Prez?" He continued, "If she's right, Maverick's killer is still out there. And if Gary's innocent, he's probably gonna run."

"How do we know she's not playing us?"

My knees wobbled. I had no defense or reasons for them to side with me. Charlie became a shield, "She's not a snitch or allies with the Porters. Gary JR just smacked her across the face."

"So?" his friend said callously.

"So, I think she pissed him off because she wouldn't give him what he wanted."

Courage found me at that moment, "He hit me because I wouldn't go back to Maine with him. I'm not sure what he wanted, but I know too much, apparently. He's been watching me and using my conversations and research to…"

"You're valuable to Gary JR?" President questioned.

"That's what he said."

"Good. Then I'll make you a deal." He scanned the room, this time for any objections. None came, so he said, "We want a cut. We'll offer you protection against the Porters if you get us the money Gary took from us; ten million dollars."

He was ransoming my livelihood for millions, a fair trade in their eyes. I just had one question for him, "What happens if I can't get it?"

Charlie bowed his head. "Then we'll get it ourselves," President said.

"Okay, but what's been stopping you from getting it before?"

"The Porters had a league of dealers who created a barrier between us and Gary. With him in prison, we weren't able to break that barrier to get to his son. Now, it seems you have a direct line to him. If you lure his son to us, we'll do the rest."

Ian at the hands of bikers was quite the sight. He deserved every blow they had in store for him. However, things didn't add up, "What about Maverick?"

"Give us the son, and he'll help us figure out who killed Maverick."

Either way, they wanted Ian. And they could have him. "Deal."

"You're quick to make deals," said President.

"I shouldn't be judge and jury, but Gary and Porter need to be out of my life forever." If they wanted their revenge, I was their best shot. They provided the protection I needed. Together, we could finally end this.

President grabbed Charlie's shoulders, "Son, I'm gonna trust her because I trust you."

That's when the resemblance shone through. "This is your dad?"

Charlie shook his head, "Nah, but he's been in my life since I was a teenager." They doted on one another, a burden lifted now that they had me to carry the weight.

President gave me a handshake, "I expect you to keep your end of the bargain."

"I have no reason not to."

The bikers resumed their chitchatting and drinks, ignoring me. I realized then what had happened. President gave Charlie a hug. Then, we were on our way out to the parking lot. Once outside, I told him my thoughts.

"The club was just a witness. They were just there to hear me say I was going to help them."

He shook his head, "It's not that deep."

"It is. They depend on me." Charlie sat back onto his bike, ready for my explanation. "I have a theory. The witness who saw Gary kill Maverick only mentioned one victim. He didn't say anything about there being other people present."

"He could have been alone."

"Why would Maverick's loyal friends leave him to meet with a shady business partner in the woods?"

He stroked his chin at my question, "So that proves the witness statement was false?"

"It proves that I don't have the full story." I sat on his bike seat. "I need my notebooks, so I can see if there is any record of the other two murders." Frazzled, I asked for Charlie's phone. He unlocked it, and I tried calling my phone to retrieve my stuff from a very furious Gavin. It went straight to voicemail. Major setback aside, I said, "During this whole investigation, I never thought about looking that far into Gary's other crimes for clues about Maverick's murder." There was someone who knew the answers to my questions. "I need to talk to Demi."

CHAPTER FIFTEEN

Charlie

CATCHING DEMI TONIGHT was not an option. The drive
up to the restaurant yielded no results. Miguel had gone
home, and I wouldn't put his life on the line by stopping by
his apartment. Ian was probably searching for me. Miguel
would be an obvious stop. Tonight, I will rest and head
back to the restaurant in the morning.

The obligation of sleep wore me down. Charlie's offer
of an Airbnb in his backyard lured me in.

The drive to his place was the most brutal. I tried and
didn't feel up for all the twists and turns on the back of
the bike. I held on, my only willpower coming from the
promise of a hot shower and a bed.

We made it to a quiet suburb about two hours from
where I live.

Used to live.

The Airbnb was actually the other half of his duplex.
It had all the amenities, except for clothes for me.

"You're on your own. I gave you money, and you gave

it back to me." The bag of money, the finder's fee, didn't sit well with me. I hadn't earned it, so I returned it.

Charlie threw the key on the counter as he gave me a tour. It was smaller than I hoped, but it was clean.

"What about Lacy or some of the girls from the club? They don't leave their stuff over?"

"I don't date girls from the club."

I leaned on the counter, "But you kissed her."

"We were only teasing each other," he said. His hair pushed back against his fingers, "I've got new toothbrushes and toothpaste in the bathroom."

"I know I gave the money back, but you can't spare just a little bit for some clean underwear?" I said sarcastically.

"You're rich, right? Aren't your credit cards on file with all the stores?"

"No." I stood, "that only happens in the movies." Now, I would hunt for a bathtub, a hair dryer, and a long extension cord. "This has been the worst day of my life."

Charlie examined my face, "How's the eye?"

"It hurts." The welt was growing into a tense pain. Charlie motioned for me to come to the kitchen sink. He wrapped some ice around a dish towel and gently pressed it against my skin. "Thanks."

"You remind me of my sister Amanda. She was always getting into fights with everyone."

"I'm not much of a fighter," I said.

He disagreed, "You can hold your own." I brushed away from him. "Never be ashamed of what you have to do to protect yourself."

"Like killing someone?"

"That was self-defense. Or at least that's what you told me."

I meant Daniel. "Someone died protecting me because I couldn't defend myself." Charlie asked what had happened. "He took a bullet for me. Then, I went on to kill someone else."

"You feel bad about it?"

"Yeah," I whispered.

"Good." Charlie set the dish towel in the sink.

"Good?" The callousness in his reply sent me over the edge. "Don't you think I should be punished for what I did?"

"The judge let you off?"

"There was no trial." He expected me to say this. "Don't act so smug, like you know me."

His hand grazed the skin next to my bruised eye, "Feeling bad means you still have a conscience. You know that every life, no matter how fucked up the person is, holds value. That means you're not a monster, or whatever it is you think you are. You're a good person who was put in a bad situation by bad people." Our eyes stayed focused on one another, "Catalina, take responsibility for what you did, and let them take responsibility for their part."

"But they're dead, and I'm not."

"That doesn't tip the scales. You're alive because God still wants something from you."

I rolled my eyes, "What on earth could God want from me?"

"Hope." He let go. "I'm going to bed."

Before he retired to his side of the house, I said, "If you were trying to make me feel better, it's not working."

Charlie grabbed the door and turned, "Pain is a part of life. Suffering is a choice." With this, he was done summing me up. "There are three locks. Use them all."

Silence filled the void he had left for me.

I sat down on the bed, readying myself for a sleepless night, the first I'd have in a while. My mind drifted over Gavin, wondering if he had gone back to his own lodging or if he was still on his way to Maine. Then Ian entered my mind. Noah had the sense to be afraid of this desperate, angry man. My escape had probably made things more difficult for him. I shrugged Noah off. Asshole got what he deserved.

I didn't think much about Aaron, fearing that things were probably worse for him than they were for me. His own brother had no idea what had happened to him. If I had my phone, I would have texted Kyle to look for him when he got back. If anyone could find the missing doctor, it would be the hunter.

A long blink cured my eyes from dryness. There was only one person left, teasing my thoughts, wishing I would think about him.

I laid down on the bed and turned to the pillow sitting next to me, cold and still. "What would you do?" I said to no one.

Daniel was merely a dream. A sweet, sweet fantasy that had taken over my life. But the fantasy was wearing off. I didn't have the flash drive, so the comfort of his voice had grown with the distance and time between us. He was no longer here, but I was. I had endured the most difficult day…second most difficult day…of my life. The most difficult day was the last day I saw Daniel. The second was today, when Ian slapped me. He probably reveled in it, giving me a taste of the pain that poured through the friend who chose his death over a life with him.

The slap had subsided, allowing Ian's intentions to come in clear. Whatever civil composure we had before would never exist again. I hated that man, as much as I hated my two-faced boyfriend. Ian stayed true to his colors, while Noah had no excuse.

At the very least, I thought we were friends. We had been inseparable for the last three months. I had wanted him in so many ways. Told him things I had never told anyone else. And with the smashing of a vase, everything we had was gone.

Noah was evil. The worst.

So, why was I crying?

These weren't hysterical tears that bombard you after an ugly, vicious breakup. They were a solemn plea to God for understanding on why everyone around me seemed to have some dark, hidden agenda that would be paid at my expense. I had no one, not a single person, who was in my corner now.

My only pillars of hope, Luke and Miguel, were far away. My sister had her own journey ahead, one riddled with disappearing clues regarding the whereabouts of her own boyfriend. At least he seemed to have a flicker of loyalty to her, even in his absence. My parents loved me, they had to, especially since I was in danger. Disappointment clouded this fact when I realized they hadn't come for me.

I was alone. Utterly, uncomfortably, alone.

Before I met Gavin, I sought solitude. Books were my closest friends, offering insight and stories. The stuff of legends. They understood me, nudging me to find myself again and again with their folds. Bringing a new beginning where I could start again.

I sat up, rubbing the rest of my makeup into my skin. A small stack of books sat in a box in the corner. I took a peek, hoping Charlie had good taste.

He didn't.

There were old motorcycle magazines, some self-help books on overcoming addiction, and the beat-up covers of old-school romance novels. The kinds where the man's hair overlapped the woman's face as he held her captive in a glance. Both characters were trying too hard. Love was so not worth it.

I reached the bottom of the box and examined my choices: pirate Fabio with the blonde busty gal or dark-haired Fabio with the gal who was surprised she was being kidnapped. The blonde seemed more of my flavor.

My shoes were kicked off, and I went to the fridge, hoping someone had left their old take-out. Nope, not so lucky. In the cupboard were several packages of chicken ramen noodles. I fired up the stove with a pot of water and sat at the table, turning to page one.

Isabella had always wanted to be a princess. The laugh overtook me. Of course, Isabella wanted to be a princess. What else was she going to do with her life? I mean, look at her!

The laugh died down. I was being judgmental, and a bad reader. Isabella deserved my attention.

She only had one problem; the brooding stable boy who looked up at her. The book closed. I couldn't do it. This man on the cover was clearly in his mid-thirties. There was nothing boyish about him.

My noodles would be done soon, so I surfed through the remaining three romance novels and settled on the brunette. Within ten pages, she had put up a fight. Her name was Anastasia, and her entire family had been killed in some type of feud.

The bowl laid empty as I thumbed through the pages, quickly rooting for my girl. Her lover was Stefan, a mysterious fellow with a strong Italian accent and unbearable burn marks on his chest.

By the time I reached page 100, I was thoroughly enjoying myself. Anastasia and Stefan were in a brawl where she had gotten away. Her instincts had narrowed as she boarded a ship to a neighboring island. I closed my eyes to imagine her brown hair caressing her face as the boat took her further and further into safety.

Stefan was quick on her heels. He enjoyed the chase, he said so himself. Their dual perspectives added a satisfying element to the story. They held my attention until I neared the last fifty pages of the book. I really wanted to know what happened between them. How they got to the end.

Yet, I was too tired. The book rested next to me, my thumb holding my place inside the pages, as I fell asleep.

↦

A knock on the door sent me soaring into a sitting position. "Open up," he said. I laid the book down, keeping my spot. Charlie knocked again.

I unsealed the door and stood in the way. "Good morning to you."

He motioned, "Can I come in?"

"It's your place."

I stood aside, and he looked around. "You get any sleep?"

"Yeah, some." My fingers pointed to the book, "I got caught up in a story."

He digested the cover, "That's one of my mom's." I nodded, still drowsy. "You wanna go see your friend, right?"

"Demi is not my friend, but yes, I do want to see her. But I need to go by Miguel's first. He has her number."

"Why don't you call him instead? It will save a trip."

"I don't have my phone," I snarled.

"His family doesn't have a phone in their restaurant?"

Charlie had outsmarted me, again. He placed his phone in my hands, and I found the number online. Miguel was working this early in the morning. He didn't have time to scold me about my shitty life choices. He offered up Demi's number with a spiteful reminder not to trust her.

After he hung up, I called her right away.

"Demi Woods speaking," she said. Even her phone greeting was pretentious.

"Demi, it's Catalina."

She paused, "Where are you calling me from?"

"A friend's phone. Mine is dead." Or lost. Or stolen. I didn't have to explain, "Listen, I want to talk to you about my lead with that murder that took place."

"Officer Dixon?"

"No, another one. Can I buy you breakfast?"

"I'm not in town. I'm back in Berkeley."

"Can you meet this evening?"

"Yeah, if you wanna drive all the way here."

"It's a date. Let's meet at that little café just off campus. It's not too far."

"Nah, I want Chinese."

"Fine! We can have Chinese."

"Can I text this phone the address?" I told her yes. "Sent. I'll see you at seven."

After I hung up, Charlie challenged our plans. "You wanna drive all the way to Berkeley on a hunch?" I told him why Demi was so important. She had a computer full of information on everything we needed. Reluctantly, he agreed. "We're not gonna be able to drive back tonight."

"Don't worry, I have a place for us to stay." Now, onto a shower and teeth brushing. I was ready in a matter of minutes. Charlie felt bad, so he leant me one of his T-shirts, which was large enough to drown me.

I figured we were going to take the bike. He struck this idea down. Charlie's plan was to ride in comfort and security. A bike was an easy target. We would blend in better if we took his Ford truck. I was bitter as I watched Charlie throw an overnight bag in the backseat.

"You wanna stop by the mall or something?"

"I'll manage." After we hooked up with Demi, I would be able to get some clothes and a hot meal. A shower with some shampoo, too.

Stay focused, Catalina. I had an interrogation to plan for.

❦

We beat Demi to the restaurant, arriving on time. Charlie reassured me when I became worried. She had every reason to stand me up, after the shit Gavin pulled the other day. His thievery justified her absence. But not by much.

We had just been seated when she walked in, darling sundress holding her body together, and flats. I should have asked her to bring me some clothes.

She dropped down next to Charlie, who was taken by her instantly. "Sorry I was late." Her Ray Ban aviators crowned her head in a stylish headband. "I stayed after to talk to my professor about my thesis."

"The one you're writing about me?"

"Yeah, that would be it," she paused to look at the menu. Charlie cleared his throat, getting her attention. "And who might you be?"

"Charlie. I'm a friend of Catalina's."

Her survey of us both brought forth the truth, "You two just met, didn't you?"

"What makes you think that?" I said.

"I've met your friends, and they are nothing like this."

"I'm a Blood Diamond," Charlie said with a splash of danger. "Heard of us?"

Demi leaned in, "Yes, I have." She turned to me, "This is about that biker getting killed?"

"Two other bikers went to Maine with him to confront Gary. Gary killed Maverick, but we don't have any idea what happened to the other guys. They were never heard from again."

"Why are you asking me about this? Miguel said you

have a friend in Maine helping you, right? Why doesn't this friend look into it?"

"You've unearthed some damn good stuff, Demi."

"A lot of that stuff is in my stolen notebook."

"I'm very sorry about that," I said with pure sincerity. "However, I read your notebook, and you didn't have anything in there about another homicide. I figured you may have come across the murders in your research, but you didn't write them down."

Her arms tucked under her sizable breasts. Charlie fought to keep a straight face. "Why should I help you?"

"Because we made a deal."

She waved it off, "That deal covers the notebook you stole."

"Well, what else do you want?"

"I want to interview Gavin Scott."

My shoulders tensed, "Why?"

"He killed Russ Huntington, and he got away with it. His father, Hank, is connected to the very drug dealer who got out of jail. Gavin's in this, and his testimony would be phenomenal for my thesis."

"Well, Gavin's gone."

Disappointment didn't keep Demi down for long. "Perhaps you can get me in touch with his father."

"I've never met him. And Gavin doesn't talk to him."

"No Gavin, no help." She didn't seem like the type to bluff. Self-assured people didn't need to. Her eyes narrowed into a squint, "What happened to your eye?"

Charlie started to explain, grasping for sympathy, I assumed. I hushed him, "It's not important." My minor injury was survivable. What I had to say next was not, "My friend is missing. Dr. Aaron White has vanished because of whatever happened to those guys." She didn't soften. "Demi, I know this doesn't have anything to do with you, but I think you're a good person. And you probably became a journalist because you want to help people?"

"*Democracy dies in darkness*," she recited.

I said, "Absolutely," while trying to find the weird comparison between my situation and The Washington Post's slogan. My words were measured, "People are dying in Settlement Island, Demi. At the hands of very dangerous people. As a journalist, you can shine some light on all this, and bring these monsters to justice."

She was torn; I could see it. Her back was placed against the booth, Charlie watching her. He had dropped the horny-teenage-boy act. He seemed moved by my speech, too.

Her long, brown lashes blinked. Then, she spoke. "What do you want to know?"

"Did Dixon mention any other murders that would have taken place around the same time Maverick, the biker, was killed?"

Demi opened up her laptop and inserted a flash drive. She surfed for a few minutes while a waiter collected our food and drink order. We would dine family-style with heaping servings, thanks to Charlie's deep pockets. I was famished, having survived the night before on only cheap noodles and MSG.

Charlie and I started feasting while Demi stayed glued

to her screen. After my first round of entrees, she turned the screen. "There!"

I set my plate aside and pulled the laptop closer. The police report was authored by Dixon. It was slightly altered from the one Luke and I had dug up. The date stamp was for two days before Russ was killed. I read it carefully. Charlie politely asked Demi to let him out, so he could sit next to me.

Dixon's report read as so:

Traffic stop on Maine Street, 9:18am

Offender: Richard "Maverick" Avery

Age: 45

Offense: Speeding (22 miles over)

Description: Avery was uncooperative. Stated that I was fucking around with him because he was a biker and a felon. Two other subjects stated that the three were not from the area, and they didn't realize how fast they were going. Avery has a warrant out for bail jumping x2 in Los Angeles County. Let him go with a citation due to an incoming call regarding a crash on Highway 11. All units were requested to respond.

"They were there," I said to Charlie. He nodded. "His last name wasn't Avery, either."

"He gave the cop a fake name, so he wouldn't find out about his other warrants. However, his alias had a warrant in the system for bail jumping because some idiot at the jail didn't realize that he had given him a fake name and date of birth." He chuckled, "It worked so well for him that he kept using it." Charlie looked over the report again, "How did you get this?"

"Public record's office. I went through a few police reports around the time Russ was murdered, thinking there was a link between Maverick and Russ." She shoveled food in her mouth. "I didn't find one."

"This still doesn't explain what happened to them," Charlie said.

"Still, they were there. All three of them made it to Maine." I checked the date stamp again, "They were pulled over right before Russ was killed." My thoughts raced forward, "What was Gary doing?"

Charlie watched me scramble for something to write with. Demi complied, giving me some sheets from her notebook. God forbid she would ever trust me with any of her research again. "Gavin's dad was running drugs for Gary during this time." I drew a line. "Hank was in Settlement Island when Russ was shot, but he never said when he came to town. So, he probably saw Gary sometime around the time Maverick was killed."

"If he was with Gary when Maverick died, he could confirm Gary's alibi," Demi added.

"No, he can't." I drew a box around Hank's name and a line to a passage from Hank's letter to Gavin. *"You don't need to make things right for your mom. I already did that."*

Demi and Charlie were invested, even if they didn't come to the same conclusion I had. I deliberated for a moment, making sure I was right. Then, I clued them in.

"Gary never mentioned Hank in any of his testimony.

So, they weren't together when Maverick was killed." I wrote *Murderer* next to Hank's name. "Hank set up Gary for Maverick's murder."

CHAPTER SIXTEEN

Accusations

I HAD TO find Hank.

"You sure about this?" Demi said with some semblance of concern.

"It makes sense," I said. "Gary destroyed Gavin's family. Everyone blamed Michelle's death on Hank because she overdosed on the drugs Hank got from Gary."

Demi thought on it, "You think this was about revenge?"

"Or something close to it. Either way, Hank probably wanted Gary out of the picture." The theory felt good. I wouldn't know for sure without cross-examining my research. *Damn Gavin for having my notebook!* With it, I would be able to know for sure if my suspicion was worth pursuing.

Charlie warmed up to the idea. Demi wasn't so sure. "Why not kill Gary instead? That seems like a far better option, don't you think?"

"I don't know. But I'm sure Hank knows the whole story." *I needed to find Hank!* Just like with my missing notebooks, my only link to Hank was through Gavin. Charlie sacrificed his phone, so I could check on Gavin's location. My phone was still off. He was ignoring me, probably. "Shit!" I threw Charlie's phone down on the table.

"Hey, remember, that doesn't belong to you," Charlie said.

Helplessness was a feeling I never wanted to experience again. "We need a plan."

"I need to finish my paper for class," said Demi. My plan didn't include her, anyway.

"And we need to find a place to sleep," Charlie said.

"We have a place."

Charlie's arms knotted across his chest. "Where?"

"My aunt's house. It's not far from here."

"You're gonna take him home to meet your family?" Demi chuckled, "I'm sure that's gonna go over very well."

I glared at her. Our truce was officially over. I set her laptop down in Charlie's empty space. "Thank you for all your help."

"Let me know if I can do more." She slung her bag over her shoulder, "Seriously, I'm here to help." My smile was unconvincing. Demi didn't hold it against me. She left without so much as a whisper of thanks for the delicious food or a leg-up with her thesis.

Charlie squeezed my shoulder. "You serious about staying with your aunt?"

"Yeah. She knows what's going on, and I told my dad I would come up here if things got bad."

"Oh, they're definitely bad," he joked.

"I used to live with her when I went to school here.

I can crash in my old bedroom, and you can sleep in the guest room."

"Catalina, it's not about the sleeping arrangements." Charlie's demeanor was fatherly, "I'm a biker, and I'm like a whole decade older than you. We shouldn't be doing this."

"Doing what?"

He licked his lips, "You have a family? Friends?"

"Yeah, but I can do this with them. All I need is you."

"Can you hear how weird that is?" Rejection was the least of my problems. I let him continue. "You shared your location with me before you even knew me. And now you're staying in my Airbnb with no money, no stuff, and no phone."

This wasn't working out. He thought I was crazy. He wasn't wrong. All this had driven me to the point of insanity. Charlie wasn't to blame. I could understand why he wanted out. I wouldn't stop him, either.

"It's a lot, I understand." One last favor, and he would fulfill his duty to me. "If you drop me off at my aunt's house, I'll see if I can get in touch with Gary and get you guys your money." His brows furrowed, "That's right, I plan on keeping up my end of the bargain."

"That's not," he paused. "Stop putting yourself at risk like this."

"You saw what Gary's son did to me. That happened after he tracked me down," I defended. "He came back into my life. I didn't seek him out. Nor did I turn my boyfriend into a liar. He also sought me out without me knowing what his real motives were."

"I know," he pleaded. "But you trust too easily." No, I didn't. Well, not anymore. Nor would I ever again. "If you want to get through this, you're gonna have to be smarter."

"I don't trust anyone."

"Except for me."

"You haven't done anything to hurt me."

"Yet." Games were not my thing. I pressed him to shoot straight. "I could have hurt you after you jumped on my bike without any hesitation."

"But you didn't." My track record was sketchy, but it wasn't a deterrent for me. "Now, do you wanna help me or not?"

He backed down. "Sounds like you have everything figured out." Charlie forked over some cash and killed his sweet tea. "Lead the way."

❧

Irving, Aunt Eloise's long-term boyfriend, scrutinized the truck as it pulled into the driveway. He had played college football before heading off to the Marines for a few years. He didn't look a day older than me. Tall, dark, and handsome. The coils on his head showed a few grays. His muscles hadn't worn down with age.

"You sure I'm gonna be okay?" Charlie said.

"Yeah, you'll be fine. Just don't mention your trips to jail or your drug addiction."

"I'll stick to the Christian stuff, I guess."

"No swearing, no smoking…just be polite."

"I am polite," he advised.

"Then you'll be fine."

Charlie opened the truck door and smoothed his hair in the mirror. My attention stayed on the colossal black man greeting me with robust arms and friendly smile.

"My sweet Lina!" He picked me up, crushing the air from my lungs. "Eloise and I were so worried when Malcolm couldn't get in touch with you."

He placed me down, "I lost my phone. And all my stuff."

Irving peered over at Charlie. "Is this Gavin?"

"God no," I said disrespectfully. Charlie gave me a sideways grin. "This is my friend, Charlie. He's been helping me out since Gavin and I went our separate ways."

Irving's hand went out, "Nice to meet you, son."

Charlie's shake was firm. "Hope you don't mind the intrusion. We were in town visiting one of her friends from school."

"Not at all. Lina's always welcome here." Another hug, this one longer. "Eloise is in the house."

I nodded, directing Charlie towards the front door. He hung back, "You working on your truck?"

"Yeah, swapping out the starter."

"Need a hand?"

"Sure." Irving guided Charlie to the other side of the driveway where his truck sat.

My thoughtful friend had given me an opportunity to catch up with my aunt without prying eyes and unspoken questions. I found her in the kitchen, mixing up some cornbread for dinner. Unlike Mother, Eloise was an amazing cook. Charlie and I were in for a treat. "Can I help?" I said.

She turned, apron dusted with cornmeal. "Lina! We were hoping you would come up this way." I felt at home within her hug. "Your father has been worried."

"Oh, I lost my phone. Can I use yours to call him?"

Eloise slipped it from her pocket. "Once you're done checking in, we're gonna chat."

I welcomed it. "I'll be a moment." I stepped down the hall into my old bedroom. It had been four years since I last stayed in this room. Luckily, the clothes in the closet still fit. I could use some of my aunt's shampoo and bubble bath. After dinner, this was my plan.

"Eloise?" my dad said. "Have you heard from Catalina?"

"I'm here, Dad."

"Honey! Thank God! I've called your cell about fifty times."

"I'm fine. How is everyone?"

"They're fine. What happened at The Chateau? I called over there and they said you had checked out already."

Nothing that had happened over the last few days would have given my father any comfort. I stuck to the perimeter of my problems, dousing any fears that burned inside him. "I didn't want to stay in one place too long. Unfortunately, my phone got misplaced somewhere, so I wasn't able to tell you."

"Go get another phone and add it to your aunt's account." He had given me a brilliant idea. Since I was on her plan, Eloise had access to my phone records. I could see who was calling. Or if I had any voicemails. "I will. Before I do that, I need to know about Aaron. Have you heard anything?"

"I'm not worried about him." He paused, "I care, but I need to make sure you're safe first. Then, I'll help your sister figure out where he ran off to." Dad's tone suggested he had lost faith in his protégé.

"I think he probably ran because of family problems."

Dad sighed, "I can't blame him for that. I just wished he was more honest with me instead of asking for time off and then just never coming back." He didn't stay mad for long, "A lot of people are scared. Officer Dixon was murdered, and another two homicides just took place."

"Who died?"

"No one you would know. Some street people." I didn't have to know them for their deaths to be a signal from Gary that he wasn't messing around.

"More people will probably die if they keep letting felons out of prison."

"Honey, don't worry about them. Focus on you."

"Will you let me know once you find out anything?"

"Again, my only focus is on you. Do you need me to put any money in your account? What's your plan?"

"I'm coming back to Settlement Island." Dad was pleased with my decision. Secretly, I knew that was the decision he wanted me to make from the beginning. But he gave me the choice. "I'll be there in a few days."

"Excellent. Let me know if you need anything."

"I love you, Dad."

"I love you, too. Please, get a phone today, so we can talk."

I agreed and hung up. Next, I went to my profile on Eloise's phone. The location was still off. On a whim, I called. It went straight to voicemail. "Gavin, it's me. If you get this, I'm at my aunt's house." What else could I say? "I'm sorry about attacking you. I just couldn't go back to Maine without finding out the truth about Gary and Porter. So much has happened since I left you, and…and I want to talk. So, give me a call back when you get a chance."

I hung up and went back to the kitchen. Eloise asked for my help with setting the table. She had already set out four plates. "That boy out there is Gavin?"

"Nah, that's Charlie," I kept my voice level.

She didn't buy my innocence. "Who's Charlie?"

"A friend." Now, for the big ask, "Can we stay the night?" Her brow came up. "Separate rooms, of course."

"Don't play with me, girl. Who's this boy?" She pointed a spatula at my face, "Tell me the truth."

I sat down at the table, "Well, we already ate dinner, so it will be light servings for us."

"Lina, I'm not gonna ask you again."

She set a tin of cornbread down. I cut a piece, "He's helping me with a thing I got going on."

"What kinda thing?"

"A Maine thing." She balled her fist and placed it on her hip. "One of my friends is in trouble."

"Does this have anything to do with your dad's beach house being torn apart?"

"Not completely." I popped a piece of savory bread on my tongue, "My absence from Settlement Island is causing me some problems here."

"Lina, you know how much I love it when you beat around the bush," she said, cutting me down.

Eloise was sharp. Cunning. Vagueness wouldn't get me far with her. "There are some people after me because of that guy I killed last year."

"How are they after you?" Her eyes advanced to the door. Irving and Charlie appeared, the door shutting and locking.

Irving looked at his concerned partner, "Honey, this is Charlie."

"I heard," her voice was skeptical with some sass.

Charlie politely asked if he could wash his hands before helping out with dinner. "I told her we already ate," I said.

"I can eat again. It smells wonderful in here." Carefully, he used dish soap to degrease his fingers while the three of us watched. Then, he washed the dishes in the sink, placing them in the drying rack. His slightly damp hand came out to shake my aunt's, "I'm Charlie Gardner."

"And what exactly are you doing with my niece?" This look she gave him was the one I should have given Charlie from the get go. Instead of being so trusting, like he said I was.

"Protecting her, I guess." He peeled off his leather, the Blood Diamond emblem visible as he placed it over one arm. "She came to me for help with a problem."

"What kinda problem?"

Charlie's eyes remained on hers, "There's this guy from Maine who's got a problem with her. I figured I would keep an eye on her until she got somewhere safe."

Eloise put her hands on my shoulders, "She's safe with us."

Charlie wasn't the possessive type. He actually seemed relieved. "I'm happy to hear that. I was hoping to get her back in touch with her family." Irving gave a surprised huff to this. "I know I'm not the type of person Catalina would be friendly with."

"I'd peg you for one of Cecilia's boyfriends," Eloise was keen on the affairs of her nieces.

No, Charlie wasn't my type. He might be my sister's, if he still had the attitude to go along with his grim past. James was actually much worse than Charlie, making him highly attractive to her. Charlie had repented for his sins and attempted to turn toward the light, where she would happily remain in the dark.

Charlie stood straight, "Listen, I'm not here to cause any problems. I only wanted to make sure Catalina was safe. Now that she's here, I've done my job."

I vehemently shook my head, "No, I don't want you to go." Even Charlie was taken aback by my protest. "We're in this together, remember? I can't do it without you."

My aunt said, "What in your life could be so bad that you need a friend like this to help you solve it?"

"Just be honest, Lina," Irving chimed in.

Everyone needed to calm down, including me. If I reined Charlie back in, I could downplay the danger we were in. "The owner of that drug operation I brought down is upset. He's been calling and harassing me." I pointed to Charlie, "I met Charlie at church. He offered to keep an eye on me. Then, someone threw a rock through one of the windows, and I got scared, that's all."

"That's not what your dad said," Eloise was too smart to fall for any more of my lies. "He said you were running for your life."

"PTSD." It was believable. No one went through what I had endured in Maine unscathed.

"If people are after you, we need to call the police," Irving added.

"I'd prefer it if you didn't call the police," Charlie smoothly voiced.

They kept bickering amongst themselves. There were accusations made from Charlie about Gary without naming him. Eloise and Irving latched on, demanding to know everything that he knew, pinning Charlie in a corner. This continued on until I said, "Everyone stop talking!" Disrespect wasn't on my agenda, so I held back. But my forceful manner brought the accusations to a close. "Sorry, I just need to think for a moment."

"Lina, if you are in trouble, you need help," Aunt Eloise said. "Go to the police and tell them everything."

"It's not as bad as it seems," I said. Charlie didn't appreciate this answer. My attitude mirrored our earlier incident where I had been slapped by Ian. My aunt narrowed her eyes at the mark on my face. "Everything will be okay once I get back to Maine and talk with my father."

Irving didn't buy my explanation, "Lina, I'd rather you settle this here, right now."

Frustration tented my shoulders. "There's an investigator in Maine who wants to speak with me. He wants to do a video interview." Again, the three surveyed my emotions. "He wants me to get back to Maine and speak with him before I talk to any other law enforcement agency. Said it was urgent." Now, to move things along, "So, we should eat and turn in early." Eloise finally released me to my room; the interrogation would continue after dinner.

I had enough time for a shower. I snuck into her bathroom and gathered up her shampoo and conditioner. Then, I drew a bath in the room that connected my room and the guest room. I locked the guest room door and let the water run. In my closet, I found some dresses and jeans hanging, along with T-shirts and undergarments in a dresser.

I laid out some clothes, just a pair of jeans and one of the three shirts I had.

Steam distracted me from my task.

Things seemed to be going smoothly with Charlie and my aunt. Irving, I wasn't too worried about. Eloise was not one to pity fools. She was a straight shooter, leaving no doubt if she didn't like you. I unlocked the guest bathroom door and peered out. They were all still standing, Charlie entertaining them with a story. Eloise shook her head at his silliness while Irving asked what happened next.

I closed the bathroom door again, and settled into the water, retrieving my book from the night before. Charlie told me I could keep it. I was doing him a favor, probably.

Anastasia was swimming away from the island, on her way to freedom from Stefan. There was a second book in the series, so I feared the story would end here.

Eloise gave me an announcement; dinner would be

ready in ten minutes. I dunked my head underwater, pulling it up and lathering up some shampoo. The wash was quick, so was the conditioning. Damp hair, I threw on some foundation, concealer, and mascara that I found in the back of a drawer. The mascara was clumpy, only spreading slightly across the hairs.

For good measure, I retrieved a large purse from the closet and put the rest of my clothes inside. I passed on the makeup. In its place, I stored two Grover books and my trashy novel. Eloise beckoned me again.

At the table, Irving had just sat down. Charlie was setting out forks, taking up my old job. "You look nice," he said to me.

"Thanks." My wet curls slung over one shoulder, the T-shirt was growing colder. I helped Eloise bring over the rest of the food. Her southern roots had dusted the fried fish, shrimp, greens, and potato salad with love.

"Where are you from?" Charlie said.

"Irving's family is from the Bay area. My family's from Louisiana." Eloise poured us glasses of sweet tea, "You from around here?"

"Washington." Charlie loaded his plate with more food. I wondered where he would put it all. "I moved here—"

He stopped breathing at the rapid knocks on the door. Irving elected himself to see who it was. Charlie, the protector, stood between us women and my uncle. The conversation between Irving and the visitor didn't last long. He turned, inviting me to join him.

I slowly abandoned the table, not able to see beyond Irving. Charlie was no help. His expression remained neutral, unable to give me any warning. I could tell by the shadow cast by the porch light there was one figure on the step. It was tall, like Ian. Broader than Noah.

Irving moved aside. I only had two steps to go before I halted.

"Hey," Gavin said.

CHAPTER SEVENTEEN

Resurrection

"Catalina, what happened to your face?" Gavin said. The concealer had let me down.

Irving stepped in to be my father, "Who are you?"

Gavin dropped his rage to look at my uncle, "Gavin Scott."

"The ex-boyfriend." Irving's robust arms didn't fold easily over his large chest. This wasn't a question, but Gavin treated it as so.

"Yeah." He pointed toward the Nova, "I have your stuff."

My grin was lopsided, "Thanks. Let me go get that from you." I coaxed Irving aside after some excessive nudging. On the lawn, I marched up to the Nova's passenger door, seeing my treasures neatly on the seat. Gavin caught my arm, pulling me back around to look at him.

"Who hit you?" he said forcefully.

Irving and Charlie crowded the doorway just beyond him. "Can we talk about that later?"

Gavin blinked a few times, "It was Porter, wasn't it?"

I grasped for words, "How, how, did you find me? My phone's been off."

He pulled my phone from his back pocket. "You have about 300 calls and texts from Noah, begging you to come back. Saying he should have stopped Porter from hitting you, and he was a terrible man or some bullshit like that." I reached for the phone, and he held it out of my reach. "Did he hit you?"

"Gavin, I'm tired. And I'm supposed to be having dinner with my family," I snapped. He bent his eyes at me. "How did you find my aunt's house?"

"After you left me on the side of the road, I followed you back to L.A. I went to all the places I thought you would be, and you weren't there. I remembered your whole story about going to Berkeley and living at your aunt's house, so I came over here. Then, I got lucky."

"Lucky?"

"I figured out your phone password." Grover's birthday. It was the only thing I could think of that would be secure. "Your aunt shared her location with your phone, so I came here right away."

"Clever," I said sarcastically.

My sarcasm was not shared. "Catalina, I'm so sorry, for everything. I shouldn't have lied to you about going back to Maine." His finger touched the skin around my bruise. "I didn't want this to happen to you." Gavin paused, "I'm not here to cause you problems. I just needed to know you're safe."

"I'm okay," I said. "I shouldn't have hit you like that."

"This?" He rolled his shoulder, "I was more shocked than anything. I didn't know you would fight like that."

"You gave me no other choice." I shrugged, "I didn't want to leave. Not until I investigated the biker lead."

His focus moved past me, "I can see that."

"That's Charlie."

"Uh huh," Gavin said.

"Don't worry, he's a good guy." There was so much I had to tell Gavin. But first, he had to be starving, "My aunt made dinner. Do you want to come in?" Gavin waited to see how Irving would react. Now, my aunt had joined them in the doorway. I put out my hand, "Come on." Gavin loosely reached his fingers around mine. "This is Gavin," I said as an introduction to all three.

None of them seemed excited.

Gavin dropped my hand, "I'm only here to drop off Catalina's stuff and make sure she's safe."

Charlie looked to my uncle for the plan. Would they take Gavin out back or would he be welcomed in to feast with us? Irving was a teddy bear, most of the time. Some encouragement from me, and he accepted Gavin on a cautionary basis.

Eloise was different. She didn't trust Gavin. The cross hanging around her neck had been the foundation for her life. Yet, she wasn't the type to be fooled. Forgiveness was on the table, if Gavin proved himself.

She stepped aside, "I'll fix you a plate." The concession was polite, mostly for me.

We all entered the house, my family taking up places at the heads of the table. Charlie sat next to me, Gavin across. An odd dinner arrangement, no doubt. My loved ones were good sports, better than my family in Maine. Dad and Cecilia wouldn't hold back. Mother would stare, undressing them with her eyes.

"This is the best shrimp I've ever had," Gavin said. "What type of batter did you use?"

"Family secret," my aunt winked. "You cook much?"

Gavin nodded, "My grandfather taught me." He regaled them with stories from his childhood, when he helped his grandfather at his restaurant.

Irving continued asking questions while Eloise slowly decided if she would let her guard down enough to ask a question. Charlie nudged me, "Let's talk." Timing was everything, and his was perfect.

Gavin was deep in conversation, plate half-empty, and without a reason to join us. Charlie and I excused ourselves, Gavin peering up to see where we planned to go. Soon, we were out the front door and onto the sidewalk.

"Careful, Gavin has serious FOMO," I teased.

Charlie put a cigarette to his lips, "Seems like it." Tension tightened his words.

"Relax. He's not a bad guy."

Charlie headed down the street, "Based on your reaction, I don't know." His wisdom shone through, "Do you trust him?" He continued before I could answer, "Is he someone who's tough enough to stand up to Gary?"

"Yeah," I said. "I mean, there are some things we need to work out. But you saw his face when he noticed the bruise."

"He's gonna kill Porter." Charlie took another drag on

his cigarette. "I guess what I'm asking is, can I leave you with him?"

I halted us, "Where are you going?" Charlie's mood felt like a good guy trying not to break my heart. "I should have known." He was leaving me.

Goodbyes didn't seem like Charlie's thing. He merely shrugged, "I gotta get back to my club."

"But we agreed to stick together," I said.

"For how long?"

"I guess I didn't think about it."

He nodded, "There have been new developments." He killed his cigarette, "The police covering up our brothers' murders means Gary has to be behind it. So, while you go shake down Gary JR for our money, we gotta find out what happened to our crew."

Foolishly, I said, "You're not going to Maine, right?"

He touched my eye, "We are definitely going to Maine."

"And you don't think it's a good idea for me to go with you?"

"Not really. I'm gonna ride on my bike." With his people.

"So, you're gonna leave me here."

"I was gonna drive you back up to your car and give you the choice. You could come with us or do your own thing." He looked back at the house, "You don't need me anymore. You're with your family and a guy who will move mountains to get to you." He chuckled, "It's kinda cute."

"Gavin and I are over."

"Does he know that?" Charlie rubbed my shoulder, "You have your phone now. I'll stay in touch, I promise."

Charlie smirked, I was crushed. "Every time, every single time, I end up losing the people I care about."

He said, "That guy who died protecting you?" I painfully nodded. Charlie shook his head, "Not everyone you care about is going to get hurt."

"A lot of people have already gotten hurt," I countered.

He knew I was right. Both hands massaged my shoulders, "Not this time. You have the entire Blood Diamond MC behind you. Gary may have the police and a network of dealers on his side, but I have a brotherhood of loyal friends protecting me. And you do, too."

Selfless, that's who Charlie was. Unlike me who only thought of how people could help me. Selfish. That is what he had called me once. I had proven him right time and time again. This time, I'd give him what he needed. "Okay. You chase the other murders and I'll see what I can find on Gary and your money."

Charlie was appeased. He knocked my arm with his knuckles, "Here I was thinking you were gonna put up a bigger fight."

"I'm not as selfish as you think."

"No, you're a martyr. And you need to cut that shit out." Charlie's admiration didn't stop there. "You are a strong and gifted person. Your heart is the stuff of legend." I rolled my eyes. "Don't let other people use your kindness to get what they need." Seriousness wrapped around us as I absorbed his words. I had finally met someone who didn't want to take anything from me.

❦

Charlie left soon after dinner. No one made a big fuss. Especially not Gavin. Irving entertained him with a game of chess while they sipped on his favorite bourbon. Eloise didn't have much to say as we washed up the dishes. She felt Charlie had made the right choice by leaving me here with them.

"That's what a true friend does. They trust you with the people who care about you while giving you space to help yourself." She definitely was my father's sister. Gavin brought a frown to her lips. "You said ya'll don't work."

"We don't." I nibbled on more of her cornbread. "He's just here to bring me my stuff."

"Does he know that?" she said. I huffed a sigh, "Lina, be careful. I had a boyfriend like him once. We were always in each other's business, being indecisive about what we wanted. Finally, I pulled the plug and went out on my own. He got married, and I met Irving."

I leaned against the cabinet. "Gavin and I aren't like that." I smiled, "I want to be like you, actually. You held onto your independence and never got married." Her brow tipped at me. "You were married?"

"I am married." On her left finger was a silver and turquoise ring. One she had worn for the better part of fifteen years.

"You guys are legally married?"

She chuckled, "Yes, child."

"Does Dad know?"

"I told him about five years ago." I snapped at her for keeping this secret for so long. "Child, you know I'm not one for fancy things. And big fusses. Besides, it happened while we were on a cruise. Irving and I were standing on the beach in the Bahamas, and we just decided to get married, right then."

A storybook romance.

I hugged her, "I'm so happy for you," I whispered.

She chuckled, "I've been married this whole time and you didn't even notice." Her eyes searched my face, "Nothing is different. I'm still the same independent, inspiring person you look up to. The only difference is I can keep a secret better than you think." Rolls of laughter erupted from us. Quieting down, her words brought everything full circle. "Is Gavin one of those problems you mentioned before?"

Alas, I couldn't escape it. I had enjoyed this evening without any dire need to run or survive on my next move. "No, he's not." I put the dish towel down.

She leaned in, "I love how you beat around the bush."

"That was a pretty clear answer," I said. More cornbread gave me strength, "I don't wanna drag you guys down with my problems."

"We're family. No matter what you're going through, we got you."

Telling my story was grueling. Reliving all the people who lied to me, taken from me, and used me for their own purposes. So, I stuck with the simplest explanation, reinforcing what I had said before. "There are some police people in Maine I'm working with. They're building a case against him."

"The man who hit your face?" I bowed my head. She didn't let me sulk for long. My chin was tilted up, "You're not a victim. Don't let him hit you again." I nodded. She gave me a side hug, "As for that boy over there winning Irving over; he can stay in the guest room."

"Thanks." Her accommodation was a sign of her respect for me, not him. She didn't hate Gavin. No, she just loved me way more than she tolerated him.

"I'm going to bed." She kissed my cheek. "No hanky-panky."

"We're not together anymore." Even without the commitment, we did manage to end up in bed together at The Chateau. He had claimed it was just sex. No attachment needed. But I wasn't in the mood for regrettable lovemaking. I had work to do.

She gave a hearty laugh, "I was in my twenties once. When things just *happened*."

"Not tonight. I love and respect you too much to bend your boundaries again." I gave her a final hug and told her to sleep tight. After she left the kitchen, I peeked into the study.

Gavin and Irving were having a great time. My uncle had pulled out his record collection, showing his new friend a few of his greatest hits. I backtracked into the kitchen, sliding down the hall to my room. Inside, I washed the day away with another shower, tying my hair up so I wouldn't sleep on a wet pillow. They continued roaring in the study for some time while I finished my book.

The ending was a cliff hanger. Anastasia barely escaped Stefan's grasp. He vowed to find her and bring her back to him. I opened my phone, almost ordering the next copy. Then, I remembered I had nowhere to send it. All the things left from my home were in this room, a few bags mostly filled with my research.

I put my phone on charge and stared into the void. It had been hours since Gavin fell onto my aunt's doorstep, and he hadn't said much to me since his arrival. We were far more dysfunctional than I thought. I shook off my disappointment, and I opened the door to the bathroom. I stopped short of crashing into him.

Gavin's eyes widened, hand ready for knocking. "Sorry, I didn't mean to startle you."

He had shed his jacket, gray shirt snug against his chest and stomach. I ruined the moment, "You're fine. I was just gonna brush my teeth."

He turned, "I'll leave you to it." I took a step in, avoiding his entire body. "I like your uncle."

"I think he likes you, too." I put up my toothbrush, "Thank you for bringing my stuff back."

"You're welcome." As I brushed, he said, "Can we talk tomorrow? About Porter and everything?"

I nodded, finishing up my grooming. "I'd like that."

Charlie was off chasing his lead, and I had my own problems to contend with. Catching up with Gary and getting the Diamonds their money was less of a pipe dream now. I had my connection to Gary within arm's reach. Gavin could get me in touch with his father, who I would strong-arm into telling me how I could find Gary. Then, I'd prove Hank was the murderer.

I'd leave the details out for now and let Gavin rest tonight. "Goodnight, Gavin."

He almost granted me a smooth goodnight. I had made it to the doorway when I felt his hand touch my arm. "I'm really sorry," he said. The makeup had washed away, allowing him to see the darkness on my skin. Gavin immortalized it with his gaze, careful not to touch it directly. "I should have protected you."

My hands framed his, "This isn't your fault. And I'm not going to let it define me."

"It's more than that." Gavin's back straightened, "I should have never left you. We were supposed to be in this together. You depended on my trust, and I wanted to do things my way, not yours."

"Gavin, it's okay."

His hands went to the sides of my face, "I'm not leaving you ever again."

Sincerity was never a problem for Gavin. He was fierce in his beliefs, clinging to them with all his might. This wasn't a promise, but his vow to me.

I lowered his hands, "Thank you for your devotion." The soul crushing truth about why I wasn't fighting him on this could wait. For now, I was ready for bed. "Let's talk more about it tomorrow."

He leaned in the doorway, "What is your plan for tomorrow?"

"Let's figure it out together." Gavin was surprised by my willingness to cooperate. "There are some things I need to tell you about, but I'm too tired to go into it now."

Finally, he relented. A short smile, and he touched my arm. "Goodnight."

"Night." I waited for him to let me go. He lingered. "Gavin, I've had a really long and terrible couple of days. I just want to sleep it off."

"I know. I just can't stop looking at you."

I nodded, "And you're worried. But I'm fine."

He moved aside. "Then, we'll continue this in the morning."

I turned and closed the door, locking it. And the door to the hallway. Then, I laid down with my phone, not quite ready for sleep. So, I decided to set my plans into motion. And I'd start with Noah.

Gavin was right. There were several texts and messages from Noah. I opened the message he had sent right after Charlie had rescued me.

"What are you doing?" Noah said. "You need to get back here, Catalina Rose! Porter's gonna fuckin' kill you if you don't get back here!"

The next message came after an assault of text messages. It was later that evening. "You need to turn yourself over, now! He's not going to stop until he speaks with you." He took some deep breaths, "I know you're scared. I'd be scared, too, but you're gonna be fine. He doesn't want to kill you, I said that out of context." He paused. I could hear someone talking in the background. "Right, all you have to do is just meet us at the airport, and everything will be okay. Just…just get back over here."

The next message came the following morning. "We're still here at the airport." Hoarseness overpowered his voice. "There's still time to meet with us." He sighed, "He's not gonna hurt you. I don't know why you don't believe me. I know you got hit, and I should have done something." More sighs, "Just get back over here as soon as you can." Another voice muffled, "Now! Get here now!" Noah hung up.

The messages slowed until this morning. "Catalina Rose," Noah's words were slurred. "We're gonna find you. There's no place you can hide."

The texts and voicemails stopped.

I went to the second voicemail where someone was clearly talking to Noah. My earbuds went into my ears. *"You need to turn yourself over, now! He's not going to stop until he speaks with you. I know you're scared. I'd be scared, too, but you're gonna be fine. He doesn't want to kill you, I said that out of context."*

The voice coaching him should have belonged to Ian. But it wasn't. "Tell her to meet us at the airport and everything will be okay," Ben said, confirming Demi's part of the story.

That's right; Ben Ryan *had* teamed up with Ian Porter. How did that happen? I had all my evidence, Demi's notebook, and the woman herself right up the street. She would be eager to share her thoughts, getting more dirt for her thesis.

She answered my text with a condition of her own: Gavin gives her details about Russ's murder. I agreed. She had class most of the morning, but she could meet off campus at this café I had raved about.

Instead, I invited her over to my aunt's house. No public places; Ian liked to hide in those. If he planned on coming for me, like everyone said he would, he'd have to make it through the door. And I would be waiting for him.

CHAPTER EIGHTEEN

Silhouettes

"WHY ARE WE doing this again?" Gavin said as I assisted him with the cover for the Nova. We should have done this last night, but I was too focused on Noah's messages. And my exhaustion.

"Because Ben's here, and I don't know if they're following you."

Ben was not in the car when Noah took me hostage. Unless he was hiding in the back. But I'm sure Ian would have used him as a shield when the bikers showed up. So, if Ben wasn't with Ian on his way to the airport, was he tailing Gavin?

I texted Charlie what I knew about Ben, explaining why he was important to our cause. He said he'd keep an eye out, but I could tell he wasn't too worried. Why would he be? He had the protection of an entire biker gang, who were currently with him. I only had my angry ex-boyfriend and a model. A model who would be here in an hour.

Irving and Eloise had left early this morning to open up

her shop. Their decision to leave was reluctant, but she had a business to run. And I had Gavin. We had made breakfast over small talk, me withholding the truth about Hank until much later. Knowing Demi, she would tell him everything about my assumptions. That his father was responsible for Maverick's murder. Hank probably set Gary up to even the score.

For now, I focused on Noah and Ben. What led them to work with Ian? Noah had said he owed Ian. But I didn't have more than that.

"Have you gotten a hold of Noah?" Gavin said as we reentered the house and sat at the table.

Coming up short with answers was becoming my specialty, "He hasn't answered any of my texts or voicemails." I had called him throughout the morning and sent a few messages with no reply. I didn't care about Noah, but I had to be civil. Pretend to care long enough for him to play into my hand.

"If Porter's pulling his strings, he'll call you sooner rather than later." Gavin grabbed my coffee cup and went to the coffee maker to fill it. When he sat down, I had already pulled out my notebooks and laptop.

"Before Demi gets here, I want to talk to you about something." The knock at the door prompted us to freeze.

"Amazon package?" Gavin said. I shrugged. The knock grew louder. We got up, "Stay behind me." He inched toward the door, gun tucked in his jeans. He removed it, holding it out front. The door opened.

Demi stepped back, "Dude, what the fuck?" Gavin lowered the gun.

"I thought you were going to be here at eleven?" I said.

"I got out early, so I thought I'd head over now." She pushed her bag up her tan shoulder, "Should have called first."

"It's the polite thing to do," Gavin put his gun away and stepped aside.

Demi came in and admired all my aunt's artwork. "Nice." She waited for me to guide her to the table. Then, she set herself up right next to me. "I brought everything I could think of."

I offered her coffee. She took it, with sugar and cream. Gavin sat across from me, Demi peered down at her notebook. "You can have it back."

Her lashes advanced to Gavin, "Only if you answer my questions."

"What questions?"

Demi charged ahead, assuming he would be onboard with her interrogation once she started. "You took my notebook, so you owe me some answers. I want to know about Russ's murder."

His shrug surprised me, "I read your notebook; you know everything you need to know."

She clicked her pen and turned to a new page in her book. "What did you and Russ argue about before you shot him?"

"We didn't argue, Demi."

Her pen tapped the paper, "So, you shot him out of the blue?"

"It was self-defense."

"Right, so you argued about something that made him defensive?"

The question held weight. I waited for an answer. Even Gavin respected her wit. "I saw a fight on the side of the road. I hopped out, Russ came at me, and I shot him." Not mentioning Hank wasn't an oversight.

"There's more to the story."

"And you know it." He shifted, his shirt stretching across his chest, "Now, tell us about Ben."

"You're not brushing this off, Gavin." Demi dug in, and his eyes darkened like a turbulent storm.

"I don't owe you anything," Gavin said. She trapped me in a glance. "What does Catalina have to do with this?"

Demi's ruthlessness laid the foundation for a welcomed attack against Gavin. Or me. The flicker of fighting stayed within her until she heard my quiet pleas. I had cheated her. Gavin wouldn't give her a story. My failure gave her permission to leave. But she stayed, despite being used for our benefit.

"She said you would tell me about Russ for my thesis."

Gavin didn't spare me, "I have nothing else to say about it." Demi hissed a sigh. "If it helps," he said, "you can add in a direct quote from me."

Demi rebounded, pulling out her phone, "Three, two, one. Gavin Scott, is everything I have written about your account regarding the murder of Russ Huntington true?"

"Yes, Demi." He stared at the camera, "I regret my actions, and I'm sorry to everyone I hurt because of them."

She cut, smiling as she said, "I can't believe this." She typed in a note in an email and saved the file. "Thanks!" Gavin seemed regretful, but he didn't wallow. Demi charged on, "You want to know about Ben? There isn't much to tell," she said. "Catalina, you knew Ben was in town when we spoke at breakfast the other day. I don't have any updates beyond that. He never showed up when he promised to meet me." Demi opened up her laptop, "I can check my notes, I guess."

Our previous conversation was coming back to me. Noah and Ben had become Ian's puppets. Judging by Ian's demands for loyalty, his alliance with the two went against all his values. Ben had worked with Blake, and Ian would never forgive him for his role in leveling his business. Unless Ben was out making offers he couldn't produce.

"Noah and Ben could have traded their sentences with Ian for help with finding me."

"That's not a surprise," she sipped her coffee. "Ben blamed everything that went wrong in Settlement Island and Anders on you. He made you out to be a demon."

"I killed his friend," I said. "It's understandable. But why didn't he come to my doorstep? He knew where I was the entire time."

"He's a fuckin' coward," Gavin said.

"You never mentioned me to him?" I said to Demi. "Once we met?"

"Are you asking if I told him where you were?"

"Yes."

Her response was thoughtful, "No. He never asked about you." She tapped her pen, "Our whole conversations were about what you had done in Maine. He would talk on and on, answering my questions, but never asking any of his own." She paused, "He did say he was looking forward to my article and thanked me for helping him get justice for his friend."

Gavin chuckled, "He was setting you up to do the research for him. For Porter."

"If Ben wasn't asking any questions, he wasn't getting any research for Porter," I said. "He was just spreading lies."

"That's where Noah comes in," Gavin said. "Ben was the guy who kept Demi informed, so when she confronted you about your past in front of Noah, Noah would be able to record whatever you said, giving Porter all the details."

"Why not just have me give the information to Ben directly?" Demi said.

"Because Porter didn't want Ben to know everything. Information is leverage to him, so keeping Ben out of the loop helped him advance his plans without Ben being able to use them against him."

Gavin drew out a diagram, "Porter's using these two idiots to spy on Catalina. Putting Ben out there was a good move, because it covered up Noah's identity. It would explain how Porter knew things that he shouldn't without giving away his mole. Then, once Catalina knew Porter was onto her, she would confide the rest of her plans in Noah, her so-called boyfriend. That set up Porter to make his next move." He threw the pen down.

"What did you do to Ben to piss him off this bad?" She corrected herself, "Other than killing his friend."

Gavin didn't know the entire truth, either. Since he didn't really keep up his end of the bargain with her, I figured I would tell Demi something that would pay for her time. "I met Ben when I was helping Porter last year. I traveled up north, close to Canada, when I stopped to get gas. He started hitting on me, and I soon found out that he was a drug dealer."

"He worked for Porter?" Demi said.

"He was selling drugs that were stolen from Porter."

She made a note, "Who did he work for?"

"Six and Jude, who worked for Blake, the guy I killed." I gave her a rundown of everything, skirting around the parts starring Daniel. Gavin didn't need to hear that. This led back to Noah and Ben. "Noah could have worked for Six and Jude, too."

Demi had filled a page with her notes. "If he did, that would explain his debt to Porter. He was willing to clear his debts if he turned you over."

Her perspective was interesting. But, "I've spent a lot of time with drug dealers, and Noah doesn't fit in their world. If Noah owes him for something, it can't be because of the stolen drugs and money."

Gavin nodded, "It would have been better if he just paid him back."

She turned a page, "You said Porter picked you for his mission because you weren't in the drug scene. I'm sure Noah's in the same spot." Demi drew a box and some arrows, "Porter has lost his business." She put his name in the middle of the box. "Ben has a direct link to Blake." His name went under an arrow. "Here you are." She put a heart around my name. "Ben is here, and you don't know why he came to L.A. other than the fact that he was my connection to the violence in Settlement Island." She drew an arrow between our names, Ben in the middle. "Porter hired Noah to spy on you, because he couldn't have Ben do it. You knew his face. You wouldn't trust him." She drew a final line.

"None of this matters," Gavin added. "I already explained how Noah and Ben arrived here."

"You're missing something," she educated him.

He, in turn, educated her, "Ben, Noah, Porter: they are all the same person. Porter uses people to do his dirty work. And the people he usually picks are low-lifes."

"All of them?" I said.

"Except for you."

"Nice save," Demi said before another sip.

"I was going to say that, anyway." Gavin took her pen and drew an X across her diagram and put a line between me and Porter. "All this started because of her relationship with him. Noah and Ben are not important. He will use me, you, them, whatever it takes to get to Catalina."

Demi took no offense to any of his words, "Okay, Genius. What does he want with her?"

He wrote in large letters GARY.

"Noah came into my life before Gary was released from jail," I said. "Ben was talking to her before then, too." I posed a threat to his theory, "Whatever he wants with me has nothing to do with Gary, unless he already knew he was going to get out of jail several months ago. And he thought I could help in some way."

"Before your investigation turned to Gary," Gavin said, "you and Luke were doing your own research into another murder, right? All the stuff on your murder wall?"

I sat back, reflecting on my fractured conversation with Ian. He had forced me to reveal some of the details regarding his father, but not once did he ever say why. Or how this information would benefit him. "He's been watching me since I started looking into Hank, Russ, and Gary. Back when I was just trying to figure out why Russ died." I muttered, "When I was just trying to get the answers Blake was looking for."

"Yeah," Gavin said.

Truths rushed me all at once, clicking together, "It wasn't until I took a deep dive into Gary that everything changed. That's when Porter decided to come for me and collect on what I knew."

"You spooked him," Demi said.

"I was getting too close." I nodded, "Porter didn't want me searching for answers anymore." The rush continued, "If I kept going, I would have figured out who framed Gary, and he doesn't want me to know because he already knows who it is. And I can't have that leverage over him."

"You think Porter knows who framed Gary?" Demi said, unconvinced.

"It's very possible."

Gavin dug in, "He probably used your research to figure it out. Now, he wants to get to that person before your biker friends do. Then, he and Gary can get their revenge before it's stolen from them." Gavin looked down at Gary's name again. "I think you solved it."

Sweet relief! I found my answer! Ian just wanted my research, so he could use it to prove his father had nothing to do with Maverick's death. I grinned. I could live with that. If Ian and Gary went after this person, they would satisfy part of their debt to the Blood Diamonds. The other part would be on them to sort out.

They didn't need me. I could go back to my boring life, a single girl just enjoying the beach, and—

"There has to be more to it than that." Of course, Demi would think this. Her questions and inquiries were always life ruining for me. "If Porter's Gary's son, he had to know all about the Blood Diamonds, especially if they were in business together. And Porter would have probably started looking into who framed him once he went to prison."

"Gary and the Diamonds were in business before Porter took over the company," I said. "Gary probably didn't tell Porter about the money he owed them." Now, the framing, "Porter probably didn't tell anyone about his research into his father's wrongful conviction. He didn't want to sip anyone off?"

"Why not?" Demi said. "If he offered up a reward for the truth, he would have gotten way more leads."

Her points hit hard.

Having Demi on our team was actually a benefit. She forced me to think outside myself and find answers to questions that moved my plans forward, not against me.

"Let's say you're right, Demi. Gary did tell Porter about the Diamonds. And Ben and Noah are here because they wronged Porter and they need to make it right. How does all that relate to Aaron? He went missing the moment Gary was released from prison. Porter told me he didn't know where his brother was. Instead of looking for his brother, he comes looking for me?"

"You're forgetting a key detail," Gavin added. "Dixon was killed shortly after Gary got out, too."

"Dixon was helping Aaron? Gary?" No, that wasn't right.

Demi's head shook, her loose curls bouncing slightly. "Dixon wasn't a fan of the Porters. He worked for Blake, remember?" She said, "Unfortunately, Dixon's dead. Aaron's missing. And we don't know how all these people fit together. But we do know Porter wants her. His motive is our motive. We need to find out why."

"Gary wants us, so he can twist our testimony to prove Blake had a motive to set him up for the murder of that biker," Gavin said. "Porter might want to bring Catalina in to meet his father."

Demi tapped on Gary's name, "Which means he doesn't know who killed the biker. But he wants some insurance in case Porter doesn't find the right person."

"Why can't Gary just come to California himself and shake down the Diamonds for some information? Or me?" I said.

Gavin drew a drink from his coffee. "He's on parole and a flight risk. He can't leave the state. If he does, he'll go back to jail."

"Okay," I sighed. "So, the only logical reason is Porter came here to take me back to Maine to face his father. His father probably wants to meet with me, personally, much like Gary wanted to meet with you, Gavin."

The motive was flimsy, but it gave me a starting point. I waited for Demi to add in her rebuttal. She didn't let me down, "*Still*, there has to be more to it than that. If Gary wants to use you two to set up Blake and Russ for murder, he'd have to use way more resources than it's worth. At this rate, he could choose anyone to pin the murder on, including a member of the Blood Diamonds. He could easily say they set him up because of the bad business deals he had with them."

"And they killed their own guy?" Gavin said.

"He could spin it and say Maverick was against them. It doesn't have to be the truth, it just has to be believable." Now Gavin and I were the skeptics. She continued, "If he's just trying to pin the murder on someone else, he doesn't need you two. He could scare or coerce anyone into making up enough evidence to prove his innocence. Why are you guys so special?"

"He's assuming I'll help because Gavin needs me to keep Gary off his back," I said.

"He has leverage on me," Gavin said. "Gary covered up parts of Russ's murder because if he didn't, the police would find a line right back to him."

"How?"

"One of his dealers was involved."

"You mean your dad?" The recoil was stark. Demi soothed him, "You're right, I did look into the murder before I questioned you. I had the whole story, except I didn't know if your father worked for Gary. And you just told me, for sure."

He flew up, towering over her. "Demi, don't fuck with my family."

Demi didn't cower. Nor did she boast. Her eyes held a bit of kindness, "I'm not coming after your family, Gavin.

I just want to know what Gary promised your father in return for his silence."

"What makes you think he promised him anything?"

"He's alive, right? Judging by the way the Porters operate, they are quick to silence anyone who can do damage to their business. Porter's killed plenty of people. So has Gary. But he left you and your dad alive."

Gavin put his hand on his chest, "If Gary killed me, it would be a direct link back to him."

"Because you worked for him, too?"

"I'd never sell drugs, even if I was living on the streets." He tousled his hair, "The only enemies I have are on Gary's side. If something happened to me, the police would assume it was Gary or one of his employees."

"Except for Blake," I said. "Six shot you. He hated Gary, too."

"Regardless," Gavin hissed, unaffected by memories from the worst day of his life, "Blake came after me because of Gary's role in his father's death. His focus was on me, but his ultimate beef was with the Porters."

"Okay," Demi said, "that eliminates you from the equation. But what about your father? If he was dealing drugs for Gary, why did Gary spare his life?"

"He didn't." My thoughts went back to the letter. "Something happened between Hank and Gary. Then, after Russ's murder, Hank ran." Gavin sat down again, having nothing else to say. Demi sat silently while Gavin and I absorbed my revelation. "Why didn't Gary kill Hank?" I said after some time.

Demi didn't have an answer for me. But Gavin did. "Someone's protecting him," he said.

Gavin's confusion told me he didn't know who this person was. "It has to be one of Gary's enemies," I said.

"He's got about five-thousand people who want to take him out," Gavin said.

"And whoever is protecting your father is probably someone on the west coast, not in Maine," I confirmed. Hank had fled, first to Houston and then to Tucson. Tucson was close enough to Mexico. He could still run drugs for his new bosses and run across the border if things went south. It was perfect.

Gavin took Demi's pen and started a new drawing. In this diagram, there was a line between Hank and Gary. Every arrow that spun to me, Gavin, Noah, Ben, and even Ian himself was born from this relationship, not my deals. "I need to talk to my father." He threw the pen down and got up, leaving me and Demi alone at the table as he stepped into the backyard, slamming the door.

"He's really something," she said sarcastically.

"Can you blame him? He just got confirmation that his father is the reason behind whatever the hell Gary is up to. And we're somehow involved."

She gave me a forlorn stare, "Catalina, I don't think Gavin's involved in this. If anything, I think Porter is using him to get to you. And Gavin knows that."

"Gary wants us both," I corrected her.

"Or he just said that to lower your guard." I was growing tired of Demi and the impending doom she had brought to the table. "Think about it. Gavin was in Maine this whole time. In the hospital, all vulnerable. They could have taken him out or questioned him at any moment. But instead, Porter put all his resources into you? He started working with people he doesn't trust to pursue you? You're a much bigger threat than Gavin."

"I'm more valuable," I muttered. "Alive, at least."

"Then, if he catches you, don't tell him anything," she said, like this was a spy novel or movie.

"Demi, isn't a game."

"Yes, it is." She took my hand, "Porter's playing you like a chess piece. He's moving you here and there, using you to take out other pieces on the board. No matter how much he intimidates you, he can't lose you until the game is over. In this case, I'd guess the game ends when Gary goes back to jail."

Melancholy turned to hope inside me. Demi's speculation was brought home quickly. "If I play into his hand, I help him save his father."

"But, if you figure out what game he's playing, and who's involved, you'll be able to beat him." She revisited her pages, "Hank is the key. He's the only person you know who worked for Gary before he went to jail. He would be your best source regarding the Blood Diamond murder." She leaned in, "You told me yesterday that you thought Hank framed Gary. You need to see if that checks out."

I paused, "It'll kill Gavin if it's true."

"It's better than not knowing." Demi threw arms around me, smelling the sweet floral scent of her hair, her tan skin holding a comforting warmth. She believed she had solved one of my problems and given me hope at the same time. "I'm here to help you, no matter what."

"Thanks?" I said, rejecting her enthusiasm. My head throbbed, my brain tired from all the thinking. I missed overthinking, where I could just dismiss the thoughts as stories or superstitions.

It was time for her to get back to campus. Again, I offered her notebook back. "I think you need that more than I do."

I walked her to the sidewalk where her Uber was waiting. She gave me one more "boost" of encouragement. "Don't forget, democracy dies in darkness."

"What do you mean by that?" I said, genuinely curious. "I'm not a reporter, so it's not relevant to me."

"But you're exposing these people and their businesses for what they are. You're holding them accountable for all the lives they have ruined and destroyed. The Settlement Island government has failed you guys. So have the people who are supposed to be protecting you. It's up to you to make this right for everyone." She smiled, "And can do it, Catalina."

I had been wrong about her. So very wrong. Demi's convictions rivaled everyone's, including Gavin and Ian's. She lived and bled what she believed in until it saturated every part of her life, her being. She was powerful and fearless all at once, carrying a light that forced her opponents to challenge her, if they dared.

And they wouldn't.

Demi understood the people I was dealing with. Sure, they held guns that were aiming, ready to shoot. But underneath their terrifying pasts and the bodies that had piled up at their hands, they were cowards.

Cowards who took to hiding behind a romantic relationship with me to get what they wanted. Cowards who teamed up with my enemies to "fool" a young college student and feed her information to reach me. Cowards who reduced themselves to slapping me across my face when I refused to give up the names of those I was protecting.

Ian claimed to value loyalty in people. But his admiration disappeared when that loyalty was not devotion to him.

He would soon learn from his mistakes.

A raging wildfire had been lit within me. And I would consume any hope Ian had of me cooperating with him willingly. Whatever he wanted, he'd have to beat it out of me.

CHAPTER NINETEEN

Father

"As MUCH AS I hate Demi, she made some really good points." Gavin had come into my room to share his insights. He sat down on my bed as I started packing up my things.

"She's been right this whole time. Instead of finding the person who murdered Maverick, I should be figuring out how I fit into the puzzle. Ian wants me for a reason, and I need to beat him at his own game."

"What do you want to do?" Gavin said.

Time to come clean. "I want to go see your dad." Gavin shuffled against the comforter. "He knows about Gary. And he knows what happened that night you got arrested."

"Catalina, me and my dad don't get along."

"I know," I said somberly. "But you know how important he is to all of this. You said you have to talk to him, too." Heaviness expanded beyond Gavin and filled the room. I abandoned my task and sat next to him. I hadn't forgotten about his feelings and how what I was commanding him to do had etched away at his heart. "It was only a suggestion."

"No, it wasn't." He turned and put my bags aside, "If my dad's a part of this, you deserve to meet him."

The mood shifted into silence. He grappled with my request and didn't know what to do when I didn't fight him on it. Honestly, I was tired of fighting. I'd give it my all when I finally saw Ian again, giving him a few punches of my own. He needed to be punished for putting his hands on me. With everyone else, I wasn't interested in disagreements or feuds. That extended to Gavin, too.

"We shouldn't go see him," he said. "It's a complete waste of time." Gavin dug his nail into his jeans. "He's worthless."

"Maybe as a dad's worthless, but with Gary, he's your ticket out."

"Nice reframe," he said.

"I'm not wrong." Gavin's face remained unreadable. Even from the closeness we shared. I couldn't tell if he agreed or not. I placed my hand on his knee, "Maybe we should find another way." He chuckled, "Why are you laughing?"

"You've been hell bent on seeing this Gary thing through until the end, no matter how far you have to go. Now you're on my side?"

"It's not about sides, Gavin. You and I want the same thing." The confession relaxed his shoulders, "You came back to make sure I was alright. I don't take that lightly. And we're a team," I offered. "We make decisions together."

"Okay, if we didn't go see him, what's your idea?" he said.

I had exhausted all of my resources here. Demi had been a blessing, and Miguel was my rock, but I had to go back to Maine. Tattered, torn me was the missing link between Gary's past and whatever plans he had for the future. Plans that I had to stop.

"I'm ready to go home."

Gavin measured my response. "Okay, well, first we're gonna have to make sure Porter and Noah don't know you're there. Maybe we can stake it out for a day or two, change the locks…"

"No, I meant Maine."

That's when I knew. His show about moving to California was just that, a show. Gavin lit up at the notion of going back to his forest. It was complicated, and downright deadly, but it was home for him.

"Alright, then." His smile brought my heart some joy. At times, I liked giving him what he wanted.

"Let's drive back down to L.A. so I can pack more stuff, and we'll hit the road."

He stood, "If you're ready, let's do it."

The nod had barely taken place before he started grabbing my things and putting them in the Nova. I sent Eloise a text, letting her know that we were on our way back to Maine. She told me to promise her that I would keep her updated on my progress. I'd call her every morning and night until I got back.

I promised.

From here, I texted Charlie and gave him the news. He said he'd call me in a couple hours, after he had a meeting with the club. I felt special being privy to the inside details of the biker gang. The smirk fell from my lips. Gavin had reentered the room.

"What's wrong?"

"Nothing, actually." But I knew that mood on him. It was the one that put him at odds with me. A lie that would break what little trust we had.

"Just be honest, okay?" Gavin turned his phone to an email. It was an acceptance letter from Stanford. "You got in?"

He nodded, solely. "Yeah, I did."

My arms thrusted around his shoulders. My lips grazed his skin, saltiness touching them. "Be happy! No one gets into Stanford, Gavin!"

He pushed me away, slightly, so he could see my eyes. "With everything going on, I don't know if I'll be able to go."

"We'll figure it out." I rushed out, "Which academic year?"

"Next fall."

"See!" I exclaimed. "We have plenty of time to get Gary back in jail, kick Porter out of our lives, and move you back in time for your first mixer!" He shook his head and shrugged. "Stop being so mopey." I grabbed my purse, "And dinner's on me."

I kicked him onto the porch and locked up the house. The Nova was pristine, untouched by Ian or anyone working for him. Gavin opened the door for me, and I reached over and unlocked his door. Once he was inside, I continued.

"You're gonna love college. What are you studying?"

"Philosophy."

"Really? What are you gonna do with that degree?"

"I love the encouragement," he said. "Economics."

"I didn't see that one on you."

He leaned into the seat, "I live in a small town that died right after the lumber yard shut down. That's why so many people turned to drug dealing and working for the Porters. They were starving for money, and tourism didn't work for their lifestyle."

I had seen the abandoned barns and blue-collar hallows. These were working-class people who had no work. "You want to teach them how to make money."

"I want to run for mayor and actually make some changes in town. Level the playing field for everyone."

A noble quest. "My father will expect tax breaks."

"I know, he told me."

He had? "You talked to my dad about this?"

"He was the one who told me to reapply. Said I should go into business or science." He continued defending himself, "Look, I had a lot of time to do stuff after you left. I bought a computer, started watching online videos about business and finances."

His progression only bothered me because I wasn't a part of it. "How often did you see my dad?"

"He was my doctor, you know? After I got released, I stayed with Brianna during my recovery. Your dad and mom felt bad for me, so they would stop by once a week, just to make sure I didn't need anything. Your dad even came out to the cabin to help me get it ready for winter when I moved back over there."

"My dad went to your cabin?"

"And your mom." He smiled, "She gave it a woman's touch. To her, that meant new towels, a better shower curtain, stuff like that."

"I think she missed her calling as an interior designer," I scoffed.

"She paid for it all, too."

Part of me figured my family would have shunned Gavin after I left. But he had saved my life by putting himself in the way to take some bullets. "And they never told you where I went?"

"No," he tapped the seat. "When I'd ask, they said it wasn't their place to share your personal life without your permission. They were being nice because they wanted to be there for me. But in the end, you are their daughter. They would respect any decision you made."

During this whole time, I couldn't afford to miss them. They seemed fine, but that wasn't the point. Hearing Gavin sing their praises made me miss them. A lot. "They never asked me if I wanted to speak to you."

"It was better that way," he said stoically. "You came out here to start over. I had to get better and heal. We both needed therapy or else we would fall back into our old habits."

In the past, we were trauma bonded. That's what Dr. Wong had called it. And it was why we never seemed to work. Our relationship was built on all the things that had happened to us. Not on the love and experiences we so desperately longed for from one another. Take the trauma out, and what were we left with? Nothing, probably.

"Well, I'm happy my family was there for you. And you're going to Stanford!" My voice wasn't allowed to break. "You deserve this!"

He grinned wholesomely, "I'd be lying if I said I wasn't happy."

My hand rubbed his cheek, "Be happy."

In a normal relationship, we would have celebrated with a kiss. *We weren't normal.* I settled on, "Let's get through the Gary thing, and then you can focus on your new life."

A minute passed, and he shifted closer to me.

The kiss was going to happen, even if it wasn't good for us.

Our eyes had met, admiring what the other was thinking. I braced myself, my chest rising and falling with each beat of my heart.

"Alright," he said while moving back to his side of the car. It roared, vibrating its power beneath the seats. Gavin threw on some Ray Bans and told me to buckle up. We didn't speed down the streets. He seemed patient, giving me the impression that he wanted to spend as much time with me before we'd have to go our separate ways.

The beach house was still. My father had a security company come out and sweep the rooms, removing whatever cameras or listening devices Noah had installed. There were more cameras installed, fit to capture all intruders. And the alarm would sound the moment anything changed without my consent.

You move, Ian.

I flicked on the lights with an app. We had agreed we

would stay the night here and get an early start tomorrow morning. Gavin plopped down on the couch, leaving me to prep for our trip. I packed a suitcase and another duffle bag with more clothes. Kyle never kept much worth taking, so I didn't have anything of his to add to my things.

I set my bags down by the door. Next, I packed lunch with whatever I could find in the fridge. A few sandwiches with turkey and lettuce, mayo for better taste. I shouted to Gavin about his thoughts, and he said he didn't mind what I came up with. He'd fallen into some type of scrolling on his phone.

"What's James saying?" I said as a guess.

"Things are calm," he stood. "I'm gonna go take a shower." His phone slipped in his pocket, but he stopped midway across the room. "Nah, I'm too tired."

Gavin didn't mind sleeping on the couch, but I offered up the guest room. The cleaning lady had come, changed the sheets, cleaned up the mess in the living room, and put everything back to where it was supposed to be.

Gavin didn't yield to my hospitality. "I'm gonna sleep out here, next to the door, with my gun."

Speaking of guns, I went into my bedroom and hunted for the gun Kyle had given me. Again, it came up missing.

He was no longer avoiding me, so I asked Kyle about it. "Sorry, darling," he said in a text. "Yeah, I took it." I was relieved to know it was safe, yet now I was dependent on Gavin.

Having Gavin in the living room wasn't a bad idea, after all. But he didn't have to suffer. I rearranged the cushions, making a proper bed.

"Why didn't you do that the first night I stayed over?"

"I didn't think about it."

He rolled his eyes, for once. The thud of his stuff hitting the floor rippled through me. Loud noises set me off, sometimes. A few calming breaths, and I centered myself. We were fine. The couch was comfortable. Gavin was tough, tougher than most people. So, why did I feel conflicted about leaving him out here alone?

I turned on the TV to the movie channel. Another black-and-white flick was on. "Thanks."

I stripped the guestroom of its bedding and brought it out for him. "What do you want for dinner?" I said.

"Delivery pizza is garbage." He kicked off his boots and walked over to the kitchen. "You got any food?"

"Nothing you would want," I replied.

He went to the pantry, then the fridge. He overlooked my sandwiches, sifted through whatever was left. A meal was on his mind, something he hadn't made for me before. "Can you order some lean ground beef, Italian sausage, and veggies?"

"Spaghetti?"

"Yep. Sounds good, doesn't it?"

It did. I placed the order and went back to my room to shower. It went by quick, given the fact that I was starving. When I got out, I threw on an oversized tee and checked on Gavin. Sauce was boiling, bread was in the oven, and he was cutting noodles. I didn't disturb him.

I called Luke to check in. It had been a while since our last chat, and he had no idea where I was headed next. He would be happy to find out I had taken his forgotten advice and befriended Demi. Well, we were friendlier.

I ended up leaving him a voicemail. Same with Demi, Miguel, and my own sister. Dad kept his message short. He and Mother were at a fundraiser in Anders.

It seemed like everyone was moving on...except for me and Gavin. New surroundings, old habits. He still cooked me dinner. Made magic out of whatever scraps I had discarded in the fridge as unusable. I made a place for him, a nest of softness and warmth for us to lie in.

We had our roles, even if the reason behind them had gone.

Gavin appeared in the doorway, "Dinner's ready."

He was surprised when I filled a large bowl full of pasta and sauce, sitting down on the couch.

"Your mom would faint if she saw you eating spaghetti on her white couch," he teased.

"I'm still alive; that should be enough for her." My fork wrapped around the fresh noodles, savory butter and herbs, sitting it on my tongue. My eyes closed, relishing the complex flavors of his cooking. "I missed this."

He watched my indulgence on his food. "Got any wine?"

"No." I made him wait until I had another bite, "I have lemonade."

"That'll do." He poured us both a glass. I set mine down on the end table, refusing to spoil this delicious feast with sour lemons. "We can watch something else while we eat."

"How about *Independence Day*?" I suggested.

"That's a pretty random request," he said.

"It's my dad's favorite movie, and I haven't seen it in so long."

He pulled the remote from the side table. I made the purchase and dimmed the lights with my phone. "Is there anything your family doesn't own?" he said.

I shushed him as the beginning of the movie trapped my attention. Gavin would glance over at me, here and there. After I finished my bowl, I tucked the blankets around me, the movie becoming my reason for living. Gavin rested in his jeans and T-shirt, gnawing on a chance to say something to me.

We made it to the end credits. I expected Gavin to fall asleep, but he didn't. We were just there, sitting next to each other, me under the blankets and him on top.

Last time we had enjoyed a movie together, we ended up having sex. Tonight, apprehension sat between us. It weighed the cushions down, causing Gavin to move closer to the edge.

"Well, I guess I should get to bed. We gotta leave early tomorrow."

"Yeah." Gavin picked up the remote and surfed over to the movie channel. I inched off the couch, and he reached out clutching my wrist. "Wanna keep me company out here?" I didn't quite know what "company" meant until he said, "Just sleeping this time."

"O-okay." I pushed back on the couch and dimmed the lights completely. Gavin stood, peeling off his shirt and his jeans. He turned and retrieved some sweats from his bag. His back muscles flexed as he dressed.

He turned around, and I averted my eyes to the TV. The smirk was subtle, illuminated by the TV lights. He crawled underneath with me, careful to keep some distance. The couch shifted, and I rolled over, just a little closer to him.

"Goodnight," he said. "See you in the morning."

A glimpse of his bullet wound made me shutter. I hadn't apologized for hurting him. I had, but it wasn't a slow, thoughtful apology, like he deserved. Teeth sank into my lip as I touched the skin. "I'm sorry for hitting you."

"I'm sorry for being an asshole." Gavin didn't reach over and release my lip, like he normally would. The action didn't seem to bother him. "We should go to sleep," he said.

"Yeah." But I didn't want to stop talking. I ached for him to touch me. To kiss me. The courage to make the first move faded when he closed his eyes and turned over.

He loved me.

But he didn't want me.

I knew it.

Once was enough, I guess. It filled him up while leaving me yearning for more. I closed my eyes, waiting for sleep to come. It would, several hours later.

CHAPTER TWENTY

History

THE MORNING LIGHT passed by me and faded before I woke up. Gavin had eaten breakfast and was checking the fluids of his Nova. It sat in the detached garage, next to my car. I looked in on him, and he shooed me away. Gavin told me to get some breakfast, so we could leave shortly.

On our trip, we would take I-10 east, traveling through the Southwest before turning up north. I wanted to make the most of our time on the road. I lugged my bags to the car, leaving my laptop and notebooks out.

"Gonna work while I drive?" Gavin said as he lowered the hood, wiping his hands on a rag.

"I figured we could piece together a plan before we come face-to-face with Gary."

"Smart." He followed me into the house to wash his hands and wait by the door, giving me space.

The walls, the aroma of breakfast, the sun beaming through the blinds, brought a few unexpected tears. Despite Noah and his cameras, this tiny beach cottage was etched into my heart as a sanctuary. My haven. My home for the last year.

My room was perfect, a complete reflection of me. Even the murder wall wasn't able to tarnish the happy memories I had made here. I peered into the guest room. I swore I saw Kyle's shadow cross me as he sat on the bed, reading some instruction manual for a project at work. He looked up at me, smiling. I blinked, and the bed was stripped, the furniture clean from his debris.

"We need to get going," Gavin said. I turned to speak with him, crashing into his chest. "The sooner we get on the road, the more distance we can put between us and Porter."

I nodded and passed him, landing in the kitchen. I pulled out three-hundred dollars and put it in an envelope for the housekeeper.

"That's awfully generous of you," he said, opening the door for me.

"She's a good housekeeper," I locked the door and checked the camera; no one had snuck into the house after I secured it. Gavin took my hand, something he hadn't done since we dated. "I'm not going anywhere."

Gavin's response rolled off his tongue, "You're gonna come back here, Catalina. I'll make sure of it."

I held onto him, walking in sync. A tribe of roller-bladers circled past us, one smiling at me. We looked so comfortable, our fingers interlaced loosely, love draped over us. Not in a quick hurry. Just the boardwalk disappearing into sand and then stiff concrete.

He opened the passenger door, and I got in, shoving

my things aside. Gavin shed his jacket on this warm day. He tossed it into the back on top of his bags. We left the garage and I clicked the app, closing the door, sealing my car inside. I had traveled all over the state with both Gavin and Charlie, leaving my car, my freedom, behind.

This time felt different.

We were going to be together, for several days, passing several states. If I didn't want to be with Gavin anymore, I would have to find my own way to Maine. Or back here.

This was my leap of faith. A show to God how far I would go to make things right and get the freedom we both deserved.

Gavin put on some sunglasses and so did I. I'd get started on my research. But first, I'd say goodbye to my ocean. The sun and sand looked good, framing the many people enjoying the beach.

"You'll be back," Gavin said.

A fair assumption, but I wasn't so sure. "Maybe I'll stay in Maine."

"And do what? Date Luke, get married, and have three-hundred kids?"

"Luke and I are just friends now."

"I've heard that before."

"Well, he's not interested in me. He's been out on a few dates with some other girls in town." He was also spending more and more time with my sister. More time than he had spent with any of the girls he was haphazardly pursuing.

"And he told you about them?" Gavin said.

"He asked for advice, which is a joke. I don't know anything about dating."

"Other than Noah, have you dated anyone else? Had feelings for anyone?"

"Not really," I said, leaving out Daniel. He was dead, and there wasn't much more to say about it. "Dating wasn't really a priority."

"How'd you end up with Noah?"

I shrugged, "He was nice and persistent. Seemed like someone I could talk to and take things slow with." Gavin gave me some long, interested nods. "I'm guessing you didn't date?"

"Dating's not my thing, remember?"

"You don't get lonely?" The question slipped.

"No," his huff was more of a laugh than a scoff. "I've got tons of people to talk to. I don't need a girlfriend." I understood the sentiment. I never wanted to date ever again.

Gavin was a man, though. Didn't he miss sex? "What about—"

He shifted in his seat, "What are your plans after all this? The serious ones."

"Serious ones?"

"Yeah. What's your big dream?"

His inquisitions paused me. Then, I said, "If I don't come back to California, I'm gonna buy a bus and convert it into an RV."

"But you don't know anything about converting any-thing into anything," his tone was cheeky. "Have you ever driven a bus before?"

"I'm sure James will help me. He owes me for helping out with his remodel."

"You held up two two-by-fours and ordered pizza." My perplexed stare made him laugh, "Yes, of course he told me about it. After you left, I tried to figure out what caused you to flee all the way over here."

"And what did James tell you?"

"You came to him for advice about Porter and drug running. He told you to leave it alone."

Such a clear recap of my conversation with his dear friend. James didn't mention anything about Daniel, which was a plus. James was more reliable than I thought. This comment helped me steer the conversation away from Daniel and toward his father.

"Your dad was a drug runner for Gary, right? Nothing more?"

"What else would there be for him to do?"

"Murder?" I treaded as cautiously as I could. "Framing people?"

"No, my dad's not a murderer. At least not like I am."

And I was. "We're part of the club, together. Not a club I like being in."

"Me, neither." Gavin hit traffic. He slowed down, finally looking at me. "Aside from all the murdering, are you doing okay?"

"I..." I took in his question. "Things were great, mostly." My body turned toward him, "Very nice, actually. I have thoughts about Blake, but I've channeled them into my research with Luke. Having an outlet gives me some balance."

He put one hand on the steering wheel, the other in his lap, eyes forward, "That's good. I wish I had your strength."

He sighed, "I think about Russ all the time. Every day since it happened."

"How many years has it been?"

"Nine."

That gave me little hope. The break in the nightmares and guilt were just that; a break. Not progress toward not thinking about it anymore. "What do you think about?"

"The whole thing. Everything that led to me pulling the trigger." His head tilted toward me, "I never told the whole story. All the details." I geared up, pen in hand, paper ready. Gavin shook his head, "Please, don't write this down."

"It could help us," I softly pleaded.

His hand raked through his hair, giving it some volume. "Please, Catalina. If you have any questions, or need me to explain something again and again, I will."

Reluctantly, I put my laptop and notebooks into my purse. "Where do you want to start?"

"My dad had come to town for my birthday. It was the first time I had seen him in a while. He left because he and my grandmother got into a huge fight."

"What did they fight about?"

"Me," he said. "She wanted him to make amends with me. He said he'd visit us for my birthday. Instead, he asked her for some money. She said no, so he left. I was on my way back to the house when my dad called. Said he had to get out of town, but he wanted to see me before he left…"

To make the story stick, I closed my eyes, meditating on his voice.

He arrived at the spot, his father already there with Russ. Gavin pulled over, letting the Nova rest on the side of the road, behind his father's truck. Gavin got out, unsure of what he was seeing. It was dark, but he recognized his father's truck and his voice. Russ's back was to Gavin, shielding his face. The struggle brought Hank to the ground, the man overpowering him.

"Get the fuck off my dad!" Gavin shouted.

Russ scuffled with Hank some more, Hank crying out for help. The wails brought out something carnal in Gavin. He advanced, grabbing Russ from behind, and pulling him back. Still, he couldn't see his face. The man got up, turning his anger to Gavin, leaving Hank in the dust.

Gavin was a scared teenager. A fatherless child who didn't know what to do. The gun left his waist band, pointed forward. The shot hurt his ears. He had hit Russ in the chest, killing him instantly.

Gavin's hand went limp, the gun dangling there as disbelief clouded his judgment. He wanted his grandfather, because he would know what to do. Stuck with his deadbeat dad, Hank was full of ideas.

"I gotta get out of here," Hank said, evaluating the murder scene and wanting to erase his imprint from it.

"We gotta check to see if he's alive," Gavin said.

"No, I need to leave town. Gary's gonna have my ass if I get caught up with this much dope. I'm not supposed to be up here."

"Dad!" Gavin said, tears coating his eyes, "I don't give a fuck about Gary! I just fuckin' shot a guy." He crowned his head with his hands, the gun resting on his scalp, barrel up. He took to pacing the narrow shoulder, impending abandonment coming between them.

Hank hushed his son's overactive imagination, "Son, listen to me." Gavin didn't slow down. "Hey!" He pulled his boy to a stop, "Listen to me! This isn't your fault." A tear fell down Gavin's cheek. "You had to kill him or else he was gonna kill me. That's what you're gonna tell them."

"What?"

"You tell them that it was self-defense." Hank let go of his child, "Hell, you're just a kid. They'll probably let you off with probation and community service."

"What about you?"

Hank took a step back, "I can't be here. No one can know I was here when this happened." He turned, bravely walking back to his truck, knowing Gavin still had a gun in his hands. No, Gavin wasn't going to let Hank off the hook. After Hank opened the door, Gavin got between him and the driver's seat. "Get the fuck out of my way, boy."

"You're not leaving me here to deal with this shit on my own, Dad."

"Do you want me to end up dead? That's what's gonna happen if I lose all this dope."

"Why?"

"Because I'm supposed to be hours away in Florida, delivering all this shit to some dangerous people. If he knew I was here, he'd think I was ripping him off or something."

"Are you serious? I just killed someone for you, and you have the audacity to make it seem like this is a big problem for you?"

"Get out of my way."

"Fuck you, Dad!" Hank laid his hands on him, forcing him aside. Gavin put the gun up. Unarmed, Hank knew it was time to do things Gavin's way. With his free hand, Gavin grabbed the notebook.

"What are you doing?" Hank demanded.

"Insurance. You say Gary would be pissed if he knew you were here. Well, I know this is your drug ledger." He fanned to the last entry. "It's right here, your last trip to Settlement Island. All I gotta do is show this to Gary, and your alibi is crushed." Next, he opened a duffle bag full of money. "Where'd you get all this?"

Hank only said, "You think you can blackmail me?"

Gavin ignored him, grabbing a stack of cash, "This is my fee for helping you. It should pay for a fuckin' good lawyer when I go to jail for fuckin' killing someone!"

Sirens neared the scene. Hank had one more card to play, "I'm getting in that truck. And if you shoot me, there goes your self-defense claim." Gavin only had a minute. Maybe two. The decision no longer belonged to him. Hank pushed past him, hopped in the truck, and sped away.

Alone, Gavin only had seconds to save his defense. He put the money and notebook in the bushes, knowing they wouldn't help his case. The blue and red lights lit up his face. Russ hadn't moved. Blood had streamed down the road, a nice crimson that clutched Gavin's stomach.

Gavin leaned over, throwing up from nerves.

"Drop the fuckin' weapon!" Officer Dixon shouted. Gavin complied, the gun leaving his left hand and resting on the gravel. Dixon's vendetta against Gavin wasn't there then. That would come much later. As Gavin stood, Dixon saw the fear and regret pouring through his face. "You do this?" the officer asked. Gavin gulped for air, nodding. "Is it just you here?" Gavin nodded again.

He couldn't breathe. His actions weren't a silent plea for his own life, but the compounding regret for killing an innocent man. "I'm sorry," he said. "So sorry," he cried, body shaking, knees wobbling.

Officer Dixon broke protocol and put his gun away. He was

young, too. Inexperienced. Instead of seeing a murder scene, he saw a kid melting away after committing a horrible mistake. The officer walked over and put his arms around Gavin, allowing him to cry for a moment before he had to suffer his fate.

"You're gonna be okay," he said. "You're gonna get through this."

Dixon released Gavin and sighed. He took a look at the victim, his friend's father. Dixon stumbled back, rebuking the impulse to draw his gun again. How would he tell his best friend his father was now dead?

◈

"I was then arrested, booked, Gary got me out, and now I live with that horrible day etched in my mind forever," Gavin said. He looked over at me, unaffected.

I couldn't be so cool. Hank had left Gavin when he was just a kid. Took him to school and never picked him up. That was the first strike. Leaving your son to clean up blood you shed covered every strike Hank could ever earn.

I proudly let him see how disturbed I was. "You begged him not to go, and he did. How could he do that?"

"He's an asshole," Gavin said nonchalantly.

"How could anyone expect you to believe in love or have hope after something like that?"

"Now you know why I didn't want to get close to anyone." He continued, "My crew had been there with me before the murder, and they didn't care what I did. They had my back, and so did my family. Their love for me never wavered, even if they didn't know what happened that night."

Curious, I added, "Is that why you never dated? Because holding this secret was too hard?"

"You know what it was like to date me," he scoffed. "I did everything I could to hide my past, and you still fuckin' figured it out. And you didn't grow up in Settlement Island." I could tell he didn't want to tell me the next part, "That's why I chose Ronda. She was just there for the sex. She didn't care about my past, either. Never asked about it."

"But she was so trashy," I said out of spite. "Why didn't you pick Molly or Adrienne?"

"Molly talked way too fuckin' much." He changed lanes onto I-10. Finally, we were on our way out of the city. "Adrienne was too shy. And plain."

"I'm shy and plain," I said. Today, I blended into the crowd. Ripped jeans, converse shoes, white T-shirt, hair in a ponytail. Minimal makeup because I wasn't trying to impress anyone.

"Shy, yes. Plain, hell no." Another dream escaped his lips, "When I first saw you, I knew I was in trouble."

"Please," I said while shifting my notebooks back into my lap. After my next statement, I'd get back to work, "You don't believe in love at first sight."

"You're right about that." His lips were licked, bringing out their pinkness. "But when I saw you, I was intrigued. I wanted to know you."

His tone dismantled my belief for just a second, but I knew better. Last night, if Gavin still wanted me, he would have made a move. He didn't.

"Do you regret our relationship?"

"No," his confidence was stellar. "Even if I lived another lifetime, I'd never live long enough to earn you."

He didn't want me…so why was he saying this? "I don't regret you, either."

"Good. Because we are stuck together." He shook his head as I tried to refute his words, "I meant what I said. I'm with you until we solve this."

And then what? I didn't ask Gavin this. It would complicate things further. And we didn't work…

"Thank you for being so agreeable lately."

"Agreeable?" he teased.

"Yeah. Since you've come back, you've been so easy to get along with."

"As opposed to when we were dating or just friends?"

"We were never really friends," I corrected him. "Our relationship was built on lies and secrets, which is not healthy. But you were a loving, wonderful boyfriend until I found out you were a killer."

"Then, everything changed." He didn't fret, "Now you know why I lied," he said. "It's not an excuse, but I didn't want to put that on you. Especially since my entire life is a big fuckin' red flag."

I chuckled, "An After-School Special is more like it."

He laughed for a moment, "You're too understanding."

No, I wasn't. "I should have respected your privacy, but I couldn't. My curiosity was selfish, but I just wanted to know you more."

"Because you loved me," he confirmed.

"Exactly. And you were my first."

Gavin sighed, "I should have been honest and let you make up your mind."

"I did. We broke up, you got shot, and I ran away." My nail dug into my flesh, "Then I shot Blake, which pretty much put me right in your shoes."

"You're an After-School Special, too," he teased.

"And a red flag." The casual cadence of my voice bothered me. "I'm still doing all this for Blake. To give him the justice he deserves."

"Sadly, if you really wanted to honor Blake, you'd have to shoot me."

That seemed like the obvious retribution, but it wasn't what Blake wanted. "Even though you pulled the trigger, he knew Gary and Porter were behind his father's death. And your dad's shitty act the night you shot Russ is proof of that." Yet, one thing didn't add up. "Your dad took the drugs and left, but Gary never sent Porter after him to retrieve the money and drugs he was carrying that night."

"I highly doubt Hank actually finished the delivery. He left, probably shoved all that dope into his veins, and Gary was arrested before he could cut him down. The cops combed through Gary's operation, looking for evidence, so Porter couldn't go after all the dealers that had shorted his father without looking guilty for all the drug running. His claim was he was in charge of the construction side, and he didn't have any knowledge of what was going on with the drugs."

This wasn't true. "He actually did." I opened my laptop and put in the flash drive. It took a moment, but I found the file from that year. The ledger showed the payments that came in, slowly, for the dealers who had hefty balances. Porter got the family money back. The only people who got away were the ones who had small balances, only a couple hundred dollars.

"You said the money your dad had was enough to keep him underground for a while, right?"

"It was around one-hundred thousand, easily."

"Porter would have wanted that money." I leaned back, "If it wasn't Gary's, where did he get it from?"

"Not my grandmother. She only gave him about two-hundred dollars to help out with gas to leave town." I wrote a note.

"So, he really was broke when he came to town. And he wasn't expecting such a large payout." I flipped a few pages of my notebook, "What did Hank mean when he said he had made things right with Gary for your mom?"

"I have no fuckin' clue," he said. "He's full of empty promises and threats."

I tapped the page. "If Gary didn't give him the money, maybe Maverick's killer did. Or, someone paid Hank to kill Maverick."

"Sure."

"Sure?" I said with strong investment into the lead. "Hank is involved."

"He probably is," he said matter-of-factly. "We'll see if I can hold my temper long enough to get it out of him."

"Maybe going to Tucson is a bad idea."

He lowered his glasses, "I love a good bad idea."

CHAPTER TWENTY-ONE

Tucson

"I DON'T RUN from things," Gavin said. "Hank does, and I don't want to be anything like him."

"You're nothing like your dad."

"Sometimes I wonder if I've fallen into the same shit he's in. I haven't seen him in a long time," he admitted. "Like actually see how he's been living. Where he's at with his addictions. If he regrets anything."

"Are you looking for closure?" I backtracked when he didn't have a clear answer for me. Closure was what he sought, but the allure of violence wasn't far behind. "You're not gonna kill him, are you?"

"Probably." His fingers went through his hair. A tic. Every time his fingers cut through that hair, I worried that he was cracking under the pressure to produce an outcome for me that wasn't his to give. "This is a waste of time. But it's worth a try, if you want to give it a go."

Patience was always lost on Gavin. Especially since he hated his father. However, I wouldn't run from anything, either. Even if it seemed like a bad idea. "Do you have any bargaining chips?"

"Not kicking his ass?"

If that was the case, "Let's skip Tucson," I said. He took it back, all his negativity on the matter. Too late. "We're better off just getting back to Maine and teaming up with Luke."

Gavin didn't mean to extinguish the dim candle I held for optimism. So, he corrected the course, "I'll bury the hatch long enough for you to get some answers."

"Thank you for wasting your time for me," I said gingerly.

"I'll do anything to help you."

This whimsical dedication to what I wanted held deeper roots for him. He was doing this to help himself, too. There was more behind his motives. "You can use this to your advantage. Get some closure out of it." Without the prospect of closure, Gavin wouldn't have caved in so easily. Even though he still loved me. "Closure helps both of us move on."

"He'll never give me that." Gavin's change of heart had come after some profound thinking. "He'll always do things to save his own and never apologize for it. We need to get what we can on Gary and get the fuck out."

His assessment was that Hank would be a fool to reject us if we brought up Gary. Honestly, his assumption wasn't bad. The impression that we had more cards in our deck than he did would convince Hank that we already knew who killed Maverick. Then, we'd let him hang himself.

"I like the way you think," I said. Gavin smiled, and

the car fell into silence. If we were going to see his two-timing father, I had to prepare my questions. I folded my notebooks open in my lap as I surfed through my ideas.

The more I surfed I realized Hank and Gary were very good at hiding their acquaintance. Even Hank's notebook didn't spell out the complete picture of their relationship. No bank transactions or files held both their names. Their destinations didn't intersect. They were known to each other, they had to be, but I wouldn't be able to prove it without Hank's damning testimony.

I spent a few hours just reviewing all the timelines that I knew of. Most of them were ones we had been through before, yielding nothing new. That's when I looked up and saw we were close to Phoenix. And I had nothing to show for my silence and research.

"Want some dinner?" Gavin said.

We had killed the sandwiches a couple hours ago. Gavin had pulled off into a parking lot, quietly watching me struggle through the little bit I knew about Hank based on what Gavin had told me. While I battled through my notes, he sent texts to James for updates. Back and forth, he huffed at some of the texts and didn't say much to others. By the time we arrived in Phoenix, he had hoped to have more information for me.

"James doesn't have anything for us," he said. "Gary's still underground, the streets are quiet, and dealers are keeping to themselves. He thinks they're icing him out because of me."

"They're scared of you?"

"They know Gary and I aren't on good terms, so they

don't want to do anything that will piss me off. As for Gary, they don't want to look like they're helping me out." Quiet streets weren't a bad thing. "I'm thinking In-N-Out for dinner?" he suggested.

"That sounds good." I put my things away and checked my phone. Luke had called twice. Impatience layered my voice when I heard his. "Hey, we finally get to chat."

"I know," Luke said. "What's been going on?"

I gave Luke the run down regarding Gavin, Ian, and Demi. He listened through my long explanations. So did Gavin. We fought through traffic, picking a restaurant in the very southern part of town. Luke overheard Gavin ordering us dinner.

"Where are you?"

"Phoenix," I said. "We should be back in Maine in a few days."

There were voices rumbling in the background, "Sorry, I'm out with your family."

"It seems like everyone's spending time with my family without me," I said, including Gavin in my comment. I swallowed my jealousy, "What are you guys doing?"

"We're at the clubhouse. They're having a dinner for your dad."

"Why?"

Luke continued with caution, "He's getting a reward. Big plaque. People kissing his ass, stuff like that."

My dad and family were out celebrating? "They understand I'm going through a terrible time, right?"

Luke didn't regain his confidence. "Well," he said.

Slowly, out came the other part, "You're on your way back home, and—"

The phone shuffled, and Cecilia assaulted me with, "We talked to Eloise, and she gave us the rundown. Gavin showed up, saved the day, and now you're on your way back here. Have we missed something else?"

"I've been on the run, Cecilia. For several days. From a guy who I thought was my boyfriend who teamed up with the guy who has been trying to kill me for years." I dug in, "Met some of your friends at the strip club, learned that you were a drug dealer, I think, which is both disappointing and embarrassing. And living through a few kidnapping attempts isn't easy," again, Gavin was included in my summary as a kidnapper. "Don't be so reductive, Cecilia."

"But you're okay. That's all that matters." Her response was too casual. "Your boy is bringing you back here, and then everything will be right with the world."

I charged on, "In the meantime, have you heard from Aaron?" She said something to Luke and he laughed. "Cecilia!"

"I'm done with Aaron." I asked when this happened. "I don't really know. It just feels like we've been drifting apart for a long time." Gavin handed me the food and backed the Nova into a parking space, so we could eat. "He's a great guy, but I need more."

"He's *missing*, Cecilia." Her disregard for his life and safety was a new low.

"He *left* me, Catalina. Instead of sticking around to protect me, he ran off. I don't want a man who bolts when things get hard."

She had a point there. Gavin's swift departure when I was in the hospital had led to the fracture in our relationship. The reality of him keeping secrets also brought down the hammer on what was left between us. Still, he did come all the way across the country to find me. And he was doing a great job protecting me now. Bending to whatever I wanted. "Does Dad know?" I said to distract myself.

While I waited for her response, I watched Gavin bite into his burger, eating his messy dinner with grace. He licked his fingers, savoring the salt and sauce on his skin. I couldn't look away fast enough. "Want a bite?" he offered.

"No, thank you," I replied, even though I did.

"Yeah. He's not happy about it," Cecilia said.

"Huh?" I had lost track of our conversation.

"I said Dad's not happy about my decision to end things with Aaron. Said he was good for me."

"He's a great guy," Luke said, his tone vain. With Aaron gone, he was able to build a real friendship with Cecilia. One he wouldn't want to share with her boyfriend.

"You have to say that because you're a great guy, too," she said to him. "But you've done a much better job being there for me than he ever has."

I rolled my eyes. Aaron adored my sister. Gave her whatever she wanted, despite her sharing her time and body with other men. "Does James know you're single?"

"Single adjacent," she said, "And yes. He calls me every morning and night to make sure I'm safe." Luke said something to her that I didn't catch. "Luke and James don't like each other."

"For good reason," Gavin chimed in as he took another bite.

"This doesn't concern you, Gavin." She and Luke passed another joke between them. "Okay, Kitty Cat, I need to get back to the party. Get your ass over here, so we can finally talk in person."

Right away, Cecilia. Then, we could sort through all her relationship drama, completely ignoring my own deadly problems. "I love you, and I'll see you soon."

"Bye, you two!" She hung up, not giving me a chance to say goodbye or bother Luke any further. She had become so possessive of him; I felt like I was losing my best asset and friend.

He sent me a text, saying he would call me after the party. I told him to enjoy himself and we would talk tomorrow.

Gavin noshed on some fries, phone in his other hand. "Why did you make that comment about James and Luke not liking each other?"

He stopped eating, eyes stuck to his phone, "James is still in love with your sister. He hates anyone who is trying to take what he thinks is his."

"My sister is not property. She is a person," I defended her.

"Relax, he thinks she's a goddess. His goddess." One more bite of his burger, and he was done.

"Kyle wants her, too." I nibbled on my burger, knowing that my shirt was bright, and I was clumsy.

"You can take bigger bites than that," he said.

"I don't wanna ruin my clothes."

Gavin turned and opened his bag. He tossed me a button-up shirt, "There. Now enjoy it."

"How romantic." He winked. I carefully placed the food down, put on the shirt, and closed it. "I'm surprised you're letting me eat all this messy food in here."

"Eat all you want. I'm getting my car detailed when I get back," he popped a fry, just to prove his point.

I didn't hold back. I had been starving. After inhaling my portion, Gavin smirked, "I love watching you eat."

"Why?" I said, my mouth nearly full.

He shrugged, "I just do." He went back to his phone and scrolled through the screen while he sipped his shake.

"What are you looking at?"

Gavin tilted his phone, "News articles. Seeing if there's any news on Gary."

"Anything interesting?"

"Not from the looks of it. My other informants say he's keeping a low profile because he has to go back to court in a few days. But business is still booming, even though the dealers are staying out of sight. They say he's still gunning for the guy who set him up, but he's doing it behind closed doors." Gavin scowled, "They know more, but like James's contacts, they don't want to get involved with me."

"They have nothing to fear," I said. "Nothing we are doing is hurting Gary or his business. Porter wouldn't have come out here if things back home were falling apart."

"I'm not so sure. Porter's priorities don't seem to line up with his actions." Gavin went on to explain, "Within the last week, Gary's been able to get his business in line while interrogating people about who framed him. Six months ago, his legit company and his drug deals were pretty lean, barely making ends meet. And that whole time, while dealers were scraping by, Porter was fixated on you." He spoke again, "Gary's a simple man, but he probably noticed. I don't really know where they're at with their relationship, but I do know how Gary operates. Porter be damned. Gary just wants to run his drug empire and expand his business. He'll do whatever it takes to stay out of prison long enough to see his vision through."

"My dad said two people were murdered. Did Gary do that?"

"The idiots who got shot were low-level dealers who couldn't give Gary a name. James said he left their bodies in public as a warning. He doesn't want people thinking he's gone soft."

"And these informants haven't heard from Porter?"

"Not a peep." Gavin watched as grimness pressed down on me. Ian's obsession with me put me inside even more crosshairs. "Don't worry. When we get back, I'll make sure he doesn't know where you are."

I sat back and decided to accept Gavin's determination. I also accepted my father's advice to not concern myself with these new murders, since they were at the hands of Gary, not his demented son. Or at least I couldn't until we spoke with Hank. I set my sandwich down and made a note in my notebook to ask Hank about Gary's potential proximity to these murders. How close he actually was.

"When do you want to go see your dad?" I said.

"Once we get to Tucson, we're going straight over there."

I thought there would be more involved. "Don't you need to get his address?"

Gavin pulled up his map. "Paula gave it to me before I left."

I nodded. "What's the plan? We rush into his house and force him to tell us the truth?" Then I remembered the notebook, producing it for Gavin to see. "We also have this. Once he sees we have it, he'll know that we're onto him."

"Something like that," he started the Nova. "Ready?"

I hadn't finished my meal, but the sun laid heavy in the distance. We had to get going if we wanted to get to Hank tonight.

❧

Hank's neighborhood looked like a war-torn settlement. His neighbors had put up fences, some with old cars and rusted projects sitting in the yard. Others had brick houses with roses and the makings of a garden. Everyone was barely getting by, dodging unemployment and eviction at a given notice. I swallowed my pity for Gavin's father. We weren't here to rescue him. We'd take from him and be on our way.

Gavin pulled around a corner and stopped at a brown house with two broken-down vehicles, a work truck, and a hole in the fence. Grocery bags tangled into two of the cacti guarding the outline of a walkway.

"This is it?" I said.

Gavin looked past me at the house. "Yeah. His last wife took his other house, or so he says." He pushed his car door open and slammed it.

I jumped out, chasing him through the yard to the

entryway of his father's *new* house. He pounded his fists with no regard to how late it was. "I don't think he's home." Gavin pumped his fist against the wood again, almost splintering it.

One of the neighbors' porch lights came on. An older Mexican man peered over the low fence, asking why we were making so much noise. In Spanish, I told him that we were looking for Hank. He said Hank had left a few days ago, but he should be back this evening. Before Hank left, he had asked the neighbor to keep an eye on the place. The neighbor said he didn't care about Hank's property, and he hoped he would get evicted. So many flies buzzing in and out, the smell was awful, so on. I relayed this to Gavin. He stepped back from the front door, examining it. Swiftly, he went around to the backyard, me tagging along close behind.

"Should we be doing this?" I said. He didn't entertain me with an answer.

In the cover of night, Gavin pulled out a pocket knife, the blade springing free. This window, to whatever room it led to, gave the best option for entry. He pulled off the screen, pulling the glass to the side. "You good?" he said to me. I nodded.

Gavin climbed in first, checking the room. Then, he put out his hand, guiding me inside. We stood on a twin-sized bed, the springs buckling under our weight. This had to be someone's bedroom, I thought. "Watch out for needles," he said.

"Your dad uses needles? For what?"

"Shooting up." My top lip turned up, and my feet

stayed planted. Gavin put on his phone light and walked to the doorway. A light came on, and I felt relieved. No needles grazed my shoes.

This room didn't hold Gavin's interests. He went to the hallway and turned on another light. "Have you ever been here before?"

Gavin said, "No," as he turned on another light. Then another one. Soon, the house was completely illuminated. "I don't see any needles, so we should be good."

This was excellent news, but only for a short while. Like Paula, Hank had a bit of a hoarding problem. Each room had a narrow pathway to the other, items and junk lining the carpet. The stretch of rotting food and mildew sang in the air. "What's your plan?" I said while breathing through my mouth.

He glanced around, "If he's involved in Maverick's death, we're gonna find something here."

His idea held value. There were stacks of papers, trash, clothes, and vehicle parts throughout the house. Before we started, Gavin opened the curtains slightly, stilling himself for a few minutes. Then, he pulled the curtains back and let me know that everything seemed clear. Despite our encounter with Hank's neighbor, no one cared if we were trespassing or not.

"I'll take the bedroom," Gavin said.

That left me in this room, I assumed. The living room was dwarfed by various things, boxes containing most of the space. I opened the first one sitting next to the couch. A few flies buzzed past my face. Gavin reappeared, "Be careful." He handed me a slip from an exterminator for a bed bug treatment.

"I'm done." Dirt was one thing; bed bugs were another problem I didn't care to deal with. I went to the sliding glass door, opening it and standing in the backyard that was mostly trash and dead grass.

I sat down on the concrete step, wondering how I had landed here. Not just with Gavin, but here in this situation, like I had many times over the past year and a half. Despite the how, I had to press on. The backyard wouldn't be fruitful. Putting my trust into Hank's graveyard of trash, praying for something redeeming, was not the way to handle this.

Gavin sat down next to me, "The receipt was from six months ago, if that helps."

"Bed bugs can live up to a year without eating," I replied.

He tossed the receipt on the ground and nudged me. "Hey, we need to get through this. I'm gonna keep looking. If you want to hang out in the car, I understand."

No, I wouldn't be a coward. "Needles. Bed bugs." I got up, "What else could be in there?"

He shrugged, "That big bag of cash my dad had when he left."

Looking around, I was sure that money went into his veins or up his nose. "That would be fantastic."

Gavin stood, "Let's just hunt around for an hour, and see what we can find."

Against my better judgement, I nodded. We went back into the house, and I resumed my work in the living room, begrudgingly. Seemed safer here. I reopened the box and pulled out some papers. It was a stack of bills for someone named Camilla Ortega.

"Hey, Gavin?" He shouted back. "Do you know anyone by the name of Camilla Ortega?"

He came to the living room again, "That was his third wife, I think." Gavin took the bill and looked at the date. "This one is from two months ago."

"He's living with her?" I said.

"I wouldn't put it past him," Gavin said, handing the document back to me. "He tends to go out of town a lot, spending all his money on drugs and hookers. Living here would give him a place to stay for cheap."

"And you're sure this is his house?"

"It was a few months ago." He paused, "He asked Paula for some money, and she asked where he was living, so she could mail a check. He gave her this address."

"Mailing a check is a terrible idea. He could use it for identity theft."

"Brianna tore up the check and refused to send him any money."

My lip ticked up into a slight grin. Gavin excused himself back into the master bedroom. I followed, wanting to get a look at what he was up against. The action proved to be the right move.

The bedroom had been towering with even more boxes, the ones on the floor soiled with an oil or liquid. I thought the kitchen was the source of the spoiled food smell, but this room proved to be ten times worse. Much worse.

I grabbed Gavin's arm. "What is it?" he said.

"That smell."

"It's pretty fuckin' bad, I know."

No, it wasn't that. "It's a dead body."

"How would you know?"

"My dad's a doctor. He did a house call a few months ago where the resident had died, and no one noticed. He said the smell was suffocating." Which this smell was. I pulled Gavin back and searched the room, forcing myself to head in the direction of the closet.

The closer I got, the more saturated the boxes were.

And so was the bottom of the closet doors.

Gavin relieved me of my duties and took on the task of opening them. I thought he was going to faint, but he recovered.

Flies buzzed past us, filling the ceiling above. Below, on the ground, was a mangled body far past the early stages of decomposition.

We gave up our search at the same time, rushing out the front door. Gavin bent over heaving while I pulled out my phone, calling 9-1-1. "We..." I took a breath, "We found a body." I asked Gavin for the address and he passed it to me in between his heaving.

The operator asked me several questions and I politely declined to answer any of them because I didn't know any-thing. Nothing that would help here, that is. Gavin grabbed the phone and hung up.

"We need to get out of here," he said.

"No," I protested. He placed his fingers around my wrist, but I wouldn't let him move me. "We didn't do this."

"That doesn't matter, Catalina."

"Yes, it does."

"We just broke into the house of a deadbeat drug dealer and found a dead body. We don't need this right now!"

This was a gift in disguise. "Once the police show up, they're going to want to talk to Hank about this."

"And his neighbors have probably told him that his house is swarming with cops."

"Exactly! If they did, he'll probably come home to check it out. So, we stake out, and we wait for him to arrive."

"You've lost your fuckin' mind!"

I had to admit, I had gone crazy, but this had to be the best option given our circumstances. "He's gonna come back, Gavin." The sound of sirens grew near. "Trust me. This is how we find your father."

He ran his hands through his hair, "Fuck!"

I laced my fingers in his, waiting for the blue and red lights to come closer. And closer. And closer.

CHAPTER TWENTY-TWO

Stakeout

"How are you two related to the victim?" the detective asked us. I found it odd that he would interview me and Gavin together. My only indication for his decision was he didn't seem to think we were involved. Mostly because the neighbor, who was also being interviewed, had mentioned he had never seen us before. Add in the Maine license plate on the Nova, Gavin's Maine driver's license, and my California one, and we were looking less and less guilty.

"My dad, Hank Scott, lives here, I think," Gavin said. His voice was solid, no wavering. Countless encounters with police had made him confident in his words. "I picked her up in California and drove through here to see my dad."

"Did he know you were coming?"

"No. We're not really on good terms."

"Which is why you broke into his house?"

Gavin nodded, "He's a drug addict. He had told his neighbors he was out of town, but I thought maybe he was holed up in there, shooting up." I sighed. Hearing how dysfunctional Hank was became a godsend for our case. The police had found plenty of evidence of drug use, helping our story. "My mother died of a heroin overdose when I was a kid. My dad has dealt drugs here and there for most of his life."

"Yeah, we're aware of your dad." The detective handed both me and Gavin back our licenses. "The victim has been in and out of drug treatment facilities for some time, too."

"Do you know who it is?" I said.

"I can't say for sure. But this is Camilla's residence. She was reported missing by her family out of Houston six weeks ago, but we didn't have any reason to bust down the door. Every time we came by to speak with Camilla or Hank, no one was home."

"So, what happens next?" I said.

"We're going to detain you two just a little longer." He pointed to some lawn furniture, "Take a seat."

Absolutely not. Gavin and I chose to stand, an officer keeping us company. The scene was busy, guarded by a ring of crime scene tape. The medical examiner went in and out of the house, talking to our detective and then going back into the house.

Charlie had picked the most convenient time to call. I shot a text to him, saying that I was busy. He texted back, saying he had made it to Phoenix. The bikers were on their way to see Hank as well based on some digging they had done. I told him not to come because the police were onto Hank for something else. And I didn't want him to get caught up in all this. After the text, I put my phone away, making sure the officer didn't see it.

Then came waiting.

We stood, in silence, until the detective came back, joined by an older black female detective. Her name was Jones, and she would escort me to her police car to answer some questions. I agreed, and Gavin was escorted to another police car. Unafraid, I decided to stick to most of the truth, opening myself up to gain her trust, in hopes she would give up some information about Hank.

She put me in the seat next to her, "Ms. Payton, I'm Detective Jones, and I have a few questions for you." I nodded, and she continued, "You and Mr. Scott have traveled here from Maine?"

"California. He drove to California from Maine about a week ago. We decided to go back to Maine together."

"Why did he come to California? Did he see his father before he saw you?" The first question required a bent answer. One that didn't involve any backstory. "He was thinking about going to school at Stanford. We were friends when I lived in Maine, so he wanted to visit me before he went back home." Now, the next question. "I'm not sure if he saw his father before he came to visit me. You should ask him directly because I don't want to assume anything."

She nodded but didn't write anything down. "You and Mr. Gavin Scott were going back to Maine together? Why are you traveling across the country with him if your residence, your life, is in California?"

"I was gonna visit my family," I said quickly.

"Are you traveling in the same car?" I nodded. "And you plan on returning to California after your visit?" Again, I nodded, "How were you planning on getting back to Maine?"

"In the Nova, probably."

"That's Mr. Scott's car?"

"Yes."

"He's bringing you back to California?"

"Yeah, he promised he would."

She started writing, "And he still lives in Maine?"

"Yes." The flow of questions made me slip. "I mean, I might come back in the Nova. It just depends."

"On what?"

"A number of things."

She put her notepad on the dashboard, "Catalina, we don't think you and your friend had anything to do with Ms. Ortega's death."

"So, you think Camilla is the one who…" I said, interrupting her.

"More than likely. It's going to take some time for the medical examiner to make a positive ID, but based on the size of the body, the missing person report, and this being her residence, we feel pretty confident it's her. Now," she put her arms around her chest, "why are you lying to me?" I stumbled around with reasons for the inconsistencies in my fragile story. She paused me, "Like I said, you're not a suspect. So, just be honest."

Her kind demeanor was an act. A very good one. "What exactly do you want to know? I've answered all of your questions."

She didn't compromise her suspicions. And I decided not to yield. My own investigation couldn't afford it. Jones settled on, "Tell me your timeline from when you met with Gavin Scott until today."

I hesitated, "Is he in trouble?"

"You tell me."

"He had nothing to do with this," I said with defense. "I thought you said neither one of us is in trouble."

She tapped her pen against the pad, "We want to make sure your story matches his."

They thought Gavin was guilty. I knew he wasn't, and I'd protect him at all costs. "Our stories will match. We've been together for the last several days."

"Again," she prepared to write a statement, "tell me your timeline."

"He came to visit me in California because he was thinking about going to Stanford."

"When was that?"

"A couple days ago. Closer to a week."

"And you spent the entire time together?" The vacancy in my answer placed one of her cards on the table. "I'm already aware of who Gavin Scott is." My brows furrowed. "We did a background check on the two of you." So, she knew about Blake, too.

I tightened my grip around the fragments of my slipping composure. "You know about me?" She nodded. Giving her affirmation, how was I supposed to explain myself, a killer? How would I save myself from being persecuted for this death, too?

The panic rumbling in my stomach vanished when

her hand touched mine. "Despite what happened last year, I don't think you did this."

"Then why are you pressing me so hard?"

"Hank Scott is a wanted man. He's been hiding from us for months, pending some serious drug charges we have against him."

I dared to ask about Gary, but that was dangerous territory. "The only thing I know about Hank is what I heard when I was living in Maine. The whole town had it out for him because of the drugs."

"That's another reason for Hank to hide."

"What do you mean?"

"Ms. Payton, let's stay on topic. I need to know—"

"No, no, no, what do you mean?" Her lips were pursed. "You know something about Gary Porter?"

Jones regretted this line of questioning. But not for long. "I haven't heard that name in years." Her head tilted toward the car holding Gavin. "Does your friend have any association with Gary?"

"No." This answer wasn't a gamble. I trusted Gavin and what he told me. "There is something, though." I overlooked any details that would harm Gavin. If they were looking for a way to jam him up, I wouldn't be it. But I told her about what was going on in Settlement Island. How Gavin came to me because he was worried that Gary getting out of jail would hurt us, along with everyone else in Settlement Island. And how we had come to Tucson to check on Hank, since he was a known associate of Gary's. Gavin thought his dad was back on drugs, and we broke in.

She wrote down every single word I said, not para-phrasing, but direct statements. Then came her evaluation, "Before Gary Porter went to jail, he had a network of drug dealers here. Not very large, but enough to get our attention. We suspect he may have been involved with some of the larger drug organizations in the state, but our witnesses and informants never gave us enough to put anyone away."

"The Porters have a way of making people disappear." I told her about the most recent murders, for which she continued to write more details down. It seemed as though I was a lottery of information, yet I didn't learn anything new from her. Once I finished, she told me to hold tight. She left the car and I opened my phone. Charlie had ceased his text messages. I sent him a quick one, asking to meet up. Detective Jones opened the door and told me to hop out.

Gavin was still talking to the detective we had met with before. He wasn't in cuffs, which was a good thing. He leaned against the car, arms folded, nodding at the officer as they chatted back and forth.

"Okay, Catalina. Before you go, I wanted to share a few things with you."

She explained that we were not considered suspects or persons of interest. However, because of Hank's shady past, they were curious to know how we had found the body buried in the closet.

"My dad's a doctor." I explained how we discovered the body; the flies, putrid ooze, and all. This led to her writing more things down.

"The body was covered?"

"Yes." Then, my shoulders slouched, "Someone knew she was dead."

"That's our theory."

"So, they killed her?"

She stopped writing. "We can't discuss that at the moment."

"Hank was living here," I blurted. "He did something to her?"

"Why do you think Hank is involved?"

I needed to stop talking, "I don't know anything about Hank, other than what I told you. I don't know about Camilla, either. I'm just speculating."

"Based on what?"

"Based on nothing. Just my own speculations."

She finished her notes and gave me a card. A step forward, "Catalina, I appreciate your transparency regarding Gary Porter and Hank Scott." Her tone turned motherly, "Be careful. Gary Porter's a dangerous felon with a far reach." The warning ended with a need. "If you hear from Hank, or if you remember anything else, let me know. You're free to go."

I thanked her, my eyes planted on Gavin. He had wrapped up his interrogation with a handshake. A warm one.

Gavin and I met in the middle, "You okay?" he said as his hands rubbed my shoulders.

"Yeah. I think I may have incriminated your father." Gavin tilted his head toward the Nova. We stepped under the crime scene tape, and he let me in the car. Once his door shut, he had more to tell me. "My dad's been incriminating himself."

"How?"

"Detective Smith over there told me that my dad's been under investigation for some drug dealing out of Texas. Police found some drugs in his truck, and they filed possession charges against him. Since then, Tucson police have been watching him because they think he's been dealing with a cartel down in Mexico. They've been looking for him since around the time Aaron went missing."

This unfortunate death had developed into an incredible clue. "Do you think…Is it possible…Are Aaron and Hank working together?"

"No fuckin' way," Gavin said. "Aaron hates Hank just as much as I do."

Hatred aside, we had to look at the facts. "They both went missing around the same time, right when Gary got out of jail. Now, we can't say Hank disappeared because of Gary, but Gary has to be the reason Aaron left town." He didn't interrupt, which was his way of supporting my curiosities. "One of these three people is the common denominator for the other two. Once we talk to Hank, we'll know which one."

He tapped his lip, "I like your idea about staking out until my dad gets here."

"I don't think he was living in that house," I said. "It would be impossible to stand the smell in that bedroom."

Gavin pointed to a corner of the backyard, "There's a broken-down motorhome over there. I bet that's where he was sleeping." He started the Nova and pulled it away from the crime scene, turning down the side street, and back around. We faced the intersection between Hank's street and the main road. "The other side of the street is a dead end. If he comes back tonight, he'll have to drive past us." Smart. "And we can watch the crime scene unfold."

"Thinking about sneaking back in once they're done?"

"Hell yeah." Gavin pulled out his phone and dimmed the light. "Dim the light on your phone, too." I complied. He shut the car off and pushed the seat back.

It was after nine o'clock. If Hank's neighbor was right, we should see him at any moment. "Should you call your dad to see where he is?"

"Nah. He hasn't answered any of my calls. Or texts." The distance didn't bother Gavin. Not like it would if it were my dad reaching out to him. I sent a text to my family, letting them know I was okay. Eloise had been added to the group chat, and she had a few ideas regarding my relationship with Gavin that created an uproar. "Your aunt has a lot to say."

Gavin had been reading over my shoulder. I pressed the phone to my chest. "Excuse you!"

"I told you to dim your phone."

"I did." He grabbed it and turned the light down even more. "Happy?"

"Yes." Gavin kicked off his boots and put one leg up, "I don't wanna see my dad."

"He's not gonna want to see us, either. We just sent the police to his house, and they are pulling his dead ex-wife out of the closet." The irony; his secrets were literally in the closet. "Do you think he killed Camilla?"

Gavin watched the investigators. The medical examiner had retrieved a stretcher from the van and it was brought to the front door. "They're bringing her out?"

"That's what it looks like." I asked my question again.

"Did he kill her?" His pause lasted too long. "I don't think so. I mean, he made me kill Russ." That was a cowardly move.

"Did he ever put his hands on you or your mom?" His nails dug into his flesh, confirming his answer. "I'm sorry."

"He said it only happened once when my mom was so high, she went crazy. I don't believe him, though."

Reluctantly, I said, "What about you?"

"Only a few times before I was strong enough to fight back." Gavin pointed to the scene. My eyes trained on him, reading into his expression. He remained steady in his interest in Camilla's fate. Blue eyes caught me staring, "They're bringing her out."

I looked ahead. Two men carried the black bag and put it on the stretcher, belting it into place. She was wheeled across the barren front yard to the van, the medical examiner walking behind while on the phone.

"Just like that, it's over," I said.

Gavin checked the rearview mirror and then his phone. "It's almost ten."

"Think he's gonna stand us up?"

"He's probably on his way to Mexico." Gavin groaned, "I don't want to leave until we interrogate him."

"Then we stay as long as it takes." My answer surprised him. "If anything, you can get some closure."

"We're past closure at this point." Detective Jones

walked to her police car. "What did you tell her?" After I shared my account, he chuckled, "Our stories were almost identical. That's part of the reason why they let us go."

"Our alibi was pretty much see-through," I said.

He agreed, "But there was no way we did it, so they had to let us go. Plus, our stories matching helps our case. We're free and clear from any future charges, too."

Silently, we contemplated the detectives' banter. So jovial after finding a gruesome death. They had spent most of their time outside grilling us, not embroiled in the flies and smell beating down the people inside.

"I've seen more dead bodies than anyone should," Gavin said.

"Me, too."

We didn't say anything else for a while as the detectives went to more neighbors' homes, asking questions. I yawned, leaning my head against the seat. I checked my phone, and it was after midnight.

"I don't think your dad's coming home."

"Maybe someone tipped him off."

"Who?"

"I know you think his neighbors hate him, but they may have their reasons for helping him out."

"How so?"

"They might be customers."

That was a fair guess. I tried to stretch out, unable to spread my legs completely. "Should we get a hotel room?"

"I wasn't planning on it."

"At all?"

His head rolled to my side, "Not tonight. I thought we

would talk to my dad, then drive through the night and get to our next destination before we rested. The sooner we get to Maine, the better."

"Detective Jones," I said, "wanted to know how I was going to get back to California after my trip to Maine."

"I'll drive you back."

"That's a very long drive."

"I don't care." His voice was supportive without any regrets. "I owe you for deciding to come all this way for me."

"And myself," I corrected him. "I have some business to tend to as well."

"Noted," he mocked me, slightly. "You were fine until I came back into your life."

Unknowingly dating one of Ian's guys didn't make me fine. Naïve, of course. But not fine. "If Hank doesn't show up, what should we do next?"

"We get back on the property, this time getting into the trailer." Gavin's lashes tempted him to sleep. The blinks were growing closer, shorter pauses between them.

I relieved my feet of my shoes. My knees curled up as much as they could, my head resting on my right arm. It was still warm at night, creating a nice cocoon around me. I watched the scene wind down. Detectives stuck to their cars, venturing away to talk through their notes with one another.

The night winded down. The body was gone. The detectives left. The crime scene tape stayed up. Two uniformed officers leaned against a cruiser, talking over coffee. They were waiting for something. Or someone.

I turned to say something to Gavin, but his eyes were closed. They stayed closed for over a minute, giving me the impression that he was asleep. I turned up the light on my phone and tried to see if I could find anything online about Camilla. I thought I found an article where she was accused of running from the police, but I couldn't be sure since I didn't have a photo of her. And her body was unrecognizable.

Gavin's breathing deepened. No need for any black-n-white flicks to aid him in sleeping. We were so unaffected by death, it was alarming. Even I struggled to stay awake. Gavin made sleep look so good.

I put my phone on the dashboard and accepted the notion that we weren't getting back behind that tape tonight. Sleeping in the car for a few hours would reward us with a window of opportunity. It had to. The universe owed us. It should have pity on us.

My lungs took in a deep breath. My eyes ached for rest. My head nestled into the corner of the seat. I didn't bother with relaxing. I'd manage with whatever sleep I got.

⦕

Gavin shifted next to me. My body had found his sometime last night. Now, my head rested on his shoulder, comforting me enough to enjoy more sleep than I thought was possible.

A low rumble from a large engine trailed down the street toward us. Gavin heard it, too. We pulled our weary bodies upright, seeking the sound that had awakened us.

It was a tractor trailer, stopping short of the turn off to

Hank's street. The sun was barely up, hiding the identity of the driver.

Had we been lucky?

"That's him," Gavin said, brushing his fingers through his hair as he looked in the mirror. He opened his door, slamming it to meet me on my side. The door opened, drawing in a soft morning breeze. His hand came out. "Are you ready to meet Hank?"

CHAPTER TWENTY-THREE

Hank

I HAD NEVER seen anything like this. Hank jumped out of the truck, unsure about what he was seeing. Police had taped off his house; crime scene yellow never meant anything good. His blue-gray eyes mirrored his son's. Everything else was different. He was taller than Gavin, slightly. Hair dark brown and to his shoulders, brows thinner than Gavin's. Husky, pouting pink lips.

Gavin looked like a model and his father looked like a rock star. Black leather jacket, thick leather cuffs on both wrists. The tattoos hid all his track marks. He looked healthier than I thought. Stronger than all the other drug addicts I had met.

But he was no match for his son.

Hank didn't stand a chance.

Gavin wound up, clocking Hank straight in the jaw. My hands went over my lips. His father absorbed the blow, his back going flush against the truck's steel. Gavin huffed, ready for round two.

"Did you kill her?" he demanded.

"What are you talkin' about?" Hank said, his voice low and grainy like gravel.

"Camilla. We found her body last night, stuffed in a fuckin' closet."

Hank's brows didn't crease. Nor did he seem surprised. "Nah, I didn't kill her."

"How did she get in the closet?" I said. He didn't say a peep. "There were boxes in front of the doors, hiding her. Did you do that?" He didn't budge.

Gavin slammed his fist down again, hitting Hank in his jaw. "Answer the question!"

"Fuck you!"

Gavin was mid-hit when Hank grabbed his fist and landed one of his own. His son stepped back, and Hank rushed him, knocking him down to the dirt. They wrestled around, punching one another. I wasn't sure who was getting the upper hand.

"Gavin, stop!" I said. If this went on, they were bound to gain the attention of the police.

Neither one of them slowed down. Rolling around, Hank fought dirty, reaching for Gavin's face. In a last effort to win, Gavin elbowed him, and got on top. His punches hit Hank in the face. He had nowhere to go.

I had joked about Gavin having rabies before. This time, he lived up to it.

Each blow was fierce, dedicated, and cold. "Gavin, enough!" I said. His father wheezed, growing tired of the assault but unable to put his arms up to save his face.

I had to do something.

The moment my hands grabbed Gavin's shoulders, I expected him to throw me off. Instead, he turned, heaving hard, darkness in his eyes. "This is not who you are!" I said.

My words broke his violent trance. He dropped his fists and got up. Hank rolled onto his side, his face broken. He may have been a monster, but Hank was still his father. And a person.

I went back to the Nova and grabbed a bottle of water and one of my T-shirts. "Here," I said as I poured water onto the shirt and wiped the blood from his lips and face.

He took the cloth from me, "Thanks." Soon, the bloody garment was tossed onto the ground. Hank waited until Gavin backed up several feet before climbing up with my help. A sound mistake when I saw his blood on my arm.

Gavin had taken a walk, leaving me to manage his drug addicted dad on my own.

Some friend.

Hank went to his truck and yanked the door open, his back to me. "That was a bit much," I said to Hank. He faced me, a joint hanging from his battered lips. He lit it up, drawing in as much smoke as he could until his lungs would have burst. The smoke bellowed from his nose and mouth, he offered some to me. "No thanks."

"How do you know him?" he said.

Judging by the way he asked, I knew Gavin had never mentioned me to Hank. This was probably for the best. I held onto the brilliant idea and shielded my identity. "From Settlement Island."

"What the fuck is he doing all the way over here?"

This answer was best kept unsaid. "He was traveling

through." Another scan down the road, Gavin was still nowhere. "He shouldn't have hit you," I said to gain some kind of understanding with him. He wouldn't like me once he knew who I was. However, kindness might be enough to persuade him to tell me something valuable.

"He's always had issues with his temper. But he took it too far this time." Hank's hand shook as he gulped down another puff on his weed. "He can't fuckin' accuse me of killing Camilla."

"I mean, someone killed her. Or hid her body," I reasoned.

"I'm not a killer," Hank said. "Gavin sure as fuck is." The sentence slipped off his tongue like venom. He was a threat. Much worse than the letter had spelled out. "Did he tell you he fuckin' killed my best friend over drugs?"

That wasn't the story. It was a lie, one that was said to damage Gavin's reputation and absolve Hank of any wrongdoing. "No, he didn't mention it."

"Yeah, he fuckin' shot him because Russ caught him selling drugs on the side of the road." Hank nodded vividly, stretching to make his story more plausible.

The lies piled one on the other, tipping the stack over to make Hank look more suspicious. I could correct him, or I could see if he would incriminate himself. The latter sat better with what he deserved.

"I didn't know Gavin sold drugs," I said in a low tone, like I was ashamed for him.

"He did back then." Hank threw his hand into his hair, much like how Gavin did at times. "He's always been a real fuck-up." He kept going on and on.

"When was the last time you saw Gavin?" I said to slow the insult train.

Hank took another drag and put the remainder of his joint out on his boot. "I mean, why would he think I would kill Camilla?"

"It looks like you did." The more he insisted he didn't kill her, the more he seemed guilty.

"She ODed."

"And you stuffed her in the closet?"

"Why are you fuckin' askin' me this? Who the fuck are you?" he said.

"I'm Catalina. And you're Hank, Gavin's father. I've heard about you."

"You're *the* Catalina." Hank sat back, "My mom told me about you. You dated my son, didn't you?"

My cover was blown. "Yeah, but we're not together anymore."

"And he didn't tell you about Russ?" His obsession with Gavin and Russ was becoming uncomfortable.

"No. He's big on secrets."

"It's a good thing you broke up with him," Hank said, closing the truck door. He motioned to the house, still guarded by police officers who hadn't noticed the big fight between Gavin and his dad. "What the fuck am I supposed to do now?"

"You can tell them the truth about Camilla," I said.

"They would never believe me." His concern turned to accusations. "You tell them anything?"

"We don't know anything," I said.

"Then how did they end up here? You found Camilla, and you called the police?"

I shrugged, "She was dead! What were we supposed to do?"

"Why the fuck were you in my house?"

A fair question. "We came to check on you. Gary, Porter's dad, got out of jail, and Gavin was worried about you."

"Bullshit! He came here to jam me up with Gary. Probably tryin' to pin shit on me."

Maybe a little sympathy would help rein him in, "I lived in Settlement Island. I've heard of the Porters and how bad they are. They've killed a lot of people, and I told Gavin we should stop by to check on you before we went back."

"*You* wanted to check on me? You don't even know me."

"You're his dad," I said, sweetening my answer with a smile. "I know you guys obviously hate each other, but you need to be careful. Gary's on a war path, and he's been stacking up bodies."

Hank crossed his arms, "What makes you think he wants to come after me?"

Either he was playing me, or his question was genuine. To push up my appearances of sincerity, I said, "Porter and Gavin have beef. I figured you and Gary aren't on good terms, either." I paused, and he just taunted me with his silence. "You know Gary's looking for the person who framed him, right?"

"Of course, I fuckin' know." The attitude was getting old. "Again, why do you think I did it?"

Another shrug. "I don't know who framed him, so I'm not ruling anyone out." More convincing was needed, "You're a drug user, and he sells drugs. Maybe you guys crossed paths when you were buying drugs from him."

"That's all you got on me?"

Beating around the bush was harder than it should be, "You also sold drugs for him until you left Maine for good. Which happened around the same time he went to jail."

Hank's frown showed he was working things out. "What exactly do you want?"

"Why do you keep asking me questions without really answering any of mine?" I said loudly. His paranoia and dodgy behavior were warranted, I guess. But he was projecting it in the wrong place.

Hank stepped up, "I can do whatever the hell I want. You broke into my house." Invading his space had brought on this attack. I could use this, if he got out of hand. "You guys were in there looking for drugs or something?"

"No," I said.

"Then why are you here?"

This circular line of questioning wouldn't yield unless I did something about it. My sigh made him narrow his eyebrows, "We shouldn't have broken into your house. Or called the cops when we found the body." I took a breath, "But you know things are only going to get worse, Hank." He tilted his head, laughing. "I'm trying to help you, and you're laughing?" Brokenness for Gavin possessed me. "Everyone was right about you," I started. "You don't care about Gavin or the fact that your relationship with Gary has destroyed his life!"

"His life?" Hank's laugh grew in size, "That boy…"

"…was just six when his mother died of a drug overdose. And nine when you abandoned him at school." The flood of memories kept coming, "And seventeen when he shot and killed Russ for you."

"You said he didn't tell you about that."

I bucked up, "He did."

Hank paused, intimidation stepping between us. "Then you know about my deal with Gary?"

"What deal?"

"Are you playing games with me?"

"No." At least not anymore.

"You didn't mention your connection with Gary." The drugs hadn't dulled his mind from searching for a way to jam me up. "I heard about you killing Blake." What did that have to do with—"Yeah, news from Settlement Island travels all over." He became more determined, "You're here for the money, right? All that cash I took that night Gavin got locked up?"

"I'm sure that money's all gone."

Hank looked down the street, "No, Gavin wants it. Or he'll settle for turning me into the cops, so they know the real story about what happened that night." He was talking so fast, I couldn't keep up. "I'm not going back."

He opened the truck door. I expected him to flee, but instead, he was grabbing onto me.

"What are you doing?" Hank rustled in the cab as he latched onto me. "I'm not going anywhere with you!"

"I'm not taking you anywhere." He struggled to keep me in place while he hunted for something. "Just need to make a quick phone call to Gary to see if your story checks out."

I was wrong. Gary and Hank were in touch. And I needed to get out of here. Now.

I had been here before with numerous assailants. But this time, I was smarter. I dug my nail into Hank's bruised face, the pain causing him to recoil. Then, I jetted, running toward the direction Gavin had gone. "Gavin!" I yelled, again and again. "Gavin!" I screamed.

He emerged from sitting on a rock on the edge of someone's yard. "What did he do?"

My arms thrusted around him, "We need to get out of here!"

The allure of fighting his father again rose. But I tugged him another way.

No more explaining was needed. Gavin put me behind him as we advanced toward his car. By the time we were in range of the Nova, Hank had fired up his truck, drawing the attention of the police. A hat and dark glasses covered his face, leaving them to wonder who was behind the wheel. I stayed focused on safety. We got in, and Gavin quietly drove us away from the scene.

My hair was wet from the shower. Gavin would take his afterward. Now, he was rinsing the blood from his hands. His ribs were bruised, but his face was perfect. Hank looked like a mess, prompting me to wonder if the police had been informed regarding their fight. For now, our phones were quiet, and we were hiding out at the Omni, a treat from my dad.

"And you're sure he wanted you to talk to Gary?" Gavin said while he stood in the doorway of the bathroom.

I brushed my teeth and then answered, "Yes," I said. "To confirm my story." My fingers grazed his bruised knuckles. "You shouldn't have hit him, Gavin. But he kinda deserved it."

"He totally deserved it," he said nonchalantly.

I asked him to step aside, and he did. He flopped down on the bed next to me. "He's sharp, though. I started with a lie and he ended up seeing right through me."

"*To be a good liar you have to know when people are lying to you*," he recited. "Or some shit like that."

"Where did you hear that? A Hallmark greeting card?"

He laughed, "What kind of Hallmark greeting cards are you reading?" Gavin continued, "My dad used to say that."

"Such good advice," I mumbled. The day's events left me puzzled. "I was wrong. Hank's not hiding from Gary." My nail dug into the blanket, a tiny line of red blood outlining my nail. I thought I had gotten it all out.

Gavin sat in front of me, pulling my body closer to his. My legs crossed, and his knees bent, closing the space between us. "Are you okay?"

"Yeah, I'm fine." He raised his brows, "Seriously, he freaked me out, but he didn't hurt me." His fingers grazed my arms, then he slouched. "He had nothing but bad things to say about you," I said. "And he totally twisted the whole story with Russ, like he was a saint and you're a demon." Gavin gave me some long blinks. "He needs help."

"I shouldn't have left you alone with him." His fingers recoiled into a fist, "He just made me so mad."

"Because of Camilla?"

"And everything else." His arms rested on his knees, my hands planted in my lap. "He was just using her for money and a place to stay. He didn't love her, like he didn't love my mom." I started to interject, but he railroaded me. "I always thought my anger came from all the trauma I've experienced. Losing my mom, my grandfather, and shooting Russ. But today I finally saw it…the source of all my hatred and pain." He took a moment to think, "It's my dad."

I had known this for some time. All the outbursts and desperation to get better were in vain. Gavin would never be completely healed until he found a way to deal with Hank.

"How do you feel now that you almost killed him?"

"Horrible." I reached out and pulled his hands into mine. "After the adrenaline fell off, I regretted hitting him, even though he fuckin' deserved it." Gavin's expression became sullen, "I replayed how I would handle seeing him again. How I would give him a piece of my mind. And today, I just…" he swallowed, "I just went crazy."

"You did," I said honestly.

"That was embarrassing. I'd understand if you were afraid of me for the rest of our lives."

Anger, much like fear, only has power if you let it control you. Anger had controlled Gavin, but I wasn't afraid for myself. "I'm not afraid of you but rather afraid for you." My next words brought him some solace, "When I told you to stop, you did."

"You brought me back." He rephrased, "I wasn't going to kill him. But the moment I heard your voice, I realized what I had done. And something snapped in my brain. I didn't want you or anyone else to see me like that." He blinked fast, "I don't want to be that person anymore. I don't want to be angry."

"Then don't," I said simply. Like it was a switch he should flip to realign his brain and his heart into wanting the same thing. Lusting for revenge was hard to beat. I knew. "It will take some time, but you just have to decide to do things differently."

"That's why I went for a walk to clear my head. I just needed to reset for a moment and calm down."

When I had seen him again, he was calmer. "I'm proud of you for walking away and calming down. Keep that up," I said lightly. Now, onto the main reason why we had gone over to Hank's. "He's not gonna tell us anything now."

"Yeah, I'm sure I fucked that up." He held in his frustration, "I'll find another way to connect all this together."

"It was my fault, too. I could have done a better job interrogating him."

"You did fine." He tapped my legs, "Tomorrow, let's head to Maine."

I nodded.

Gavin smiled and moved back, but not by much. This casita was a king-sized suite, one bed that we would share. The timing was all wrong. Our friendship was rocky, at best. But the attraction I had to him was hard to kick.

"Thank you for being the voice of reason," he said to lessen the tension between us. "You're such a good person. Way better than I could ever be." He glanced at the clock, "Let's get some sleep. I'd like to leave early—"

This kiss came from me. I pressed my lips to his, mindful of the blow he had taken against his cheek. Gavin pulled away. "I shouldn't have done that," I said.

He moved back, "It's okay." Gavin licked his lips, "I thought you didn't want…us anymore."

"It's just sex, right?" I leaned in to kiss but he blocked me.

"No, it's not." He sighed, "I shouldn't have said that because it's not true." Gavin painfully said, "You're the love of my life, Catalina."

I should have been the one to worry about falling in love again and growing an attachment to him that would ruin my life. But he had fallen first, before me. Love was still painful, and it came at a great loss. And I still didn't want it. "Gavin, we've been through a lot. And we're still healing from all the stuff we went through."

He nodded, "And you're still in love with Daniel."

He shouldn't know that.

My voice was run over with shakiness, "Who told you?"

Gavin looked over at my purse, "You left your notebook full of love letters to him." He rushed out, "I didn't read them. I opened the book to see where you might go, and I saw his name at the top and the words 'I love you' at the end with your signature."

Gavin knew I loved someone else, and I was still the love of his life? That was a mistake. He had to know more of the truth. "He saved me when Six and Jude were going to kill me."

He put his back to the headboard. "Tell me about Daniel. Why do you love him?"

"Why do you want to know?" I said.

Gavin said, "Because it seems like you have no one to talk to about it." His eyes glanced up, "I'm probably not the right person for you to share all your undying love for another guy with, but I assume you wouldn't be writing letters in a journal if you had someone that would listen."

A cruel joke this had to be. Gavin and Luke had played tug-o-war over me for so long, both staking deep claims for my heart. Gavin won, then lost, then won while losing again.

Jealousy wasn't the issue. It was his own lies and mistrust that had obliterated our relationship. "Okay, I get it. You don't want to talk about it," he said after my long pause.

"What's the catch? Why are you being so open about this?"

"Because that's what you do when you love someone." His voice held the comfort that lured me in.

"Daniel was something else," I started. The story tipped off my tongue, recalling everything that had happened since Ian had sent me the letter. Mindfully, I didn't hold back as I took him on the ride, the abrupt ending to my love story coming with these words. "He told me he loved me and then he died."

Gavin and I sat in silence while I waited for my heart to succumb to the sting of losing Daniel. It was mild this time. Much milder than before.

All Gavin had to say was, "He loved you, and you love him."

"Loved him. It's silly to love someone who died."

"I still love my mom, and she's not here."

"That's different."

"How so?"

"Because you'll always love your mom," I said matter-of-factly. "I'll always appreciate Daniel and love him for what he did for me. But he obviously wasn't my true love." He asked why I was so sure. "God is love, and He would never do something so devastatingly heart-breaking like that."

Gavin pointed, "Now, that belongs in a Hallmark card." His eyes drifted over to the clock again. "I've gotta get some sleep."

Sleep was smart. Yet, the urges to be close to someone overruled me. "Gavin, can I have a hug?"

He chuckled, "Sure."

The embrace was warm. Tight, but not suffocating. I rested my chin on his shoulder, reminiscing on Daniel's smile as it faded back into its place as a memory. Gavin was here, a living tragedy who harbored such strong feelings for me. Feelings of love that I had turned my back on.

I tugged at his shirt, pulling it up. He stopped me, "Catalina, I can't. Not while you clearly don't feel the same way about me."

"It's not sex," I said. I held onto the hem of his shirt, "I just want to see something."

His protesting died down. I pulled the shirt over his head, dropping it onto the bed. The bruises marred his smooth skin. They represented the enemy I had been fighting, not the man.

"Daniel loved me so easily because he was happy," I said. My finger touched his bruise, "And you love me despite everything in your life that has told you that love doesn't exist." My finger went up to the bullet wound, touching the sacrifice he had made for me. I leaned in and kissed the skin, "I shouldn't have been so harsh to you."

Gavin didn't know about the anger that had gripped me because of him. The silent pledge I had made to never love again. But here, right now, he would know the truth, the moment I had learned it, too. "You would have died for me, too."

He nodded, "I had planned on it."

But God had spared him.

We were a mess. And we never seemed to work until now. Until he came within inches of his father's face, choosing to lay his revenge down and walk away. Until I had bared my soul about Daniel and accepted his death completely.

Daniel was gone.

His memories would stay tucked into my heart.

But, for now, Daniel was gone.

And I could finally move on, my heart a little fuller, knowing that my love for him didn't have to end. Yet, I couldn't hold love for Daniel and anger for Gavin in the same heart. Making amends with Daniel had sweetened my soul. An apology to Gavin would redeem it.

"I'm sorry," I whispered while looking up at him. "I'm sorry for throwing you aside before. For abandoning you when you needed me most. And for being so careless with your love. That's not who I want to be."

He stopped me from talking with a kiss. A hesitant one, that felt like it would get us into trouble. I returned the kiss, giving him permission to take it further. But he didn't.

We were both breathing hard. "The next time we do this, I want you to want me as much as I want you," he said.

A few breaths later, and he backed away. Stiffly, he got up. "I'm gonna take a shower. Then, I'm going to bed."

The light flew off. I relaxed into the pillow, trying not to overthink it. But I knew it was futile. I was slipping back into bad habits with Gavin. And I didn't want to fight it.

CHAPTER TWENTY-FOUR

Separate Ways

"And Hank just went crazy?" Charlie said. We had finally caught up in the morning while Gavin went out to get a part for the Nova. Nothing serious, he said, just something, so we wouldn't burn too much fuel.

After our night together, I wasn't going to overthink our interactions. He wasn't avoiding me. We were on our way to becoming friends, and that was that. Nothing more or less, I guess.

Back to Charlie. "Yeah, Hank went berserk. At least I know he's working with Gary."

"He probably never stopped working for Gary."

"What did you find out about Hank?" I said.

"He ran some of our shipments for Gary from time to time," he said. "We found his name in our contacts under Gary's organization. Around the time Maverick got killed, Hank was doing some runs down to Florida for us. Gary had met some guys overseas who were interested in our product, so they gave Gary a huge sum of money for a shipment. He chose Hank because he was relocating to Arizona, so he'd be close enough to manage the deal with us."

"Was the shipment ever delivered?" I interrupted.

"Yeah. One and only delivery that happened to these people. We never heard from them again after that. Gary got locked up, and Gary JR didn't want to continue the relationship. We want to shake Hank down for details about the money."

"Hank had a bunch of cash before he left town. It's probably yours."

"That's what we want to ask him about. Our books balance out, but we never received a payment from him or Gary. Or Gary JR. So, where did the money come from?"

"Wait, I don't understand?"

"The balance was $150,000. Gary never paid us, but we were never short that money. That's why we didn't think about it until now."

"And it's not a bookkeeping mistake?"

"We've had three different accountants look at it, and they came up with the same balance." He told me to hold on while he spoke with one of his buddies. They were going to be in Tucson soon, and Charlie was hoping to see me. "Let's look at the books together. Can you meet me in an hour?"

"Yeah. Gavin's gonna pop the part into the Nova, then we'll be on the road."

"Where are you?"

"Omni resort. I'll send you the address."

"Perfect. We'll meet you there, then we can all caravan up the coast like one big happy family."

His concern was out of place, "I thought you wanted to be with your people, and you wanted me to stick with my people."

"You're stretching the truth. I said I needed to get back to my club. I never said I didn't want to ride up with you."

Sure. There was no bitterness in my thoughts, but I remembered things differently. "Either way, there is safety in numbers."

"Sounds like you don't need safety from us." Charlie laughed, "Gavin's my kinda guy."

"He almost killed his dad."

"I know, but it sounds like his dad deserved it."

"I thought you were a Christian?"

"I am." Charlie shuffled the phone, "Hank is hiding something."

"He's a liar," I said.

"Sure, but no one would get that belligerent unless they felt threatened. You were getting too close, my friend." I asked him to continue with his suspicions. "If Hank is trying to pin Russ's murder on Gavin, and pretend like he wasn't there, he probably had a bigger hand in it."

I blinked, not sure why I hadn't thought of that. "Do you think he set Russ up?"

"Nah. That would mean Gavin was in on it, and I don't see how he would benefit from killing a stranger."

"Sounds like we need to take another look at what happened that night."

"Go easy on Gavin," Charlie said. "If Hank set him up to murder Russ, Gavin's gonna kill him."

I nodded, "Regardless, the only story Gavin has is the one his dad told him. Just like Blake, Gavin needs to know the truth, too." It was clear. Hank had lied. And it was infuriating to think he had gotten away with it. "I don't let Hank off easy." My belief dug in, "You get the truth out of him because he has a chance to warn Gary."

"Warn Gary about what?"

"Gavin and I are obviously digging up stuff from Gary's past to figure out who framed him."

"Isn't that what he wants?"

Sort of. "Gary's got a lot of skeletons in his closet. By investigating his past, we might stubble on some evidence related to some of the other murders he's probably committed."

"What a great guy," Charlie said. "No matter what, the club is going to back you up."

"Thanks." I looked over at the clock. Gavin would be back soon. "I'll talk to Gavin about it and see if he's up for talking to his dad again."

"Good. I'll see you soon."

We hung up. With this new idea planted, I called Luke. "You finally caught me at home with nothing to do," he said. I asked him where my sister was. "She's out shopping with your mom. Apparently…" he stopped short.

"Apparently what?" I said. Luke said he probably shouldn't tell their business. "Luke, this is my family. I need to know what they're up to."

"Cecilia's redecorating your room at the loft. You know, for your homecoming."

It wasn't a homecoming. Just a long visit. Or a short one, depending on how successful Gavin and I were. "That's really nice," I said.

"They're really excited."

"Why didn't they call me to tell me that directly?"

"They wanted it to be a surprise. Along with a surprise birthday party for you."

My family had forgotten the whole reason why I was coming back. "I don't need a party. And I won't have time for one. I mean, do they understand that Gavin and I are trying to solve this deadly mystery?"

"They just don't want to dwell on it." Of course not. After all, none of this applied to them. "Hey, don't be offended."

I rubbed my face, "I just don't get them sometimes." But it could be worse, "Oh, I met Hank, finally." I told Luke about Hank and Camilla. Finding her body, the fight father and son had, Hank's erratic behavior. "So, you can see why having a birthday party is not at the top of my list."

"Maybe one day you'll finally have a normal life." The pity in his statement gave me a little smile. "Once you get back, I want to spend time with you. We can have lunch or go sailing."

A flash of light crossed my face. I looked out the window to the parking lot. The resort was secluded, hidden from traffic. If anyone came rolling up, I would see them before they saw me. "I'd like that." I closed the blinds and sat on the bed, "Charlie thinks Hank is way more involved with Russ's murder. He thinks Hank set Russ up."

"Does Charlie want to go sailing with us?"

"No, why?"

"Because I tell you I want to hang out, and you change the subject." My apologies went to deaf ears, "I know this is important to you. But I'd like to do more than just chase low lifes all the time."

"I'm sorry, Luke. It's just hard to think past all this."

"I understand," he said. "But after we're done with all the murder stuff, I want to be real friends."

"We're gonna be real friends, Luke," I stressed. "I mean, we are real friends."

"Good." The phone shifted. "Okay, let's talk about Hank and Russ. If Hank set up Russ, that would mean…"

"…Gavin had to be in on it, which is impossible." I bit my lip, "Gavin didn't do it. He would never kill someone on purpose."

Luke considered all the possibilities before hitting on a conclusion. "Hank could have planned on killing Russ, but Russ got the upper hand. Then, Gavin showed up and killed him."

Gavin had told me the story. Line by line, every single thing that led to him killing the man. Yet, Hank had twisted the facts enough to make Luke's thoughts valid. "Gavin had a gun that night, but I don't know if Hank did. Gun aside, if Hank did intend on killing Russ, what was his motive?"

"Maybe they were in a drug deal that had gone bad."

"Russ wasn't into drugs. He was at odds with Gary

over the drug business." My phone buzzed. "Gavin's calling. Gotta go."

"Okay. Ask him if his dad had a reason to kill Russ."

My stomach tightened. The phone beeped again. "I will. Talk to you soon." I clicked over. "How's the Nova?"

"Amazing. I figured I would check in and see if you were ready to go."

"Yeah," I said. "Charlie wants to meet."

"About what?"

"Your dad. He has some questions for you. And so do I."

"What kind of questions?" he said.

"Did your dad have any reason to hurt Russ?" I said.

"Hurt him how?"

I treaded softly, "You said they were fighting on the side of the road. I wonder what they were fighting about."

"He never told me," he said. "We can talk about it when I get back. I should be there in ten minutes."

There was a knock on the door. "Sure. Look, someone's at the door. I'll see you soon." It was getting close to check-out, so I hung up and threw the rest of my things into my bags. The knock grew louder, but only slightly.

"I'm coming," I said, padding to the door. Then, I opened it.

Father and Son

I lied about needing a part for the Nova. It was fine. Catalina was fine. But I couldn't let this shit go.

Hank had crossed a line this time.

I downplayed the situation to Catalina, so she wouldn't see what I had to do next. The lengths I'd go to for her. The muscle I'd have to flex to get this fucker to final give up the truth.

Gary has been a problem for him since I've been breathing, but he's not gonna hide behind his shitty life choices anymore. I owed it to Catalina to sort this out, for her sake.

His truck was still parked down the street. The crime scene tape had been removed. I kept the Nova out of sight, just in case. Music blared from his camper window.

I dialed his number, expecting it to go to voicemail. So, when he answered, I hesitated before I spoke.

"What the fuck you want?" he said.

"They let you go?"

"Who? The cops? They didn't have anything on me."

"You fuckin' killed someone."

"I didn't kill Camilla!" I could see him holding the phone away from his face, screaming into it as his vein popped. "You don't know what the fuck you're talking about."

"Tell me your side."

"Fuck you, kid! Seriously, I'm done with you!"

I pounded on the door and waited. He didn't say

anything. I pounded again, "Open the damn door!" The phone stayed connected for a moment, and then he opened up. Dear Old Dad had on a dirty wife-beater, ripped jeans, his hair loose and sweaty. "Need a fix?"

He folded his arms, "You wanna help me out?"

My brows tightened, "Fuck no." I walked past him, stepping on a used syringe. I sat down on the table after pushing some stuff on the floor, my boot sitting on the filthy chair. "So, what happened to Camilla?"

"Your girl didn't tell you?" I told him no. "She ODed. That's all."

"And you stuffed her in the closet? That's real classy, Hank."

"You can go fuck yourself." His face was marked up and purple, lending to his bad mood. He was in lots of pain with nothing to curb it. And I was loving it.

"I shouldn't have hit you," I said to gain some points with him. Fake some sympathy, so he would eventually give me what I wanted.

Hank blocked the door, "You came this close…"

"…to what?" I kicked the chair at him, causing him to step back. "Of the two of us, I'm the only one who has pulled a trigger." Hank tossed the chair aside and marched up. I stood, clearly ready for a match. He was an old beaten-down man, and I still had my rage. "You don't want to fight me again." He pushed me, and I fired up to push back. *It will take some time, but you just have to decide to do things differently,*" Catalina said in my ear. Do things differently. "I'm not here to fight you. I just wanna talk."

Hank stared me down, then laughed, "You backing down? Did your bitch put you up to this? Is her c—"

Sorry, Catalina. I grabbed the straps of his wife-beater and held him in place, "Call her a bitch again…"

Hank knew my loyalty to the people I loved was not worth rivaling. His hands peeled mine off his shirt. "Get out of my house."

Holding back, I had to reason with the bastard. "Look, let's just get straight to the point. You didn't kill Camilla?"

"Fuck no!"

I studied him for a moment, not ready to believe him. My grandmother said that when my dad lied, he always looked to the left. He had done this since he was a kid. Granddad would stand next to Paula, and Hank would look over at him for approval, to see if the lie had gotten past him.

Hank's eyes were still on mine. No lie here. "Okay, you didn't kill Camilla. Got it." Eyes narrowed, "Why did you go after Catalina?"

"I didn't."

"She said you were holding her hostage until you got a hold of Gary. Why? What is she to him?"

"I never did that," Hank said. He looked over my left shoulder.

My boot stepped on his toes, the pressure slightly there. "I just need the truth from you, for once."

"You have a lot of nerve coming at me like this," he growled. "Like you don't have your own arrangement with Gary. You're just mad cause I was gonna use her before you had a chance."

My fists balled as I thought about what Catalina said. I didn't have to drop down to his level. All I needed was one thing from him, and he was pushing my limits. "What's up with you and him?"

"None of your business," he snarled.

My head tilted, "I've got better leverage with Gary. If you keep pushing me, I'll use that leverage to get the truth out of you."

Hank rose to the threat, "You think playing along with Gary's plan gives you leverage? I thought I taught you to be smarter than that."

"You didn't teach me a damn thing, and you know it."

"We're gonna rehash your childhood?"

No, we weren't. We needed to move this along, for both our sakes. "Look, what's Gary got on you?" My first attempt at faking sincerity had failed. This time, I dropped the angry expression and my arms, pretending to be concerned for him.

The act fell apart once he snickered at my lying. Hank was a good liar, and I just couldn't fake it like he could. Hank also knew he couldn't dick me around. His damaged face was proof.

He conceded from fighting, a little bit. "Your girl asked me the same question."

"So, answer it."

He huffed a sigh, "Boy, my business with Gary is nothing that concerns you."

"Gary got you that scared?" I said to instigate him. He remained quiet, so I pressed further. "My guys have been keeping tabs on who's been meeting with Gary." My tongue clicked as he rubbed his stubble. The DTs would set in soon. Then, I'd lose him. "They gonna find anything on you?"

"Depends."

I tapped my finger on my jeans, something I did when my patience was running out. They tucked into a fist as I was torn between this high road Catalina kept going on about and the best way to get results. "If you answer my questions, I'll leave you alone for the rest of your fuckin' miserable life."

This bargain enticed him. "I haven't seen Gary in fuckin' years."

"Of course not." I rolled my eyes, "And it's just a coincidence Camilla's dead, right around the same time Gary's out of…"

"She died weeks ago," he said, pulling the focus back to where we began. "And I was handling it until you broke into my house and fucked up my entire situation here. I got police asking me questions, and now you're in my face about some shit with Gary. If he's after you, boy, that's on you."

He droned on, and I fell into a trance, grasping to remember the layout of the room. We didn't know Camilla was there until Catalina found her in the closet. No needle in her arm, no vomit, no other evidence of a drug over-dose. Not like when Mom had died. She slept like an angel, needle not far from her arm, tiny bits of blood on the light blue comforter. The sheet under her crumbled, hiding the baggie with Gary's insignia.

I jetted out of the door, sailing over the shit in my path.

I yanked down the crime tape and forced the door open. He arrived at the room shortly after I did. On the bed were several baggies, none with any insignias except for two.

"This is Gary's shit," I said to Hank. Now he was held up against the wall. "You gave her Gary's shit!"

He stammered through his excuses as he pushed me back. "If she got it from Gary…"

"Gary was in fuckin' jail when she ODed!"

No more mercy.

"You fuckin' killed her, then you stuffed her in a fuckin' closet!" When I stepped forward, we were chest to chest. A fever had set into him, his body rejecting sobriety. "Why did Gary want her dead?"

"You don't know what you're talking about!"

I freed my right hand and grabbed my gun. Barrel next to his temple, I said, "I'm gonna ask you again. And the next time you answer, it better be the truth."

His body shook, maybe from withdrawals or from fear of me, but the gun did the trick. "I didn't get it from Gary. I got it from Jensen when I came through Texas."

"Who the fuck is Jensen?"

"He's one of Gary's dealers. He owns a steakhouse and brothel. I passed through on a run, and I bought some shit off him."

"You still working for Gary?"

His eyes shut for a moment, the sweat pooling onto his skin, "I never stopped."

Quick wit helped me piece it all together. "Police caught you dealing, and you told them that it was a cartel out of Mexico who hired you. Smart."

"Gary and Porter can't afford to lose any more money."

"I know," I loosened my grip on him. "You kill Camilla cuz they wanted you to?"

"I didn't kill her," he said. My grip tightened. "I gave her the drugs, and she died."

"Did you mess with her dose?"

"Nah, but Jensen probably put some fentanyl in there. He's been upping the dosage, so he can collect more on each deal."

"Did you know he was doing that?"

"Yeah," he snapped.

"So you knew her shot was fatal?"

"Now, hang on—"

"You already fucked yourself, Hank. Now come clean."

He looked at the stain where her body used to be. His head smacked against the wall over and over. "She's got some family in the cartel business in Sonora. They were stepping up on Gary's business in Tucson, so Jensen gave me the bags to straighten it out."

"Rival dealers?" I said.

"She was a mule for them when I met her. I told her to come work for Porter, and she refused cuz of family loyalty and shit. I was able to keep them apart for a while, until her people saw how good Porter was doing."

"You tell her?"

"Didn't have to. She saw the money and product I was bringing in, so she worked it out on her own."

Then, Hank gave her the shot, and she killed herself. My eyes winced. Hank had a habit of killing people without ever pulling the trigger. I focused on him, "What does Gary want with Catalina?"

"Nothing, I don't think." The barrel pushed into his skull, "I'm being straight with you. He doesn't care about her."

"Then why did you latch onto her?"

"Just to scare her into leaving me alone." His voice dropped, "With her around, I knew you would figure out what happened with me and Camilla."

He slouched forward, exhausted from my questioning. My elbow planted against his chin. "You know who killed Maverick?"

Hank huffed again, "Who's Maverick?"

"The reason Gary went to jail." His brows narrowed. "He was a biker out of California who came up murdered in Maine. Police put Gary in jail for it."

Hank swore, "I knew he caught a murder charge, but no one told me who."

Another look over my left shoulder, and I grabbed his shirt. "Why are you lyin'?" I screamed into his battered face.

Hank grappled with me for a hand hold, but I was too strong. "I don't want to get involved!"

"You're already involved. So cough up some answers."

"Victor Lloyd!" Hank's eyes stayed firm. "I heard a rumor that the guy who called the cops to report Gary was the guy who did it."

"Who'd you hear that from?" Hank held onto his silence. "Fuckin' tell me!"

"Some bun head fucker Ben Ryan. Blake's friend."

I let go, "How would one of Blake's friends know who framed Gary?"

He straightened up, "Ben found out sometime last year, when Blake was fucking over Porter and stealing his business. Asked Porter to spare him if he gave up the name of the person who actually framed Gary. Said he'd heard this guy Victor claiming that if things went south, and they couldn't kill Porter, they could at least frame him like he did Gary, or some shit like that."

"So, this fucker Ben's known the whole time?"

"Yeah."

"Motherfucker," I said, my hands on my sides. "Let me guess: Victor's gone missing?"

"Left last year and no one's seen him since then." Hank coughed violently, and I stepped back, not wanting to catch his shit. "Listen, boy. If your girl is trying to find Victor, she's gonna run into trouble. He's a fuckin' hero to a bunch of Gary's enemies. He's well protected by Gary's competition. He's been feeding them information. If she fucks that up, and he gets caught, they'e gonna kill her."

"Don't worry about her," I hissed.

"She needs to stop looking into this."

Hank was weak. He never had it in him to do the right thing, like Catalina did. "I don't believe you. I believe Victor's just some low life who's taking the fall for someone else. And, judging by everything you told me, that person is probably you."

He latched onto my arm, "Boy, I didn't kill that biker!

"But you know who did." His eyes feigned left for a second. "Who did it?"

"Remember what I said about Gary's new dosage?"

"The fentanyl?"

"Ben's the one who gave it to Victor."

Ben Ryan had killed Victor Lloyd? I couldn't confirm if this was a lie or not. Hank bent over, throwing up right in front of me.

"You're pathetic." He reached up and held onto me. "Just leave Catalina the fuck alone." I yanked my arm away and stepped into the warm desert air. Hank was on his own.

✦

Gavin shouldn't be here this soon. And he had a key. My stressed level fell with the words, "Housekeeping" spoken through a deep male voice.

Shit! I had to get out before we got stuck with another night's tab. "Sorry," I said through the door. "Can I have a few minutes? My ride's on his way back." Silence on the other side of the door made me nervous. Then came another knock. "Yes, I heard you!" I opened the door, and everything stilled.

The man's voice wasn't Ian's, but he stood in the doorway.

CHAPTER TWENTY-FIVE

Collection

"You have the good sense to be afraid," Ian said as he stepped into the room and closed the door.

His harrowing shadow touched me. I kept my distance, "Gavin will be back soon."

"Yes, I know." He took out his phone and turned the screen, "Noah put a tracking device on his car." Ian watched me breathe, admiring the fear I swallowed with each passing second. "Relax, I'm not here to hurt you." My body tensed. He looked at the screen, "We don't have much time."

"For what?" I said. "Another conversation?"

"No, we're done talking." He opened the door again, and Noah came in. "Get Ms. Payton's things and put them in the car."

"Ian, I'm not going anywhere with you." My protest was audible, but confusion had stolen the spotlight. "Whatever you have to say, you can say it here."

He put his hand in his slacks pocket, the other verifying

Gavin's whereabouts, I assumed. "You missed your opportunity for that." He snapped at Noah, prompting him to search the room for my luggage.

Noah grabbed my purse, the notebooks shifting behind the flap. I latched on to it, my life line. "Catalina Rose, just relax."

I tugged it from his hand, "Don't touch my stuff."

"Enough with the theatrics," Ian said and advanced. "They are beneath you."

"So is hitting a woman," I growled.

He narrowed his eyes, "I am sorry about that." He tilted my head to look at my face. I backed away. "Catalina, we can talk about this on our way back to Maine." Noah had gathered up my things, handing my phone to Ian. I reached for it, but he slid it into his pocket. "Now, Ms. Payton, you can either go with me willingly or I'll drag you out of here by your hair. Your move," Ian said.

Time to fight. I swung toward his face, but he grabbed me. "Wrong move." He whistled, and Ben Fuckin Ryan came into the room.

"Malibu! How I have missed you!" I would have swung at him, too, but Noah had appeared at his side, protecting him. No allegiance to the girl he claimed to love for months. Not that I cared. Ben grabbed my arm, Noah grabbing the other, "Hey, Baby, don't be like that."

"Don't be an ass," I said.

Ben smirked, and Noah followed Ian out of the room like a loyal puppy, me dragging along. The Porsche had been repaired. This time, Ian and I sat in the back while

Ben accompanied Noah who was driving. Ben had a gun pointed in my direction.

"For insurance," Ian said.

He didn't need any. Charlie and Gavin would have no idea where I had gone. I slouched in the car seat, Ian watching me contemplate my situation. A poker face wouldn't help with the man who seemed to read my thoughts.

"Where are we going?" I said.

"Takin' a trip back to Maine," Ben said.

"Benjamin, please do not speak unless I tell you to," Ian said.

Ben peered over at Noah. Noah didn't have a problem following orders. His thoughts remained to himself. But Ben didn't shut up, "You came to me for help, Porter."

"Indeed. Don't make me regret it."

Ben laughed, "I've been good to you, brother." I should have warned him about Ian's impatience. But losing Ben to homicide wouldn't be so bad.

"Noah, let's go," Ian said in place of reminding Ben that he was the one in charge. We pulled out of the parking lot and climbed up the hill to the main entrance. Ian pulled out his phone, "Take a left." The driver complied. "Now a right." Ian zoomed in and out of the screen. "One more left and we should be good."

"Where is Gavin?" I said.

"Closer than I'd like." Ian shut his screen down, his attention on me again. "You went to an address on the south side of town. Is that where Hank is living?" That was not my secret to tell. "Catalina," he said while brushing his pants, "things will go a lot smoother if you continue this conversation."

"You know everything already, don't you?" I snapped.

"If I did, I wouldn't be asking." His shady eyes came up, "What did Hank have to say?"

"He wouldn't talk to me," I replied. This was not a lie at all since Hank had left me in the dark. "I tried to get him to talk, but he was high out of his mind and crazy."

Ian snapped his fingers at Ben who didn't appreciate this. His nostrils flared at being summoned. "Hand me the book," Ian said.

"What book?" Ben asked.

Ian's frustration rose, but only slightly, "The one with Catalina's research."

Ben grabbed my purse and turned it upside down, the contents scattering on the floor board in front of me and Ian. "See what you're looking for?" Ben said.

Ian rubbed his forehead, "Catalina."

"No," I said. "You can't have it."

He tsked me, "I've been very, very patient with you, Catalina." His back went to the corner of the seat, "You should know better than to test me."

"It's not a test," I reasoned, "it's just personal." Ben huffed a small laugh. "There's nothing in those pages that will help you find out who framed your father."

"That is for me to decide," Ian snapped his fingers for Noah to pull over.

Ben's next task was to clean up his mess and officially hand the book to Ian. To do this, I was removed from the car and held captive by Noah. Ben tossed around my items, winking at me when he found the notebook in question. Ian took it. Next, Ben threw my things back in the bag, and got back into the front seat.

Noah walked me to the passenger rear. I shrugged him off, "I got it!" The door shut behind me. My attention went to Ian, fuming. This was an invasion, almost as bad as the cameras in my house. But it was three against one, and I had to survive this. Lashing out wouldn't help me move my agenda forward.

Ian opened the cover and carefully read the first page of diagrams and notes. At this rate, we would be at this until we set foot in Settlement Island. "What are you looking for?" I said. He didn't answer. The page turned, and he read more. I sat back, thinking about what page he could be on.

"So," Ben said, "what's in Catalina's purse?"

"Touch my stuff and die."

"Temper, temper," Ben teased. He pulled the flap open, pushing through my things until he found my wallet. "Got any pictures of me in here?"

"Put her things back, Benjamin," Ian said. He turned another page.

Ben looked over at Noah, who backed Ian's play, "Put it down."

Ben discarded my bag on the floor. Boredom didn't last long for him. "Malibu, you dated old Noah here?" he said. Noah shifted in his seat. "I wish you I got that privilege."

"Your responsibilities led you elsewhere," Ian said as he turned another page.

"And you knew my face from upstate. Or do you

not remember because you were too busy getting Molly killed?" I said.

Ben shrugged, "Please. Molly put herself out there." He put his foot up on the dashboard.

"Benjamin," Ian said.

He complied with a bit of a grudge, his foot landing squarely on the carpet. I latched onto this, "You do everything he says, even though you hate him?"

Ben's eyes darted at me, "You're one to talk. You had your deal, too."

"I never hated Porter," I said. Ian paused on his reading, just staring at the page. "I take responsibility for what I did to him."

"Fuckin' Kyle, right? Did he ever get to fuck you as thanks for all your help?"

I hissed a sigh, "Do you really want to have this conversation right now?"

"We've got time. Several days until we get back to Maine," he winked.

"Maybe I'll put you on a plane and spare us all the misery," Ian said as he turned another page. His disdain for Ben was mutual. "Ms. Payton had the dignity to quietly take her punishment and do her time."

"So, you fucked her?"

Ian tutted at this. "Noah, pull over."

At this time, Gavin probably had to be back at the resort, wondering where I was. My phone had been turned off, so there was no way he nor Charlie could locate me. This must have given Ian the confidence for what he wanted to do next.

Noah took the exit which led down a long desert road. Ian told Noah to keep driving some ways.

"You can't do anything to me," Ben said. "Remember, I am your life line to the dealer network that's keeping tabs on Victor Lloyd."

An interesting development. Ian and Ben had found Victor? How was that possible?

"Noah, pick any spot," Ian closed the book and sent a message from his phone. Then, he gazed at me.

"Look, I'm sorry for what I said about Catalina," Ben whined. Ian's fixation peered into my skin as he ignored Ben. "Malibu, we're just kidding around, right?"

Ian raised an eyebrow. "I, um," I stammered, not satisfying Ben with an answer.

"That settles it," Ian said. The directive remained the same; found a quiet place for us to park.

Then, Ben's punishment would come at my expense.

I didn't care what happened to Ben. If anything, leaving him here in the desert didn't seem like a bad idea. The sun was mild enough to give him a chance, if he got back to the highway before dehydration really set in.

Optimism drained from Ben's jovial teasing, replaced by daunting fear. "Malibu, you gotta say something."

"Ben, I…"

"Spare your breath, Catalina," Ian said. "It won't help him." Noah pulled the car to a stop. "Noah," he motioned for him to get out.

"You can't touch me, Porter," Ben said with shaky arrogance. "We've made alliances." His door opened,

"Man, you're on my side, remember?" Ben said. Noah reached for Ben, but he wasn't easy to subdue.

They rustled, Noah struggling to get the upper hand. I thought about Gavin's fight with Hank. Gavin was able to overcome and beat his father almost to death without much effort. Noah was going to lose this fight if he didn't get any help.

"Catalina, care to lend a hand to your former friend?"

"No," I said without hesitation. Ian turned his brows down, "I'm not hurting anyone." Ben had rustled Noah to the ground, holding him there in a chokehold. Ian sighed and pulled out his gun. "What are you doing?" Ian's door opened, and he stepped out, holding the gun down in the direction of Ben's head.

I threw my door to the side and started running away, toward the highway. It was still hot, even though it was autumn, and my throat burned from thirst. But I kept going, down the dirt and rocky road, kicking up pebbles. Ben's distraction had to give me time. They couldn't just leave the dead man there, unguarded, for some cattlemen to find. No, they would have to let me go. They would—

Noah caught me by my shirt, rushing me to the ground. I clawed at his face for a moment until he pushed my wrists down by my head.

"Let me go!" I said forcefully.

"Catalina Rose, calm down," his voice was soothing and irritating.

"He just killed Ben."

"No, he didn't."

It would be hard to lie about this. Either he was alive,

or we would be digging a grave for him. He couldn't be both. "Noah, let me go." He clung tighter. "Get off me!"

"Catalina Rose, there's no way out. You have to do whatever he says."

"No!"

We wrestled, my aggression was laughable against his need to please Ian. "Just stop!" he said. "You're not gonna win."

"Why are you doing this?" my voice broke, screaming for some water to relieve it. "I thought you were my friend." Noah didn't skip a beat. He hoisted me up, marching me back to the car, hand clenching my bicep. Ben was kneeling on the gravel, Ian's gun resting on the crown of his head. "What's he gonna do to me for running away?"

Noah said, "He doesn't want to hurt you."

"He slapped me, and you did nothing." Noah's grasp loosened. "You just let it happen."

"What was I supposed to do?"

"The right thing!" I twisted, unable to break the tether between us. "You know I don't deserve this. Noah, please!" He was almost dragging me, sharp edges from the bushes piercing my skin.

Ben's head was bowed to the ground, hands up. Ian told Noah to bring me over. Then, they traded, Noah taking possession of the gun, and Ian gaining control over me. His grip on my arm was strong. "Benjamin, look up," he commanded. Ben sucked in two breaths and complied. "Apologize to Catalina for your vulgar remark." Noah pushed the muzzle further.

Noah's support nudged Ben to get on with it. "I'm sorry."

Ian turned to me, "Do you accept his apology?"

"Yes, now let him go," I said, my voice strained. Ian nodded to Noah. Out came a syringe from his pocket. "Don't!" It plunged into Ben's neck before he could react.

"The fuck!"

"Relax, Benjamin. Literally," Ian's instructions to Noah were to help Ben into the front seat.

"Is he gonna be okay?" I said, the shock absorbing into reality.

"Did I kill him? No." Ian peeled off his jacket, a spot of blood on his white shirt. "We can all use a break from his incessant talking. Especially you." I wasn't allowed to enter the car without Ian's candid advice. "The next time you run away, you'll catch a bullet in your back. Do you understand?" A slap across the face. A bullet in the back. Promises of violence were his only way to gain my compliance. "Do you understand?"

"There's blood on your shirt," I replied.

He looked down at the spot then back at me. "Pull a stunt like that again, and there will be even more blood on me."

Ian wasn't a coward. This must have been the person everyone else saw. Robert Porter who didn't pity fools nor keep them alive. Ben had been given a gift by only having to endure a beating, not the sudden ending to his life.

I selfishly believed I was different. "You wouldn't," I challenged.

"I wouldn't do what?" he hissed.

"Kill me." I dared to continue, "Or you would have had Noah shoot me instead of bringing me back."

"If I were you, I wouldn't tempt fate."

He nodded to Noah to place me back in the car while Ian got in on his side.

"Sorry, Malibu," Ben slurred, his body hunching into the window. Some blood sat on his neck.

"It's alright," I said, analyzing the last couple of minutes.

Four people had gone into the desert, and all four were coming back. Ben and I had been lucky. Another flare up from either one of us, and that number would continue to dwindle down until only one was left. And that one person was bound to be the man at my side, reading my thoughts, page by page, unraveling my research and my plans.

We stopped twice for fuel. Ian read my words like they were gospel. Noah kept his attention on the road while Ben slept in the front seat. I imagined he was in incredible pain. So much pain that he was probably glad that he was sleeping through it.

Ian closed my notebook. "Noah, take us to the resort."

What? He had made reservations? I wasn't sure where we were, but Noah seemed to know where to go. And this resort was merely a chain, but one of the nicer ones. My bags were kept in the room next door, where Ben and Ian would be staying. I figured Ben would take a literal stab at Ian in his sleep, but the doors were unlocked on both sides, and opened, giving Noah a lead into the room if something happened.

Besides, Ben was handcuffed to the bed the moment he sluggishly dragged himself into the room. And Noah administered another shot to help him sleep better.

I was not restrained. I guess they assumed I wasn't strong enough to fight back.

What they didn't see was the plot thickening in my mind.

These arrangements made them vulnerable.

Noah would be my companion on account that he had been my handler this entire time. And Ian wanted to enjoy a full night's rest. I could use this to my advantage.

Noah took the bed closest to the door. "If you promise to behave, I won't tie you down."

"Lovely," I snapped. "Do I get access to my things?" I said.

There was a knock at the door. Noah got up and answered it. Two men came in. "Is he here?" said the one who looked like he played high school football. He could have been Luke's older, more confident brother. Noah nodded.

Ian emerged, "Jensen, it is always good to see you." They shook hands. "And Erickson." Another handshake, "Thank you for coming."

"Of course," Jensen said. "I figured you would pass through Texas on your way to Maine, but I wasn't sure." He glanced over at me, "Is this her?"

"Please, let's talk about this over dinner. Do you know of any good steakhouses?"

The men laughed, "You're still the owner and operator of *Porterhouse*, sir," Jenson said.

"And the house is still operational," Erickson added. "Want us to get you there tonight? We got the plane."

"No need. We'll drive," Ian said.

"You sure?" Jensen said. "I can send someone for your car."

Ian seemed flattered, but his answer remained. "We'll stay here tonight, if you two wouldn't mind keeping an eye on Benjamin and Noah."

"Not a problem."

Jensen motioned for me to sit down on the bed. I complied, after I noticed the gun on his hip. Once in place, he sat down next to me, draping his arm over my shoulder, while Erickson helped Noah with our bags. His eyes stayed forward as he spoke with Ian about a bit of chitchat. Different cuts of steaks Ian would enjoy. How business had soared this year, despite Blake's efforts to crush it.

And not once did he ask any more questions about me. Nor did he even look at me while he gushed. It wasn't like he was avoiding me. Instead, he was just so engrossed in his conversation with Ian than he was with studying me. They were true...friends.

Jensen abandoned me after Erickson called him over to discuss Ben's condition in the other room.

"Is Ben gonna be alright?" I said.

"He'll be fine," Ian took out his phone, sending a text.

Now, for the next question, "Jensen and Erickson work for you?"

"A lot of people work for me," he said.

He seemed disinterested in the topic, which made me think he wanted me to fade away into silence. Which I didn't plan on doing. "You care about Jensen." Not in a romantic way. More like a best friend. Or even… "He's your brother." Ian didn't snarl at this, so my guess had to be true. "How many brothers do you have?"

"Just two, no sisters," he said. "Not that it's any concern of yours."

"I'm just surprised. I know Aaron's your brother through your mother. Jensen is Gary's kid?"

"His mother and my father were never married." I did feel privileged to know this.

"Does Aaron know about Jensen?"

"No. I keep it that way, so he and I can continue with our affairs uninterrupted." Then why was he telling me all this? "I trust you will keep this information to yourself."

"Why would I? So, you don't hit me again?" Ian smirked at my words. "You shouldn't have put your hands on me."

"Ms. Catalina, I've been known as someone who never gives second chances or holds their temper. The fact that I only hit you once took a great deal of self-control."

"So, you think I deserved it?"

He grabbed my arm, his strength pronounced. I winced, knowing this assault was gearing up to be worse than the last. "If you stop challenging me, you'll be fine."

Backing down didn't seem like a smart way to show my own strength. But I didn't quite have the leverage he did. After all, I had only killed one person in self-defense whereas he had killed many people who were just obstacles. People who had disobeyed him.

"How many people have you killed?" I said.

"Why do you feel entitled to having this conversation with me?"

I didn't. My assumption came from curiosity-driven plotting. This plot included my revenge against Ian, of course. But I also planned my escape. The steps were easy, if I could adhere to them.

First, remain docile.

Second, make him believe I felt fearful of his retaliation for crossing him.

Third, retreat into finding a way to get my things and return to Gavin.

"I was only wondering. I mean, you know all about the person I murdered."

"Indeed, I do. But that doesn't give you the right to bait me."

Lying and being evasive were not my thing. Even when my life depended on them. So, I leaned into the truth, tempting him with it. "I only challenge you because I'm unhappy. I don't like being held hostage. Or spied on." That snap was against Noah who hoovered in the doorway, monitoring Jensen and Erickson's efforts to keep Ben alive through the night.

Where was the guy I had dated? The one full of life and love? I knew he didn't care about me, but did his deception go this far? Far enough to make him a shell person? Quiet and uninteresting? He just followed Ian blindly. And I assumed it was because he knew his days were numbered. Once he lost his usefulness, he would be dead. And so would I.

"Tomorrow," Ian said to Noah. "When we arrive at the steakhouse, I want you to take our bags into the guest suit and find a place for Ben. Just tell the front desk attendants who you are, and they will help you. Then meet us in the restaurant for dinner at seven P.M.."

"Yes, sir," said the puppet.

"Ms. Payton, tomorrow you will attend dinner with me, my brother, and my associates." He leaned in, "Tonight, I want you to rest." Erickson appeared, relieving Noah from his duty. Silver handcuffs dangled from his fingers. "So, you'll behave while I'm sleeping," Ian added. He left the other bed and the room entirely, leaving me to be shackled up by Erickson, who took over the empty bed.

Behaving would be for my benefit tonight. It would allow me a chance to find Ian's weakness and use it to become his undoing.

CHAPTER TWENTY-SIX

Steak

THE REST OF the night was uneventful, with the exception of Noah being dispatched to run an errand with Erickson, and two other guys standing guard outside my door. I slept fairly well, only because I was so tired and couldn't keep myself awake for long. We were up early, in the car quickly, and on the road before the sun got too high.

Jensen and Erickson loaded Ben in the back of their truck. He had been sleeping since yesterday, a constant stream of drugs pumped into his veins to keep him silent.

"It's better this way," Ian said as he filtered through my pages again.

Noah sat in the passenger seat, the driver was some unknown Asian man with young features and a rigid demeanor. No one told me why he had taken over for Noah, nor did I ask. I leaned into the silence, using it to plot out my escape.

I knew our next destination; some steakhouse. A place with sharp knives, piercing forks, and maybe a road I could hitchhike on. One call to my dad's office, and they'd send the brigade to rescue me. All I had to do was my part; get out.

Getting out meant picking the weakest link to Ian. Noah.

I'd put that steak knife to his throat and promise death if he didn't let me go.

My eyes stayed forward on his seat. Not much movement from him. A shy little lap dog waiting for his next order. In his mind, he was innocent from what laid in wait for him.

❧

The steakhouse was more like an upscale gentlemen's club. The car was brought up to valet, and Noah followed Ian's instructions. He opened up the trunk and handed the doormen his keys. The rooms were upstairs, so he wouldn't stray very far.

Ian turned to me, putting out his arm. "Will you have dinner with me?"

"I prefer not to. Steak isn't really my…thing," I said as a fact.

He tucked his hand into his pocket, "I imagine breathing is your thing. Preferably without the assistance of a breathing machine. Or a hospital bed." Ian's threats were becoming more obscure. Perhaps it was all the traveling that had made him grow tired. Reason crossed his face, "Resisting my generous offers is not only disrespectful to me, it will lead to this journey becoming more and more difficult for you."

"How difficult?"

"You saw what happened to Ben, didn't you?" I bowed my head. He tilted my chin up, "Then, we have an understanding?"

My eyes veered off to the fortress sitting behind him. Some wars took more patience than others. And my war on Ian would take not only patience but precision. The precise mistake on his part met a golden opportunity that I would create right here by letting him think that his intimidation was working.

I put my arm in his, walking in unison with him up the steps and through the double doors. That's when I saw the gun on each doorman's hip. This was Texas, after all.

We were guided through a large waiting room full of people in nice dresses, cowboy boots, and hats. Ian motioned to a hostess who came rushing over.

"How can I help you, Mr. Porter?" Great, she knew his name.

"Ms. Payton and I need more suitable attire for dinner. Can you please gather up some clothing for us?"

"Of course. Would you like to clean up as well?"

"Yes, please."

"Right this way," she said.

Ian pulled me behind her. "I have my own clothes," I said.

"I know." He wasn't detoured.

The dear hostess invited us into a small parlor on the main floor. Inside were three women attendants. "Mr. Porter," said a black girl with bounding hair and a tight dress. "Jensen gave us a heads up. We have your suit pressed and ready."

"Thank you, Keisha." He turned to me. "Ms. Payton will need something from the closet as well as makeup and styling."

"Of course."

He approached me, "Be good." He leaned into Keisha's ear, whispering something that made her laugh. Then, he disappeared through a door.

"Right this way," Keisha said as a blonde and a brunette attendant followed us. Porter's army. She turned on the light to a large room full of men's and women's clothing. "You're a size small?"

"Yes," I said as I admired the walls full of designer dresses. "Where did all this come from?"

"The business. Mr. Porter and Mr. Jensen provide us with whatever we need."

I nodded, still speculating. "So, what is it that they do here? Other than running a steakhouse."

"They do a lot of things," said the blonde.

"Like what?"

"Ms. Payton, Mr. Porter will be expecting you shortly." Keisha told me to strip, and I told her no. "If you want a shower, you'll need to get ready."

"I would like some privacy," I snapped.

She sighed, "You can shower alone, but you can't close the door." The other two girls stepped up next to her.

"Fine," I walked through the door to the modest bathroom. Then, I stepped into the shower and released all my clothing, throwing them over the rod. I washed up quickly because the water was on the cold side, not warm. I peeked my head out of the curtain, and the girls were in the bathroom waiting for me. The brunette handed me a towel. "Thanks."

I ran it through my hair and wrapped my body. The curtain opened, and the blonde offered up a cute white sundress and cowgirl boots. This was not the wardrobe for a fighter. But they reminded me that they were short on time, and they still needed to do my hair and makeup.

I turned away from them, throwing on my bra and underwear, then the dress. Next, I sat down in a chair in the salon. Keisha blow dried my hair, straightening the curls and adding in loose waves. The brunette did my makeup while the blonde kept an eye on everything.

Soon, I was in cowgirl boots, ridiculous lashes, and soft curls.

Ian met me at the door, in all black, a smirk on his face. His arm went out for me to take again. And I didn't hesitate because there were too many people staring at us.

And they were all a part of his dedicated army.

Jensen greeted us at the front of the steakhouse, wearing black jeans, a black button-down with rolled-up sleeves, black cowboy boots, and a black cowboy hat. "Ready?" he said to his brother.

"Lead the way," Ian said.

Jensen walked around a few tables with men tipping their hats to him. Next to these men were women wrapped in tight dresses, big breasts, and too much makeup. Some giggled while others sat on the men's laps, teasing them with alcohol and cigars. We were invited into a quaint little dining area that had curtains blocking it from the rest of the room.

The curtains were opened. Ian, Jensen, and I were joining Noah and Erickson. Noah had cleaned up, too. His blond hair slicked back, plaid shirt tucked into Levis. His hat was a sandy brown, complimenting his eyes. I looked over at Erickson who pulled the chair out for me. He had brown hair, unremarkable features, and a large hat in dark brown. White shirt and jeans. Ian pursed his lips.

"Erickson, when you are at the steakhouse, I'd prefer it if you wore all black, in case you need to handle a problem," he said.

Meaning, in case Erickson had to beat the shit out of someone and hide the blood. "Understood," he said as he took a seat next to Jensen.

The table was a circle, allowing each of us to keep an eye on the other. Or mostly me.

"Where is Ben?" I said.

"Resting," Erickson replied. "He's had a long day."

We all had. Enough with the small talk. Two women in barely-there dresses came over, big blonde curls, and tarantula eyelashes, much like mine.

I wasn't in the mood for steak. Or anything for that matter.

"Are you ready?" the waitress asked.

"Yes, I'll have a porterhouse rare and a side salad," Ian said. She wrote furiously.

"And you?" she said to me.

"I'm good," I said.

"No one passes up a steak from a steakhouse," Erickson said to humble me.

"If you don't eat now, you won't be able to eat for the rest of the trip," Noah informed me.

I didn't care. "I made my decision."

She didn't wait. She went on to the other patrons, collecting their orders. Noah had ordered a modest steak, getting shit from Jensen and Erickson for being a light-weight. Yet, he remained true to his order, something I wish he would have done with us. Clung to his humanity and decided not to hurt his friend.

"Round of bourbon, please." Jensen settled into his plush chair, putting his arm behind Erickson's, "Porter, Gary's looking to expand the business. Is this place on his list?"

Ian shook his head, "He has no recourse here. No ownership."

"I'd like to keep it that way," Jensen said. "Gary's welcome to come and check things out, but he can't stay."

"I'll keep him occupied, so you don't have to worry."

Jensen smiled and whispered something to Erickson. He got up. "You find out anything else about that fucker who got him locked up?" Jensen said.

Ian remained quiet. The waitress returned with a tray of bourbon. We were each offered one, rejecting it was not an option. After she left, Ian said, "I'd rather not talk about that in the midst of our guest."

His brother narrowed his eyes at me, the only time he acknowledged me since yesterday. "You're right," Jensen said. He licked his lips and turned his attention back to

Ian. "Looking for some company tonight?" Ian's head tilted toward me. "I can have the girls watch her for you. And Noah."

Noah perked up at his name, "I'm here to help you, sir."

Ian paused. Erickson came back, black bag in tow. "This is what I have my eyes on," Ian said. He unzipped the bag, stuffed with money. "Business is better than ever."

"Thanks to that new connection you found for us," Jensen said. He held his glass up, "To you and your good business connections."

I left my drink on the table, knowing it was probably tainted with a sedative. Ian leaned in, "Catalina, you are being rude."

"I don't want to be here," I said. Steakhouses with dangerous cowboys were also not my thing. Nothing about Ian was my thing.

He leaned in, "I don't really care about what you want."

That was a given. "Why exactly are we here? This dinner isn't necessary. We need to get back to Maine."

Giving orders to Ian was not smart. But I had to toughen up if I held a chance against the Porters. Jensen, not sure if that was his first name or last name, wasn't much like Ian or Aaron. He was his own person, with his own agenda. His exterior also seemed reinforced, not much room for me to encroach and learn more about him. So, I tried my luck with his brother.

"The sooner I can see my family, the better," I said.

"We'll go back to Maine when I'm ready," Ian said.

I expected Jensen to ask why I was in such a hurry,

but he didn't. Instead, he waved the waitress over. "Get us a round of bourbon and some cigars." Once she was dismissed, he spoke to Noah. "When we're done with dinner, I need your help, boy."

Noah didn't contest. And Ian didn't ask what Jensen's plans were. They moved forward with the conversation, something to do with their predictions on how the business would perform next year. Jensen was the risk taker, and Ian was the bank, I assumed.

I had enough of this. I needed to get out of here and explore my options. Hunt for exits and blind spots.

I stood, and Ian grabbed my arm, "Am I a prisoner now?" I said.

"That's obvious." His eyes threatened to kill me right there. Jensen sat up straighter, ready to support his brother.

"I need to go to the bathroom."

"Bullshit," Jensen said. He shuffled in his seat, "She's been eyeing the front door since we sat down."

The bastard was astute. But he wasn't clever. "Fine. Can you have one of your girls escort me, so I can't run away?"

"And have you claw her eyes out?" Ian motioned for Keisha to come over. She had been in the wings, waiting to be summoned like a glamorous puppy. "Please escort Ms. Payton to the restroom." He snapped his fingers at Noah, "Go with her."

Keisha was a robust woman, the figure of a pin-up. She could probably take me without thinking much about it. "We'll be fine," I said.

Arguing with Ian in front of his brother and workers

landed another blow to my face. This slap was just as hard as the first one, strategically placed on my cheek for the loudest clap. Heads turned as the patrons watched me push my hair back. Noah bowed his eyes while Keisha gasped.

"Keisha, pull her together," he said.

She recovered with a nod, "Yes, sir." Her hands went to my shoulders, helping me up, even though I didn't need it. I marched to the bathroom, Keisha rushing to catch up, and Noah chasing her.

I threw the door open with all my might, slamming it against the drywall, pushing in a tiny part with the door lock. "Fuck!" I said, my hands tugging on my hair. Keisha and Noah had entered the crowded space, Noah closing and locking the door.

We had stepped into a parlor room with stalls down a short hallway. The lights were low, dim, making it almost impossible for me to see the bruise that was rising under the makeup.

"Ms. Payton," Keisha said cautiously. I put my hands on the vanity, dropping my head down just to catch my breath. "Ms. Payton?" her slightly chilly fingers touched my shoulder.

I shrugged her away, taking a step to face her. "Don't you fuckin' touch me." Her hands rested on her sides.

"Catalina Rose," Noah said, "you need to get back."

My hands went to his chest, and I pushed him into the wall. This was all his fault. "Noah, how could you do this to me? You just served me up to these monsters, like the sick little lapdog you are. You're pathetic!"

"Ms. Payton, please," Keisha said. "You need to calm down."

"Or what? Ian will come in here and slap me again?"

"Who is Ian?" she said.

"Porter. It's his first name," I answered while looking back in the mirror at the slap mark.

"Master's first name is Robert," she replied.

I turned to her, "You call him Master?" She nodded. Noah put his hands in his jeans, embarrassed. "What is wrong with you people?" I took a step toward her, "Keisha, this isn't 1818. You're not his slave."

She became offended, "Girl, this isn't about race. Master and Jensen own this establishment, and we live and work for him."

"You live for him?"

"I mean, we all live here, upstairs. And we work for him."

"Sounds like slavery to me," I quipped.

"It's not like that," Noah chimed in.

Keisha added, "We get paid for our services. Some of us work in the restaurant only. And others work upstairs, servicing guests."

As if things couldn't get any worse. "This is a brothel." Keisha didn't deny it. "So, men pay you for sex?"

"Only if we want to. Jensen doesn't force us to do anything we don't want. If you can't work in the restaurant or upstairs, you can be a courier."

"That's enough," Noah said. She obeyed him.

Being defiant, I continued my questioning. "You think Porter's going to make me a brothel girl?"

"You're too opinionated to be a brothel girl," she said. "But whatever you do, don't piss him off. People who piss off Master and Jensen tend to go missing."

I knew this. However, I couldn't just let this man keep hitting me without retaliating. Noah sensed this. He invited himself into our conversation, "Just get through dinner, and everything will work out," he said to save himself, not to give me safety. Or support.

"No," I said. If my disobedience had a say in what happened to him, I'd drag him down, too. "I'm not going to let him put his hands on me anymore." I made sure they both heard me when I said, "I'm getting out of here."

A knock on the door didn't affect us.

"Catalina Rose," Noah said, "you're not going to win this."

"I'm not weak like you, Noah. I'll do whatever it takes to save myself."

The knock was replaced with a loud thud as the door was kicked open. Jensen popped in, casually checking to see what was taking so long. "Porter is waiting for you, Noah," he said.

"Sir?"

"Take Ms. Payton back to the table. Then, get the house ready."

Noah's hesitation made Jensen's eyes narrow. "Yes, sir," he said slowly. I didn't move.

Jensen didn't request compliance. He drug me out of the room, tossing me to walk in front of him. On the way, he kept an eye on me while I walked alone. Almost like he didn't want to be held responsible if I bolted out the door.

Cigars were lit, and Erickson was chatting with Ian on a topic that was too important for me to know. They hushed their tones, Ian telling him, "Give us a moment alone." Erickson's glance at me was short-lived. He joined Noah who stood next to the table. Ian gave him a little bit of encouragement, "Erickson, take Noah to the house and get it ready."

The men didn't spend too much time lingering. Erickson walked off, while Noah stayed behind to send a grimace my way before being waved off by Ian.

Ian's eyes were softer than before. "Catalina, I know you are upset with your situation, but heed my warning. As I've said before, I am not a patient man. And I have no more patience left for you."

"You're not an honorable man, either," I said, lighting a fire within him. Might as well pour gasoline on that fire. "You hit me. Twice."

"You cannot defy me in front of my business partners and employees."

"The same ones who call you Master?" I leaned in, "I know you need me or else your father will go back to jail. So, the way I see it, we're equals. I need a ride back to Maine, and you need me to solve your little legal problem." His fingers grazed his chin. "I don't care what you do, Ian. Really, I don't. But you will never lay a hand on me *ever* again. Do you understand me?"

He smirked, "You are not in any position to make demands."

"It's my human right. I have the right to protect myself."

"If I don't comply," he said, "your beloved Gavin will put me in an early grave? Or your Blood Diamond friend will beat me into oblivion? Idle threats and promises of harm do not worry me." Now his face was closer to mine, "Being difficult will only make things worse for you, not gain you your freedom."

"You do not control me. Nor do you own me."

There was monumental silence before he dared to touch me again. This time, he moved the curls that were guarding the mark on my face. Mesmerized, he said, "Truly, I am sorry that our relationship has taken this turn. Before, I really was fond of you."

I appealed to the grief he felt for the girl who adored this man. "Ian, I'm willing to do whatever it will take to get back to Maine."

"You won't," he replied. He hushed my rebuttals, "Catalina, please do not insult me with your fake pleading. I know you are plotting your revenge against me." He tucked some curls behind my ear, "Pretending to like me is not only going to make our relationship worse; it's beneath you."

"Okay, then," I said thoughtfully, "if flattery won't help me, what will?"

He held my stare, still unnaturally close. His hand touched my mark once more. Then, I felt the prick of the needle in my leg. I pushed him away, "What did you do?"

"It's only a sedative," he said sweetly, "Nothing more." Adrenaline pumped through me, but I knew I wouldn't be able to make it to the door before sleep violently rushed me. "Your wild antics are getting the best of you. So is your fear."

"Fuck you, Ian."

"That is not the correct conduct for a lady. Nor is it the right response from someone who is in my mercy."

Soft tingles touched the top of my scalp. My mind vehemently denied what my body was telling me. I was falling asleep, fast. Ian continued brushing my hair, giving me the same attention a spider would give its food before feasting.

"You're gonna pay for this," I said with the limited amount of energy I could find.

"No, I'm not." My body leaned against his, which he enjoyed. "Just sleep now, Catalina. Because when you wake up, I have something in mind for you."

He took me in his arms, like a considerate lover. Like he actually cared for me. I rebuked his tenderness because it wouldn't stop the inevitable. I'd fall asleep, and when I woke up, if I woke up, no one would be there to save me.

CHAPTER TWENTY-SEVEN

Killing

GAVIN WAS NOT there when my eyes cracked open. And he was not saving me. Yet, Noah's face made me realize I wasn't dead. Unless he was dead, too. But if we were both dead, why was he free while my wrists were held above my head, holding my body up? A chill prickled my skin. The buzz of a generator shuttering also meant I was still alive, I think. If this was Heaven or Hell, it was really loud.

"Catalina Rose?" Noah said.

"Wha…?" I tried to say.

"You need to get up," he said with urgency.

A kick hit my back. I screamed. "Up and at 'em," Jensen said.

The jolt was enough to open my eyes wide, but I still couldn't speak. "Wher…"

"Now, Catalina, I've got some questions for you," Jensen said. I tried to ask where I was again. "Wait, I haven't asked you any questions yet."

"She probably doesn't know anything," said another

voice. I slung my head to see him tied up next to me. "Hey, Malibu," said Ben. He, too, was a prisoner. My heart tightened; we were in this together. Unlikely allies crashed together by two sadistic brothers.

"What's," I paused, "happening?"

Jensen turned to me, so I could see him, "I've got some questions for you." He held up my notebook. "It's about Gary."

"Your dad?" I said.

Jensen looked over at the corner, "Loose lips sink big ships."

Ian leaned against the wall of the room, long black coat on. He had my phone in his hand. "Focus, Jensen."

This call was enough to reign his impatient brother in. "Alright, Kitty Cat! You're here because we need some information from you. Give us what we want, and you'll live." I'd been in this situation before. Nothing new, just another crazy dictator trying to scare me into submission. This time, I would be wiser.

Gary needed me if he wanted to stay out of jail. All my research would be invaluable in convincing the law that he was innocent, which sadly, he was. So, I wasn't too worried about my fate. All I had to do was placate Jensen and learn his true intentions for me.

My expression fell into fear and compliance. "What do you want to know?"

"That's a good girl," Jensen said as he took to pacing short distances in front of me and Ben. Why Ben was strung up didn't cross my mind. My sole focus was my own survival. "Porter has looked over your little diaries, and you've been quite busy with your investigations." The mockery in his voice hit hard against the headache forming in my temple. "What do you know about Maverick?"

"Only what's in my journals."

Jensen snapped his fingers and Noah produced Demi's notebook for him. "You found a connection between Russ and Maverick?"

"Everything that you need to know is in those pages." Jensen didn't seem to like this answer, so I elaborated. "I wrote everything down, so I wouldn't forget it."

"You have memory problems?" he said while looking up from the open book. "Too many slaps messing with your head?"

I wanted to pounce on him, but I refused my instincts. "No, it's just a lot of information."

Jensen grew bored with his own vagueness. And Demi's notes. "Aaron White," he paused for unnecessary effect, "where is he?"

"I don't know," I said, glancing slightly at Ian who was still examining my phone. If he knew me well, he would figure out the passcode. Jensen stepped between us, blocking my view. "I've been trying to find him."

"Why?"

"Because he's missing."

"I mean, why is Aaron important to you?"

"He works for my dad."

"And he's been dating your sister," Ben added. Leaving this key detail out wasn't an oversight but rather my way of saving her.

"I'm sure she's moved on by now," I said.

Jensen perked up, "What's the matter? She's lost her gravy train?"

"No, she's got her own ways of making money." If she worked for Jensen, she'd be his biggest cash cow. "She doesn't like being ignored, especially by the men she dates."

"So, she doesn't know where he is, either?"

"No. He just left, no note. And he won't answer any of our texts or phone calls."

Jensen nodded, but his tightened shoulders made my stomach turn. Ian loved Aaron; he would never do anything to hurt him. And he wouldn't let Jensen near him, either. Unless, Aaron had betrayed Ian, which is why he fled.

"Answer the question," Jensen demanded. I had shut him out while I pieced the frail picture together.

"I'm sorry, what did you ask me?" I said with pleading eyes.

He latched onto my thoughts, "What were you thinking about?"

"I was trying to figure out why Aaron would leave," I said as a cover. I didn't know the answer to this, but maybe Jensen would give whatever he knew away. He wasn't perfect. He could slip and divulge something I could use against him. "Since I left Maine, I haven't seen or talked to him in over a year."

"What about your sister?" Ian said as he left the comfort of his wall and strolled up to me. "You think she might help us?"

"I don't think so," I said sheepishly. They passed a subtle look. "Only because," I continued, "she probably doesn't know anything more than I do."

Jensen shifted his weight while Ian's disappointment seared into me. He faced my phone toward me. "Call her," Ian said. The dread on my face was unmistakable. "Catalina, if you don't, there will be consequences."

"What kind of consequences?"

Ian pulled a gun from his waist band and shot Ben in the head. It happened so fast I couldn't even stop the scream that enveloped the entire room. Ben slung forward, blood on me and Ian. My body trembled as Ian continued, "You're next."

I panted a few breaths. This had been his plan the entire time. Kill Ben so both Noah and I would know to stay in line. No bright ideas or heroics. Just blind submission to our evil master.

Ian lit up the screen again, "Passcode, now."

"Grover's birthday," I said against the terror climbing up my throat. Ian punched in the numbers, then scrolled through to find Cecilia's name.

Then, the phone started ringing. I bit my lip, a tear falling for Ben who caused his own death. And a second tear for underestimating Ian's nonchalance to violence.

"Oh my God, Catalina! Where the hell are you? Dad's got the police looking for you, Mother is a mess and Gavin…he's lost his entire mind," she rushed.

"She's in good hands," Ian said coolly, the gun going back to his waist band. He motioned for Jensen to bring out his gun and point it at me.

"Who is this?" she said with an attitude.

"Robert Porter, darling." He put a hand on his hip, "Now, I have a question for you."

"You have a question for me?" her voice snapped. "You take my sister, and you think you can just have a casual conversation with me? No, fucking, way! We're doing this my way! First of all, we're going to start with you answering my questions. Where the hell are you?"

"I'm not interested in your questions," he said with force. "I need you to…"

"I don't need to do anything for you, you punk ass bitch. If you do anything to my sister…" Ian motioned for Jensen to fire a shot. The bullet whizzed by my scalp, causing me to scream. "Catalina!" The shrill from the phone was so high, Ian had to pull it away from him. "Catalina!" she screamed again mixed with crying.

Ian stepped closer, "Deal with this," he said.

The tears were drowning me, but I got out, "Cecilia?"

"Catalina?" she said, fighting her own flurry of tears.

"Yeah." I took another breath, "I'm okay." She cried loudly. "We need to do whatever he says, okay?" She didn't respond. "Cecilia?" I said softly.

"I'm here," she said between her stream of crying.

"Alright, Ms. Payton," Ian said. Jensen folded his arms, satisfied that he had rattled me and my sister into surrendering. "Where is Aaron?"

Cecilia pulled herself together, "I don't know."

"You want me to believe he didn't tell you anything?"

"He didn't." She swallowed some air, "He just left one day, no note or text or anything."

Ian and Jensen weren't sure what to do with this information. Jensen took the phone, "If you're lying, we're gonna put a bullet in your sister's head."

"I'm not lying!" she said. "I'd serve Aaron up a million times to keep my sister safe. Fuck it, if I see him, I'll hand him over. Please, just give me back my sister!" Jensen looked at his brother again. Ian nodded. Another shot rang out, coming even closer than the first one. "What are you doing?" Cecilia screamed.

"She's telling you the truth!" I said in return.

Jensen walked up to me, gun gripped in one hand as he used his free hand to fist my hair. My head was pulled back, "Cecilia, you gotta do better than that. Or else the next bullet won't miss."

"I don't know where he is!" she said.

And she wouldn't be able to find him. But I knew someone who could.

"Call Gavin Scott," I said, hoping my plan would work. I feigned a pause in my words to regain my sanity after being shot at twice. My head went down, my eyes looking over at the screen, which had put Cecilia on hold and was now calling Gavin. The moment the line picked up, I started talking before he could say anything. "Listen, I'm stuck in some steakhouse and brothel in Texas. I know you don't know where Aaron is, but I think you can find him if you get Luke's help. Ben's dead, so he can't help, but Jensen and Porter aren't going to stop until they find Aaron. So hang up and call Luke. Tell him everything." The line went dead.

Ian looked down at the black screen. "She gave up on you…" The phone rang. It was Cecilia. He answered.

"Catalina? What happened? Are you there?"

Jensen's brows tightened, "Did you call Luke?" he said.

Her next words brought on my execution, "What are you talking about? Why would I call Luke?"

Ian scanned my call history, seeing Gavin's name. He showed Jensen, "He knows." The rage built. He shut the phone off and dropped it, crushing it with his shoe. Now, the fury was directed at me.

Another tear stained my damp skin. This was it. Ian pulled the gun back up, pointing it at my forehead. Noah had broken his indifference toward me, his chest heaving loudly. My death would be his fault, too, towering over him for the rest of his inevitably short life.

Staring at the barrel of Ian's gun brought sadness, not fear. I'd die here, in this cold slaughter house in Texas, nowhere near my California beaches or the cold shores of Settlement Island. My dad's medicine wouldn't be able to bring me back. My mother's desperate prayers for my life wouldn't be heard by God. And my sister would live the rest of her days, replaying our last conversation, help-lessly clinging to Luke for support that he wouldn't be able to give.

They would have to find a way to go on because I'd be a part of the sky tonight. Welcomed into it by Daniel who had left this cruel angry world, the same way I was about to. Death had yanked him away from me. Right before my eyes, he had vanished. Gone from me, but not forgotten. I closed my eyes, expecting him to be happy that I had finally joined him.

A few breaths into this fantasy, and he wasn't there.

He had given up his spot to someone else.

Tossed dark hair, blue-gray eyes, softer. He had become my stars, my sun, and my moon. My darkness.

My heart ached for him. For my life.

Daniel may be watching over me, but Gavin was coming for me. And he would bring hell to earth to stop anyone who got between us.

My eyes opened. Ian didn't seem like the type to hesitate. After all, the shot that took Ben's life rang out seconds behind the decision he had made. Planned or unplanned, it happened, and the interrogation went on.

So, why had things halted? Slowed down to a crawl that left Jensen itching to take over and Ian unable to move.

His chest throbbed violently, conflict crossing over him. Killing me went against his destiny. Without me, he would lose the last bit of his humanity, and he wasn't ready. Not without giving me one more chance to buy my redemption, my life. To beat the odds and prevent his own murder, too.

If I died, Ian would die.

He knew this.

Gavin wouldn't have any reason to hold back anymore. Taking me, the love of his life, away would fuel a fire that would burn not only Ian's family and his business down, it would extinguish any hope, any plan, he would ever have to escape his final judgement.

Jensen grew impatient while Ian grew more desperate.

He needed a way out, I hoped. To save us both, I created one.

"The flash drive," I offered.

Jensen stepped up, "What flash drive?"

"Daniel gave me a flash drive," I said to Ian who held

his gun steadfast. "It has files and documents on it. It's where most of my research stems from. There might be something on there that will help you find Aaron."

Ian's eyes searched mine, a spark of prosperity inside them. "Noah, bring me Ms. Payton's things." Noah sprinted to the door, disappearing in the darkness.

Jensen looked at me and then Ian, "Brother, we're gonna have to do it."

"No," he said.

"But she's just sent Scott here. If he finds out about…"

"I said no," Ian said. Calmly, he sweetened his objection, "If she's right about the flash drive, we'll spare her."

Jensen's nervousness was a first. "She's a liability." Ian's angry eyes challenged his brother's determination. "You said we'd get rid of her and the kid."

Indecision plagued for a minute. Just one. "We'll have Noah do it, when he gets back," Ian said. Noah busted through the door, all my bags dangling from his arms. "Where is it?" Ian said to me.

"There's a pocket inside my purse." He motioned for Noah to dive in.

Noah started rifling through my bag, unable to produce anything valuable. Jensen stomped over and snatched it from him. He turned it upside down, all my contents spilling onto the house floor, landing in Ben's blood. Jensen then opened the inside pocket, pulling out the flash drive.

Ian and I stayed frozen, our eyes locked. Jensen grabbed him, "We need to get out of here," he said with energy. To Noah his direction was, "Take care of her."

I blinked, and the two were making their way out of

the slaughter house door. Now, I was at Noah's mercy. He came up to me, pulling out a large knife.

"Noah, please," I said hoarsely.

He didn't say anything as he cut the restraints, my body dropping down to the ground. "Catalina Rose, we need to get out of here."

I didn't have any time to inform him that we didn't have a plan. Nor did we have a way out. But Noah put me on my feet, pulling out his gun, and taking my hand. We were running out of the door when headlights hit us. Noah tried to pull me into him, but I didn't need his shelter. The reeving of engines belonged to a tribe of motorcycles and an angry muscle car. It slid to a stop on the gravel. The grass was slick, but I started running at full speed.

The car door slammed shut, "Catalina!"

"Gavin!"

My pace quickened. He crossed the headlights, bolting toward me.

I collided with his open arms, entrapped in leather and warmth. The hysterics overwhelmed us as I felt alive next to him. We fell down to the grass, him pulling me into his lap as I held onto him. To say I was crying was an understatement. I collapsed into my feelings, the man I loved just rocking me.

"It's okay," he said. "I'm here."

More boots crunched on the grass, creating a hedge of protection. But I didn't need them. I had the only thing I needed right here, protecting me. And I'd never let him go.

CHAPTER TWENTY-EIGHT

Wounded

GAVIN WASN'T QUICK to get up. He just rocked back and forth until I had the strength to gather myself. When my head lifted, he looked relieved. If he had been through what Cecilia had heard on the phone…

"I need to call my sister," I said next.

Gavin brushed my curls aside, "I told her I'd call her once I found you."

Charlie, one of the sets of boots protecting us, crouched down, "Is that another bruise?" Gavin narrowed his eyes at it in the dim light. Charlie shook his head, "I'm gonna hit the shit out of that guy," he said as he stood again.

"Where is he?" Gavin growled.

"He ran off with his brother," I said, my voice hurting.

"Aaron?" Gavin said.

"His other brother," I replied.

"Jensen," Noah confirmed. "He owns the property."

"Where are they going?" Charlie said to Noah.

"To look for Aaron," Noah took a step into the circle,

watched like prey. "They told me to kill Catalina, but I let her go instead." This didn't win him any favors with Gavin or Charlie.

"That was so kind of you," Gavin snarled. He looked up at Charlie. "You ready?"

Charlie nodded. "Hell yeah."

Gavin looked in my eyes, "I'm gonna get you out of here."

"Not yet," I said. Climbing to my feet, Gavin got up with me. "I need to find Ian."

"They couldn't have gotten far," Noah hoped his helpfulness would grant him safety with the crew. "They're probably up at the steakhouse, getting ready to leave."

Guns drawn, the bikers advanced. Gavin wanted to hold me back, but I wanted my revenge. Together, we all approached the front door. Two bikers clobbered the valet guys. Next, Gavin put me behind him as Charlie stood to his side. They nodded and in unison, their boots hit the two doors, a loud crash announcing our arrival. Gavin and Charlie walked in first, passing the scared hostess and heading to the dining room.

Inside, customers and working girls paused on their dinners. Charlie nodded to one of the Diamonds who stepped up on one of the lavish tables, machine gun in hand. He fired a precession of bullets into the ceiling, causing everyone to jump.

"Ladies and gentlemen," Charlie said. "I'm looking for Porter and his son-of-a-bitch brother. Give 'em up, and no one will get hurt." Minutes before, this room was crowded with food, drinks, drugs, and men hoping they had enough money to get lucky. The silence that followed our commanding entrance was so vast, it swallowed up everyone's sins, leaving them speechless without any direction toward either brother. "Seriously, I don't want to hurt any of you. I just have some unfinished business with the Porters, and I'm not leaving here without them."

"Master isn't here," Keisha said. She trembled, having betrayed her prized employer. "He and Jensen drove away about ten minutes ago."

"In what car?" Charlie said.

"The Porsche."

Charlie turned to two of the Diamonds, "Check with those dipshits in the front and see if it's true." For the other Diamonds, he had something else in mind, "Tear this place apart and make sure they're not here."

The league of bikers got to work, turning over tables and exploiting the place. Patrons ran for the door, stopped by three bikers who checked them head to toe before letting them flee. Charlie's aggression turned to concern for me. His hands went to my shoulders, "What happened?"

"I…" I stammered. My hand went to wipe my face, only to find blood on me. The trembles came back. "I…"

Charlie hushed me. Gavin took my hand, "I'll get you cleaned up." I remembered the bathroom with the shower. Somehow, I managed to lead him there. He checked it thoroughly before he locked the door. He threw on the water, checking the temperature. Once the steam bellowed, he sat me down in the same chair Keisha had put me in to do my hair and makeup.

Gavin turned me away from the mirror, peeling the

boots and socks off my feet. Then, he threw off his jacket, and rolled up the sleeves to his button-down shirt. Next his boots and socks came off. Finally, he told me to stand. Slowly, he unzipped the bloody dress, exposing my naked body to him. Instead of marveling at my feminine form, he placed his forehead on mine, thankful that I hadn't been shot, too.

He brought me into the shower, his clothes drenching with water as he placed me in the warm stream, the blood slipping off my skin and onto the shower floor. Gavin nursed me back to health, water touching the crown of my head, shampoo lathering my curls, soap washing away all traces of Ben.

The tenderness of Gavin's care, his carefulness, gave me the clarity to tell him my story. "He almost killed me," I said. Gavin stopped. "Ian was about to kill me before I gave him the flash drive. It's gone."

"We'll worry about that later." He shut the water off. "All I care about is getting you somewhere safe." He cradled me in his arms, "I was so scared he had killed you." His chin rested on my head, "I lost it, just thinking about him taking you away from me."

I pulled my head back, "You came for me."

"Always."

He had lost himself until he found me. Now, I was losing myself in the blue-gray hope in his eyes. So, I kissed him. He returned the kiss, and we fit perfectly within each other.

There was a knock on the door. "We need to talk," Charlie shouted.

I broke the kiss. "Give us a minute," I said. "I need some clothes." Gavin nodded and handed me a towel. I raided the closet again, this time finding a southwestern style layer skirt with a jean top. My hair went up into a messy, wet bun. Gavin asked why I was putting makeup on when we were clearly on a time crunch. "I don't want people feeling sorry for me," I said, referencing my bruise. "He doesn't get that power over me." I tossed the concealer on the counter.

Anger crushed what little humility I had left. "I'm going to kill him, Gavin."

He leaned against the vanity, his back to the mirror, wet clothes dripping over the makeup. "Catalina, you can't kill him." My fury wasn't going to be reasoned with. He put his hand on mine, "This is not who you are."

"He made me this way!" He didn't so much as blink at my statement, another slap in the face. "He put a gun to my head after he killed Ben to scare me. And now he's going to kill Aaron." A dangerous thought crept in, "And he's probably going to kill my sister once he gets back to Maine." Gavin rubbed my hand. I released him from me, "I have to do it, Gavin. It's the only way."

Gavin's hands cupped my cheeks softly, "If you kill him, Catalina, you will never survive it. The guilt will cut you down."

It was a card I shouldn't play, but it was relevant, "It took some time, but I survived killing Blake."

"This is different."

"How?"

"Because Ian is your friend."

"*Was.*"

"Okay, *was.* Still," he said, "you know him. You guys had some sort of friendship before you found out who he truly was." He tapped my chest, "In your heart, you're still friends with that version of him. And if you kill him, you'll kill that version, too. That will be damaging. You'll never escape that kind of guilt. It will consume you."

"You weren't there," I stressed. "You guys have had your fights, but he's never put a gun to your head. He's threatened you, sent people after you, and when it came down to it, you were fine. Not even Kyle's come this close to being shot by him. No, he's been holding out for me. His final act of revenge against you and Kyle is to make an example out of me!" My finger jabbed into my chest, almost breaking it. Gavin slowed his breaths. "You're not saying anything because you know it's true."

Gavin tucked his arms around his body, pausing to think. "Who stopped him from pulling the trigger?"

It didn't matter who stopped him. When I said this, Gavin pushed me just a little further to relive the worst seconds of my nearly-shortened life. Finally, I had an answer, "Jensen said that they had to stick to the plan to kill me. That I was a liability."

"So, Jensen stopped him?"

"No, he was cheering him on. But Ian wouldn't do it. He said no."

Gavin finished his thought, "Porter could have killed you, but he chose not to. He held back because deep down, you're his friend, too."

I pointed to the bruise, "He hit me. He kidnapped me,

drugged me, took me away from you, and killed Ben right in front of me. Friends don't do that to each other."

"I'm not saying he's a good friend, but he cares about you, Catalina."

"Look where that has gotten me."

The smile curling his lips bordered an insult, "He saved your life." My rebuttal flashed like lightning, gone before it had started. Gavin was right. Just for insurance, he added, "He could have shot you, or he could have had his brother do it. But he put the task in Noah's hands because he knew Noah would let you go. It was all an act."

"It felt real," I said.

"He needed it to be believable. That was the only way he could protect you from Jensen or someone else doing it."

"That doesn't make us even, Gavin." My anger would not be deterred. "He has to pay."

"And he's going to." His next words were strong, "If you pull that trigger and kill him, you'll remember that one time he had the chance to take your life, and he didn't. He did the right thing, and the way you repaid him was by doing the…" he paused, noting my narrowed brows. Gavin's wisdom wasn't compelling enough. So, he sweetened it, "Leave Porter to me and Charlie. He's gonna make it right for his friend Maverick, and I need to settle this for you, for me, and for my mom." He took my hand, "Let me carry that burden for you."

Having a man pledge to kill my enemy seemed sickly romantic, in a dark, twisted way. But Gavin didn't have to sacrifice so much. He had already earned my love. And he wouldn't lose it again.

It was my turn to put my hands on his cheeks, "I'm not gonna make you a murderer again, either."

"Trust me, it wouldn't be a big deal. Porter and I are not friends. Not now, not ever."

"If I can't kill him, neither can you." Morbidity had hijacked my morals. This was wrong. And sick. "What has gotten into us?" Gavin sighed. "No one is killing anyone anymore. We're better than that." I thought Gavin would perk up at my concession to his will. Instead, he seemed to sink further. "What is it?"

"This is my fault," he murmured. "First, I ruined your life in Maine, and now I'm fucking up your new life. If only I had left you alone."

Self-punishment wasn't needed. Nor would it change anything. "Listen, what's done is done."

He cut into my speech saying, "Don't be so dismissive."

"I'm not dismissing anything. You've apologized hundreds of times, and I've forgiven you. Now, we just have to get through this." *One more thing.* "Our days of killing people are past us, no matter who it is. We need to focus on saving lives, not taking them."

"Then, our next move is getting to Aaron before Porter does," he said. I nodded. Gavin asked if I was ready, and I gave him another nod.

He unlocked the door and Charlie stood on the other side. "You're all wet."

"Took a shower with my clothes on."

"Okay, then." Charlie told us to step into the now-destroyed dining room. "We tore this place up, and they're not here. We rounded up all the employees, and the boys are questioning them." Charlie handed me some sheets of paper. "Thought you would find this interesting."

The thin stack of papers was a sample of Maverick's case file. "Where did you find these?"

"Christian Jensen's room." Charlie looked over my shoulder, "Are they the same as the ones you had?"

"Not all of them." I flipped through the pages. Some of the pages were identical, with the exception of three pages. There was a medical report from Aaron White, Medical Intern. He wrote:

Decedent Description: Caucasian male, aged between 40-50 years old. Several tattoos on arms, back, and stomach. Will be used to identify patient when next-of-kin is notified. Height: 6-foot, 1 inch. Weight: Approximately 250 pounds.

Clothing: Levi jeans, fairly decomposed. Black T-shirt, fairly decomposed. Black boots. Leather jacket with words Blood Diamonds MC, good condition.

Date of Death: Found July 20th.

Manner of Death: Probable Homicide. Gunshot wound located on back of head.

Death Location: Wooded area alongside Lazy S River, near Porter Construction LLC.

More Information: Decedent is not a resident of Settlement Island, ME or Anders, ME. Found by Victor Lloyd. No other information regarding manner of death or body discovery provided by Mr. Lloyd.

I pressed my hand to my lips. "He lied," I said. Charlie and Gavin waited for my big reveal. "Aaron's only a few years older than you, Gavin. He would have been what, twenty-one, twenty-two years old? He couldn't have been a medical intern."

Aaron's timeline was a blur for me. But Gavin didn't think it mattered, "Aaron's been volunteering at the clinic in Settlement Island and at Anders General since he was a teenager. Maybe they had him write it up."

Good thing my dad was head of the hospital now. He would never let a teenager write up a medical report for a homicide investigation.

Charlie tapped the name Victor Lloyd. "That's the same guy in the other police reports."

"Yeah, he is. He reported the death, I think."

"How did he find the body?"

I didn't remember. Not without my notes, that were now covered in Ben's blood. "I don't know."

Again, Gavin didn't think it was relevant. "No one knows what happened to Victor Lloyd after the report. I've been fed some lies about him bragging about setting Gary up, but they're just lies."

"The other Diamonds that went to Maine with Maverick disappeared, too. Seems like everyone involved has come up dead or missing," Charlie added in. I had also forgotten that fact, too. Three men go to Maine, one comes up dead, and the other two are still missing. "Maverick was a big guy; he would have been able to take one guy, but not two," he said. A conclusion was brewing, "How does Jensen figure into this?"

I put myself in Jensen's thoughts, seeing it from his angle. Porter's motivations were clear; help his father anyway he could. They were close. But what made Jensen tick? Why was he so determined to help? And why would Porter turn to one brother to cut down the other? "Porter probably reached out to Jensen after Aaron went missing. Jensen works for Gary, too." I scanned the medical file again. "It's possible Jensen did some digging of his own and that led to him believing Victor Lloyd was probably the killer. And he thinks Aaron helped Victor cover up his crime."

"Aaron's not involved," Gavin said.

"Why did he run?" Charlie said.

Gavin didn't speculate. But I did, "What if Victor Lloyd convinced Aaron to write this? And Aaron ran because he knows who Victor Lloyd is."

"That would be enough for Porter, Jensen, and Gary to want him dead," Charlie said. I nodded.

Gavin disagreed, "Porter wouldn't kill Aaron. He loves his brother too much. And he wouldn't let Jensen do it, either."

"Jensen's got a room full of manifestos for Gary," Charlie clarified. "He's trying to prove to Gary that he's a better son to him than Porter is. He'll do anything to win his dad's approval, including turning Aaron over."

"But Porter would never let Jensen hurt his brother," I said. "Plus, Jensen has a huge crush on Porter. You should see the two of them together. Jensen was ready to jump in front of a train, just to prove his blind loyalty to his brother."

"Well, if Jensen feels that way about both of them,

imagine the situation he's in." Gavin had a point. "Jensen will probably do anything to help Porter, unless his dad gives him a better reason to betray him."

"Gavin, you're right. Jensen's loyalty will go to the family member who can give him what he wants: acceptance. But Porter's not insecure like his brother." Ian would never betray Aaron. Yet, he'd have to make it look like he did. To ensure his brother's safety, he would have to do what he did best: hide. Hide his true agenda from Jensen and cover his own tracks. "Remember, Porter knew Noah wouldn't kill me, which is why he told him to do it. He needed to give Jensen the impression that it would get done." And he was doing the same with his brother. "Porter has to know where Aaron is. It's the only way he can throw his enemies off Aaron's trail."

"Why would his enemies want Aaron?"

My stomach jumped, "Aaron has to know who Victor Lloyd is. And so does Porter." We only had one shot at the truth. "If we want to find out who killed Maverick, we have to go to Aaron. Of the two of them, he's the only person who would probably tell us the truth."

"You sure about this?" Charlie said.

"Absolutely." I turned to Gavin, "We need to get back to Maine."

"That's been the plan this whole time," he said to be a smart ass. I slapped his stomach. "Get as much of your stuff as you can, and I'll meet you at the Nova in five minutes."

I stepped over the mess that covered the floor, brushed past the terrified employees and barely-dressed girls, and went out to the slaughter house. My notebooks had been left abandoned where Jensen and Ian had stood. Ben slung forward, blood sitting below him, creeping toward my notes.

"I'm sorry, Ben," I said as I gathered up my things. My purse was ruined, so was my phone, but my wallet and…

"Mali-bu," Ben said slowly.

I flung back, pages scattering. "Ben?" I said, my heart tightening. He gurgled. "You're alive?" He gurgled again. Blood had caked his hair, but I moved it aside to see the wound. I wasn't a doctor, but it was obvious that Ben was on borrowed time. Frantically, I groped around for my broken phone.

"Don't leave," he pushed out.

"I won't," I promised. I shouted for Gavin. "We're gonna get you some help."

"We?"

I shouted for Gavin again, "Yeah. Gavin's here."

Gavin rushed into the room, stopping only when he got to me. "What's wrong?"

"He's still alive."

Gavin knelt down in front of Ben, tilting his head up. "Shit, he is," Gavin pulled out his phone and called 9-1-1. The call connected, and Gavin stood, stepping outside.

I put myself in front of Ben. "Hang in there. We're gonna get you some help."

"Malibu," he said again, strangling his words.

"I'm here. I'm not gonna leave." I clasped his hand. They were still warm, which was encouraging.

"Jensen?" he muttered.

"He's gone. So is Porter."

"Where?" he said.

"He went to Maine." I redirected the conversation to focus on Ben. "Don't worry, he's not gonna get you."

"Aaron."

"He's not gonna get Aaron, either," I said, unsure why he was concerned.

"Scott?" He was using too much of his energy to talk.

"Ben, just rest," my voice was soothing with care and concern.

"Scott Senior," Ben said.

"Scott Senior?" I said.

Ben lifted his hand haphazardly, tapping a page in my notebook. "Senior knows where Aaron is."

Scott Senior. I looked down at the page where Hank's name had been circled. The puzzle took a minute to solve. "You're talking about Hank, Gavin's dad? Hank knows where Aaron is?"

Ben nodded then fell silent.

CHAPTER TWENTY-NINE

Breathing

"Like always, all roads always seem to lead back to your dad," I said as Gavin stood in Ben's hospital room. We had done the right thing and gotten Ben some help. Doctors expected him to be okay, even though he had taken a bullet to the head. Apparently, it was somewhere between a flesh wound and death. This made me wish Aaron was with me, so I could ask him for his own medical opinion for my own reassurance.

No, Aaron wouldn't be coming to Ben's rescue. He was behind some veil Hank had known about this whole time.

Ben was sedated, and he hadn't said anything else that could help us connect the line Hank and Aaron held. Still, Gavin studied him as Ben's chest rose and fell with the beeps of the machines. Gavin's last conversation with his father ended in blows and me reasoning with them both to set aside their hatred so we could get some answers. They hadn't spoken since, Gavin's messages and threats going to voicemail.

"Your dad's gone?" I said, my eyes watching Ben struggle to breathe.

"Probably," Gavin let go of his phone, slipping it into his pocket. "If we're lucky, we'll be able to get to him before he gets to Aaron," he said.

"Do you think he's going to hurt Aaron?"

Gavin seemed unsure. For my sake, he toyed with a more optimistic idea. "If he was going to, he would have done it by now." His response brought little solace.

"We gotta find Aaron before Jensen does. He's the key to solving this whole thing." And he was a human that deserved to live.

He put his hand on the side of my cheek, "Porter's not gonna let Jensen anywhere near Aaron. But we should find him sooner rather than later."

"Onward to Maine, then." I got up, glancing down at Ben. If he had anything else for us, now was the time to spill it. Nothing came from his lips, just more breathing, the machines giving me the answer I wasn't looking for.

Gavin walked beside me, weary and beaten. "You need sleep. So do I," I said.

"I'd rather get the fuck out of here first."

We were still in Jensen's territory, some small town outside the big city. One thing I knew about small towns is the monsters tended to stick together. And Jensen's monsters were out to get me, Gavin, and the bikers who had just left us to find somewhere to crash. Lucky for them, they were being trailed by a truck that had supplies for fixing the bikes and gear for sleeping on the side of the road. We were welcome to join, but Gavin had held out. He wanted to spend just a little bit more time here with Ben, hoping he would wake up.

But he hadn't.

And we could only go so long without sleep.

"Where should we go?" I said.

He took my hand, "We'll drive a little bit, get the fuck out of here, and find somewhere."

One more check-in with the nurses to confirm that Ben was useless to us, and then we were at the Nova. I was dead on my feet, but I couldn't just fall into sleep. "I don't like Ben, but I'm happy he didn't die." I sat down with the door open, my legs and body facing Gavin who was ditching his wet clothes for dry ones. He had spent the last two hours drenched and cold. Miserable, he held it together until now, which I appreciated.

His shirt came off, followed by his jeans. Sculpted, chiseled, muscles taunted my sleepy eyes. He tugged at his boxers, winking. My hands flew up to shield his body, embarrassed by my intrusion. "Relax," he said, as he changed, his bare skin lit by the rising sun. The parking lot was barren, but I was mindful of prying visitors gazing at what had once been mine. He pulled fresh jeans on and a black shirt. "Better?"

"Yes." He motioned for me to get into the Nova and shut the door. After he got in, he said, "It's not normal for people to cheer on the death of others."

Oh, yes, we were talking about Ben's near demise. "Ian and his crazy brother didn't seem to have a problem with it."

"They are psychopaths. And when I find that son-of-a-bitch, I'm beating the shit out of him." Gavin looked over at me. It was far too late, or early, for that much energy, even if it was directed toward a man I wanted to kill myself. "Sorry." Gavin turned, placing his back against the window. "Come here," he said.

I moved over, placing my head against his chest, my feet tucking up against the passenger door. He kissed my hair, his arms cocooning around me. "We should probably get on the road."

"Yeah? Is that what you want?" he said in a low tone.

No, I wanted to sleep, right here, in his arms. After what was probably a minute that had turned into five, I said, "Can we just rest for a bit?"

"Yes," he said. His body slouched, too, bringing me further into comfort. He moved, only to put his leather jacket over me, shielding me from the chill that grazed my arms. I expected him to heave into sleep, leaving me here to fall on my own. Instead, he brushed my curls with his fingers, allowing me to fall into peaceful dreams first.

"Catalina," Gavin whispered to me. I swatted his chest, needing more rest. He moved my hair and kissed my ear, "Catalina…" he said, playing with my heart.

"Mmmm."

"We gotta get going."

"A few more minutes."

"I gave you five hours." With this, I sat up. The sun had woken up and climbed high in the sky. "Hi," Gavin said when my eyes discovered him.

"Oh, we need to get going," I said.

He pointed to a Porsche. "He wants to talk to you."

Startled, I got out the question, "Who does?"

"Noah."

Gavin's sigh mirrored my disdain for him, too. "What does he want?"

"Just to talk." Gavin sat up straight, "I was gonna tell him you weren't interested, but I thought it would be better coming from you."

"How long's he been here?"

"The entire time we've been here. At least that's what he said." Gavin read my thoughts, "I'm not crazy about you going over there, either, but he won't let it go."

"What did he tell you?"

Gavin ran a hand through his hair, knocking it back into place. "Just some shit about how he messed up, and he wants to help you."

"Now he wants to help?" I hissed.

"Apparently. Says he has some clues about where Jensen and Porter might be headed."

"Why didn't he tell you?"

Gavin chuckled, "He hates me. I mean, I did cuckold him," another smirk.

"We weren't married, so you didn't cuckold anyone. Besides," I looked over at the Porsche, "he lied about everything. He could be lying about this."

"He swears he wants to come clean, and then he'll leave you alone forever."

"Not likely," I said. Surly attitudes aside, if he could give me just one piece of evidence to find Aaron, a temporary truce would be worth it. "Did you check him for guns or kidnapping stuff?"

"Yeah," Gavin pulled out his gun, "but one more check won't hurt."

We got out of the car at the same time. Noah hopped out of his vehicle, too, stepping up to Gavin against his better judgement. "You have a lead on Jensen and Porter?" I said as we came to a stop.

Noah put his hands up, "Yes." He was smart enough to keep the distance between us. Gavin had lowered his gun, but it was still brandished. "I'd like to talk to you about it. Alone, if that's okay."

"You've had a hand in my kidnapping twice now. Why would I trust you?"

He knew my skepticism was planted on firm ground. Not to mention the three months he had lied to me, pretending his way into my heart. Noah measured the situation, hunting for approval from us both. Gavin would take my lead, only if I made the right decision.

"I'm sorry about my role in this."

Not good enough. "Just tell me what I need to know, and we can end this."

"I'm willing to tell you anything you want to know, without him."

"Whatever you want to say, you can say in front of Gavin, too." We were standing close, arms touching, showing our unity on the topic.

Noah didn't heed to the compromise, "I'd rather talk to you alo—"

"Why not? Of the two of you, he's affected the most by

whatever Jensen and Porter are doing." Correction, "And so am I. You drove him to my door, and you have to do whatever it takes to make it right for me…and him."

"Nice save," Gavin teased.

"I don't think…" Noah started.

"Whatever you have to say, come out with it," I said.

Noah didn't concede. Instead, he remained silent until Gavin offered, "What's your plan, anyway? What's the point of being so secretive?"

"She can tell you everything after we're done," Noah didn't posture. His request remained humble.

"He's scared of you," I said to Gavin.

"I'm not scared."

Gavin nodded, "Yeah, you are. You know I'll cut your ass down if you so much as breathe on her."

"I'm not gonna do anything," he pleaded. "It would just be better if I spoke with her."

"Which means," Gavin interrupted, "whatever you want to tell her has to do with me."

"Something like that," Noah said.

Enough with the games. Gavin and I had to get going. I ended the stalemate with a condition. "If you and I talk alone, you've gotta give us something. Insurance, that is."

Noah's brows knitted, "What do I have that you want?"

"Your phone."

"I'm not giving you my phone, Catalina Rose."

"Mine is crushed, and you have a direct connection to Porter and Jensen. I need it."

"No, that's nonnegotiable."

Right here stood an even bigger clue. "You're waiting

for them to call." I rushed out, "When are you supposed to call them?" Noah shied away. "Noah?" His name was sharp on my tongue.

Gavin stepped up, "Would you like us to help you make that phone call?"

Noah wasn't a big fan of this. But Gavin was larger and intimidating. "Listen, I just need to tell Catalina Rose what I need to, and I'll be on my way."

"Where?" I questioned. Noah hadn't prepared a lie. "To Maine, right? Because that is where Jensen and Porter want you?" After he had killed me. Noah had let me go, so he would have to answer for his maleficence. Disobedience was a direct hit on whatever Jensen and Porter had planned. "Just talk," I said.

"I will, once it's just you and me." He remained focused on his intentions.

This provoked me, "I need something else in return. I want you to call Jensen while you're with me and tell him to give you instructions on what to do next."

Noah's position was tough, I guessed. Teaming up with us would put him at odds with Ian. And that would lead to his death. So, I sweetened the deal, "They won't know that you helped me."

"Once Jensen finds out what you did to his steakhouse, he'll figure it out."

"Not if they believe you were one of the casualties." A lie, maybe two, would secure that fate. "Just lay low, and we'll make sure everyone thinks Gavin shot you," I said.

"Why would you cover for me?"

"Because you have information that will help us," I

advised. "So, in exchange for that information, I'll cover for you. We'll make it look like you and I both disappeared, so no one would know the truth. Then, when I see Ian again, I'll tell him what happened to you."

"You'd lie for me?"

"A lie for a lie," I said.

His sigh was confirmation of his agreement to my wishes.

Gavin took it upon himself to pat Noah down, removing the firearm from his back and another one from the driver's side seat. Keys in hand, Gavin opened the back door to the Porsche. "This way you can talk to her in private without driving off." Noah got in, and I opened my door. "Please, be careful," he said.

I nodded and shut it on him. Noah fidgeted before he faced me. I headed up the conversation, "You stood there and let him hit me. And then, you stood there as Porter let his brother almost kill me."

"Jensen went off script. Porter never wanted to hurt you like that."

"He shoved a needle into my body, and then he hung me up in a slaughter house!" My teeth bit hard together.

Noah panted, "His brother put him up to it. Believe me, Porter just wanted to get the truth out of you and then leave you safe. I promise."

"Why? And why did they try to kill Ben?"

"Ben overheard a conversation between Porter and someone. He killed him for it and to make you give up whatever you knew about Aaron and Gary. I feel bad about what happened, but there was nothing I could do."

"You need to work on your backbone, Noah." The insult seeped deeper. "Porter's put a leash around you, and you just go wherever he tells you. You sit by, loyally, as he hits me, almost kills Ben, and…"

"Ben's alive?"

"Barely." Noah sighed as I continued, "Don't act all concerned."

"Ben is my friend. I never thought Porter would take it this far."

"Well, he has!" I huffed past my anger, "So tell me, what is going on?"

Noah was frantically shifting in the car, the seat unable to comfort him. "Porter doesn't…" He calmed himself, so he could get out the remnants of his thoughts, "He doesn't know where Aaron is. Or who framed Gary. He lied to buy him some time while he keeps looking."

"He took the flash drive. That has everything that I know. It should be enough to help him piece everything together."

Noah said, "It's not enough. And Gary's getting impatient. He knows you have a relationship with the Blood Diamonds. He still thinks he can use you to get out of his murder charges and take care of the bikers."

"How?"

Noah gulped more air, "You are leading the Blood Diamonds to Maine. Once they are there, Gary's gonna plan his attack on them. However, you can stop it if you can turn Aaron over to Gary."

This was, in fact, the flimsiest plan I had heard. The only way this plan would work was if it was planted on a lie. "Aaron knows who killed Maverick."

"That's the assumption. And Gary plans to beat it out of him. You gotta find Aaron and get the name for Gary."

"I don't know where Aaron is."

"But Hank does. Gary's been calling and calling Hank, and he won't answer. Ben told me that he overheard a conversation with Porter and Hank. A short one where Hank said he didn't want to get involved in this. And he didn't want to know anything else about what was going on with Aaron."

"That seems like a stretch."

"It's not. Jensen told Porter that Gary had evidence that Hank saw Aaron the night of that biker's murder. And Hank was making arrangements to leave town right after everything went down." I pondered his theory. Noah said, "You think there's something, too?"

"Is this what your call with Jensen and Porter was about?"

"No," he stammered, offended that I hadn't been impressed by his revelation. In truth, I needed more.

"Call Jensen."

"Catalina Rose, I'm so sorry, but if they find out I helped you, they'd kill me." The pleading continued, "You have to understand that the rest of us don't have the same favor with Porter that you do."

"What is his leverage over you?" Noah became shy. "Seriously, why are you still protecting him?"

"I worked for Ben and Jude after they took over Porter's place. Nothing crazy," he clarified, "just holding some drugs and money for them, keeping them out of Porter's reach." He blinked, "After Blake's death, Ben convinced me and some of the other dealers to turn ourselves over to Porter to save our lives. We returned the drugs and money we had. Porter spared me and Ben, killing everyone else right in front of me."

I would say I was sorry, but Noah had earned his fate. "Why did he spare you two?"

"Ben wanted to do whatever he could to make you pay for Blake's death. He claimed to have some inside information about Porter's competition. After he shared that, Porter told him to befriend Demi and use her to find you. She was more than willing, not knowing that she was setting you up to be caught. My job was to befriend you and let him know if you came up with anything he could use."

"You fake dated me," I cleared up.

"The only way I would be able to get more information from you was to pose as your boyfriend." He caught himself, "But my feelings were real, just based on a lie."

My head shook, "You never cared about me, Noah. Or else you would have been honest."

"I did," he said. "That's why I never had sex with you, even though I wanted…"

"Thanks for the information," I said as I flung the door open. I didn't need his apology or the illusion of boundaries for my sake. Damage was done, and he'd never earn my trust.

Noah scrambled after me as I approached Gavin who was leaning against the front of his car. "I wasn't done," Noah said as he rounded the Nova to gain my attention.

"Looks like you're done," Gavin said.

"Catalina Rose, Hank's on the run because he is

holding onto the last pieces to Victor Lloyd's identity. So is Aaron."

"If you know something about Hank, you better cough it up." Gavin watched his prey squirm. I tugged on his arm, "Can I talk to you?"

Gavin yielded after I asked again. We took a few steps to the side, "What did he tell you, Catalina?"

"Gary knows about the Blood Diamonds. And Noah confirmed that Hank and Aaron know who Victor Lloyd is. So, we just need Noah to call Jensen."

"What for?"

"To get an update on where Jensen and Porter are," I said. Gavin asked for more details. "We have to know their plans. Noah can help with that." To Noah I said, "Make the call."

Reluctance was no longer an option. Gavin's patience had left before the conversation began. And I just stared at Noah, my face sullen, losing all hope for a good outcome. The mixture of our responses took him down.

"Fine."

Noah hit a button and the phone started dialing. After a few rings, Jensen's hurried tone said, "You get it done?"

"Yeah, but I gotta lie low. Scott showed up."

"The girls told me he tore the place apart and Payton was with him."

"He thought he was in the clear, but I killed Catalina Rose when they were in the parking lot at the hospital."

Ian's voice pierced my ears, "Did she suffer?" A note of sadness drifted from him to me. Noah felt it, too.

"No. It was quick." Noah shifted his weight, "I had to

leave in a hurry. Scott and I had a shootout in the parking lot, and I don't know if I got him."

"You're good, we got you. I've got one more assignment for you, and then you can head back to Anders," Jensen said.

"What's up?"

"Hank went by the pawn shop an hour ago, looking to offload some stuff for cash. One of those items was an old cell phone."

"You want me get it?"

"Grab it, and head on up north."

"Sure thing."

The line went dead.

"What's the address for the pawn shop?" I said to Noah.

We never got it. A shot rang out. Gavin pushed me to the ground. The windows to the Porsche shattered. Noah panicked, crawling his way to the side of the Nova. Another shot passed his head.

"Fuck! It was a trap!" Noah crawled past me, heading toward the protection of another sedan.

Gavin was quick. He grabbed me, pulling me under the Nova. By the time we were shielded, Noah was up on his feet, shots flying past him as he ran into the brush. A pair of boots came up next to the Nova.

"There's no one in here!" said a male voice.

"It doesn't matter, he lied."

"Where's the girl?"

"Probably in the hospital. Ya'll go inside and see if she's there. The rest of us are gonna hunt Noah down."

Hesitation came from one of them. "Torch the Porsche, right?"

"What about this thing?"

"Nah, it's still got the tracker on it." With this knowledge, Gavin looked under his car, carefully feeling for whatever device they had referenced. "We'll need that to find them."

A set of gunshot rang out. "We need to get moving before the sheriff comes."

Crunching of glass, rocks, and metal overshadowed the chaos around burning the vehicle. Nevertheless, it was engulfed in flames.

"Got it," Gavin said as he pulled the tracker off his car. "Fuckin' Porter will stop at nothing."

"What should we do?" I said.

Carefully, he peered his head out. "Wait." Slowly, he climbed out, leaving me to examine our surroundings for a second. Then, he retrieved me, wasting no time to get in the car, and punch it into gear.

"They're gonna be on our ass the moment they find out we bolted." He tapped his phone screen, "Dad, I gotta talk. Gary's onto you, and some guy said something about you pawning an old phone? Just call me back." Gavin ended his voicemail.

Everything was a blur. "If he doesn't call us back, what do we do?"

Gavin smirked. I assaulted him with a frown for his blatant disregard for our wellbeing. Then, I saw the name on the caller ID: Hank Scott.

CHAPTER THIRTY

Vow

"Boy, you have a way of really putting yourself into shit," Hank said.

"Nice to hear from you, too." Gavin wasted no time delivering key highlights from our most recent events. I expected there to be more bickering. All I got was the slightest impression that Hank had been caught, and he knew it.

"I don't know where Aaron is."

"Why do Jensen and Porter think you do?"

"It's probably because we left town at the same time."

Gavin's head shook, "There's more to it than that, or else you wouldn't have called me back."

"You said they knew about the pawn shop. Someone's been spying on me, and I want to know who."

"Join the club." Gavin rolled his neck, "Give me something."

"I'll tell you like I told you before; stop chasing this shit."

"You only say that when I'm getting too close." Hank didn't refute this. "Is the cell phone thing true?"

"Pawn shops don't take old phones." Hank ignored Gavin's next question about what he was actually selling. "I don't know anything. So, stop asking."

"Where are you?" Gavin asked.

"On a run. Since you ruined my situation in Tucson, I gotta keep going."

"Where are you running to?" I said. Gavin had wanted to keep my presence a secret, but there was no point.

"Just working until this blows over." Hank didn't elaborate. He claimed someone was calling him, and he hung up.

"I really thought he was gonna tell you more," I said. It didn't make sense for him to call Gavin back just to lead him on. "Why does he do that?"

"You mean being completely unhelpful? That's just who Hank is."

"I mean, he acts like he wants to care, but he never seems to come through."

"Welcome to the last twenty plus years of my life."

Sarcasm aside, I read between the lines. Hank only called to tell his son to stay out of Gary's way, the same thing he had done in his letter. That letter had been a warning about Gavin's relationship with Ian. The fights they had over Michelle's death. Hank had said he made it right with Gary. But Hank was working for Gary? Double crossing Gary? Or was he working for Victor Lloyd?

Only someone with more allies and a longer reach would be able to take down Gary. This begged the question, "Had you ever heard of Victor Lloyd before Gary went to jail?"

"No." Gavin watched my brows tighten. "What's up?"

"If Victor Lloyd was able to take down Gary, he would have to be pretty well-connected." The thoughts flowed, "Even if his name is an alias, his name would still be known."

"So, what are you thinking?"

"How did he know where Maverick would be? And how did he know about Gary's connection with the Blood Diamonds?"

"You thinking it was a Diamond who set it up?"

No, I wasn't. My questions were merely inquiries until Gavin proposed this option. "It makes sense. If there was bad blood within the club, someone may have set up Maverick and Gary at the same time. And they made up Victor Lloyd to hide one of their biker friends."

"Get Charlie on the phone and see what he has to say."

"I can't. I don't have a phone."

"Then, I guess we'll have to wait until we cross paths with them In Settlement Island. Tonight, let's just get some rest, and we'll make the final push tomorrow."

Gavin and I were still exhausted. With a good night's sleep, we would be able to cover more ground tomorrow, maybe even making it home before the bloodbath began.

✑

Gavin asked me to take over driving while he called his dad over and over. Hank's phone went to voicemail, giving us no hope of finding him. Undeterred, Gavin said there was a good chance he was already in Maine. We had pulled into a motel somewhere, tired from driving into the night. Now, we were laying on our respective beds, his closest to the door while mine was safely pushed against the window.

This small spot was on Hank's route, the one he had stayed in while running drugs for Gary. Gavin had come up with the idea. He figured we could learn as much as we could about Hank if we followed his footsteps. I had my notebooks which were mostly preserved aside from the blood on the covers. I had cleaned them off at some roadside gas station, carefully, allowing them to dry before opening them up again.

The owners of this place remembered Hank, but they hadn't seen him in a while. A few months, actually. They claimed he was no longer involved with Gary, which I found odd. To them, Gavin and I were perfect strangers. They didn't owe us any information or apologies. But they insisted on giving us Hank's cover regardless.

"They're creating an alibi for him," Gavin said. "Helping him conceal his tracks." He leaned against his stacked pillows, "You're right. There's something to be said about Gary and Hank being connected. And my dad leading us to Aaron."

"*I told you so,*" *wasn't necessary.* "So, you think Noah's probably told Porter the truth? If he's still alive?"

"I don't care about Noah." Gavin sighed, "We gotta get back to Maine to see for ourselves. That's all I care about."

"We can take turns driving and sleeping," I suggested. "I'll drive during the day, and you can drive at night."

"I think we can make it home, if we don't stop."

I nodded. Now, it was time for bed. I pulled my comforter down, tucking it around me. "I guess I'll see you in the morning."

"Do you want to talk about…"

"No."

"You don't even know what I was going to say."

"It doesn't matter." I said, now leaning against the headboard. "No more talk. We just need to act. Get this done with," I said.

"Okay," he said with confusion.

"Sorry, I'm just tired of talking about things and speculating. We just need to figure this out and move on. Seriously."

"And we will," he affirmed. The softness brought down my mood. "I have a confession to tell you."

"What brought this up?" I said.

"I thought about what you said to Noah. About him lying to you. Well, I went to see my dad, right before you got caught up with Porter." He explained everything to me. Unlike with Noah, I didn't feel betrayed. Gavin's move had helped us, not hurt us. "You're not mad?" he said.

"No. You did it to help me, like you do time and time again. You've been trying to protect me, in your own way. And…" Here came my own truth, "when I thought Ian was going to kill me, I only thought about you." No quip came from him. "I know I've been hot and cold with you, but I'm just scared, Gavin. We seem to keep pulling each other down, and it's not good for us."

He climbed off his bed and sat across from me. "I know." His chest continued to rise and fall, not from nerves, but from comfort. "I never wanted this to happen to you. Part of me feels like I should have never pursued you. But I don't regret loving you, Catalina. Not for one second." He always knew what to say to make everything worse. I rubbed my eyes, "Then we decide, right here, right now," he said. I peered out beyond my fingers. "We decide if we want to work on this and grow this…whatever it is…into something healthy. Or we walk away. No more flirting, no more sex, no more leading each other on. We either choose each other or we walk away."

The notion was admirable, but would it work? What if one of us decided to stay while the other decided to leave? How do we reconcile that?

"This is dangerous," I said.

"But it's better to draw a line in the sand, once and for all." Gavin laced his fingers into mine. "Catalina, I want to grow with you. I want to become a better friend for you. And I'm willing to do the work, become the man I know I deserve to be, and be all in with you." His eyes lit up, "No more lies, no more secrets, no more running. I'm all in, until I draw my last breath."

I gasped, "Are you asking me to marry you?"

He gave me a sly grin, "Not without your dad's blessing. And yours." Slight disappointment hit me. "I'm a mess, and I don't have much to offer you, but I'm growing. And right now, I promise to continue working on myself, my anger, and just everything that doesn't help me."

I leaned in, "You sound like a textbook," I said.

He rolled his eyes, "I'm not good at this stuff."

I rubbed his fingers, "I know."

He straightened up, "I want to be good. Healthy. Strong." A huffing sigh, "Healed."

"For me?"

Confidently, he shook his head, "For me. I have to do this for myself first, then I can focus on serving you." I couldn't stop him from getting down on one knee, "Catalina, I love you. And I vow to never, ever, be an asshole to you ever again. Or decide for you." My brows came together. "I'm talking about that time when I tried to drag you back to Maine, and you left me at a rest stop." Yes, that time. "I vow to listen to you, and be kind, and…"

I pulled him up, "Gavin, just be yourself." I caressed his cheek, "When we dated, you were perfect for me. And you didn't have to make any vows or pick up a self-help book to earn me. You were just you. So, be that guy, and don't worry about anything else, least of all what I think or need. Don't ever change for anyone, including me."

He nodded, relief crossing over him. His lips kissed my hand. "So, that's settled. After this is over, I'll make sure you get back to California, and maybe I'll see you from time to time when I'm at Stanford."

He lifted off the bed, and I grabbed his wrist. "What are you talking about?"

"This is it, right? You're choosing to walk away."

My head shook, "No, I'm not."

"I thought—"

"I mean," I measured my sigh. At the risk of sounding unsure, I just spoke from my heart. "We're a mess, Gavin, not just you. And we can't change all the shit that happened between us. But at one time, we did work. And I was the happiest I had ever been in my whole life."

And I was happy, not because Gavin made me feel like a worthy person. But because I had loved him without apology, the way I always wanted to. No overthinking, no pressure, just laying with him, learning about what he loved and telling him what I loved. He was my best friend, my strongest supporter, and the person who gave me the most space to grow. I wouldn't have been able to fight Blake, leave for California, tear down Ian, or survive everything I had without him. Running from him, being broken by our circumstances, had taught me that I had always been strong. A diamond in the rough I had trapped myself in. He brought out the fighter, the determination, and the soul I had hidden away.

"I wouldn't be the person I am without all the stuff you put me through."

"I don't think that is a good thing," Gavin said.

Yet, it was. "I didn't become the person I was because of you. I finally started to decide for myself because I didn't need you."

"That's hurtful."

I laughed, "What I mean is, I created my own life because you forced me to think outside myself. And all your drama finally made me meet myself and accept myself for who I am. And who I will become." My fingers laced around his, "We've seen each other at our absolute worst. We're both killers. You understand me. And I think that if we can survive this, and become whole people, we can be together."

"So, our relationship depends on whether or not we graduate from therapy?"

This was becoming unbearable, so I kissed him, "All we have left is growing together. And giving this a real try. One where we fight with respect and apologize. Where we move in together and see if we kill each other. Where we talk and decide what would be the best thing for the other."

"Now, you sound like a textbook." His plea was, "Just tell me from your heart."

Instead, I showed him. I kissed him again and again. "I love you, Gavin." Another kiss. "A lot."

He returned my kiss with a few of his own, "I'm obsessed with you." The line could have been cringe-worthy, except he put on a grin. "Will you be all in with me?"

I nodded, "Will you be all in with me?" He nodded.

Our kisses came on faster and faster. I pulled off my shirt, tugging at his jeans. He stopped us, "Wait."

"For what?"

Gavin sighed a few times. "I'm all for this, I just want to slow down." He licked his lips, eyes widening. The next kiss was more meaningful, sultry. "Remember how I said I was obsessed with you?"

"Yeah, and it was a little weird," I said. He kissed my neck.

"Let me show you how obsessed I am," the huskiness in his voice made me laugh.

"Gavin," I gave him a kiss, "please stop." He winked at me. "Seriously, just be yourself."

He kissed me deeper, the motion putting me on my back. I made a dash for his jeans again, but he stopped me. Before I could rebuttal, he placed his finger to his lips, calming me. The kiss went down my cheek, to my neck, lowering down to my navel. I was ready and willing to receive whatever it was he had offered me. Then, he halted.

Frustration crowned my head. "Why are you stopping?"

He came back up and made eye contact with me. "Remember how I didn't want to have sex with you because I wasn't sure if I was the one for you?" Unfortunately, yes. "Well, I don't want to rush this. I mean, we just…"

I pushed my lips onto his. He sat up, and I followed, sitting in his lap. "It's okay. I'm ready. More than ready."

"So, all that talk about being all in was just, so you could bed me, Ms. Payton?"

I kissed him again. "Yes. Now, as the object of your obsession, I demand you prove it to me."

Gavin grinned, "Yes, ma'am." He continued his trail of kisses, this time leading to destinations unknown.

❧

We probably should have stopped sometime last night, but we couldn't help ourselves. Everything Gavin did seemed heightened this time, given the fresh start we had created. His so-called obsession left me gasping for air as he willingly showed me how much he adored my body. Each kiss, each motion we made together, brought us closer and closer. And this time, instead of wondering or overthinking, I woke up this morning, in his arms, safe at home.

We would have to make up for lost time, of course. But for now, we had gotten dressed, checked out, and were getting breakfast at some pancake joint. Sitting next to each other, we shared a plate, syrup dripping from my lips as he fed me a triangle of cake and butter.

"We need to get it together," I said after chewing.

"I know," Gavin replied as he dropped the fork onto the plate, one arm around me as the other landed on my thigh. "But I just want one more second of bliss with you before we have to deal with Porter and his bullshit."

I agreed. "When we finally put an end to him, we can have 365 days of bliss," I leaned in, "and good sex." I kissed him, "And talks about the future. Like what happens when you go to Stanford."

He tilted his head, "Will you wait for me?"

"I figured you would want me to go with you."

"And leave your best friend in L.A. or your family in Maine? I would never ask that of you."

Such a noble act. I gave his lips a peck, leaving syrup on them. "Yes, I'll wait for you."

And just like that, perfection had been crushed by a phone call. This time from a known number, belonging to an unknown person. Gavin answered it with force after putting the phone on speaker, "If this isn't Aaron White, I'm going to kill whoever this is."

"It's Victor Lloyd."

CHAPTER THIRTY-ONE

Victor Lloyd

GAVIN STARED AT the phone, like he didn't believe our luck. I did. That voice belonged to the one person I figured knew the most about Victor Lloyd. "Aaron," I said, relief feeling like a strange friend. A mystery had been solved, bringing an unfortunate fact along for the ride. "It's been you this whole time."

"Catalina, what in the hell are you doing?" he scolded. "You're supposed to be happy and free in California."

"That life was a lie." I didn't have time to explain the details. "Aaron, where are you?"

"Trying to stay one step ahead of Gary, which is pretty fuckin' difficult."

"You should have thought about that before you framed him for murder, Victor," Gavin joked.

"Gary's got it all wrong. Victor didn't frame him for anything. He's not even a real person."

"Then what happened?" I said. He started to backtrack, realizing that I wouldn't leave his vagueness be.

"Aaron, do you know how many people have been screwed over by your supposed lie?"

"A lot. But I'm taking responsibility, and I'm handling it."

"The Blood Diamonds are on their way to Settlement Island." The silence on his end of the phone could have echoed for miles. "Gary and the Diamonds are going to fight it out, unless you tell the truth."

"If I tell Gary I made Victor up, he'll kill me, no questions asked."

I had to ask, "You didn't kill Maverick?"

"No! Come on, Catalina," he said with disgust. "I know we're not that close, but you should at least know I'd never kill someone."

"If you're so against killing, why are you helping the person who did kill Maverick?"

"Listen to me, Catalina. Don't worry about who killed Maverick. I'm gonna take care of Gary, and get Gavin and Gary off, okay?"

"How am I mixed up in your bullshit?" Gavin said.

"Gary needs a way out. Without the pieces that tie Victor Lloyd to Maverick's death, he's gonna pursue the lie that Blake and Russ had a role in Gary's wrongful conviction. He'll need you for that."

"Gary's plan is flimsy, Aaron," I protested. "It's a stretch, and no one would ever believe Blake and Russ had the opportunity and the means to pull off murdering three people." He probably entertained this idea himself from time to time. I mean, he had to consider it. "You took off because you knew Gary doesn't want me and Gavin.

He's just throwing the Blake theory at the courts to buy him some time. The only way he can get his conviction overturned is to bring the real killer in. And right now, that person is you, *Victor*. Unless you can prove otherwise."

The chasm of silence returned. Gavin tapped the table, thinking. He put the phone on mute. "If Aaron is Victor, the Diamonds are gonna want his blood, too. That's why he's stalling. He's in over his head, and the person he's covering for isn't helping him anymore."

I nodded and unmuted the phone, "Aaron, Ian and Jensen have teamed up to find you. At first, I thought Ian knew where you were, but it seems like he doesn't."

"My brother doesn't know anything. He just knows I'm missing."

"Has he tried to call you?"

"I blocked him." Damn. I thought Ian was protecting his kid brother, but at the end of the day, they weren't even talking. "I heard my brother has been making your life hell, Catalina. Stay away from him."

"I've been trying to," I said, stopping my excuses at once. Aaron wouldn't care about the sacrifices I had made to keep Ian at bay. I had failed. That's all he would hear. "Your brother is nowhere near me. He's on his way back to Maine, with his brother Jensen."

"What's the deal with Jensen?" Gavin said. "What does he want from all of this?"

"Gary's enlisted Jensen for some extra muscle." The phone shuffled.

"What about Hank?" I said. "He's been acting really shady."

"More shady than normal," Gavin corrected. "Someone told us Hank knows where you are."

"That's a lie. I haven't spoken to Hank."

"Why would he lie about this?"

"Everyone's been pointing fingers at each other to get Gary off their backs. They know Gary wants to talk to me about the medical report I signed for Maverick. When he couldn't find me, he started shaking people down for leads. Since Hank's not living in town, someone must have pointed the finger at him to get out of being questioned." Aaron answered my sighing with a request, "Catalina, don't come back here. Just stay out of it, for once."

"No," I said with strength and determination. "I can't. Not with everything Porter's done to me. I have to end this."

"What did he do?" I told Aaron only highlights of the last couple of days because Gavin was mindful of the time. But Aaron had to know exactly how his lies had led to Ian becoming the threat that he was. "He tried to kill you?" Aaron said with surprise.

"Gavin thinks he staged the scene, making it look like your brother was going to kill me. But I don't know for sure." I switched gears, latching onto Aaron's disbelief that his murderous brother would choose to murder yet again. "Why are you so shocked?"

"Because my brother likes you," Aaron's voice was muffled by some shuffling. "He's always liked you. That's why he's always given you all those second chances. And he told you his first name."

"And the gifts," Gavin interjected.

"Exactly," Aaron said. "You're the closest thing to a friend he's ever had."

Gavin smirked at Aaron's confirmation of his theory. Ian, somehow had, at one time, cared about me. "I don't think he cares about me anymore."

"He knows *I* care about you. We're family, even though your sister has probably moved on by now." He saved me from answering by continuing, "I've gone to bat for you with Porter a million times, begging him to not hurt you. He said he wouldn't. He promised."

This very smart man was incredibly naïve. "Giving you his word doesn't mean he would keep it, Aaron."

"You don't know him like I do. We live very, very different lives, and I can't stand him most of the time. But, we do have one rule: if I tell him someone is off limits, he can't hurt them. And if he gives me his word, he can't break it." Aaron's voice stilled. Then, after a pause, he informed me of his next move. "Catalina, if you come back to Maine, I can't protect you. Neither can my brother. He can't go against what Gary wants. If he could, you'd be free to frolic on the beach, and I'd be sitting at home eating a bowl of Rice Krispies with my girlfriend."

"You don't have to protect her," Gavin assured him. "My crew is there. Plus, the Blood Diamonds have a very soft spot for her. Not to mention, I'm sure Malcolm has hired the National Guard as a backup." He leaned into the phone, "I won't stop until Gary's out of the picture, and she is safe again."

A chill feathered down my spine, brought on by the vow we had made to one another.

This testament of love and declaration unfazed Aaron. "Love and allegiance mean nothing during a civil war, which is what we're about to see. Gary's got numbers, and the Blood Diamonds want vengeance for their brothers. We're all fucked."

The outcome was grim, but so were many outcomes I had faced before. Disobeying Ian and saving Kyle had been the first challenge I had survived. Next was the inevitable death that encapsulated Blake by my own shaking hands. All this was followed by a cross country trip along a highway lined with gun fights and carnage; the final destination an invitation to an unavoidable war.

And I wasn't afraid.

Freedom isn't given; it's earned.

I had earned mine every time I survived one more outcome. One more meeting with the wrong person. One more leap of faith into the wrong hands. One more hope that had turned into a nightmare.

Aaron was now dwelling in the same place I had been when his own brother had placed me there. Now, it was my turn to help him survive it.

"Everyone is talking about protecting me, but no one has been protecting you, Aaron." I licked my chapped lips, still hitting little drizzles of syrup on my softened skin. "I know what it's like to be the glue that holds all this together. The fear and loneliness that comes from making the worst decisions imaginable. So, I'm willing to help you. I'll protect you, if you help me send Gary back to jail."

"That's sweet, but there is nothing you can do for me."

A wicked idea formed a wicked grin, "I have proof that will put Gary away forever."

Gavin muted the phone again, "What are you talking about?"

"The flash drive."

"You don't have the flash drive."

"I can get it." I unmuted the phone, "Daniel Sullivan gave me something that will cripple Gary and any plans he has to stay free for the rest of his life."

"Really?" He sounded as unimpressed as Gavin looked.

"Yes. I just need to go see your brother."

"Catalina, I don't know where my brother is. And if I did, I wouldn't tell you because I don't want you to get hurt."

"You said your brother promised not to hurt me."

"I also said I didn't want you to come anywhere near Maine! For the love of God, just stay out of sight until this blows over."

My skin prickled at this statement. "Is that what you're going to do? Just put your head in the sand and hope every-thing works out?"

"Yes. Trust me. Porter doesn't want this Gary thing to keep going. He wants to get his business back in line, with or without his dad."

Aaron had unknowingly given me his biggest tell. "I understand," I said slowly. Gavin's brows bent. "I'll let you know when I get to town."

"Catalina! I'm serious! This is not a game!"

Yes, it was. And this game was one I was willing to

play. "We gotta get on the road. I'll call you when I'm back in town."

I hung up, pausing until my shoulders unknotted. I looked over at Gavin, "Porter's protecting Aaron. He knows why Aaron ran. He also knows why Aaron lied on the medical report. And why Aaron's protecting Maverick's killer. The reason has to be so good, Porter's willing to keep Gary in the dark about Victor Lloyd." I thought my observation was enough to impress Gavin. He only blinked a few times. "Porter has to know the full story about what happened that night. And he's keeping Aaron alive, because whatever Aaron knows will help Porter in some way."

"I think you are overreaching." Gavin dunked a piece of pancake into some syrup.

He took one bite, but I stopped him from taking the next. "I think Hank is the one who killed Maverick, and Gary put him up to it. And Aaron knows it was Hank."

Gavin choked on his father's name. "What?"

"Hank wanted to get back at Gary for Michelle's death. And Gary wanted out of his deal with the Blood Diamonds. So, Gary leveraged his failing relationship with the Diamonds for his revenge. He invited them up for a talk, and he told Hank his plans. Hank would pull the trigger and pin it on some rival dealer named Victor Lloyd. Hank accepted the offer to be the hitman, because he wanted to set Gary up. Hank went out to the woods and shot Maverick. He used the delivery down in Florida as an alibi, but everything fell apart when Russ got involved. You shot Russ, and Hank left you at the scene, so Gary would think the job went off without a hitch. Then, he made up Victor Lloyd to pin Gary to the crime scene!"

"How does Aaron fit into that?" he said cautiously

"Hank must have convinced Aaron to write the fake report, because they both wanted Gary gone. Then, Porter found out the truth, he confronted Aaron, and Aaron pled for forgiveness. Aaron came clean, your dad hid in Tucson, and Porter didn't say anything because he couldn't incriminate his brother!"

My theory seemed solid compared to everything else we had speculated.

In return, Gavin drummed his fingers on the table. "So, how is Russ involved?"

"I don't know. Maybe he saw Hank driving away from the scene, and they got into a fight about it," I said.

"Russ hated Gary. He wouldn't fight with Hank to defend Gary. Nor would my dad have told him anything. He would've lied to get Russ off his back and keep him out of the crime scene."

"The evidence is there," I stressed. "Aaron's fake medical records. Hank's weak alibi during the time Maverick was murdered. They both hate Gary." I shrugged, "What's missing?"

"If you want to gloss over Russ, you still have another problem. Porter." His finger caressed the patch of skin on my face that had been beaten by that man one too many times. "If Aaron betrayed his brother by putting Gary in jail, Porter would never forgive him. Add in that time Porter's entire business fell apart because of Blake, and Porter would have blamed Aaron, not me, for destroying every-thing he had built. He would have made his brother pay."

"Business was great after Gary went to jail," I exclaimed. "It was a win for him and Gary."

Gavin dropped his hand, "Let's say Aaron schemed to put Gary behind bars. What was his motivation? Getting rid of Gary didn't stop drugs from coming into Settlement Island and Anders. It didn't stop all those murders. His brother took over the drug enterprise, and Aaron didn't benefit at all."

"Maybe he thought Porter would have given up the business."

Gavin's head shook, "Aaron knows Porter better than anyone. He would have known better than to assume Porter would've had a change of heart."

Deflation robbed me of every ounce of joy I had built on my almost certainty…

"Honestly, it's a good theory. Unfortunately, it doesn't work." He quickly put a few fluffy triangles in his mouth, drowning them with coffee. "We need to get going."

Now our trip was clouded by my vain attempts to best the other players in our game. "I thought I had it," I said as Gavin opened the passenger door for me. He had closed his own door when I continued, "Aaron and Hank are involved." He sighed, his hands dropping from the steering wheel. "I'm sorry, but I can't let this go."

"It's not that," he said, eyes still forward.

I reached over, lacing my fingers in his hand, "What is it, then?"

I expected another parade of apologies. Another round

of Gavin taking full responsibility for my role in this shitty situation and how I should have never been brought into this. Or at least an acknowledgement that whatever was waiting for us in Maine would be far worse than anything we had ever dreamed up in our short, tainted relationship.

So, when he said, "I know where Aaron is," I almost didn't catch it.

"You do?"

"Yeah?" He started the Nova.

"That's great news," I said in an effort to cheer him up.

"I just wish I had figured it out sooner," Gavin pulled the car into gear.

"Hey, we all make mistakes." Again, my words didn't cheer him up. "Is that all?"

Gavin put the car back in park. "When we see him, I'm gonna have to deal with my past." His ominous replies gripped my chest. He soothed the panic attack before it rose to the surface. "His family has an estate on the outskirts of town. Not many people know about it. I only know about it because my mom had my first birthday party there. I've got pictures of it in my bag."

"Oh." My hands sat in my lap.

"After her funeral, Aaron's parents had a reception at the estate. My grandparents, Brianna's family, and a small group of people were invited. I remember Brianna chased me around the yard for like an hour until my grandmother told us to stop. Then, Paula took me aside and we went on a walk next to the river. Close by was an old mill and one of Joseph Settler's old cabins. The estate belonged to the Settler family until it was bought by Grover Capshaw White."

"You're kidding?"

He shook his head, "Nope. The estate should have been in my family, since I am a descendant of Joseph Settler. Instead, someone in my family tree let the property get foreclosed on due to back taxes, and Grover bought it at auction. Some of his books were written there."

I scolded the giddy girl inside. "That's awful."

"That's why the Whites offered to host my mom's reception there. And it's the only place I can think of where Aaron would have gone."

"How do you know?"

"Because no one knows where it is unless they have been there before. Grover had it removed from public record, so he could write there in peace without all the journalists and reporters finding out about it. Apparently, after his first few books came out, the press alone was a nightmare."

I was too young to remember this. But it made sense. Grover had mentioned in his autobiography how he liked his privacy. The houses he owned were never in his name. Nor did he do interviews regarding his questionable past and the gaps in his personal life. That's why I had never drawn the line between Grover and Aaron being related. Nor did I ever hear about Ian in any of Grover's books.

This memory from Gavin was a gift. An opportunity. I thanked him for it. "Don't thank me yet. I might be completely wrong."

Regardless, it was the effort and the willingness to try

that counted. "If you're right, great. And if you're wrong, that's okay, too. We'll find him."

He grinned, smitten with my relentlessness. The kiss on my hand lasted for a blink. Then, he put the car in drive. I released my thoughts, letting them fade into a distant memory. They traveled out the window and into the cold air. Soon, we'd be back in Maine. Back to where it all began. And I welcomed the closure that would greet us once we arrived.

Either way, no matter which way the coin landed, I knew this was the last trip I'd make to Settlement Island, Maine.

CHAPTER THIRTY-TWO

Maine

MOTHER SAT ON the porch, a mug in her hands, her hair seated over one of her shoulders. She was beautiful, young. Peaceful as the morning sun rose across the lake barely waking from a night of rest. The roar of the Nova was loud, startling her to her feet.

I hadn't seen her in months.

Each time she visited me at the beach house, she overlooked the time and distance that had kept us apart. She had projects she wanted me to oversee. Chores she wanted me to master. And recommendations about how I could make the small cottage a better home.

This time, on her turf, her eyes were filled with tears. The mug was left behind as she bounded toward me, a large sweater robe bouncing against her small frame. Her arms wrapped around me, the smell of her lavish conditioner and designer perfume telling me to never leave home again.

"Hi, Mom," I said, unable to let go. She was, in fact, keeping me warm.

"Baby, I missed you so much."

I had missed her, too. More so now that we had been reunited. "I missed you, too." Mother didn't cry. Ruining her makeup wasn't really her thing. In place of balling came a reluctance to let me stand on my own.

Dad rushed out the front door, pulling us apart. "My God, Catalina. Are you alright? I've been calling you, searching for you, losing my mind over what happened to you."

"I'll give you all the details after I get some food and a shower." I pointed to Gavin, "And this one needs a very long nap."

Gavin had driven through the day and night. After the lead on Aaron's whereabouts, he didn't stop. His eagerness to get me home outweighed his need for sleep. I could tell by the way he was leaning against the Nova, he was tired. I had slept most of the night, my head on his shoulder, his jacket over my arms.

Now, his duty was done. His reward was an incredible meal, a steaming shower, and Mother's layered bed in the guestroom.

Dad put out his hand to Gavin's, shaking it, "Thank you for bringing her home."

"It was my pleasure."

"Come in, come in!" Mother chanted. "Gloria is making breakfast."

"Who is Gloria?" I said.

"Your mom's new housekeeper," Dad said under his breath. "She's a hell of a cook. Made up a really nice dinner last week for Luke and Cecilia."

"I need to call them," I said.

"I'll let them know you're here. And I'll have my assistant bring out a new phone for you on our plan as well."

"You have an assistant?"

"Well, yeah. I'm a busy doctor." Dad ushered us into the dining room for breakfast burritos, Mother's guilty pleasure food.

"Can I eat this while I take a shower?" I said.

"Catalina, don't be a savage," Mother scolded me. We were sinking back into our old habits, and I loved it. "Gavin, are you hungry?"

"Yes, Mrs. Payton."

Mother stood aside and let Gavin be served by Gloria. I was next. Then, Dad commanded us to all sit together and eat before we ran off to our various tasks. "I've cleared my schedule for the day, just for you."

Dad never took time off from work. "How did you know I would be home today?" He pointed his burrito at Gavin. "He gave me a heads up yesterday."

"I can only imagine the things you two have been through," Mother nibbled on her food.

The story we had to tell was worth hearing. Yet, I couldn't get my mind off my sister. "Where is Cecilia?"

"She stayed the night at the loft."

"I told her we were on our way home," Gavin said. "I'm sorry I didn't let you talk to her before. Everything happened so fast, and then you fell asleep in the car."

"She'll be happy to see you. So will Luke. They've been here at the house every day, waiting for you to arrive,"

Mother said to alleviate Gavin's guilt. "Finally, I had to tell them to go about their business until you came back."

"Your mom has been our rock through this all," Dad said.

I struggled to see how. The hurtful answer was she didn't care about what happened to me. If I had disappeared as a result of my poor decision making, that was my own doing.

The revelation behind her peace came from the very large, heavy cross hanging from her neck. "I put my faith in God that you would return safely."

My reaction was just a smile. Mother was a believer, I assumed. But her faith always seemed like an afterthought. Something to brush off when things didn't go her way, never a place to go for daily practice.

"That's good," I affirmed, unable to come up with something more encouraging.

"I'm serious. Luke's mother and I have been going to church every Sunday. And I've cut back on drinking, too."

"And what prompted you to make all these changes?" I said as gently as I could.

Her smile beamed, "Too much drinking causes cancer and wrinkles." This was a well-documented fact. "As for church, I needed some place to go when I was worried about you being so far away. I felt so helpless." Dad ate quietly while watching his wife. "After you left, I had a hard time coming to terms with you being gone. Not being able to comfort you when things are bad." Mother bowed her head, "I wasn't a good mom to you." Her napkin dabbed her eyes.

Again, Mother never cried. It wasn't her thing. Or at least it hadn't been her thing…until I abandoned her. I left my chair and knelt down in front of her face, seeing the glistening tears for myself. "I'm okay, Mom," I said with relief. I reached up and hugged her, "You were never a bad mom."

Through her curls, I could see Gavin hold space. He missed his mom, too.

"I told you she still loves you, Sally," Dad said.

"I never stopped loving you, Mom." In truth, "You'll always be my first love."

The tears continued as Mother took advantage of the closeness between us. She gave me one more hug. I looked over at Dad for an enlightening explanation. "Menopause," he mouthed. I nodded. "And," he whispered, "she really did miss you."

Dad rescued me, "Sally, we should let these kids get settled in. Catalina, the upstairs guest room is ready for you guys."

I let go of my mother who was slowly recovering from her speech. "I thought I wasn't allowed to sleep with a guy under your roof."

"You can sleep next to a guy," he said in his deep tone. Gavin regretted the offer. "You're a grown woman. I need to start treating you like one."

"I've been grown for several years now," I said.

"No," he shook his head. "Eighteen doesn't make you grown. A car, a job, your own house, those things make you grown."

"But I live in one of your houses." Saying this wasn't

making my case. Gavin gave me a wink to stop while I was slipping behind. "Thank you for treating me like an adult. Finally."

"No *finally* needed. Do you know why I've been so hard on you?" Mother and I groaned for Dad to spare us from one of his lectures.

"Malcolm, just enjoy our daughter being home," she said.

"I was so hard on you," he continued, "because I always expected more from you. You're smart, hardworking, and extremely gifted. When I look at you, I see a lot of me. And I never wanted you to fall into the same traps your sister did."

"Cecilia turned out to be a fine young woman," Mother defended. If only she saw the stuff her darling child had swept under the rug.

"Cecilia's *finally* figuring out how life works," Dad said. "She's standing on her own two feet instead of chasing after some man to give her the world. But you never did that. You always stood for what you believed in, no matter how much we hated it. So, I always held you to it. And I never wanted you to settle for less than what you deserved."

"Thanks, Dad." I meant my appreciation.

All these years, I thought I had been invisible to him. That who I was as a person was never good enough. His condescending attitude toward my wants and needs trapped me in my childhood. Held me there as proof that I couldn't provide for myself. Yet, in my silent rebellions and frustration for never earning his respect, I had finally proven my worth to him when I had proven it to myself.

"If we act like children, you're gonna treat us like children."

"Bingo!" Dad had finished his plate and handed it to Gloria. Then, out came his phone, "Your guy Grover has this quote I really like." He started scrolling frantically. "Hang on, I know it's here." I chuckled. "Ah, found it." He stood in dramatic fashion, "*Let your children remain children until they see their own light.*" He put his phone down, "I'll be honest, I'm not sure what it means, but I thought it would make sense to you."

"It's a line from a poem about standing in your parents' shadow," Gavin said. We turned our attention to him. "A child can't stand in their own light if it's constantly being eclipsed by their parent's greatness."

Dad pointed, "Exactly!" He grabbed his phone, "Now, if you'll excuse me, I have some phone calls to make."

Mother said to Gavin, "Honey, you need some rest."

"I think I can manage until I get upstairs."

"Let me help you," I said.

I showed Gavin to the room that was across from Cecilia's old haunts. The sheets had been turned down, the shades drawn. Gavin threw his jacket on the couch sitting at the base of the bed. Off came the boots. Jeans, shirt, and socks still on, he collapsed. "Wake me in a few days."

I sat down against the pillows, inviting him to put his head on my lap. My fingers brushed through his hair, this single action shortening our conversation.

"Thank you for bringing me home."

"Uh huh."

"I didn't expect my mother to be so emotional."

"She's your mom." Gavin's eyes remained shut, his body refusing to move from the nest of blankets.

"I know, but I kinda feel bad for putting her through hell. And for causing Cecilia so much grief."

"Mmm."

"I'll let you sleep."

"You can keep talking," he mumbled. "I can't guarantee that I can keep listening."

My fingers slowed, still brushing. And he fell asleep immediately. I left him there in the room, tiptoeing to the door and closing it. Gloria met me downstairs, informing me that Mother had left to retrieve some things for me and Gavin. Dad was on a conference call. She offered to draw me a bath, which I accepted.

As she prepared the tub, I stood in my old room, seeing some clothes in my closet. I picked out a sweater and jeans, a pair of beat-up Converse shoes to match. All my books were either at the loft or in California, so I went to the library in one of the other rooms.

Traditionally, this was a craft room Mother would never use. However, I was surprised to see a few half-full scrapbooks and the beginnings of a crochet blanket. Beyond these things were two bookcases on the wall. Most of the books were from Oprah's and Reese's book clubs. A lot of self-help remedies and biographies from celebrities. Seeing that Mother was personal friends with many of these people, I figured she already knew their stories.

To humor me, I found three books by Grover.

Mother had bought these when I was in high school. She said she wanted to know why I was so obsessed with a man who wasn't remarkably good-looking and talked in circles. His allure was lost to her, but I was relieved that she had kept the books anyway.

The bathroom door closed, and I set the book down on the bath tray. Jasmine and lavender misted the air, loosening my tense shoulders. The water cupped my skin, softer than anything Los Angeles had to offer. My eyes shut, just enjoying the simple things, like this warm bath and a good book.

I couldn't get lost in this.

On the other side of this sanctuary was the intention for my homecoming. The war I'd soon be thrown into. The town that would be brought down to rubble.

We had traveled down Maine Street on our way in. Buildings still stood. Couples took walks on paths next to the lake. Boats rocked against the waves as sailors didn't dare enter the frigid waters.

Settlement Island, Maine was idyllic.

Unharmed.

So, where had the threat gone? Where was Gary? The Blood Diamonds?

My eyes mournfully opened.

Later, I'd find my answer to these questions. I'd receive my new phone, rally the troops, and I'd find and fight Gary for my home. My family. My town. Like the good Settler I was.

The word Settler remained on my tongue.

I opened the book, turning through the pages until I found the poem Dad had referenced. Indeed, Gavin had been right. Grover had warned parents against stifling their children. He pleaded his case that kids learn best when they are in the teeth of the wolves.

Okay, that was a little bit extreme. And that was probably the reason why I had forgotten he had written this poem.

I moved on, the word Settler still close in mind. As secretive as Grover was, he probably nodded a clue toward his make-believe Settler roots.

There, I found it.

The Settler Man's Ballad

Washed in wisdom they were. These men claimed this land for their own. They battled a landlocked sea for the island they would call home. Maine's winter had been mild, pushing them into the marshes where waterfalls had given them abundance. Elk forging, one brought down by the prick from an arrow. The men cheered, they laughed, they got to work, adding a few more days to their starving bodies.

I was never a Settler because I refused to settle. But the woman I love is. She had grown here, her father taking her to the resting place of this elk's bones. Her mother was washing their clothes in the laziest river they had ever known.

That's where her first love had taken her on their first date.

She had fawned over these grounds where her family had picnicked, camped, and told heritage stories. She invited him along, though he wasn't a storyteller. The art was lost on him, but the love he had for her pushed him to try. To imagine. To dream with her.

Before she became the character in my stories, she was his. Yet, he failed to be hers.

She held little heart for the tall brawny man with wicked dreams of conquering a landscape that refused to produce fruits from his deceitful labors. Despite it all, she had faith that this town, the land where more elk bones had come to rest, would break him of his dreadful songs.

Songs and ballads to a wise God who had no interest in changing this place. The Lord had something else in mind for this man and this woman, and only she would heed. Her sun was named Ian, a light that gave her the strength to return to the land of her people. To teach him how to be a Settler and what ballads he would sing. Ballads and stories that had given him his namesake.

I heard her song, a tearful melody about losing love. About a man dusted in the winds of strife, longing to find his way back by the waters of that lazy river.

I followed her to the cool waters where she bathed her baby while he played. She had come home.

I sat beside her, admiring her beauty as her child gazed at his treasure. She had become my treasure, too.

"Darling, what is it you need?" she said to me.

"I need a name for the song you sing."

"It's nothing special, just an ode to my father. He gave it to me as a wedding gift a long time ago."

"So, darling, what is your father's name, so I can name this song after him?"

"Victor Lloyd."

The book dropped into the water, which was unfortunate. I needed it as evidence. Without it, Gavin, nor anyone, would believe me.

"I solved it," I said after the rush of connections came through me.

Aaron had gone missing. Someone had told him to go. So, he went. His absence was hedged in a layer of protection from the only person who could offer it.

A promise had been made between brothers. Aaron would comply, like he always did, as long as Ian had given him something in return. Fearfully, Ian agreed, only if Aaron agreed to alter my course.

Ian knew I was looking for answers. He knew I had to know why I had to shoot Blake. I had to find a way out of the pain. Instead, I had found a way into the plot Ian had gracefully hidden behind Russ's assassination. A murder that secured his future and saved his fate.

Aaron had been a good and faithful servant. But the conspiracy didn't come from him, but rather his father's lips. Aaron could deny it, but this poem concealed Ian's most damning secret.

Ian is Victor Lloyd.

CHAPTER THIRTY-THREE

Consent

"I NEED MY phone!" I said as I rushed to the kitchen, hoping Mother was still here. Then, I remembered that she was retrieving said phone, and both of them were nowhere to be found. My focus shifted to Dad who was locked away in his office. Banging on the door, it was Gloria who relieved me.

"Mr. Payton stepped out for a quick house visit."

Okay, no Mother, no Dad, and no phone. That left Gavin upstairs to help me. I took the steps, two at a time, which was difficult seeing that I was barely 5'7" and the steps were a healthy spacing apart. I made it, without grace, opening the door while breathing hard.

Gavin hadn't turned over from his stomach. His soft snores brought on sudden guilt.

All I needed was his phone.

Which was probably in his pocket.

Selfishness competed with compassion for the man that had driven himself crazy to get me back here.

But I needed to make this call.

Out of options, I shifted through his jacket pockets, hoping the phone was there.

The phone fell onto the carpet with a thud.

Gavin didn't stir. I grabbed it, sealing the door behind me, and headed back to Dad's office where I knew he had several cords and power stations to charge his many devices. I set the phone to charge, anticipating a glow from the screen. It came some two-three minutes later.

Passcode: My birthday

Contacts: Luke

Just Luke, no last name.

I pressed the phone to my ear and waited for the ringing to be replaced with Luke's voice. "Hey, man. It's great to hear from you."

"Ian is Victor Lloyd!"

"Catalina?" His voice perked up.

"Luke, Ian Robert Porter is Victor Lloyd!" The shouting and cheering from my end had drowned out whatever he said next. "I solved it! I solved it! And I have proof!"

"What proof?" He cut in.

"The poem that Grover wrote. It's there, in black and white, damning evidence that Ian framed his own fuckin' dad for murder!"

"You're sure about this?"

"Yes!" I wanted to take the phone to get the book, but it wasn't charged enough. "Hang on, and I'll read it to you." No response of compliance was necessary. Luke hung out while I brought the wet book into Dad's office and placed it on the desk. Turning the wet pages was difficult, but I was undeterred. Finally, the passage was soggy, but the words were still legible.

I read it slowly, ensuring that he didn't miss a single clue. At the end, I announced Ian's alias, and pushed the book further on the desk, protecting it from any damage.

I didn't ask what Luke thought. My assumption was sound.

He began with, "Grover is Aaron's dad. So, Aaron could be Victor."

"He already tried to pass that lie to me." I told him about my conversation with Aaron. "I wanted to believe him when he told me, but some things never made sense. This does."

"You seem so sure…"

I had to interrupt, "Luke, it has to be Ian. He's the only one who has a foot in both camps. He's Jensen's brother, which means he has to keep up the act about who framed their father. Aaron forged those medical documents because he was protecting *his* brother. If Gary knew Ian framed him, then he would surely kill him."

"But what's his motivation?"

The original theory stood. "Greed. By putting Gary in jail, Ian would inherit the business." I folded my legs on the chair, "It was doing better under Ian's leadership. He's making more money now. Or he was until Blake ruined it. Regardless, Ian was the only one who did it. He knew about the relationship between Gary and the Blood Diamonds. Once the police looked into Gary's past, he knew that they would believe that Gary did it. So, he made up that whole story about Victor Lloyd being the witness, when in reality, Victor Lloyd was the killer. He had to be."

"Huh," Luke laughed. He stammered over his thoughts, landing on, "I think you nailed it."

The tidal wave of relief and understanding brought me to the ground. I had my leverage against Ian. I held all the cards. I held his fate in my hands. "How do I use this?"

"Well, when you get back to Maine, we can figure it out."

"I'm already here."

Luke's voice rose in volume. I was required to tell him where I was before I spoke another word about anything else. Then, he was on his way.

❧

I stood on the porch, like my mother had, when Luke pulled up. He was a new man. He stood taller, dressed better, hair tousled, jacket snug against his muscles. His hug lifted me off the ground with no effort.

"God, I'm so glad you're here."

"I missed you, too," I said. His blue eyes were brighter than they had been when he claimed that he loved me. "Please, come in."

He closed the door behind him, placing his coat on the rack. Strong was an underestimation. God-like, a warrior, was closer to what my friend had become.

"You were serious about going to the gym," I said.

"My trainer has me on this new program. It's intense, but I'm seeing results right away."

With this body, he should be the trainer. "Okay, now that you're here, can you gush with me about Victor Lloyd?"

"Where's Gavin?"

"Sleeping upstairs."

"So, I'm the only person you've told about Ian?"

"Yes. I called you the moment I found out."

He nodded and put his hands in his pockets. "Before we jump into the whole Ian thing, can I talk to you about something?" My brows furrowed. What could be more important than solving this case? "I just, um, need to talk to you while we're alone."

"Okay, sure," I said, my skin tightening. We sat down on the couch, facing each other. "What's up?"

Luke nodded, his eye wishing to twitch. "You've been gone for over a year. And things have changed a lot around here." He paused, and I wished he would speed up. "You'll always be my best friend. And I know you love him, and he loves you…"

"Oh, no!" I put my face in my hands. This was about Luke's inappropriate feelings for me. Why couldn't I escape this?

He laughed, "It's not what you think. At least, I hope it's not." Luke pulled my hands from my face. "I'd like to ask if it's okay for me to start dating Cecilia."

"What?" I said, recovering from my horror of reliving a love triangle again and being thrust into another awkward love arrangement, this time involving my own sister.

"I like her, a lot. And she likes me, but we don't want to pursue anything if it will bother you."

"You like Cecilia?" He nodded. "Since when?"

He grinned, "I don't know. It just kinda crept up on me. She's been so nice and fun. We do almost everything together, and I can talk to her about anything."

We never had that, Luke and I. Our courtship was laced with my complicated feelings for him and my curiosities about Gavin. We were never pure in our attempts to be with one another. The glow in Luke's eyes showed that he had found purity and fun in Cecilia of all people.

"Yeah, Luke. If you want to date her, I'm okay with it. I mean, she has a habit of running men into the ground, but I'm not gonna stop you from seeing if she's worth it."

"She is."

I gave him a crooked smile. "What about Aaron?"

"She's not dating him anymore. Or James. Or that guy from the gym."

"She was dating some guy at the gym?"

"They went on one date. She told me all about it, and I told her to pick a guy that makes her happy. So, she dumped all of them and picked me." He said, "I thought she told you about all this."

"Nope." Whether it was jealousy or fear that I would keep this lovely man from her, she withheld everything. "Either way, you have my blessing." He let out a relieving sigh. "Can we talk about Ian?"

"Yes." The way he positioned his consent didn't sit right with me.

"I'm sorry. I feel like I'm being a jerk."

"You're just really excited," he said.

"No, that's not it." In with a deep breath, "I have this

habit of making everything about me. Especially when it comes to my relationship with you." His face fell into the truth. He knew exactly what I was talking about. "If you're happy with my sister, I'm happy for you. And if you want to help me with my Ian problem, I'm grateful to have you."

"I told you I would help with putting Gary back in jail, and I meant it." His exterior was tough, but his touch was soft. "I would never lie to you, Catalina. And I'll always be here for you." My smile leaned to the side. He took it anyway, "Now, if we're going to prove that Ian and Victor Lloyd are the same person, we're going to need more proof."

"I have these." I dug into a bag and pulled out my bloody notebooks.

"Whose blood is that?"

"Ben's." Oh, Lord, I had forgotten about Ben. Was he still alive? Without my phone to call Noah, I wouldn't be able to know. "He might still be alive." And maybe Noah was, too.

"Shit, Catalina. Maybe we shouldn't look further into this."

There was no turning back now. "We've already done the hard part, Luke. We've got him!"

"Sort of. You're still missing some key pieces of evidence."

"Such as?"

"Well, there's Dixon, Russ, and Hank." Two dead men and a deadbeat. "We know Hank is involved for sure. But we don't know how Porter and Hank are connected. We're not clear about who killed Dixon and if Russ was actually killed because of Porter. And if we can't prove that, Porter can twist all this onto Hank, Russ, or Dixon." He turned the page in my notebook to one that had managed to be free of blood. "Hank worked for Gary, so he has every reason to frame him for murder. Blake brings Russ into the picture, because Russ was at odds with Porter's drug operation when Gavin shot him. They tried to pin it on Russ and Gary having a feud, which is only reinforced by Blake's attack on the Porters' business."

"So, you're saying Ian could spin it and make it seem like Blake finished what Russ started. That Russ originally went after the business and framed Gary."

"Exactly. And that brings in Dixon. He was close friends with Blake, which also means he was probably close with Russ. Being in law enforcement, Dixon could have planted evidence to make Gary look guilty." He circled all three characters' names, "Victor Lloyd could be any of these people: Dixon, Russ, or even Blake."

I slouched back, out of ideas for a moment. "The only way we can prove it was Ian is if we could find someone who actually saw him shoot Maverick. Or if Aaron confesses."

"Remember, Victor Lloyd has always claimed to be a witness who saw Gary do it. No one has ever claimed to be the killer. And the cops have no leads to prove it wasn't Gary." He paused, "According to Dixon, that is."

A flash of hope tainted my mind, "We need a witness. A new Victor Lloyd."

"In order to find a witness, we would have to get someone to talk. And I highly doubt anyone would be willing to do that."

There was Aaron. But judging by our last phone call, his bond with Ian was growing stronger every day. Plus, Ian had Aaron and he had the flash drive, which held the police records, videos, and every other piece of information that I could use to find more evidence.

My fingers massaged my temples, "I shouldn't have given it to him."

"Given who what?"

"I gave Ian the flash drive to save my life. It had all of Daniel's files and our research. Now, I have nothing."

"I made a copy," Luke said. My head flew up. "You didn't make a copy?"

"No, I didn't."

He shook his head, "What am I gonna do with you?"

"Right now, you're saving me." Time was not on our side. I tore a page out of my notebook and wrote a message to Gavin on where to find me. Luke had an apartment in the township, so we would end up there, after I got my new phone.

I grabbed one of Mother's coats, and we were on our way.

❧

Mother hadn't made it to the phone store, so it took some time for me to finally get a new device on the family line. But when it was finally activated, a barrage of texts, voicemails, and emails flooded the screen. From here, I sent Gavin a formal text, giving him the address to Luke's new place.

It was a studio overlooking the lake. Bigger than it seemed on video chat. Warmer than any home I had ever owned. "I've got wine in the kitchen, if you want some." His face glowed in the light of the fire he had lit.

"Thanks, but I don't really drink anymore." Now, some gossip, "And neither does my mother."

"Yeah, she's been hitting the whole Jesus thing hard since you left." He placed his laptop on the dining room table. "She's on like every committee at church."

"Well, good for her." We sat down next to one another. "How are your parents?"

"They're getting a divorce."

"Oh, Luke, I'm sorry."

He waved my concern away, "I'm glad. They should have gotten divorced a long time ago." He powered on the screen. "Besides, my mom is a completely different person. She's so happy and drinking less."

"That's good."

Luke typed in his password and pulled up a copy of every single file, photo, video, document, and speculation we had about Victor Lloyd. "Alright. Are you ready?"

"Yes."

He got up and went to his printer, pulling out a stack of blank papers. "It might be better if we write things out on these. So, we can rearrange the pages and see if there are any patterns."

"Smart."

"Okay, where do we begin?" he said.

Our options were Gary or Ian. Father or son. Or, even better, "We start with our murder victim: Maverick. We need to see what motive Gary and Ian would have to kill him."

"That's easy. Gary would want to kill Maverick because of their business deals. Gary owes them money, so when Maverick came to collect, Gary murdered him."

"But there were two other Diamonds who came with him. Maverick was the only one of the three whose body was found," I said.

Luke drug his hand over his chin. "Three against one? Those odds don't work out."

"How do you know Gary was alone?"

"A few reasons. Reason one: if someone was with Gary when Maverick died, we would have heard about this person. Everyone in his company would have hunted this witness down until they found him."

"He could have killed this person," I said.

"Maybe. But he would have needed this person's help to get rid of the bodies. That leads to reason two: why was Maverick's body left out for someone to find? If Gary did kill Maverick, he would have gotten rid of all three bodies."

I thought about it, "He could have done it to send a message."

"To a motorcycle gang that doesn't even live here?"

He was right. "So, then Gary has to be out. He had the means and the motive to kill Maverick, but he couldn't have done it." I wrote all this down and set the paper aside. "Now, we move on to Ian."

Luke started, "Ian kills Maverick because…"

"…he wants the business for himself."

"So, why would he get rid of the other two Blood Diamonds? More bodies would mean more jail time for Gary."

"And three murder charges are harder to beat than one."

This is the last thought he stayed on for a bit. We needed more information. A new, fresh lead. Luke scanned the files using the Find feature. We searched for Porter's name and any references to Maverick or the Blood Diamonds. Nothing returned. Our next search tied Victor Lloyd to Maverick or the Blood Diamonds. The only results brought up Aaron's vague police report and Victor Lloyd's witness statement.

"There's nothing here," Luke announced.

Indeed, it was lacking. But could I use it.

"It's not a homerun," I said while writing a note to myself. "We can't expect one piece of evidence to tell the whole story. No, there are layers here. And we need to pull back one layer at a time."

"Can you explain that in plain English?"

Thinking and explaining it to him would slow down my progress. So, patient Luke waited until I had written my note, complete with names, arrows, and question marks. "Officer Dixon responded to the call when Maverick's body was found. And Aaron signed the medical report. This is where we start. We get through the lies Aaron and possibly Dixon told, and we find the real line that ties Aaron and Dixon to Maverick's murder."

"But we don't know where Aaron is."

"Yes, we do. Thanks to Gavin." I pulled out my phone, "And I know just the way to draw him out."

The text was short. To the point.

Ian is Victor Lloyd. And I can prove it.

CHAPTER THIRTY-FOUR

Estate

AARON CALLED RIGHT away. "Catalina, it's not what you think."

"I think your brother framed his father, and you are covering for him. I read the poem Grover wrote about Victor Lloyd. And I have more evidence to prove that Ian did it." He sighed. Luke didn't say anything regarding my bluff, which was admirable. He didn't let Aaron know that he was with me, listening, either. Aaron also didn't know that we were sitting on the road to the Settler Estate.

Luke had found the place. I explained to him what Gavin had shared with me, and he was able to locate it on the map. There was a large gate, covered by vines. Beyond it was a house, in good shape.

We couldn't get into the gate without Aaron's blessing. Here, we would have to wait until I could negotiate our way in.

"What evidence do you have?" Aaron said.

"Let's meet, and we can talk it over."

"I can't leave here."

"Then, I'll come to you."

"I'm not going to tell you where I am."

My eyes rolled. A call beeped in. It was Charlie. "I know you're at Grover's estate, outside of town." I shot a text to Charlie, letting him know that I was in town and I would see him soon.

"Who told…Gavin."

"Yes." Playing my cards to get him to open the gate took precision. Aaron couldn't know that I was hoping he would give me something that would move our research forward. If he discovered the truth, he wouldn't let us into his fortress. I had to re-earn his trust by appealing to the desperate situation Ian had put him in. "Aaron, I want to help you and your brother."

"Don't be obtuse."

No luck. "I'm not." I prayed that what Gavin had told me about Ian and the cherished friendship he had with me would move Aaron in some way. "Your brother doesn't want to hurt me, because he values our friendship. That's what you two agreed to. You'd protect one another, and you would keep his secret only if he didn't hurt anyone else, including me. So, I want to help you and your brother."

"What does your relationship with Porter have to do with me?"

"Because you see the same thing I see in him. That your brother is just lost, but deep down, he can be brought back. He just has to know that we understand why he did it." I shifted in the leather seat, "Gary is a monster, worse than Ian. And he's gonna get what he deserves one day.

But if the Blood Diamonds find out Ian is the real killer, which they are close to figuring it out, they will kill him and everyone else who gets in their path for justice. That includes you."

"So, that's an even bigger reason for me to just lie low for a bit longer."

That was true. If I told Charlie about Ian, I would have to tell him about Aaron. Unless… "What if Ian agrees to pay the Diamonds back the money Gary owes them? As a good faith offering for the murder he committed? He could say that he knows Gary was probably involved, and he wants to make amends."

"He would never do that because it would prove that he murdered Maverick. And Gary would know Ian murdered Maverick."

"No, we spin it another way. Ian doesn't want a fight because it's bad for business. With Dixon's death, the Porters can't afford anymore complications. So, he pays them off, and no one tells the Diamonds who the real killer is. We say it was some low-level dealer that Gary put up to it, and Ian killed him."

The phone was silent. "Why would you do this for him?"

"Because I want something in return."

"Of course, you do."

"I know you and Dixon worked together to cover the murder up."

"No, we didn't."

I hissed a sigh. "Then why didn't Dixon question your paper-thin medical report? And why did he allow Gavin to go free, even though he clearly killed Russ, his best friend's dad?" Aaron didn't say anything. "I'm not gonna leave until I get the truth. From you."

"You're gonna leave Maine a very upset woman."

Time for hard ball, "Gee, I wonder what the Blood Diamonds are gonna think about your little hideout." He didn't respond. "I see a really nice fence covered in vines, and what looks like a white house on the other side. Right next to that old mill." All this posturing had to be rewarded somehow.

"Fine." The phone call ended.

"Remind me to never keep a secret from you," Luke joked.

Finally, the gate opened. We traveled up the driveway; the property on this side of the fence was magnificent. The house was a remodeled colonial, with a large wrap-around porch and plantation-style lawn. No slave quarters, I noted.

Aaron stood on the porch, black hair, white shirt, and jeans. I had never seen him so casual before. Luke and I bounced out of the car, reprieve passing over our host.

"Thank you for not bringing Gavin."

"Thank you for letting us in."

"As if you gave me a choice." Aaron waved for us to enter the open front door. It closed with a bang behind him. "Do you guys want a drink or something?"

"No, thank you." I still didn't trust anyone since everyone seemed to want to use beverages and syringes to pull the wool over my eyes.

Luke declined, which was a smart move. I expected he

would feel ashamed for taking Aaron's girl from him, but he was chill. "Nice place."

"It's my dad's."

"Gavin told me the history of your family estate."

"Dad's thinking about donating it back to the town." Such a noble idea, from such a thoughtful man. He motioned for us to follow him through the castle to the living room. Grover's book covers had been blown up into posters that lined the walls. The air smelled of vintage books and coffee.

Luke and I sat next to each other on one large couch, while Aaron sat a distance away from us on the other couch. "It's probably not my place to say this, but I always thought you two should have been together."

In unison, Luke and I moved further apart. Not that we were touching to begin with. My reason for our friendship was clear to everyone. They knew who the love of my life was. Luke's reason was sure to turn to blows between him and Aaron.

I changed the subject with, "Luke's been very helpful with all this. But it's up to me to bring it to a close. That's where I need your help." Aaron folded one leg over the other. "I just need your testimony about what happened the night Maverick died." Aaron sized me up, checking to see how confident I was in my pursuits.

"Hey, man, I know this is hard for you." Luke's compassion was his super power. "You're a super loyal person. That's why you're a great doctor. Cecilia won't stop talking about how much of a good guy you are. And how you want to do the right thing."

This broke Aaron's stoic stare. "I can't believe I've put her through all this," he said. "She broke up with me over text message." I kept my eyes on Aaron, not Luke. "Honestly, I'm glad she did. I can't be committed to her and be in this shit with Porter." He licked his lips, "I'll have to lie to her unless I disown him."

"Why have you been so close with your brother? He's the worst person in the world."

"Everyone forgets that I knew him before he started drug dealing and murdering people. When we were kids, we had a blast. He'd take me out to places, help me hit on girls. He was a normal brother. And man did I look up to him." His reminiscing formed a smile on him. "Nobody messed with Porter."

"No, they didn't," Luke said. "I'd hear all these stories about how badass he was." He pondered, "He never really started trouble with anyone."

"That's who he is. He's not one to start fights, but he will finish them. As long as you stay out of his way, he won't have any problems with you."

"I met Jensen," I said. Aaron didn't hide his disdain. "You don't like him?"

"He's a psychopath, just like Gary." Aaron paused, reflecting. "Gary never really warmed up to Jensen like he did Porter. He saw him as a threat to his business."

"And it was your brother who ended up screwing him over," Luke said.

Aaron couldn't backpaddle fast enough, "How are you two so sure that Ian framed Gary?"

"He had the most to gain," I said quickly before he

could see the truth. "His motive to eliminate Gary put more money in his pocket."

"How did you find that out?"

I held up Luke's flash drive. "There's a file on here where your brother planned to set Gary up. Text messages between Porter's number and Maverick. They talk about a meeting place and time. There's also a typed witness statement saved on here under the name Victor Lloyd. Porter even sent an email to Dixon from a bogus email address belonging to Victor Lloyd. He saved the password here."

"Where did you get that?" Aaron said.

"Daniel Sullivan gave this to me when he was alive. He told me to use it to protect myself against Ian, if I needed it."

Smoke, mirrors, and convincing eyes. Hopefully he wouldn't see through my monologue and pick out the inconsistencies.

Luke's observation helped me, "There's also some stuff on here that makes you look bad."

"How?"

"The Blood Diamonds think you're helping Gary and Porter," I said.

Aaron's sigh shook, his body tensed. Our interrogation was wearing him down.

"On the flash drive," Luke said, "Porter mentions Dixon helping you with the medical report."

Aaron spent a moment sorting through what we were telling him. But would he trust us? "If I come clean, you can't use anything I say against Ian or me." I gave Luke a side glance. "Catalina, I promise you. If Porter finds out you know the truth, he will come after you, gloves off."

"Then, that ensures my silence," I said humbly.

"Mine, too," Luke said.

Permission was given, but he took his time. I wanted to give him more incentive to start talking. If only I—

"Dixon did it as a favor for me, not Ian." Aaron asked us to turn our phones off to keep him from being recorded. No notepads, either. Once off, he asked that we put the phones on the coffee table. He checked them, satisfied that what he'd say next was going to remain between the three of us.

"Gary was getting bad. He started problems with the local dealers in Anders, and the dealers had the police in their pockets, so Ian was worried they were going to lose it all. He asked me to talk with my dad about bail money and a good attorney. I told him to shut down the business, just give up on selling drugs. Walk away. Ian told me Gary made sure that if any of his dealers or associates left the business or turned on him, they'd end up in a pine box. My brother was in too deep, so he couldn't leave. And if things started to sink, Gary expected him to go down with the ship. That's when I said something that I now regret."

"That he should frame Gary?" I said.

"No. I knew Gary had probably killed some people, but I didn't suggest framing Gary. I told Ian, *If the cops knew about all those people Gary killed, he'd never get out of jail.* Three months later, Maverick was in my morgue, and some guy named Victor Lloyd had claimed to have witnessed Gary kill the biker. I didn't know about the Blood Diamonds, but

I did know that Victor Lloyd was a character in my dad's book. Grover based him off of my grandfather, Victor Ian Floyd, our mother's father."

"You knew before he told you?" said Luke.

Aaron nodded. "I called Porter and told him to come down to the medical examiner's office. That's when Dixon showed up. He spoke with *Victor* on the phone and took his statement. As he looked over the body, he said that the statement was a little too accurate. That the person he had spoken to was probably the killer, not Gary."

"Then, you covered for Ian," I added.

"I told Jaime that I thought I knew who Victor was, and he had committed the murder in self-defense. That Maverick went after Victor, one of Gary's guys, over some old drug beef, and Victor shot him. Victor blamed Gary because Gary was supposed to be there to confront Maverick, but he left Victor to fend for himself. Dixon never liked Gary, so he was happy to go along with whatever I wrote down in the medical report. Then, he wrote his report stating that Victor was telling the truth, and Gary was the killer."

"Did he ever find out about Ian?" I said.

"He knew pretty much right away. Russ, Blake's dad, had tipped him off."

I sat up straight as a board, "I'm sorry, you said Blake's dad was involved?"

Regret shortened the conversation, "You know enough already."

"Aaron, you can't hold back now."

"If I tell you what I know, you're gonna turn it into a huge deal, and Gavin's gonna lose what's left of his mind."

"He has a right to know, Aaron!" How could he not see that? "If whatever happened that night led to Gavin shooting Russ, you have to tell me."

"Catalina, he would never be able to live with himself if he knew," Aaron said.

"That's not for you to decide!" Raised voices and confrontation wouldn't help me win this crucial piece of information. "I killed Blake, remember? And I did it to protect Gavin because he killed Russ. So, you owe me the truth. That way I can cope with being a murderer."

Aaron was there when Blake took his last breath. He comforted Blake, reminding him that he wouldn't be alone when he died. Aaron cleared his throat, holding back the emotion we shared.

"Russ and Gary were at odds for years. Their hatred for each other got worse when Russ planned on running for mayor of Settlement Island. He was going to use his title to close down Porter Construction and get the FBI to seize all the records to prove that Gary was running an illegal drug operation. One thing led to another and Russ found out about the Blood Diamonds coming to town to look for Gary."

"How do you think he found out?" I said.

"My brother used the tip line Russ had set up. People would use the tip line to report suspicious activities, and the police would check it out. Well, the dealers started using it to rat each other out, and one of those dealers was Ian. He called and said that Gary had been thinking about bringing some out-of-state bikers into town. He said Russ should have the police check it out. Ian set up the lead, so the police would track the Blood Diamonds when they came into Settlement Island. Then, when they ended up dead, the tip would lead to Gary. Ian didn't know it, but Russ decided to follow the lead on his own."

"Russ ended up seeing the murders," I said.

Aaron nodded, "Dixon told him about the bikers he had stopped. Russ found them outside Porter Construction. He followed them into the woods, and he saw Ian shoot Maverick and the other two. Ian saw Russ take off running, so he sent Hank after him."

"Hank was there?" I said.

"Yeah," Aaron said solemnly. "Hank and Ian put together the plan. My brother needed someone to help him, and Hank wanted to get back at Gary for killing Michelle. When Hank gave her the drugs, he didn't know the dose was off. And when he confronted Gary about it, he didn't care. So, it took some time, but Hank found a way to get back at Gary. He helped Ian, and Ian paid him using some money from a fake deal he had set up in Florida under another one of his aliases. The fake deal was also evidence that Gary was setting up the bikers to be murdered, too."

Charlie had told me about this. "The Blood Diamonds were doing a deal in Florida with some new drug contact. Hank was in charge of moving the money and the drugs. The bikers got paid, and they never heard from the Florida people again."

"Ian covered his tracks. The bikers had their money,

and he paid Hank out of Gary's own pocket. Then, he cooked the books, so the accountants wouldn't notice."

"What happened with Hank and Russ?" I said.

"Hank was supposed to kill Russ, but Gavin ended up doing it instead." Aaron wiped a tear from his face, "Gavin was always innocent in this thing. My brother didn't want Gavin to suffer for unknowingly defending his business, so he told Gary that Hank and Russ got into it over the drug operation. Russ was gonna bring down the whole thing, so Gavin shot him to protect the business that employed his father. Gary got him out of the murder charge as a thank you for saving his business. But Dixon had a problem with it. So did Blake. Dixon knew he couldn't publicly confront Gary or Ian about Maverick or Russ's deaths, nor could he give up the real reason why Gavin shot Russ. Ian had bought the police department with drugs and money, so Dixon had to find another way to figure out why Gavin shot Russ. That's where Blake came in. He wanted to know the truth, even though Gavin would never give it up. And Dixon didn't have enough of it to help Blake out."

Aaron put his head against the headrest of the couch, a flow of tears trailing down to his shirt.

Luke sat quietly with his hands in his lap.

And I was speechless.

The floor creaked.

Gavin stepped into the living room.

"Hank let me kill Russ to cover for Porter?" he said. Fist tightened. Blood hot. "I'm going to kill him," he said as a firm declaration.

He was gone before any of us could get up.

CHAPTER THIRTY-FIVE

Sinners

"GAVIN, YOU HAVE to listen to me," I said as calmly as I could. "We have to be strategic about this."

This was not the right move. He stepped around me, walking, not charging, up to Aaron. "Your brother has just fucked my dad big time."

Aaron's chest heaved with anger, "It's fucked up, I know. And I'm sorry I didn't tell you about this sooner. But I couldn't. I told my brother I wouldn't say anything, and he said he'd make it right. Porter regretted that Hank put you in that position. Especially since Porter gave him money and the means to leave town, leaving you to take all the responsibility."

"That bag of cash came from your brother?"

"Yeah. He told Hank that he had to go, and he could never come back to Settlement Island ever again. And if he snitched on him, one of Gary's many associates between here and California would cut Hank down."

The eruption that would soon follow was inevitable. I had seen Gavin lose it over less.

Hank had ruined Gavin's young life time and time again. And this was understandably the last straw. The foundation for all his hatred, even if he didn't know where it had stemmed from, had been laid. Like Ian had set up his father, Gavin would set Hank up for his own death.

I put my hand on his arm. Gavin took a deep breath. No raking his hair or posturing. He said, "Catalina, just leave me to get my own justice, for once."

"We made a promise that we're not going to be murderers," I said.

"Catalina," his voice was even, wrapped in stone, "this fucker costed me ten years of my life for a murder I didn't want to commit. He killed my mom, he killed Russ, and he has to die." He stepped up, "I love you, but don't get in between me and my dad."

"I'm not saying you can't get your revenge on your dad. It's just…he's not our only problem. We have to worry about Gary," I said.

"Even if he didn't kill the Blood Diamond, we can't let Gary stay out of jail," Aaron said.

"Leave Gary to me. I'll handle it." Unlike with my promises to defend Aaron, he actually took Gavin's pledge seriously. I guess he just needed a more capable person saying these words.

"Gavin," Aaron said his name with heavy compassion, "I never agreed with the way my family has handled all this. And I'm sorry you had to find out this way."

Gavin put his hand on Aaron's shoulder, "Deep down, you'll always be my brother. So, I forgive you."

Aaron silently allowed Gavin to avenge himself. Except, he had one condition, "Don't kill my brother, please. Despite everything he's done, I still love him."

Gavin's hand tightened around Aaron's shoulder, "If he gets in my way, he'll leave me no choice." Gavin's attention came onto me. "I need to talk to you." We exited the front door, Gavin shutting it.

"Gavin," I said, "you can't kill your dad."

He shook his head, "I'm gonna kill Gary, first, for my mom. Then, I'm gonna kill Hank, for me."

"What?" My breaths hit him in the face. "Killing Hank is one terrible idea, but killing Gary is going to make things a lot worse for you. You're gonna lose everything. You won't be able to go to college or start the life you've wanted." I placed my hand over his bullet wound. He softened against my fingers, "Gavin, if you kill them, you kill yourself in the process. You kill the person you were supposed to become. The person who was a little boy who was supposed to grow up to become this incredible man with endless opportunities. Don't let a split second of rage rob you of an entire life." Gavin cracked a small smile. "Why are you smiling?"

"You forgot to mention my good looks." He sighed, "I hate my dad, but I can't kill him. As much as I want to, my grandmother would never forgive me. But, I will never forgive him, so I don't know what to do."

"You don't have to know," I said. "And you don't have to give up on getting justice for your mom and Russ, either."

"Well, if I can't kill them, I don't know what to do."

I did know what to do. Sort of. "We have the full story, so we know what happened. Now, we have to find the other Blood Diamonds Porter killed."

"Then what?"

"I tell Charlie where they are, and then we all fight Ian, Gary, and Hank together."

"No, I'd never put that on you." His fingers tapped my hands, "Then, you'd carry the burden of sending three people to their deaths."

Honestly, I didn't want to carry more deaths with me. Blake's was more than enough. But justice had to be served. "Ian and Gary need to spend the rest of their lives in prison. It's the most humane way to solve our problems, but it doesn't give me, you, Blake's family, or the Diamonds justice. So, I can't be the one to decide. The final decision needs to come from all four of us."

Gavin liked the idea. "Let's talk to Aaron and Luke."

Hand in hand, we went back to the living room where Luke and Aaron were talking. They didn't stop once we arrived.

"I was just telling Luke that we could use the medical report to possibly pinpoint a location for the other two bikers. Then, we can use that to stop Gary from investigating my brother. And maybe even get the police to look at other suspects."

Gavin nodded. He turned to me. "Okay, so, um, I think all four of us have a decision to make," I said.

"What kind of decision?" said Luke.

"Given everything we know about the murders and Gary, we have to decide how we're going to handle this.

Before, it was easy to focus on getting Gary and Porter into jail, but that won't help the bikers. And Porter will probably end up killing Hank, which Gavin doesn't really want." Gavin shifted. "So, I think each one of us should talk together and come up with the best solution."

"How does that work?" Aaron said with openness.

"Well, each one of us represents a group of people who are affected by whatever steps we take next. Gavin, you have your dad to consider, so you can speak from that perspective. Aaron, you represent Porter. Whatever you decide will affect you and your brother. Luke, well…" He tilted his head, knowing that I had nothing to go on. No matter what choice was made, Luke wouldn't be affected. He had no skin in the game, unless he wanted to shed some. "Luke, you're…"

"It's okay," he said. "As a victim of the home invasions, and the one person who currently lives in Settlement Island Proper, I can speak for all the other residents of Settlement Island."

"Perfect!" Now, for me. "I represent Blake, Russ, and Maverick. I'm friends with Charlie, so I can decide for the bikers' fallen friends. I killed Blake, so I speak for him and Russ. And Dixon, I guess. I mean, at this point, there really isn't a single dead person on our list who isn't connected to me and the decisions I make."

"How so?" Aaron asked.

"I can get justice for them all because I'm keeping them all from getting justice."

"That's a weird way to say it," he replied.

"She talks like a textbook sometimes," Gavin said.

I glared at him. "Dixon, Blake, and Russ are all lumped together because I kept Blake and Dixon from getting justice for Russ. If I let Gary and Porter go, Maverick doesn't get any justice. Does that wrap it up in a nice little bow for you guys?"

"Sounds good to me." Luke said, "Let's vote, so we can start on the plan."

"Okay, Aaron, why don't you go first. How do you think we should solve our Gary-Maverick-Porter problem?"

Aaron didn't fire away with an answer. Pausing and contemplating, we all took a seat in the living room, giving Aaron the floor.

He was a thoughtful, calculated doctor. The decisions he made on a daily basis literally saved lives. They were not taken lightly or without a clear understanding of how one action could set up a deadly reaction of consequences. But he was taking a long time. So long, I expected Gavin or Luke to tell him to get to talking.

They didn't.

It was almost like they were taking this moment of silence to prepare their own decision. As should I be doing.

"I'm not worried about Gary," Aaron said. "He's not my father. And my brother sent him to prison, so I'm sure he's not too worried about Gary, either." He sighed, "My brother is an asshole. A narcissist and a psychopath. But I love him." He paused. "He's not good for me and he's not good for this town, but I love him. So, the best justice for everyone would be to remove him from society and put him away, so he can't hurt anyone else. To do that, I'll tell the police what happened to Maverick and how I covered up for my brother. I'll say I don't know how he's involved, but he had something to do with it. And they can figure the rest out."

I nodded. This was fair, and it kept Ian alive. One thing remained, though, "Are you okay with him coming after you?"

"He's a lunatic, but he's also a pretty fair person. He'll see if from my point, that I had to do the right thing, and he won't hurt me. Not physically, anyway. He'll probably disown me for life. And I'll no longer have his protection from anyone, not even Jensen."

"I'll have your back," Gavin said.

"Me, too," Luke agreed.

"And I'll do whatever I can to make sure he doesn't blame you." I moved on quickly before anyone could challenge me. "Luke, what about you?"

He didn't stand. He just sat up. "I've heard stories about Gary and Porter, but I never really had any problems with them until Blake kicked in my door and put me in the hospital. However, I've lived here for a long, long time, and so many people have been screwed over by the Porters. They destroyed businesses and turned Settlement Island Proper into a freaking mobster movie." He looked over at Gavin, "I didn't like you because of them. I thought you were the one who was fueling all this, and I was wrong."

"It's cool," Gavin said.

"It's not, though. The Porters ruined your life, and they will continue hurting people unless they are stopped. I'm good with them going to jail, but Gary got out. So..." He looked over at Aaron.

"You can say it," Aaron said mournfully.

"Maverick was a Blood Diamond, and I don't want another group of bad guys taking over our town. So, if we give them Gary and Porter, they can decide what they want to do with them."

A good, neutral decision that passed the murdering onto someone else. Aaron frowned. Next, I asked Gavin to tell us his decision.

"My tie to all this is Hank. He worked for Gary, and Gary killed my mom. Porter pushed him to kill Russ, and my dad set me up to do it. He's never been there for me, even after the one person who meant the world to me died. Hank brought these fuckers into my life. And he keeps picking them over me. Over and over." He pointed to Aaron, "But I'm with you. I can't kill my family."

Armed with this information, he gave us his final decision.

"I know what it's like to have my loved one die and not get any justice for them. My dad chose his life, and he's gonna have to live with it." He ended with, "Tell the Blood Diamonds, and let him find his way out of that."

"What should we tell them?" I said.

"That Porter's business did something to Maverick. We don't have to give them names, but we tell them that Gary didn't do it. We got a lead that Porter JR was the last one to see Maverick alive, and someone close to Porter knows more. Then, they can follow the line, and if it leads to my dad, he'll have to find his own way out of it." I put my hand on my boyfriend's. He slumped over, his elbows on his knees. Not one to dwell, he said, "Alright, sweetheart. What's your vote?"

So far, Aaron was the only one who wanted to go to the police. Let the guys rot in jail. Luke and Gavin were willing to let the three key players fight on their own against the Blood Diamonds.

Vigilant justice.

This style of justice had turned Settlement Island into a battlefield. Yet, the police had failed to protect everyone, too. They were defenseless, a feeling that had covered me almost every day I had lived here.

Poor, defenseless me had evolved, though.

I held the fate of three men in my hands. Hands that had shed blood because of them. Hands that had helped those who barely survived. Just barely.

Ben, being one of them. If he was still alive.

Still, I knew the cost that came with vigilant justice. Jude, Six, and Molly had paid that price. As the proxy for the dead, I would speak for them, too. Each one of them died for a different reason, so I had to consider what justice meant for them individually.

And what justice meant for Daniel.

He died protecting me.

He died to get me out of this place.

He'd be disappointed if the decision I made didn't involve me saving myself.

So, voting for him would be simple. He'd want me back in California, abandoning justice for everyone, and never returning again. Never visiting his grave or searching for his soul here.

It was gone. He was gone.

Daniel was in the stars, tucked away in a safe place where he could watch over me.

So, he would go wherever I would go. And I wasn't going anywhere.

My place was here. And my decision would reflect that.

"Gary needs to go back to jail, because that is where he belongs. So, we find something, anything, that puts him back there. Hank also deserves to go to jail for his role in Maverick's death. But I think you, Gavin, need to confront him first. You need to let your father go, and then let all the ugly consequences catch up to him." I nodded, confirming my decision, "We tell Charlie the truth. We lead him to wherever the other bikers are buried, and then we let nature take its course. Either Hank goes to jail or the Diamonds get him first. It's Hank's choice."

Luke and Aaron nodded. Gavin didn't say anything.

I sighed, "Ian Robert Porter is a different story." The urge to bite my lip subsided, "He's put so many tickets and debts on me. So, I have one to put on him. Before we turn him over to anyone, I need to make things right for myself. I have to even the score."

"Catalina, my brother doesn't fight fair."

"Everyone has always told me how just your brother is. That he is a man of his word, good or bad. So, if I'm deciding his fate, he needs to know it. He deserves to stare me in the face while I unleash hell on him, his business, and his family." I cleared things up, "Not you, Aaron. In fact, I don't want him to know it came from you at all. I want all this on me."

"Love the gusto, but you need to be realistic," Aaron warned.

I was being realistic. "Aaron, how many times has Porter reached out to you over the last year?"

"I don't know. Five, six times. He'd call just to make sure I'm keeping my mouth shut and I'm staying out of sight."

"Luke?"

Luke shrugged, "Never."

"Gavin?"

"I don't like this game," he said.

"I don't like it, either, but you know where I'm going. Ian rearranged my entire life, so he could have a hand in it. For some reason, I'm the most important person to him. He's obsessed with controlling me. And I'll never get my life back until he sees that I have his fate in my hands. He needs to see me as a threat. A worthy opponent. Then, I'll beat him, and I'll give him the option. He can go to jail, he can turn himself over to Charlie, or he can run. And if he chooses to run, I'll make sure he has nowhere to hide."

"And how are you gonna do that?" Aaron scoffed.

"You have me and my crew," Gavin said. "Us, with the bikers, gives you the numbers."

"I'm sure I can convince the police to help us," Luke said. "They want vengeance for Dixon's death, so the deals the Porters had with them are off."

"It's the fairest option." Aaron scratched his jaw, "Yeah, fuck it. Let's do it your way." There was no cheering or celebration. We sat quietly, while Aaron left us for the study. He returned, Maverick's medical report in hand.

"Here's where they found Maverick's body. Maybe you can make sense of it," he said to Luke and Gavin.

Gavin took a screenshot while Luke studied it. "I know these woods, but they've probably changed a lot since this report was written."

Gavin sent a text, receiving a speedy reply. "Kyle thinks he knows where this is. Said he'll send me coordinates, so we can meet him there." He turned to Aaron, "Got any shovels?"

❧

Aaron's landscapers had left three shovels at the house. Kyle brought four, along with James, Oliver, and Mark. The reunion didn't last long. The sun was fading behind the trees, and we needed whatever light God would give us. Kyle pulled out his metal detector.

"What's that for?" I said.

"Shell casings."

Kyle ran the metal detector over the land, an uneven terrain of overgrown grass and sparse flowers sitting as a small patch beyond the trees. It was a secluded meadow located about three miles west of Porter Construction. Kyle had gone hunting here, so he knew this place well.

After an hour of searching, the detector hit on a casing. "Let's dig."

The boys got to digging while Aaron and I had a moment alone. "Even if we find them here, it doesn't prove your brother killed them," I said.

"It will when the police look into the county records.

Then, they'll see that this land belongs to Ian White. Another one of my brother's many aliases."

"He will stop at nothing to cover his tracks."

"Nope."

"Hey, Doc!" said Oliver. "Think we got something."

They hadn't dug for very long, so it was highly unlikely that they had hit the jackpot so soon.

But they had.

A bone, growing into the soil, had been unearthed. Aaron checked it and confirmed it was human.

Still, we didn't know for sure if the bone belonged to a Blood Diamond. So, they kept digging. And digging. And digging.

Finally, some clothing was found under the body. It was in bad shape, but the emblem still had the letters BL DI MOND.

We had found them.

I opened my phone and called Charlie. "I found your missing friends," I said.

CHAPTER THIRTY-SIX

Diamonds

WE GAVE THE living Blood Diamonds first rites to the bodies before we called anyone else. Some of the bikers cried while Charlie remained determined. I put my hand on his shoulder, "Sorry about your friends."

He nodded sullenly, "You say the Porters did this?"

"Someone in their organization did."

"But it was probably Gary?"

"We don't know. All I know is the police report and the medical examiner pinned this as the place Maverick was shot. So, we followed the hunch, and it landed us here, the same place that Victor Lloyd guy had mentioned."

He nodded, again. "We haven't been able to find Gary."

This was not really a surprise. Gary had stayed off everyone's radar. So had Ian. This led me to tell Charlie, "He's not going to wait too long before he strikes. Once word gets out about your friends being found, he's probably going to come looking for you guys."

"That's not a chance I'm willing to take." Charlie

leaned against a tree, "We came here for Gary and our money. We're not leaving here without him." He watched Aaron direct Oliver and Mark, telling them where to dig.

"He's still on parole," I said, turning away from the grotesque scene, only seeing rows of trees beyond Charlie. "If he's smart, he won't leave the state, or they'll take him back to jail."

"A bunch of vengeful bikers out for his blood is enough to break some parole promises."

"Maybe, but that's a bit of a gamb—" A branch moved, snapping quietly. "There's something out there," I said.

Charlie looked into the tree line, "Where?"

I motioned to a sliver in the packed trees. It was black, cowering in the folds of two trees. "Right there."

He studied it for a moment. "It's probably an animal." Nothing moved. He resumed his thoughts, "We can use Gavin's crew to help us fish Gary out. They probably know where he'd go." Aaron would know better than they would. His brother was Gary's son, after all. I told Charlie my assumption. He charged up to the doctor, Aaron tensing on his arrival. "Can you get us in touch with Gary?"

Aaron was a smart man. Withholding from Charlie would make things worse. Much worse. "I don't have tabs on Gary. But I'm sure he's probably at one of his many properties. I can give you a couple of addresses." He pulled out his phone, the light bright against the darkening sky.

A large branch snapped.

Charlie heard it, too.

He drew his gun. Gavin came up next to me, pulling

me into him. His gun was also up. I kept my eyes on the horizon, watching three bikers leap over the terrain at full speed, slowing down when they rushed the person. The hooded person, in black and military fatigues, was overpowered and brought back to us.

James, Oliver, and Mark stood next to Gavin. Kyle stood on my other side, with my gun.

"Nice gun," I said. He didn't joke back. His eyes were trained forward.

The biker prospects pulled the intruder's hood down. "Noah?"

"Catalina Rose," he muttered with a blistered lip.

He was dead on his feet. One black and red eye from a punch. Another open wound on his forehead and a cut on his chin.

"Did Jensen do this to you?" I said.

Charlie stepped up, "You alone?" he said, ignoring my question.

"Yeah."

"What do you want?" I said.

"Gary's ready to meet all of you."

"Now?"

"Tomorrow morning at nine at Porter Construction. He's ready to pay ya'll off."

"No," Gavin said. "Maine Street. That way he won't be tempted for a shootout."

"He's not gonna…"

"It's not up to him," Charlie commanded. "It's either Maine Street or we don't meet."

"Fine."

Charlie nodded for a couple of bikers to give Noah a ride back to wherever he had come from. Before he left, Noah's eyes peered into me. Despite the safety of a heavily-trafficked street, he knew none of us were safe.

CHAPTER THIRTY-SEVEN

Brothers

"THIS IS STUPID!" Cecilia said as she blocked the door to her loft.

"It's gonna be fine," I said. "It's a public place."

"Fuck that!" She pulled her phone from her back pocket. "I don't want my boyfriend putting his life on the line for a bunch of wannabe thugs."

The boyfriend she referenced was Luke. He would join the crowd that was gathering on the street below in the next few minutes. The bikers and Gavin's crew were on their way.

They had spent the night at James's house, preparing. So did the bikers. I was sent to stay with my sister where it was safer. Two biker prospects had stayed in the living room, just to keep us safe.

"Cecilia, it's fine." I took her hands, "We have the police, a brigade of bikers, and half of Settlement Island on our side. We're gonna be fine," I said with a nod.

She pulled the blinds open and pointed to the street.

Scruffy, unhoused-looking men huddled together. "This is not what fine looks like!" There was a knock at the door. Cecilia brushed past the bikers, opening up. "You got some nerve coming into my house, Gavin!" she said as he walked past her.

His first line of business was to kiss me. "Hey," he said, his fingers tangled in my hair. "Listen, I just wanted to say—"

A gunshot rang out.

Gavin took the stairs two at a time, along with the prospects. I followed, Cecilia was close behind me.

Ian and Jensen stood in the middle of Maine Street. The pack of unhoused men had made a formation behind them. No Gary, of course.

Gavin, Charlie, and James were the leaders of our groups. We had slightly more numbers, thanks to the bikers and the dealers who didn't want to be a part of Porter's business anymore.

I stood behind Gavin, Charlie and James standing on his sides. Everyone else clustered forward, our organization not looking as neat. Cecilia grabbed my hand; she was scared.

Charlie spoke first, "So, what's up?" he shouted. "Where's Gary?"

Jensen put his phone in his pocket, "He said I can negotiate on his behalf." *I, not we.* Jensen was cutting Ian out. And Ian noticed. His expression dipped for a moment. But not for long. "What are your terms?"

Charlie looked over to his second-in-command who stood beside him. He was a big guy, taller and wider than

Charlie. They chatted for a quiet, brief moment then let the rest of us in. "Ya'll killed our guys, so we obviously want someone's head on a stick for that. Second, Gary stole business from us. We want compensation."

"What kind of compensation?"

"$10 million. Plus a part of the territory."

Ian shook his head, "We're not giving you that."

"Then, we'll take it."

No posturing. Charlie was serious and so were his people. They pulled their guns out, no one taking aim. Gavin looked over at James who shook his head. Their side of the crew didn't draw arms.

Jensen didn't look at his brother when he said, "Gary's business took a hit last year. We don't have that kind of cash."

"Not my problem."

"You got properties," Gavin said. "Brothels, steak-houses, and a construction company. Throw all that together, and there's your ten million." Charlie nodded.

Jensen leaned into his brother's ear, and they debated the deal.

Cecilia let go of my hand and flew into Luke's arms. I guess he had just arrived. Behind him, Aaron folded his arms, understanding why he had been dumped. "I'm sorry," I whispered to him. He pressed his eyes forward.

Jensen and Ian wrapped up their conversation. "No deal," Jensen said.

"Why not?" Charlie said.

"Because this is our business. Our town."

"No, it's not!" said a voice from the sidewalk. It was

a middle-aged woman who had stopped her shopping to watch the showdown.

She wasn't alone. The pedestrians had stopped to become witnesses. So had the park dwellers, the people on their way to the boat ramp, and everyone else who had a vested interest in how this was going to turn out.

"Jensen, you don't even live here," said James. He motioned to all the townies around us, "We're the Settlers. This is our town. And we're cool with the deal The Blood Diamonds want."

"No one asked you," Jensen said.

Ian was smarter, "James, you and the other dealers don't benefit from a biker gang taking over our operations. Why are you siding with them?"

"I'm not a dealer anymore," James said proudly. "And we made an arrangement with them. We'll let them stay if they shut all this shit down, once and for all. No more dealing, no more drugs, and no more fuckin' murdering each other. They're gonna help us bring legit businesses back to Settlement Island. And we're all gonna live in peace, all kumbaya."

"That's not really what that means," I said to James.

"Whatever! My point is, the Porters are out of business in Settlement Island and Anders, forever!"

The bystanders started clapping and cheering. Jensen shot a glance at the growing crowd of people who were happy to see someone finally standing up for them.

"Gary's not going to just walk away," Ian said once the crowd hushed.

"Well, he didn't show up for the vote, so he's out of luck," said Gavin.

"He can't be seen with a bunch of felons," Jensen said with a bite to his words. "It goes against his probation."

James said, "Running scared, like always."

"Where's Hank?" Gavin said. I hadn't thought about Hank this whole time.

"He ran like a coward. But before he left, he gave us what we needed," Jensen said. He pointed to me, "Hank gave you up, Catalina. Told us that you were the one that brought the Diamonds into town. So, this one's on you. You're helping us settle our own score, betraying your new little friends." He licked his lips, "One of our guys may have cut Maverick and those other fuckers down, but we were never able to get the rest of them up here, so we could put a bullet in each of their heads. Now, we can. Thanks to you and your little—"

A blast hit my ears. Jensen fell, blood pouring from his head.

Ian froze, looking at the remnants of his brother.

"Fuck you!" said a voice on the sidewalk. It was Noah. Gun wobbling in his hand, he walked in between the two feuding parties.

Ian recovered. He pulled up his gun and shot Noah in the head.

The rest of mayhem.

Everyone sprang into action. Gavin tackled me to the ground as bullets flew. "Get out of here!" he said to me.

"Not without you!"

Gavin kissed me and then said, "I can't run and leave my people here to fight a battle I helped start."

I searched his eyes, tears forming in mine. "No," I said in a whisper.

He kissed me again. When he released me, his eyes had their own tears. "I will always love you." Gavin shot up, shielding me as he told Kyle, "Get her out of here."

Kyle latched onto my arms, my body violently fighting against him as I watched Gavin run into the crowd. A shot ran by me. I dropped down as Kyle returned fire.

"Run, Catalina!" Kyle said. "Save yourself!" He rushed into the fight, a rifle strapped to his back, pistol in hand.

A path had been cleared for me. In the path, I saw Luke, holding onto Cecilia, him rushing her to the safety of a café.

Beyond them, I saw a man running into the building next door.

Ian.

Saving myself would be in vain if I didn't handle him first. I dashed through the fight, bullets whizzing, punches landing, and I made it to the sidewalk. Then, I slipped through the door.

CHAPTER THIRTY-EIGHT

Gunning

"YOU'LL NEVER GET another chance like this, Ian!" I said as he came to a stop. I didn't understand why he had picked this vacant building as his refuge. It had been an old shoe store located close to Pete's Garage. "Right now, it's you and me. No Gavin. No Charlie. No one to stop you from finally giving me whatever punishment you think I deserve." Ian turned to me, someone's blood on his hands and dark coat. I lifted my hands, "I'm out of second chances with you. There will be no more tickets, no more debts between us." His nostrils flared. "So if you want me, come and get me."

Ian marched up, "You betrayed me," he seethed.

"No, I didn't."

He pointed his gun toward the street below where Blood Diamonds, Gary's people, and Gavin's crew were literally fighting to the death. Mayhem and malice all wrapped up in a quest to gun their way into ownership of the town.

"You brought this to my door," he said.

My head shook sternly, "No, you did. You're the one

who framed your own father for murder. And then you sent everyone on a wild goose chase just to cover your tracks." He flinched, "I know you are Victor Lloyd. I read about you in Grover's book. Aaron confirmed it. He told me everything."

Another gun clicked behind me. I didn't have a chance to move. Gary clutched me, my back hitting his chest, him using me as a shield as he backed away from his son. "So you framed me?"

Ian blinked a few times. He held his gun up, "Give me the girl."

"Answer my fuckin' question!" Gary rattled against me.

"Give her to me," Ian's voice was calm. "She has nothing to do with this."

"Sounds like she knows everything." Gary turned me to see my face. "You know about Maverick and those other Blood Diamonds?" I froze. "Answer the question, dammit!" My eyes shut, his spit hitting my eyelids. "Don't go all shy on me now! Open your eyes!"

When I did, I made an assessment of Gary. He was a handsome man, slightly shorter than Ian. The kind of guy you would see in a commercial for erectile dysfunction. I didn't mention this to him. The veins on his forehead throbbed, his grip tightening on my arms. "Now, answer the question. He framed me?"

"Someone in your company did," I said. I don't know why I lied for Ian, but it seemed like a good idea. Of the two of them, I must have felt my odds were better if I was seated in his arms.

"You just said…"

"I was only speculating."

He grabbed my hair, causing me to yelp. "You blame her for betraying you, but she won't even give up your name," he said to his son.

"Her loyalties are remarkable." Ian kept his gun on his father. Any bullet he sent off would hit me before they scratched him. "While you're here, Dad, now is a good time to renegotiate the terms of our agreements."

"Fuck off!"

"Not until you sign everything over to me."

"After what you've done?" Gary tightened his fingers on my hair, "I gave you everything, including my name. Jensen did exactly what I told him to do. He begged for my approval, and I still wouldn't give him my name."

"And he died without," Ian said. "That gives him some dignity in death."

Gary moved up, dragging me along, "You don't have any dignity, either. Only a sick son-of-a-bitch would turn his own father over to the cops. You did it for what? Greed? You had to take my business because you couldn't build one for yourself." His fingers tightened.

"Ow!" My nails tore into his flesh, but he ignored me, only seeing Ian.

"I built all this up while you were on your knees in prison, begging the other inmates to forgive you for fucking over their families. I sent my best guys in there to keep you safe." He pointed to his chest, gun still in Gary's direction, "You should be kissing my feet."

"Ian," I said as more of my hair was ripping from my head, "stop. You're only making this worse."

Ian considered relenting, but his guard stayed up. Gary pulled on my hair tighter as a test. Ian advanced a step, longing to come to my aid. "Oh, I get it," Gary said coolly. "You love her."

"No, he doesn't," I said, not willing to believe the words myself. But as tiny as it may be, a spark of anger and worry was there in Ian's eyes. In some sad, dysfunctional way, his actions did point his compass in the direction of loving me.

Ian didn't admit to his feelings of friendship toward me, so I bought my own way out. "I can help you, Gary," I said through gritted teeth.

"I'm not into sloppy seconds."

"It's not like that," I strangled for breath. "I have proof that you didn't kill Maverick."

His grip loosened. "Where's your proof?"

Dixon was a safe card to play. "Dixon wrote a report that pointed the finger at Victor Lloyd as the killer. I met someone who knows Victor."

"You said *Ian* was Victor," he corrected me.

"I lied," I said. "It was only a bluff, a test to see if he was the real Victor Lloyd. I thought Ian was guilty, but my confidant, Demi, said that she knew who the real Victor Lloyd was, and it's not Ian. She interviewed him. Victor Lloyd's real name is Miguel."

Ian didn't bend an eyebrow at me.

"None of that means anything to me without proof," Gary said.

His skepticism became my way out. I'd lure Gary away from this place and get him on the street. Then, someone could shoot him. "I've got copies of everything at my house."

Gary squinted, "You're the doctor's daughter? I heard you moved to California."

"I came back."

"Why?"

None of the answers I had were going to cut it. "I missed my family."

"And you found out who framed me? What a coincidence."

"Stop talking, Catalina," Ian said. The commotion outside grew, more shouting and gunfire blasting. "Gary, it's over. We've lost. We're done."

Gary wasn't so sure. He held onto me, "Boy, you really fucked up this time." His grin grew wicked, "But I know how to get even." He put the gun to my head. "I always told you that falling in love in this game will kill you. After I kill her, I'm gonna kill you, and then I'm putting a bullet in your baby brother's head."

Ian's breath hitched. He knew he couldn't get a clear shot off to protect his so-called loved one. Not with the gun so close to my head. If I was going to survive, I had to get clever.

I threw my head back and stomped on Gary's foot. He didn't move. He attacked back, winding up to hit me across the face. Ian rushed him, knocking the two down. He pushed me away, putting himself between me and his mad father.

Ian was younger, stronger, but Gary never seemed to have anything to lose. His punches landed on Ian's ribs. Gary held the upper hand, landing more blows across Ian's body. Ian lost his breath, unable to retaliate.

I had to do something.

If I didn't, Ian would be dead, and I'd be alone with Gary and without mercy.

I cupped my hands and smacked them hard against Gary's ears. He fell over in pain, his gun falling by his side. I grabbed the gun and put my hand out for Ian to take. He came up, his own gun abandoned next to his father's hand.

Ian's lip was bleeding, but most of the blows had gone to his mid-section, sparing his angry face.

Gary took his chance. He got to his feet, taking Ian's gun up with him.

Ian put me behind him. I held onto his shirt, willing him to keep standing and protecting me.

The blast came through the window, knocking glass onto Gary. He dropped to his knees, blood touching his shoulders, falling with him to the floor.

Ian and I took our breaths in unison, unsure about what had happened.

Ian didn't take the shot.

Someone else had.

"Are you okay?" he said. I nodded. "Catalina, no!" he said as I flashed past him and to the window. I had to see who the good Samaritan was that had saved our lives.

The gunman lowered his rifle when I stepped into his scope. He tucked some blond hair behind his ear and gave me a nod before ducking behind the window sill of Pete's Garage.

"Kyle Workman," Ian said.

I smiled, "Aren't you glad you didn't kill him?" I said.

I had never joked with Ian before. Not since I found

out his true identity. It felt awkward and strange to be in this new limbo with him.

My eyes fluttered up to meet his. He was passing a look between my eyes and the gun in my hand. "Oh, yeah," I said, remembering where we had been only minutes before Gary had interrupted us. The mournful truth that sat in the space here with us would finally unfold. "We can't live in the same world, Ian," I said.

He stepped in front of me, "Then, do it." I knew what he was referencing without him saying another word. I held the gun up, pressing it against his chest. His heart.

I gasped, a chill running through me. I had wanted this destiny for so long. And so many other people wanted it, too.

This evil man had to pay for all the heartache he had caused them. The brokenness he had caused me. But, "I'm not a killer anymore." I heard someone call my name. Shout it, actually. Soon, they would fly up the stairs to make sure I was still alive.

Ian and I didn't have much time.

I put the gun in Ian's hand, making him a promise. "I'm giving you back your life. Now, take it and go." His brows bent. My name was shouted again. "Go!"

Ian rushed to the other side of the room, eclipsed by the darkness, as Gavin landed on the top step.

He stepped over Gary, discarding him, and pulled his arms around me. "Thank God!" he said as he held me with no intention of ever letting go.

CHAPTER THIRTY-NINE

Truth or Dare

"YOU THINK THEY'RE gonna bury Gary in here?" Charlie said as we stood in the cemetery, looking at the three fallen Blood Diamonds' gravesites. He chose to bury them here, so he could keep an eye on them.

"Hell, no," I said. "No one's come to the morgue to claim him, so they're gonna burn his body and flush the ashes."

"That's a bit harsh."

"He was harsh to this town."

"I hear that."

I tucked my arms around my body, "Charlie, you sure you want to stick around here?"

He nodded, "The guys and I talked it over. Gary owed us a business, and he's got a fully functioning construction company ready for the taking. A couple of my guys have construction experience, so they've started cleaning that up. And the ones who aren't working on the construction stuff have already started infiltrating Gary's drug business.

A few raids here and there, and we'll take possession of all the drugs and money and put them to good use. James, Kyle, and Gavin's boys are gonna help us." Charlie smirked, "Gavin's got some good guys. I can't believe we didn't lose a single person in the fight."

My brow rose, "How are you going to put drugs to good use?"

"We're gonna burn 'em. Get 'em off the streets for good and then push out any other dealers who try to bring 'em back in."

"I've heard about that crusade countless times from so many people."

"Did those people take down Gary?" I shook my head. "Well, we got this."

"What about the California chapter? Or the other chapters? Will they continue to deal drugs?"

"Now that I'm the president of the association, no. Jensen's got a few steakhouses across the country, so we're gonna take ownership of those. And the girls are free to do whatever they want, but we're shutting down the escorting and prostitution."

"Thank you," I said while touching his leather-clad arm.

"It's all thanks to you, Catalina. Not only did you help us settle our score with Gary, you brought our brothers home, and you gave us a brand-new business venture that will keep us on the right side of the law. Not to mention, this place is pretty fuckin' beautiful."

"Yeah, it is."

Charlie checked his phone, "I gotta meet with the accountant. You want a ride back?"

"Nah, there's someone I want to visit."

Charlie wrapped me in a hug. He kissed my cheek, "That's for everything."

"You're welcome." I accepted Charlie's appreciation and let him go.

Then, I walked along the path, passing Settlers and Scotts who had lived and died in these lands. I finally stopped at the one man who didn't really belong here.

"Hey, you," I said to Daniel's resting place. "So, I did it! I took care of Gary, and I saved Settlement Island, too. I know you wanted me to run, but I couldn't. I had every reason to stand up for this place. It's my home." I sat down on the grass, "I'm gonna stay here for a while until things go back to normal. And I'll come visit you, just to check in. So, you can hear about my life, and I can make sure you're still right where I left you. Okay, that was morbid." I chuckled, "I just want to hang out with my best friend, that's all. And remind you that my life is perfect because of you."

The emotions tickled their way to the surface. I shook them away, not willing to cry. I wouldn't cry today.

I got up and put my hand on the cold stone. "Until I have the pleasure of meeting you again, my friend." The turn was dramatic, but I just wanted to get out of here as fast as possible.

My eyes narrowed on him, my uninvited visitor.

Hesitation filled Ian's eyes. He knew he was wrong for standing behind me, for spying on me.

"What are you doing here?" I said. "I told you to leave."

"I know. But I couldn't go without speaking to you one last time."

"I don't think we have anything else to say to one another." I approached him. Ian was much taller than me, his frame tucked into a gray coat and jeans. No more suits. No more high fashion. The Blood Diamonds had raided and sieged everything. He was left with bad memories, no family, and an entire town that hunted for him. "I spared your life. Now go!"

"Why did you save me?" he said with awe.

I corrected him, "I spared you, not saved you."

"Regardless, you had the gun and plenty of motive. Why didn't you pull the trigger?"

"Because I'm not a murderer." Well, "I don't kill people anymore." He dropped his head with a laugh. "Seriously, this conversation is pointless. Just go already."

His head came up, "This may be a surprise, but I don't have anywhere to go. Jensen's dead, Gary's dead, Aaron refuses to talk to me, and my business has been taken over by the Blood Diamonds. I have nothing."

Pity would never fall at Ian's feet. He had crushed it and every other sympathy anyone would ever have for him. I could remind him of this, but he already knew. So, instead, I said, "Start over. Go to some place where no one knows you, and just begin a new life."

"And act like none of this ever happened?"

"No, learn from it," I said, wiser than I had ever been in my life. "Look, you know how this life ends for you. So, learn how to be a better person. A person who can earn a living without cutting other people down. Someone who can make real friends without using them. Someone who can love someone else without ruining their life."

Ian sighed, "I didn't want you to find out about my feelings that way."

I nodded, "I know."

"Did you ever wonder if I did?"

"No, not really," I said. Right here, right now, he would learn his first life lesson. "You can't hit the people you love. Or spy on them. Or try to intimidate and control them. You have to let them go and be free. That's the only way you can love them, and they can love you in return."

"I don't know if I'll ever know how to love someone the right way," he admitted with shame.

"Try therapy. The right therapist can help you figure it out."

"Therapy?" he scoffed.

I shrugged, "It helped me. And I've started going to church with my mom, which also helps."

"If there is a God, I don't think He'll ever want to hear from me again."

Probably not. "Just take the first steps toward giving something to this world instead of taking from it. Whatever that looks like will probably be okay."

Ian blinked a few times. "Even with everything I've done to you, you're still being kind to me. Even now, you're still treating me like a friend."

"I don't know if we were ever really friends, Ian," I said in a tone that provided no wavering. Steady as a heartbeat, I meant what I said. "Gavin said when the time came for me to kill you, I wouldn't because a part of me was still friends with the guy who brought me books. The guy who told me great stories and put a thoughtful smile on my face."

"Looking back on it, I was never that person to you? A true friend?"

"Looking back," I said slowly, measuring my own feelings, "that guy will always be my friend. He was real, just like you are. The only thing is, that guy tried everything he could to win my friendship. And that doesn't work for me because I only want people to be themselves around me, nothing more. So, I don't really know you, and I don't want to."

He chuckled, looking down again. "I understand." The sigh came at the same time he grew nervous. "Catalina, you're still my friend. And I promise that from this day forward, I will never do anything to hurt you, your family, Gavin, or anyone else close to you, ever again. Including Kyle, who has officially paid his debt with me."

I rolled my eyes, "See, this is why we can't be friends. I would never be friends with someone who would keep a score like that." I came a little bit closer, "The past is the past, Ian. All your debts have been settled. You're the only one holding a ledge, and no one's name is on it."

This was common for attention-seeking narcissists. Empty threats, brandishing superiority over others, making them believe that they will always hold control. You can only control someone if you have strings to hold.

Mine were cut.

"I'm walking away now." I did just that. Turned and

walked down the damp path to the parking lot where Mother's car would be. I'd fly back with Gavin to get mine this week. For now, I was using hers for whatever…

Ian's hand was on my arm, gently asking me to stop. "I'm sorry, I just want to say one more thing."

"Ian, enough. Let's just end this here."

His arms wrapped around my entire body, him needing the hug more than me. I was stiff within his acts of compassion and love, though I knew they were sincere. He pulled away, "Thank you, again. For everything."

I was prompted to speak, but a car door startled me. I turned, hearing it shut. Not many people came to Settlement Island Cemetery to visit on a Wednesday morning. But I knew one person who would.

I walked a short way, stopping to see Gavin strolling up the pathway. "Were you just talking to someone?"

I glanced over my shoulder. Ian had gone. "Just Charlie." I smiled, "He went to meet with his accountant."

Gavin nodded, putting his hands in his pockets. "Come to visit Daniel?"

"I wanted him to know I was sticking around for a bit. And I'd be checking in on him."

"I don't think he's going anywhere."

I smacked his arm, "I know that. I wanted to see my friend, that's all."

He smirked, "You know, not a lot of guys would be cool with their girlfriend visiting her dead ex-boyfriend."

"But you're not like a lot of guys."

"I know. I'm better than them," he joked.

I punched his arm, again, for being so arrogant. He

pulled me into a hug, this one I actually wanted. "And he wasn't my boyfriend."

"Well, if it wasn't for him, you wouldn't be here. So, in a way, I kinda like him." He kissed my forehead and put out his hand, "Take a walk with me?"

We laced our fingers, and Gavin guided us back up the hill. "Did you come here to visit someone?" I said.

"Nah, only you."

"In a cemetery?"

"I'm willing to go anywhere to be with you." A smile flashed across my lips. "Truth or Dare, Catalina?"

"Truth."

"You're supposed to pick Dare!"

"I've had a lifetime full of Dares, so I'm good."

He pulled us to a stop. "Just this once, pick Dare."

I sighed, "Fine, Dare."

"I'm gonna tell you a Truth."

"Of course, you are," I said with enough sarcasm to last the rest of the year.

He faced me, "I lied. I don't have a Truth for you, I have a Dare. Because the truth is, I'm so madly in love with you, Catalina, it hurts. And I know I haven't always been the best man for you. I haven't always deserved you. And I sure as hell haven't always been good for you. But I love you. That's been my truth. So, now, I have a Dare for you."

Gavin got down on one knee, in the middle of an audience of dead witnesses, and pulled out a box. He opened it, a rose gold ring with an orange diamond surrounded by chocolate-colored diamonds inside. Orange for the color of dress I was wearing when he first saw me. Chocolate for the candy bar that he had bought me. And rose for my middle name, the person I was when he found me again.

My eyes moved from the ring to him. He was shaking in a way that made me love him more. This soon-to-be-said question terrified this tough man. I terrified him.

So, I relieved the poor guy with a comment, "That's a very unique ring."

"You're a very unique woman." He took a breath, "Marry me, please, Catalina. And I'll spend the rest of my life earning your love."

I smirked, "So, where's the Dare?"

Gavin paused, "I'm daring you to marry me."

I nodded. "Yes. Yes, I'll marry you."

He wrapped his arms around me, pulling me up, and spinning me around. The kiss was long, happy, and a vow, not a dare.

He put the ring on my finger, declaring that from here on out, our lives would only be filled with Truths, no Dares needed.

CHAPTER FORTY

Storybook

W E NAMED HER Michelle, and she is our home. An old school bus we converted into the perfect sanctuary on wheels for us. Blues, beiges, and white surround me. It feels like the beach in here. It's cozy, making it the perfect place for writing this letter to you, my dear journal, the book that has encapsulated our entire love story. From that first wink in the café to this morning when my husband made me blueberry pancakes, so I would smile.

Gavin's reading the book Grover and I co-wrote that expanded on his poem, *The Settler Man's Ballad*. He's read the unedited manuscript a few times already, each time discovering a new small detail. Today, he's hung up on the story about the meadow. The one we visited on his birthday. He loves the way I described his hair in the sunlight against dark clouds.

My favorites are the silly ones. The one where I pushed him into the lake, him clinging to the rocks, his hair deflated. Or the one recapping our trip to California last year, where we found the most beautiful piece of white coral. It sits on the kitchen counter, next to the spice rack and a cutting board.

Grover loved all my memories. This book was more about me than it was about him.

"Your ring is blinding me," Gavin says, pointing to the diamond cluster on my finger.

"You picked it out."

"I still regret it." He closes his manuscript and turns to me, "Mrs. Scott, Aaron dropped this by for you." He hands me a small package wrapped in paper. "It's from his father."

"He could have given it to me at my party tonight."

"He's flying out this afternoon, so he tried to drop it at the house, but Mom said the house wasn't ready for visitors."

Of course. Since Cecilia's wedding this past summer, Mother has been doing a total redecoration of the family home. Lucky us, we were given her old decorations and linens. The couch is so soft, we fall asleep on it at least once a week. The kitchen and dining areas feature her mix of plants and earth tones, giving them a cottage feel. And our bed sits beneath a bank of windows, above them hundreds of photos of our family and friends shine down on us. Old and new. Goofy and serious. Our wedding photo, which was taken off the back deck, takes up the most space, reminding us of our undying commitment to one another.

"Well, are you going to open it?" Gavin says.

I turn the package over and take the tape off. The gift is a book. The cover is a tribute to the Scott and Settler families. A sepia-toned collage of old photos of the residents who built this place. My family's included, too. Dad and Mother smile while they hug me and Cecilia.

The inscription reads: *Catalina, my darling. So glad to take an old poem and turn it around with you. Looking forward to the next one, kiddo! Grover.*

Gavin kisses my cheek. "Happy birthday, my love."

"Thanks. I made it to twenty-five," I say as a remark to his constant fear of not making it to this very age. A fear he finally let go of this year when he turned twenty-eight.

This kiss is more meaningful. "I have something for you, but you have to take off all your clothes."

"Gavin! We are parked outside Luke and Cecilia's house, with its many windows!"

"Relax." A more passionate kiss. "We had to suffer through them going at it the whole time we stayed in their guest room." The honeymoon has been over for a while, but they show no signs of slowing down.

"It was so sweet of them to let us use their lawn for our buildout."

"Well, now they owe us," he says with another kiss.

"That's not how that works."

Kiss, "I don't care," another kiss.

I groan, "I can't. Demi and Miguel are landing soon. I gotta go pick them up."

Aaron moved on from Cecilia. He's got a thing for bossy Demi, but she's trying to win Miguel back. It's a long story, and there's no point in telling it.

Right now, I'm convincing Gavin and my body that I need to get going.

"Tell you what," Gavin says, "we'll park somewhere more remote, that way you'll feel more comfortable."

"Or, we can make love in the meadow, where I tried to steal your virginity all those years ago."

He kisses my nose. "Deal." Then, he gets up, "I'm gonna head inside and help Luke with building that thing he bought your sister for her birthday."

"The shelving unit for her craft room?"

"Yeah, that's the one."

Cecilia is nesting, and it is cute. "Tell him I said hi."

This last kiss is warm, inviting. "You gonna miss me?"

"Always." I grin, "Truth or Dare?"

"Dare."

"You're supposed to pick Truth!"

"Fine, Truth."

"No one will ever love me, fight for me, breathe for me, more than you do." I give him a long kiss. "I love you, Gavin Christopher Scott. And I will love you for the rest of my life."

He smiles, "I loved you, Catalina Rose Scott, before I even winked at you. And I'll love you in this life and the next one. And every lifetime in between."

"Alright, show off!"

He kisses me and shuts the door.

I pick up my book and something falls out of the pages. A postcard.

Catalina,

Happy birthday. I hope you have a wonderful time with

*the love of your life. Even though I will always believe
you can do better, I am at peace if you are at peace.
Grover let me read your words, and I was so touched by
how beautifully you poured your honesty into the pages.
I will always regret my part in your stories, the villain I
always seem to play. But I will never forget you and the
lessons you have taught me. I highlighted a passage in
your words that I hope will best describe them.*

Until I have the pleasure of meeting you again.

Sincerely, Ian

Is And Now

*He was always hard to wrangle until she came
along. Not a lover, like most would believe. But a
true friend who gave him hope. Belief. His need to
be a better person is more powerful than his need to
be rotten. She had become a reality that passed from
one season to the next. Their friendship would endure
time, distance, love, and eternity. He would always
be changed by her compassion and determination to
stay good, even when the world seduced her to the
dark side. Darkness would never become her. No,
she compelled it away. And I am forever grateful.*

I stick the postcard into the book and place it on the
bookshelf.

Ian is my past, and I am no longer afraid of him. I
never look over my shoulders because I don't care if he
is watching. Let him watch. Maybe he'll learn something.

Something about loving someone through all of it. Something about suffering through the hard times, like Gavin and I will have to do when he starts school at Stanford next year. Something about being a good sibling, like I had been when I gave Cecilia my hand to crush when she thought she was going to lose the man she loved to gun violence. Something about letting go, like I've done so many times, in order for me to have this life.

I've let go of my childish ways. Of hiding from the dark, even though I was running from the light. And as I hung onto the fear of being consumed by it, the darkness passed over me, touched my skin, and then released me. I had survived it, but I'd never forget it. In its absence, it left behind a love story. Our love story.

A love story that would have never happened if I didn't take that fateful Ride With Darkness.

May you find love and light wherever you go!
Love Always,
Tara

Tara Majuta is a published author, story coach, storyteller, and whale saver. Darkness Ever After is her fourth published book. Her first book, The Fascinating Files of Claudia Broadstad, is still under construction and redress, with a reprint date coming soon. Her love of writing comes from an obsession with true crime, dragons, and the Renaissance Festival. She began writing in September 2007. Since then, she has drafted more books than she can count to be published in the upcoming years. Currently, she teaches aspiring authors how to write fiction books. If you are interested in writing your novel, please visit brilliantbookscoaching.com to learn more.